# Books by Elisa Braden

## MIDNIGHT IN SCOTLAND SERIES

*The Making of a Highlander (Book One)*
*The Taming of a Highlander (Book Two)*
*The Temptation of a Highlander (Book Three)—Coming soon!*

## RESCUED FROM RUIN SERIES

*Ever Yours, Annabelle (Prequel)*
*The Madness of Viscount Atherbourne (Book One)*
*The Truth About Cads and Dukes (Book Two)*
*Desperately Seeking a Scoundrel (Book Three)*
*The Devil Is a Marquess (Book Four)*
*When a Girl Loves an Earl (Book Five)*
*Twelve Nights as His Mistress (Novella – Book Six)*
*Confessions of a Dangerous Lord (Book Seven)*
*Anything but a Gentleman (Book Eight)*
*A Marriage Made in Scandal (Book Nine)*
*A Kiss from a Rogue (Book Ten)*

Want to know what's next? Connect with Elisa through Facebook and Twitter, and sign up for her free email newsletter at www.elisabraden.com, so you don't miss a single new release!

# Confessions of a Dangerous Lord

# ELISA BRADEN

For more information about the author, visit www.elisabraden.com.

ISBN-13: 978-1-54-812432-8
ISBN-10: 1-5481-2432-X

# Chapter One

*"We all have hidden depths, dear boy. The question is whether those depths conceal treasure or monsters."*

—THE DOWAGER MARCHIONESS OF WALLINGHAM to Lord Dunston at said gentleman's annual hunt.

*March 15, 1819*
*London*

MOST MEN SAW POORLY IN THE DARK. SABRE WAS NOT MOST MEN.

Call it breeding or training or random fortune, but an alley beneath London's coal-choked sky posed no greater hardship to his eyes than a candlelit ballroom. Less, perhaps. Here, at least, the vermin did not bother with disguises.

Which was why the rat caught his notice. It gnawed something boot-shaped and motionless.

"Like bleeding pitch," muttered Drayton, a looming wolfhound at Sabre's side. "Should have brought a light."

The Bow Street runner had left the lantern with the coachman two streets over, fearing their contact would balk at being seen. That assessment might have been correct had their contact still been breathing.

He glanced again at the rodent's furtive form. Heard the whisk of rodent feet, the squeak of rodent teeth on cheap leather. It knew what was becoming obvious, if only from the odor, floating beneath the stench of human refuse and animal waste.

"Return to the coach."

Sabre's grim order straightened Drayton out of his habitual hunch. "He's a mite late, I'll grant. But he's the first source we've had in seven—"

"Late, yes. As in the 'late' Mr. Chalmers. Fetch the lantern." He moved deeper into the dark, toward the rat's feast. "Be swift, now."

Behind him, Drayton groaned. "Ah, bloody, bleeding hell."

Sabre crouched beside the corpse as Drayton's loping clomps receded. The rat flew with one hand's impatient swipe. The tang of blood entered his nose.

Three alcoves and two piles of rubbish in this alley. An attacker would have little trouble hiding long enough to dispatch a craven mouse like Chalmers. Sabre had warned him a public location was best. Instead, the mouse had insisted on this narrow spot between back doors and brick, far from the green glow of gaslights in more respectable parts of the city.

Stupidity had killed him, as it had many who entered the Investor's sphere.

Sabre searched the man's coat—rough wool suited to his recent poverty—and found only a gilt-brass watch, a wadded handkerchief, and a ruined pouch of snuff. He tossed them all aside with a curse.

This had been a fool's errand. Ending in yet another fool dead.

After more than a decade chasing the Investor like a hound hunting smoke, Sabre should have known better. But leads were few in this particular hunt, and consequently, more tempting.

One breath before he attempted to rise, he felt the prickle. Heard the *thwick* of metal leaving a sheath.

Spinning low away from the sound, he sprang from his crouch. Withdrew his own dagger from the scabbard at his hip. Sliced upward in one ghostly motion.

Caught cloth and shadow but no flesh.

Heart slowed. Eyes sharpened.

By contrast, the shadow breathed fast. Probably surprised by his quickness. Rats who inhabited the dark often were.

Sabre grinned, bouncing lightly on his toes, the long knife's ebony grip cradled in his palm like a woman's breast. Warm and sweet. Familiar. "You should have contented yourself with Mr. Chalmers." He tsked. "Your employer's name, if you please."

The shadow stilled. A blade shone in the meager light from windows along the adjacent street. The assassin must have wiped his weapon clean after withdrawing it from Chalmers's kidney.

"Come now," Sabre chided, slowly circling. Dancing. Waiting. "Few men desire an excruciating death over a swift one. Surely you are not among them."

"Y-you're him." The shadow's voice trembled and broke.

"Him?"

"The Sabre."

Sabre tsked again. "Dreadful moniker." He held up his knife, tossing it with a practiced spin. He liked the way it caught the light before returning home to his hand. "Inaccurate, as you can see. Well, perhaps you cannot, dark as it is. Knives are my preference. Portable. Efficient." He nodded toward Chalmers. "I note your fondness for them, as well."

The shadow's greatcoat shrugged nervously. "Hardly that. Only doing what I must."

His accent was warbling and odd. Part Manchester, part Dublin, if he didn't miss his guess. And young. Too young.

Sabre slowly circled, drawing the man's back around to face the street. Drayton would return soon. Better to catch the shadow by surprise.

"Your employer, old chap. Do let's be reasonable. Gutting a man produces hideous stains. Removing them is tiresome. Do not force me to it."

"Horatio Syder."

"Nonsense. Syder has been dead for nearly two years."

The shadow stilled. "His name yet lives."

Sabre inched closer, disguising his maneuver inside a dance from front foot to back. Front to back. Front to back. Light and smooth. Shifting and deceptive.

They should have called him Dancer. Or Dagger. Or something other than a weapon he'd rarely used. He did not even possess one at present. Nevertheless, he was known as the Sabre, for reasons he preferred to forget.

"I watched that butcher's blood soak an entire room, old chap. He is quite dead, I assure you."

No answer.

Sabre sighed. "Very well. How were you contacted?"

A long pause. Rough breaths. A twitch of the shadow's knife. His blade was several inches shorter than Sabre's, duller and cheaper.

"M-my wife was given a letter."

"By whom?" Front foot. Back foot. Front. Back.

"I don't know." The shadow's arm swiped a sweating brow. "A lad, she said. Syder was the only name given."

"And you did not bother to question a letter from a dead man?"

The shadow's fist clutched his knife reflexively. "Stop movin' like that."

Sabre smiled, half amused at the young man's frustration, half sick at what was coming. "There was a threat to your wife, yes? A few quid if you performed your task. Her death if you did not."

Another pause. "Aye."

The Investor understood incentives better than most. This assassin was merely a tool to be used and discarded, and scenting the trail back to his true employer would prove fruitless. If Sabre had learned anything, he had learned that. Still, perhaps he could spare the man the fate of all the others.

"You could flee. Take your wife to Dublin. Manchester."

The shadow's greatcoat shook visibly. "I cannot."

Sabre went colder. "I have no wish to kill you, old chap. Run. Do it now."

He did not run. Instead, he repeated in a whisper, "I cannot."

Then he attacked. Lunged and thrust with that short, dull blade. Desperate, inexpert jabs. Once. Again.

Sabre danced away, first to his right then backward so the shadow had only air to puncture. "How may I persuade you? Run, for the love of God, man."

Heavy breathing and another swipe, close this time. "The babe is comin' soon. I have told you I cannot."

Going still, Sabre felt old rage rising. Pure, bloody evil, that's what this was. The Investor would use anyone—a half-Irish boy who couldn't afford a decent knife. A woman who did nothing more sinister than accept a lad's delivery. A babe who had not yet taken a breath.

"I shall help you. Get you all to safety." Sabre didn't know where the offer had come from. As a rule, he eschewed sentiment. With enemies such as Syder and the Investor, soft meant dead. Worse, it meant death for anyone cherished and close. A wife. A babe.

Which was why he had neither, despite a temptation of the utmost extremity.

"You cannot help me," the shadow said. "He finds the ones he hires. Always. I kill you or she dies. That simple."

Sabre knew it was true. But the boy did not have to die

tonight. Not by his hand. "Take my offer," he pleaded. "Give yourself a chance."

The shadow's answer was a sudden lurch right, a high stroke aimed at Sabre's neck.

Sabre pivoted to avoid the slash, but it came too quickly. His forearm caught the worst of it, folded up beside his jaw to guard his head. The blade dug through wool and linen, gashed skin and muscle in a streak of fire.

His hand didn't think. It was deadly and automatic, carrying his dagger up through the shadow's belly into the shadow's heart.

The motion dispatched the threat, killing a half-Irish boy with a warbling accent and an expecting wife.

"Ah, God." The boy's words were wet. Bloody. He hung on Sabre a moment. Staggered backward, his boots slipping in something wretched, his body falling, dying, sprawling wide. His chest went motionless within seconds. The gurgling stopped, leaving a shattering silence.

Light came, golden and dancing toward Sabre, but he didn't want to see. He turned instead to face brick walls and piled refuse. A stack of discarded, broken crates. A heap of food scraps. A rat returning for a missed meal.

Light expanded as footfalls drew near. First fast. Then slow. Drayton had returned. *Too late. Too late. Too late.*

No saving anybody now.

"Bloody, bleeding hell." Gold rocked wildly then stilled into a pool amid long shadows as Drayton placed the lantern on the ground near the boy's outstretched hand. "It's Boyle."

Sabre turned, keeping his eyes upon Drayton, who knelt beside the assassin's blue greatcoat. It splayed out like wings upon the ground. "You know him?"

The man who resembled a wolfhound—dark and unkempt, shrewd and loyal—shot Sabre an outraged glance over his shoulder. "He's a Bow Street man."

"One of yours?"

Drayton scratched his unshaven chin. "Nah. Horse patrol. But I've seen him before. Christ. Only been at Bow Street a year."

So, the Investor was drawing closer. Previous assassins had been low men—ruffians and thieves, primarily. Easily persuaded to kill. Easily controlled by a bit of blunt. But a Bow Street runner was an entirely different matter.

*Close. Too damned close.*

Drayton flicked the tip of the boy's blade with his boot, setting it to spin in place. He grunted as he pushed to his feet. "You hadn't any choice."

Sabre glanced at his long knife, still streaked with blood. Moving a few steps away, he bent and wiped it clean on Chalmers's coat before returning it to the scabbard on his hip. "Perhaps I did."

"Nah. Boyle was a mite green, but he could handle himself fine. I'd wager he was given no option. Neither were you."

"His widow and babe might disagree."

Drayton's eyes flashed, that houndish face scowling. "Now, listen here. We're hunting a bleeding monster. It ain't your doing. The Investor—"

"Is no more within my grasp than he was two years ago. Or ten. I am hunting smoke, Drayton. Every time I catch its scent, my hands come away both empty and burned."

The wolfhound wagged a long chin toward Sabre's left arm. "Appears cut to me. Best wrap that."

Sabre gave his own forearm a cursory glance. His sleeve was soaked. His hand was slick and weak. Throbbing pain grew with each passing heartbeat, echoing up his shoulder and neck.

"Were there papers with Chalmers?" Drayton asked.

Sabre shook his head, sighing and rubbing a forefinger along his brow. "He may have left them behind. If he ever had any at all. Who the devil knows? The man went from being a solicitor to hiding in his brother's cellar. Clearly, he was terrified. I assumed with his ties to Syder, he must have something that would point to the Investor. Something. Perhaps he was lying."

"Hmmph. Can scarcely blame him for that." Drayton paced to the former solicitor's boots and tapped Chalmers's heel lightly. "Must have known he would end here, I reckon. You were his best chance for sanctuary."

"He was stupid. Had he done as I instructed he would be alive." Sabre's eyes drifted to Boyle, saw the pale, open hand, the dull knife, and the black-red pool spreading beneath both.

He swallowed. He hadn't vomited since his first kill, a Frenchman who'd fancied Napoleon a god rather than a tyrant. Young like Boyle, only a shave or two past twenty. Strange to think Sabre had been a similar age at the time.

*We all die the same, don't we? Paris or Dublin. Boy or man.*

After more than a decade, the price of Sabre's long, relentless hunt could be measured in blood.

He looked down. Saw his own hand dripping red onto the watch from Chalmers's pocket. It lay where he had tossed it, the sole remnant of a solicitor's comforts. He bent and plucked it up, his thumb smearing the engraved surface. Red tarnished the brass, settled into the engravings.

Chalmers had held this. Kept it close like a talisman. Sabre understood, for he held a talisman of his own.

Or, rather, she held him.

Once again, he ran his thumb over the watch's surface. Then, he tucked it into his coat pocket. Eyed the carnage of battle. Felt the fire of the Dubliner's cut.

And not for the first time, he considered whether the price of vanquishing a monster had grown too high.

# Chapter Two

*"The purpose of the season is to attract suitors.*
*The purpose of attracting suitors is to acquire a husband.*
*If you wish to be amused, I suggest acquiring a dog."*

—THE DOWAGER MARCHIONESS OF WALLINGHAM to Lady Maureen Huxley regarding said lady's recent loss of composure in the face of Lord Dunston's provocations.

*March 20, 1819*
*Mayfair*

MAUREEN'S DOWNFALL BEGAN DURING AN OTHERWISE SEDATE quadrille. She was spinning to a stop on the fourth figure of *Le Pantalon.* Henry, the dastardly devil, stood across from her, waggling his brows like a madman.

That was what did it.

She bent double, covering helpless, giggling snorts with one gloved hand while the first couple advanced and retreated between them. Although she was part of the second couple, she could not complete *L'été*. Laughter had possessed her with maniacal force. Violins continued their spirited accompaniment as she gasped rudely and held her middle.

Oh, good heavens. She could not stop. How mortifying.

She glanced across the bewildered, spinning couples to the imp who had prodded her with silly faces and pointed stares at Lord Burnley's prominent backside. Henry grinned back, his handsome features wreathed in wicked satisfaction.

He had wanted this, blast him. Yet even knowing it was true, knowing that her partner for the quadrille, Mr. Hastings, must think her positively mad, she could not stifle herself.

A convulsive hum of laughter escaped her fingers. Her eyes watered. Her ribs ached.

Stop. She must stop. But the memory of Burnley's bum waddling like a drunken duck each time he bounced from one foot to the next, flopping the tails of his coat like a pair of black wings was simply too much to bear.

She could not catch her breath. Turning her back to the other dancers to face the wall of Lady Holstoke's drawing room, she squeezed her waist harder and straightened. She held her breath. Perhaps she would suffocate and be spared the indignity of this moment.

"Bit of a cough. Not to worry. Carry on," Henry called to the other dancers before a masculine hand cupped her lower back brazenly—one might even say possessively, if one were fanciful.

"Oh, God, Henry," she chirped through her fingers. "If you dare speak to me right now, I shall ... st-strike you ..."

"Hmm, let me guess," the devil purred in her ear. "With Lord Burnley's chair? I wager it would deliver a thrashing unmatched by seats of, shall we say, lesser proportions."

Oh, no. Here it came again, bursting from her like

champagne from a shaken bottle.

Henry's steady hand steered her through the throng of appalled peers and matrons. At least, she assumed they were appalled. Tears streamed down her cheeks now. Perhaps the moisture would cool them, for she felt the prickling heat of the Huxley Flush. She was a Huxley. Therefore, her cheeks stained red at the slightest provocation.

And there was no greater provocation than Henry Thorpe, the Earl of Dunston.

He ushered her out of the crowd into a dark-paneled corridor.

She collapsed against a wall and covered her hot face before releasing a groan. "Henry, what have you done? You left your partner stranded. Poor Miss Andrews. Oh! And poor Mr. Hastings ..."

"There, there, pet." White-gloved fingers dangled a white square in her vision. "I am certain Hastings will understand. Lord Burnley's *Pantalon* was breathtaking."

Another giggle escaped. This time, she bit her lips between her teeth.

She would *not* start laughing again. She would control herself, dash it all.

Dabbing her cheeks with Henry's offering, she rolled against the wall until she could see him again.

The imp. He was her friend, although at one time, she'd been certain he would be more. Presently, his insouciance was vexing.

He grinned down at her, white teeth flashing in the low light of the tapers behind him. Full of distracting wit, Henry's masculine beauty was easily overlooked. But he was heart-meltingly handsome. Brown hair shone with hints of auburn. A high-bridged, refined nose centered proportionate features. Dancing eyes beckoned one closer, if only to see how dark the color blue could be. Full, smiling lips made a woman picture all the wicked things he might do for hours—even days—if one were the object of his desire.

Maureen was not such an object, of course. He'd taken pains to convey the message gently, but convey it he had.

Now, she tore herself from the beauty of his mouth to sigh and narrow her eyes upon his. "I should pummel you," she gritted. "Have you any idea how long I have waited for Mr. Hastings to approach me?"

"Since you discovered his grandfather's proximity to the hereafter?"

"Three weeks. And my interest is not in his title, you devil."

"Of course not. Must be the hair."

"Mr. Hastings is quite handsome; a broad forehead gives a man an academic air. I find him most appealing."

"Hmm. Broad. Yes. I'm having a bit of trouble with the 'academic' part of your description, however."

She stamped her foot. "Stop being such an aggravation. He may not have your wit, but he is not dim. He attended Cambridge."

A snort. "Precisely."

"Besides, many ladies regard a bit of ... thinning as rather distinguished. I happen to be one."

"Thinning? At this rate, he'll be entirely bald by thirty." He arched a brow. "Perhaps wigs will become fashionable again, and he may spare us the full glare of his rapier intellect."

Leaning back against the paneled wall, she briefly closed her eyes, a familiar ache shuddering in her chest. This was not laughter. This was despair. It had become a constant companion over the past two seasons.

She opened her eyes to find Henry staring down at her. "I must marry someone," she whispered. "Mr. Hastings is ..."

A muscle ticked in his lean jaw. "Not right for you."

"I fear some of us must accept our limitations."

Eyes flaring, raking her face and throat in a way that made her swallow, Henry cocked his head and gave her a faint grin. "What limitations would those be, pet?"

"After three seasons, I have no offers."

He said nothing.

"Something is obviously wrong with me, Henry."

"Don't be silly. You are perfect."

"Really."

"Of course."

"Then explain my failure. Men approach me, they appear to find me pleasing—"

"Naturally."

"And then"—she gave a flailing, forlorn shrug—"they disappear. No more dances. No more drives in their phaetons. No more lovely chats or even the mildest flirtation. I have not been kissed in ages."

His smile faded. He retreated a step.

"No," she said, pushing away from the wall. "Answer me, if you please."

He glanced left then right, giving a polite nod to a white-haired gentleman traveling from the billiard room to the drawing room. "What do you wish me to say?" he murmured.

"I have tried everything." She hated the way her voice contorted. Henry was ever the polished wit. She'd rarely seen him overcome by any emotion stronger than exasperation. Heaven forefend he should suffer a wounded heart's despair, as she had.

"Define 'everything.'" His words were hard, his jaw once again flexing, though his eyes remained turned toward the billiard room.

She wadded his handkerchief then smoothed it between her palms. Truthfully, she would prefer not to reveal all she had done to improve herself. The magnitude of her efforts was embarrassing.

"All I have ever desired is to fall in love. To marry a good man and have a home and children." She chuckled. "*Many* children. What else would you expect from a Huxley girl?"

Finally, his gaze returned to her, heated and strange. He did not smile fondly or utter a charming quip. He said nothing at all, staring down at her and gritting his teeth.

Her confidences were obviously causing him discomfort. Although they had been friends for nearly two years, and their families acquainted for longer, Henry avoided conversations of this sort—intimate and plain—in favor of lighter subjects and droll banter.

However, given that he had spoiled her chances with Mr. Hastings, she felt little remorse. Let him be uncomfortable. She needed answers.

"Something about me repels gentlemen's interest." Firmly, she held his gaze. "I have searched for the cause. I asked my sisters. Mama and Papa. I even asked John what it could be." Her brother had turned crimson before stammering that he was not in a position to judge the womanly appeal of his sister.

Henry's brows arched. "His response?"

"He fled the room as though I had threatened to set his waistcoat ablaze."

"Sensible decision." Henry indicated his own waistcoat with a casual stroke of his finger. It was ornate gold silk, the pride of his expansive collection. He tended to wear it on more formal occasions. "We are not heathens, after all."

She snorted.

He grinned.

For a moment, she remembered why she'd once thought they would share far more than friendship. But that was years ago. Two, to be precise.

Drawing a deep breath, she sallied onward. "Cease distracting me. I require your advice if I am to succeed in my aim."

"Landing Hastings?"

"Or another suitable gentleman. I must determine what is wrong with me and repair it forthwith. Three seasons constitute an acceptable time frame for a lady in my position. Four would invite pity."

He sighed. "Why me, pet?"

She raised her chin. "We are friends, are we not?"

"Certainly." Caution made the word sound like a question.

"And you are a man."

"You noticed. I am honored."

"As a man—one who might have once looked upon me with some ... admiration?" She swallowed as he gave no response. Not even a blink. "I wish to know what caused your interest to wane. Was it my gowns?" She brushed a hand down the layered canary silk of her skirt. "My hair?" She touched the curls at her temple. "My insistence on discussing Capability Brown's use of serpentine lakes in his landscape improvements?"

Finally, a smile. "None of those. You are lovely. Despite your affection for Mr. Brown's work. A glorified gardener, that one. Any fool can dam a stream and plant a bit of grass."

"Henry."

"Beg your pardon, pet. Do go on."

"I have no more guesses. It cannot be my scent. I have visited Floris numerous times, and the perfumer has attested that, while I might change my scent, there is little to improve upon."

"Has he now?"

"Yes. Furthermore, I have purchased outrageous quantities of honey vanilla soap, violet tooth powder, orange flower hair rinse, and rose milk cold cream. It is more than Papa can bear. He recently set a new budget, and he is earnest in its limitations."

"I can imagine."

"Still, I bathe quite frequently. More so than other young ladies. I am most fond of it."

Henry cleared his throat and rubbed at the corner of his mouth. "Bathing?"

She nodded. "Not the sort with a washstand and cloth, mind you. No, no. *Full* immersion. It is a dreadful lot of hauling water, and I must bribe the footmen regularly, but I *adore* the sensations of heat and wetness and steam surrounding me. Could anything be more pleasurable?"

Again, he was silent, his thumb stroking oddly at the edge of his lower lip.

She shook her head. "In any event, I have determined, after much introspection and experimentation, that my odor is not offensive, and therefore not the cause of my problem."

"I should think not." His voice had gone hoarse and, once again, he avoided her eyes. His gaze now hovered between her throat and midsection. If she didn't know better, she would suspect he was admiring her bosom. Men often did. But not Henry. First of all, it was too dark in the corridor for him to see her properly, even if he were so inclined. Second, he was not so inclined. In fact, he did not regard her as a woman worthy of ogling. His affection was more ... brotherly, perhaps. No, that wasn't quite right either. He and John were acres apart in their disposition toward her.

Dash it all, she did not *know* how he regarded her. Affectionately, warmly, humorously, yes. They enjoyed one another to an absurd degree. No one made her laugh like Henry. And, yet, whatever her feelings for him, his were strictly platonic.

"I chatter too much, don't I?" she blurted, ashamed to utter her darkest suspicion, but sensing she must force both herself and Henry to tend the matter at hand—her inability to hold a man's interest. "Gentlemen find me charming enough for an hour or two, but they tire of hearing me go on and on." She squeezed her eyes closed and straightened her spine. "Tell me truly. I can bear it, but you must be honest, Henry. I must know."

A pair of lean, elegant hands gripped the sides of her shoulders with unexpected firmness. Her eyes popped open. His palms heated her skin through his gloves and the beaded yellow cap sleeves of her gown.

"Listen carefully. There. Is. *Nothing.* Wrong with you."

She opened her mouth to protest.

He gave her a little shake before dropping his hands away. "Nothing. You are perfect in every conceivable sense."

"Of course I am not. Otherwise, I would already be wed. No. I am flawed in some critical aspect only a gentleman would discern. You may hesitate to wound my feelings, but my suffering shall be far lengthier if you do not simply tell me—"

"You choose weak men. Weak and inconstant. That is your problem."

She rolled her eyes. "You would blame *them*? I am the common thread, here, Henry. Me. Perhaps in my first season, I would accept such an answer, but not now. *You* are hardly weak. And *you* do not want me."

He fell back a full step, the ripple of his throat jostling an expertly tied cravat. Several breaths drifted by while his eyes remained locked upon her, flared and glittering.

Oh, dear. Perhaps she had gone too far. She hadn't wanted to toss his rejection in his face so bluntly. Come to that, perhaps describing her love for bathing was a bit much, as well. Conviviality was no excuse for a breach of decorum.

After a time, he spoke. "Let us return to your mother. We have been alone here too long." His lips quirked. "Mustn't set the hounds of gossip upon our heads."

As he pivoted away, she reached to grasp his arm. His violent flinch startled her, and she released him instantly. Chest heaving on fast breaths, he held himself rigid, his muscles flexing in time with his fists.

Yes, she had erred badly.

"I—I am sorry, Henry. I did not mean to disconcert you so."

A moment passed before he grinned over his shoulder in a semblance of his usual fashion. Without humor, it was simply white teeth and a hard jaw. "Never fear, pet. It takes a great deal more than your perfect self to set me off balance." He crooked his right arm and nodded toward the drawing room. "Shall we?"

UPON DELIVERING MAUREEN TO MAMA'S SIDE, HENRY OFFERED no explanations, bowing politely and uttering, "Lady Berne. Lady Maureen. A pleasure."

Then he strode away at a smart clip, his lean form disappearing into the crowd. Maureen watched him go, a queer ache in her stomach. How deeply had she offended him? Would he even speak to her again?

The impossibly affable Lord Dunston was known for brushing aside rudeness with astounding ease—a trait which led one to assume he was immune to being "set off balance," as he'd described it. He was far more likely to fire off a humorous quip than take offense, even when others referred to him as a "dandified peacock" or a "fashionable fribble."

He was neither of those things, of course. Henry had substance—warmth and wit, kindness and courage. It was not his fault that he preferred a high standard of neatness and a bit of color and ostentation in his waistcoats. Perhaps he had too many, she would grant. But it was hardly a reason for scorn.

Still, she'd rarely seen him as pale as he'd been when they'd reentered the drawing room. There'd even been beads of sweat upon his brow.

"Cease biting your lip, Maureen," muttered her mother, wielding a lace fan with vigor. "You are not a rabbit."

"Apologies, Mama."

Mama's rounded features gentled into a smile as she draped and re-draped an apricot Kashmiri shawl over Maureen's arms. "Are you well, dearest? I do hope you're not suffering an ague."

Maureen patted her hand. "A sudden cough, nothing more. Lord Dunston was most helpful."

Mama's lips tightened and pursed. "Hmm. Yes. So I noticed." She turned her eye upon the crowd. "Where is that charming Mr. Hastings, do you suppose?"

Blinking, Maureen jerked her gaze toward the dancers. Mr. Hastings stood on the periphery with Miss Andrews. The pair spoke earnestly and cast blushing glances at one another while he handed her a cup of lemonade.

She sighed. There went another one. "I believe Mr. Hastings has decided better prospects lie elsewhere, Mama."

Mama's brows arched as she followed Maureen's nod. "Well, who would want a man so inconstant, I ask you. Not my daughter, of a certainty."

Maureen chuckled. She leaned down and kissed her mother's rounded cheek. "I adore you, Mama."

"Of course you do." Brown eyes twinkled. "Now, let us speak about Lord Holstoke."

Groaning and laughing at once, Maureen gave her hand a squeeze. She should have known Mama would only accept Lady Holstoke's invitation with matchmaking in mind. The two countesses cared little for one another's company. However, Mama had no such distaste for Lady Holstoke's eligible, titled son.

"I suspect he finds me disagreeable, Mama."

A blink. "Impossible. You are the most agreeable of all your sisters."

Maureen considered the two older and two younger girls. Each was a Huxley through and through. Brave. Determined. Willful. Yet each was unmistakably her own person. Annabelle was the oldest, a natural leader with a preference for commanding others. Jane was the shy one who preferred books to society. Eugenia was the brat with an unhealthy fondness for hats and footmen. Kate was their little performer, dancing, singing, and acting out scenes from *A Midsummer Night's Dream* at the barest sign of encouragement.

And Maureen? She was the unremarkable one, often called the "prettiest" or "most pleasant" Huxley girl as if nothing more notable could be said.

"That may be," she answered her mother, "but Lord Holstoke spoke only six words to me the entire time we sat together at the arborist's lecture last week." She held up her fingers to count. "'Lady Maureen,' twice—once in greeting and once in farewell. And 'no,' when I inquired whether he agreed with the speaker's assertions about proper clumping of trees."

"That is only five."

"He repeated the word. Perhaps for emphasis. To be fair, the arborist's claims were preposterous. Concentric circles, indeed. In any case, John was there, and even he agreed Lord Holstoke and I do not suit." Maureen frowned and eyed the door to the dining room for signs of Henry's return. He'd been dreadfully pale. Had she damaged their friendship permanently?

"Nonsense." Mama's lips pursed with stubbornness.

Maureen sighed and returned her attention to the matter at hand. Leave it to her mother to dismiss Lord Holstoke's disinterest with a word and a sniff. Mama had already matched her two oldest daughters, Annabelle and Jane. Annabelle had married an earl's son, and against all odds, Jane had become a duchess.

Mama did not countenance failure.

Maureen found her arm grasped firmly in a maternal clutch before being hauled past the ladies seated along the longest stretch of blue wall. The older ones awaited the return of their charges; the younger ones sought relief from their status as wallflowers—or, as Jane had often called them, the Oddflowers. As far as Maureen was concerned, her sister could refer to them however she liked, given she had once lived amongst their ranks.

"Mama, where are we going?"

"To greet Lord Holstoke."

"I have told you, he does not like me."

"Nonsense."

"You may speak that word a hundred times, but—"

Her mother stopped, drawing Maureen to a halt at the end of the Oddflower row. Mama nodded politely to Lady Darnham before facing Maureen and hissing, "Some tasks require persistence, young lady. Have I taught you nothing?"

"Just because Papa agreed to let you acquire another cat does not mean—"

"Persistence gained me what I desired, did it not?"

"My persistence has lasted three seasons. I am growing weary, Mama."

"Nonsense." Mama's rounded chin rose, her eyes flashing. "Straighten your shoulders."

Knowing this would end faster if she did as she was told, Maureen complied.

"Better. Now, let us remind ourselves of Lord Holstoke's finer qualities." Mama made a show of fluffing and resettling Maureen's shawl while whispering her list of qualifications. "He is an earl. Some suggest he possesses more than moderate means. Not as handsome as some, but a sound lineage and no signs of peculiar excesses."

Oh, dear. Mama was examining prospective suitors for "peculiar excesses"? Worrisome, indeed.

"He is an excellent prospect. Further, despite his father's well-known daftness, he appears to be more ... intellectually inclined. Hence, the arborist's lecture."

"*He* is the reason you gave me the literature? Oh, good heavens. I should have known."

Mama sniffed. "I am your mother. I have done appropriate research in pursuit of your lasting happiness."

"You've asked Lady Wallingham, in other words." The Dowager Marchioness of Wallingham was Mama's dear friend—and the reigning empress of all ton gossip. Jane and others referred to the white-haired, fragile-boned, inexplicably powerful woman as a dragon. The description was apt.

"Her sources are impeccable."

Maureen rolled her eyes. "So she often claims."

Mama gave her shawl a sharp tug then smoothed it with small strokes. "Persistence, Maureen. Now, remember to smile. Bigger. Pretend you have not recently eaten putrid meat. There you are. Lovely."

He stood in the corner near the entrance. Tall—several inches taller than Henry, who was a scant inch shy of six feet. Hair as black as coal and cut severely short emphasized high cheekbones and ascetic features. More than anything, however, one noticed his eyes. They were the palest, eeriest shade of green. Expressionless. Assessing.

After cordial greetings, she and her mother stood before him for long, awkward seconds, waiting for him to speak. Which he did not. It had been the same at the arborist's lecture. Lengthy silence and little expression. Perhaps now Mama would understand why Maureen had dismissed him as a prospect. Even if she ignored his obvious disinterest, she found little to like in the odd, chilly man.

Besides which, he was dreadfully tall. She preferred a man of Henry's height. Like all female Huxleys, she was short of stature and did not enjoy extreme disparity.

Mama broke the silence. "How long have you been in London, my lord?"

He blinked slowly and tilted his head as though puzzled why Lady Berne was speaking to him at all. "A month."

"Just long enough to regret it, I daresay." Maureen did not know why she uttered the impertinence. She'd grown accustomed to bantering with Henry, she supposed, and it had popped out like her mother's new cat—pouncing and mischievous.

While her cheeks heated, however, the most astonishing thing happened. Pale, eerie green fixed upon her. Then lit. Then warmed with ... interest. Those straight, ascetic lips curled at one corner.

"Indeed," he confirmed. "I comfort myself that it could be worse. The plantings in Hyde Park are sensibly arranged at present."

To anyone else, it would seem a banal observation. But Maureen was not anyone else. She grinned. "Can you imagine? Concentric circles. Honestly."

Then, he laughed. Well, chuckled, really. But she liked his

voice, low and quiet. And when he smiled, she thought him rather ascetically handsome.

He stepped closer, tall and dark and so very *interested*. "Do you concur with the criticism of Capability Brown's tree clusters?"

Her eyebrows arched. Her heart fluttered. Her breath stopped.

Oh, good heavens.

Her mother had been right.

Not so bad a prospect. Not so bad at all.

# Chapter Three

*"To claim uncharted territory makes one a bold explorer.
To invade territory occupied by vastly superior forces
makes one a suicidal simpleton. Perhaps you would like
to reconsider such adventures, hmm?"*

—THE DOWAGER MARCHIONESS OF WALLINGHAM to the Duchess of
Rutland, upon receiving an audacious invitation to her grace's
competing weekly luncheon.

HOW WAS IT POSSIBLE FOR A MAN TO BE AFIRE IN THE BONE-
chilling damp of a London night? Henry only knew that he
was. He suspected the cause, of course.

She wore canary yellow silk. Her skin flushed brilliant

pink. And she made him hurt.

Closing his eyes, he leaned against the brick of Holstoke's town house, tugging his hat lower and bracing the elbow of one arm with the wrist of the other. Absently, his thumb stroked his lower lip.

He should stay away from her. But he'd never found the strength to resist making her laugh. She did so not only with her mouth or eyes or even the dimples in her soft cheeks.

No. Lady Maureen Huxley laughed with her whole body.

Her lush, curved, sumptuously tempting body.

She'd accused him of not wanting her. How he wished it were so. For both their sakes.

Holstoke's front door opened, shining a narrow beam upon dark cobbles.

"... too soon to call upon her father?"

"Depends. When would you like to bed her?"

A sigh billowed in the wedge of light. "Presently."

Masculine laughter rang out along Park Lane, flaring against Henry's already scorched nerves. He pushed away from the wall as the door closed behind the two men. "Hastings. And Walters, is it?"

Heads swiveled toward him. "L-lord Dunston," Hastings squeaked. "Didn't see you there. Gave me quite a fright, I don't mind telling you."

Even in the dark, he could see their faces. Hastings had more to fear than he knew.

"Fear not, my good man. Simply awaiting my horse." Deliberately, he remained in deep shadow, held very still.

Walters cleared his throat. Shifted from one foot to the other. "Perhaps I'll go round to the mews and see if I can't hurry things along," he said before scuttling away.

Hastings's companion was more discerning than Hastings himself, who could best be described as a dullard. Entirely ill-suited to a woman of Maureen's curiosity and wit.

Henry tilted his head as he eyed the dullard with the

"broad" forehead and "quite handsome" visage. "So. Hastings. Contemplating the parson's mousetrap, are you?"

"Er—well, I suppose I must." He laughed sheepishly. "Walters compares it to the theatre. To enter, one must purchase a ticket."

Intellectually, Henry knew his comment was a mild jest of the sort many young men made. Certainly nothing to kill over. But, at the moment, his intellect was a prisoner of the heat, stretching and itching beneath his skin, flushing him hot and cold. His head spun and pulsed. His hands hummed with the desire to realign Hastings's "quite handsome" features.

But violence would only beg questions he had no wish to answer. Instead, he kept his tone casual. "Some tickets are costlier than others, I daresay."

The dullard grinned like the balding imbecile he was. "Indeed. One may only hope the performance satisfies in equal measure."

Later, Henry would blame the heat. It took him in a wave, propelling him toward Hastings, balling the man's lapel in his right fist, and using their combined momentum to slam the other man's back against the stone column left of the door.

Hastings's hat flew. He sputtered a curse. "Bloody hell, Dunston! Are you cup-shot?"

Henry's fist tightened and shoved until Hastings's balding head bounced against the column's fluted surface. "Were I you, my good man, I should reconsider this particular purchase. Spend too lavishly, and you may find yourself beggared."

"I—what the devil are you—"

"Your grandfather plays often at Reaver's, does he not? What would happen if he took the wrong advice or played a wretched hand at the tables? You might find his fortune quite ... diminished long before it reaches you." Henry rarely chose such a direct method of dissuasion. He preferred intermediaries and strategic rumors untraceable to him. But Hastings was a special case. An urgent, dense, infuriating case.

"Are you ... threatening me?"

Good God, the man was a lackwit. "Yes, Hastings. That is precisely what I am doing."

Hastings glowered and rubbed the back of his head where it had struck the column. "To be frank, my lord, I'd no idea you were this fond of Miss Andrews. After you abandoned her in the midst of a quadrille, I assumed ..."

"Miss Andrews?" Henry's fist loosened.

"Yes. That is the—er, ticket we are discussing, is it not?"

He released Hastings's lapel. Miss Andrews. He struggled to recall the chit's face. Thin. Pointy nose. Not a dimple in sight.

Instantly recalculating, Henry pretended to stumble back, shaking his head as though he were dizzy. In fact, he was, though not because of drink. "Miss Andrews is a spleen—*hic*—splendid girl, Hastings. Mustn't speak of her in such terms, you know. If she's to be your wife, keep a gentlemanly tongue. Is only right."

Hastings's befuddled frown eased as he blinked and straightened his coat. "Yes, I see your point. I shall endeavor to do so in future. Be assured I have the utmost regard for Miss Andrews. My intentions are honorable, though perhaps my words were not. For that I beg your pardon, my lord."

Henry waved sloppily and made a show of losing his balance as he bent to retrieve Hastings's hat. He presented it to the man with a flourish and an affable smile. "Think nothing of it."

Moments later, Walters returned, followed by a groom leading three horses. Henry promptly bid the men farewell and rode into the dark, listening to Hastings remark that drunkenness made the Earl of Dunston a prickly and unpredictable fellow.

By the time he arrived home, Henry's head was spinning, his stomach queasy, his flesh flashing hot beneath his clothes. Though he'd not had a drop of anything intoxicating, he struggled to coordinate his steps across the marble-floored entrance hall of Dunston House.

"Henry!" It was his mother, garbed in her usual pink dressing gown and ruffled cap. She carried a cup of tea in one hand and her cane in the other as she bustled through the west corridor, apparently on her way to bed. "I did not expect you to return this early. Was the Holstoke affair tedious, then?"

He huffed and placed his hat and gloves on the sideboard near a silver tray. The low candlelight glinted strangely on its surface. It flickered and drew close. He caught himself on the edge of the table just as his mother shouted his name.

A teacup shattered. His mother's warm bulk grasped and held him upright with surprising strength. Her voice echoed in his ear. "Henry! What is wrong, son? Dear God, you are burning up." Her hand lay cool against his cheek like when he was a boy. "Stroud," she bellowed. "His lordship needs help!"

Henry's valet appeared, his spectacles awkward upon an aquiline nose. "My lord, are you ... Let me ... your arm round my shoulders ..." Stroud was a good man. Strong and capable. But his voice kept fading in and out. And when he reached for Henry's arm, agonizing fire raged.

Someone roared and swung a fist into an aquiline nose. Henry thought it might have been him. He was nothing but pain now. Pain and heat.

His mother screamed and wheeled back.

Nursing his injured nose, Stroud quickly returned on Henry's opposite side. He looped Henry's right arm over his shoulders and maneuvered them both toward the stairs.

Unflappable. That was Stroud. And deadly, upon occasion. Henry supposed he was fortunate the valet was also reluctant to retaliate against his employer.

"... get you into bed, my lord. Then, we'll ... physician. Appears ... septic ..."

Next, Henry heard his mother's voice, though he couldn't discern what she was saying. Probably ordering the maids to clean up the mess he'd made. She'd dropped her tea, hadn't she?

He blinked and he was outside his bedchamber. Blinked again

and he was undressed and lying between cool sheets. Blessedly cool. He glanced at his left arm, now naked of its wrapping.

Streaked, crimson flesh. Oozing white and yellow. Swelling between neat stitches. Septic. Yes, the gash had gone septic.

His mother was there again, her hand stroking his hair away from his forehead. "Stroud ... the physician. He'll be here soon. Henry." Her voice twisted. "What ... your arm, son? How ... such an injury?"

He closed his eyes and breathed deep and fast. What sort of lie would suffice? Ordinarily, they came with ease. But pain and heat were like a steam cloud, obscuring his vision and disorienting his balance.

"Happened while I was fencing with Blackmore," he murmured. "Foolish accident. Didn't want to worry you."

"Well, I am worried now, you silly boy." Her hand cupped her mouth, and she turned her head away. "I cannot lose you," she choked through her fingers. "I cannot go through it again."

"Only a fever, Mama. I'll be fine."

"... furthest thing from fine!"

"Survived worse."

A long, choking silence. Throbbing, concussive heat.

Distantly, before sleep swallowed him, he heard her say, "Good God, son, what could be worse than this?"

HE KNEW HE WAS DREAMING. FOR ONE THING, THE COLORS were wrong. His papa had worn blue, not green that day. The weather was different, too. It had been overcast and windy, the gusts rocking the coach into a creak-and-shudder symphony.

In the dream, summer sun streamed yellow-orange through the travel coach's windows. It heated his cheeks and made his skin itch.

He remembered rain, first slow then harder. Also, he'd been chilled rather than hot. But everything else was the same. The scent of his father's tobacco. The ache in his spine after six hours. The dried mud on the toes of his boots.

"Another day or so, and we shall have all of London to explore together. Have you decided what you would like to do first?" his father asked, tucking an enameled snuffbox away.

Henry set aside his book and pursed his lips. "Harrison says I should visit a book shop. But I only read books when there is nothing else to do. He likes reading much better than I."

His father chuckled and leaned forward to ruffle Henry's hair. "You are a man of action, son. A Thorpe through and through, like your papa."

Henry grinned back and nodded emphatically. "May we go riding first?"

Sunlight caught the edges of his father's queue. Red played among the brown. In his hazel eyes, mischief sparked. "The very moment we arrive, we shall spring from the coach and demand our mounts." His arm playfully swung in a wide arc, pretending to brandish a sword. "We shall gallop across Mayfair, declaring for all to hear, 'The journey from Suffolk could not defeat us, good sirs! Witness our triumph!'"

Henry held his middle and laughed helplessly, enjoying the deeper peals of Papa's laughter alongside his. He liked when Papa laughed. It made his stomach glow.

Light shifted. The world cracked.

A shot, loud and piercing.

The carriage lurched and slowed, meandering oddly to the opposite side of the road.

Hoof beats. Masculine shouting.

Henry found himself lifted into his father's arms and carried to the floor while another shot rang out. It was dark beneath Papa. Hot and dark.

"Stay still, son," Papa whispered above his ear. "No matter what happens, stay very still and quiet."

Henry's opposite ear was pressed to Papa's chest, so he could hear the larger heart inside booming a rapid pace. It was not as fast as Henry's own. Sweat sprang forth upon his body, lining his skin and sweeping his neck with ice.

The carriage drifted to a stop.

"No matter what happens, son. Still and quiet. If you hear another shot, run. Hide. Do not stop until you find safety." Papa's words fell moist and hot against Henry's scalp, his strong arms clutching so tightly, Henry couldn't draw a full breath.

Papa kissed his head and pulled away.

Dark became light as the door opened.

Henry remained frozen, huddled on the floor of the carriage. Still and quiet, just as Papa had commanded. Beside his knee, his book lay sprawled and ungainly.

A bridle jangled. Hoof beats approached. Slowed. Stopped.

"Lord Dunston." The man's voice was oddly muffled, his speech rounded in the manner of a servant.

"If you know who I am, then you know you will hang for this. Leave now and you may stand a chance of escape."

"'Ave you any coin, m'lord? Gold, if it please ye."

Henry shook. He didn't mean to, but the tremors arose from inside, like when he played too long beside the streams of Fairfield Park in winter. He was cold now. Cold and burning.

"Very well," came Papa's voice, low and calm through the coach wall. "I have some in my pocket. Permit me to—"

A shot.

Agony twisted Henry inside out. Every shallow breath squeezed until he thought he might be dying. Wished he was dying. But he did not move. He stayed. And shook. And gasped for enough air to chase away what he knew to be true.

He'd felt it. Heard the hard thud of a man collapsing onto a muddy English road.

*Still and quiet. Still and quiet. Still and quiet.*

He should run. Papa had told him to run.

He could not move.

"Hmmph. Not so bloody powerful now, are ye?" Those words were clearer than before.

He heard rustling. The huffing and grunting of the man with the gun. The muffled clink of coins inside a purse.

He needed to move. To run. Or, at least, to see.

His hand shook where it braced beside the sprawled book. One finger by the next, he clawed that hand forward, his palm scraping the floor of the coach, sweat making his path slick.

His body shook as he crawled forward, frozen and stiff and burning. Finally, grasping the leather strap beside the door, he pulled himself higher until the bridge of his nose topped the edge of the window.

The man wore black. Black hat. Black coat. Black breeches and boots. But he wore a red scarf. It was pulled down, bunched over his throat. Henry saw his face in profile. Oddly, he did not look like a devil. He looked like a blacksmith or a farm laborer. His face was pitted. Dusty. Framed by lank brown hair. There was a dark mole on one side of his flat nose.

In his hands were sheets of parchment, folded in a square and apparently withdrawn from Papa's pockets, for Henry recognized Papa's unbroken, red wax seal.

The red-scarfed man's shoulders stiffened. Suddenly, he swung his head toward the carriage.

Henry ducked and curled himself into a ball, hugging the tufted leather of the door. Perhaps the glare had disguised him behind the glass. Perhaps the red-scarfed man hadn't seen him at all. He tried to listen for approaching footsteps, but his heart pounded and swished. Pounded and swished. Twisted and ached and pounded and swished.

*You should have run, Henry. Should have run.*

He was being squeezed by every second that passed. Harder and tighter. Hotter and colder.

Then came the creak of a saddle being mounted. The snap of reins. The receding of hooves on hard-packed earth. That was when the rain came in earnest, pattering glass and murmuring a heavy sigh.

For the longest time, Henry could not move. He lay amidst the loud rain, the baleful gusts, the gray light, and the cold sweat that itched and burned and made leather sticky against his cheek.

Slowly, though, he gathered himself. Papa needed him to be strong.

He opened the door. Climbed down without knowing quite how he did so.

Saw Papa's boots. Saw red rivulets forging the mud. Smelled the acrid tinge of recent shots.

Rain gusted his face. The coach door gouged his back.

He staggered forward, shivering with cold and heat.

The dream went dark. But he remembered the rest. Hazel eyes open to the falling rain. A dark hole where one should never be.

The consuming urgency of finding help, though help was useless. Three men dead. John Coachman, their footman George, and ... Papa.

Henry remembered running. Finding the inn just as the sun set.

But in his dream, he was back home. His mother cradled him and stroked his hair away from his face. She'd been swollen with a babe when he and his father had left Fairfield.

Mary, his sister, was born a mere week after Papa had ...

His mother sang to him now, off-key and humming as though she'd forgotten the words. Strange how her voice was rustier than it had been then. Deeper. Older. Sadder.

He was older, too, he knew. No longer a boy. But still frozen inside himself.

Still burning inside himself. Why was it so bloody hot in here?

He ached and tried to turn over.

"Settle yourself, Henry. Thrashing about will only do you injury."

His mother again. She'd been there before. After his father's murder.

Letting her tuneless humming soothe him, he drifted again. Now, he stood on a terrace in Yorkshire beneath a bright, slumberous moon. Around him twirled sprightly dancers— ladies with flowers in their hair, clapping and laughing and springing in rhythm with a country tune. Only one caught his notice. Held him fast.

She glowed. Beneath moonlight and torchlight, she glimmered and shone. Her hair was not simply brown, but forever lit with streaks of gold. Her nose was round and dainty, her cheeks delicately dimpled, her lips plump and ripe and curved as though they strained against a secret. Tonight, she wore a crown of daisies and heather, and as she spun one last time, she bestowed upon him a midsummer gift: her blushing, beatific smile.

He wanted to kiss her. He wanted to lift her. Carry her away from the Duke of Blackmore's south terrace and down to the fish pond she'd admired earlier. He wanted to lay her down upon the grassy bank and lift her skirt and debauch her senseless. He wanted to breathe her inside. He wanted all the sticky heat of an August night to soak his fingers and heighten into a crescendo of lust and pleasure. He wanted his teeth on her inner thighs, his hands clutching her hips.

He wanted to devour her white skin and lush breasts. Discover if she tasted like vanilla and salt and orange blossoms on his tongue.

In his mind, he took her hundreds of times in dozens of ways—laughing and gentle, hard and brutal, fast and deep, slow and thorough. In reality, he could only watch. She was Harrison's sister-in-law. An earl's third daughter. Young and enchantingly soft.

She would break apart on all his hard, hidden edges.

Oh, but she laughed like light on water. No. Deeper. Like currents and eddies and riptides. She sucked a man in before he knew he'd been taken.

He wanted to drown.

He *was* drowning.

In flame and thick, suffocating air.

"Maureen," he called. But his voice was hoarse, soundless.

She danced away, holding her flower crown atop her hair. She twirled and laughed with her whole body, shimmering and taunting.

"M—Maureen," he panted. "Stay with me."

"You must drink, my lord." When had Stroud come out to the terrace? And would someone douse the bloody torches? He was sweltering.

"Come. Head up. There we are."

Cool touched his lips. Slid down his throat. It tasted bitter at the back.

Soon, more cool covered his forehead. "That's better, now, isn't it?" Stroud again.

"Good man," Henry rasped, not bothering to open his eyes.

"Yes," came the wry, nasal rejoinder. "A good man with an offensive nose, apparently."

"Where is ... my mother?"

Long silence. "Resting. We thought it best she not be present whilst you are insensible, my lord."

Henry's body ached as though it had been trampled by a coach and six. His head throbbed. And that damned heat flashed up and down his skin, despite Stroud's efforts to cool him.

Opening his eyes, Henry was thankful the room was dim, with only a low fire and a single candle to brighten it. "I've been saying things, then?"

Stroud nodded and avoided Henry's gaze.

"How long?"

"Five days. The fever appears to be receding. Dr. Nettleford believes you will recover within a week or two, provided you do not overexert yourself."

Henry glanced down at his bandaged arm, then let his head loll toward the window. His vision swam, but he could see violet light edging between the draperies. It must be evening.

"Has ... anybody else sent inquiries?"

Again, Stroud avoided his gaze, busying himself rearranging the basin and tea tray on the bedside table.

"Stroud?"

"No, my lord. You've had no callers apart from a brief visit by Mr. Drayton. He wished me to assure you he has made arrangements for Mrs. Boyle's relocation."

Henry sighed and closed his eyes again. Of course there would be no other visitors. He'd long kept friends and acquaintances at a safe distance—even his best friend, Harrison Lacey, the Duke of Blackmore, who currently despised him.

Perhaps he would regret his choices less keenly were it not for his infatuation with Harrison's sister-in-law. The woman who made him burn, even without this damnable fever. The woman who thought he did not want her.

Laughable. In fact, he would laugh if he did not feel so bloody awful.

Sleep wafted and dragged over him.

He fought it, forcing his eyes open.

Stroud was a dark blur, puttering about with damp cloths and pitchers of water. "Go on and sleep, now, my lord. Should you receive inquiries or correspondence of particular interest, be assured I shall inform you straight away."

He did not wish to sleep. He did not wish to dream any longer. Not of anything or anyone but her.

It claimed him nonetheless. And in the darkness of his fevered head, he was once again reminded why Maureen Huxley could not be his.

# Chapter Four

*"The line between honesty and rudeness is a delicate one.
Allow me to demonstrate. You are an odious toad
in grave need of a valet with a functional sense of smell.
There, now. We appear to have located the boundary.
I am gratified to have been of service."*

—The Dowager Marchioness of Wallingham to Sir Barnabus
Malby in response to said gentleman's observations about
Lady Berne's plentiful figure.

"I have offended him; I am certain of it," Maureen said
with a sigh and a sip of stout, faintly floral tea. "It will be a
wonder if he ever speaks to me again."

Her sister, Jane, lowered herself slowly onto the opposite sofa, leading with her shoulders and bracing with her hands. "Ugh," she wheezed, laying a small hand upon her very large belly. "When did I agree to give birth to a rhinoceros? I don't recall the conversation."

Maureen snorted and shook her head. "You're not that big, dearest."

Jane raised a brow and pushed her spectacles higher on her nose. "Perhaps you should inform my lungs and my back, for both are wearying under the strain of my not-bigness."

Indeed, she was rather alarmingly large, although Maureen dared not say so. Beneath the folds of her claret silk gown, Jane's belly swelled like a great, round pudding. Except bigger. Much bigger, even, than their oldest sister Annabelle's belly had been before giving birth to their niece. Initially, Jane had been dismayed by her increasing size, for she'd long been a bit on the plump side and worried that she'd endangered the babe through overindulgence.

No sooner had she begun to trim her portions at dinner, however, than her husband had taken umbrage and put a stop to it. Harrison was obsessively protective—a tall, forbidding, ensorcelled duke who would sooner starve than see his beloved wife forgo her favorite gooseberry tart.

"To whom were you referring?"

Maureen tore her gaze from the aforementioned belly. It was bulging along one side as the babe pressed and kicked. "Hmm?"

Jane smirked. "The man you've insulted. Holstoke?"

Shaking her head and reaching for a biscuit to soak in her tea—a treat reserved for these private visits with her sister—Maureen sighed again and bit into the newly moistened sweet. "Dunston," she clarified after nibbling and swallowing. Honestly, biscuits were too dry without the addition of Clyde-Lacey House's delicious tea. "I accused him of rejecting me."

Dark, round eyes flared below a fringe of equally dark hair. "That was ages ago. What made you bring it up again?"

Maureen felt her face heating. "I asked him to explain what is wrong with me. From a gentleman's perspective."

"Oh, dear."

"It made him dreadfully uncomfortable."

"I should think so."

Maureen dunked and nibbled a bit more.

"When did you speak to him?"

"The Holstoke ball. He made me laugh. We had a moment alone together."

"Mmm. A moment in which you asked him to inventory your faults."

Narrowing her eyes upon her sister, Maureen set her tea and biscuit on the table beside her. "Gauche and presumptuous, perhaps. But I am weary of guessing, Jane. I require answers. This is my third season, and something must be done."

Lightly strumming her belly, Jane tilted her head, those dark, intelligent eyes probing. "It is possible you are too attractive."

Maureen rolled her eyes.

"No, really," Jane insisted. "You are lovely, Maureen. Perhaps men find you intimidating. You even look splendid in yellow."

"How is that a measure of—"

"Yellow flatters no one. For example, wearing the same canary gown which, upon you, resembles a beam of sunlight, I would instead be mistaken for a lemon left too long in the larder. Sickly and defeated. With hair that refuses to curl and skin of curdled milk."

Releasing a sharp laugh, Maureen eyed her plain sister who was perhaps more plump than some ladies and, yes, wore spectacles. Jane was shy with strangers, but with those she loved, she was both a charming wit and a loyal lioness. "You are beautiful, Jane."

"That's what I mean. Lovely."

"What?"

"You find me beautiful."

"Because you are."

Jane shook her head, smiling affectionately. "No. I am not. You sound like Harrison."

"He is right. We both are."

A wry grin curved her sister's lips. "He would be gratified to hear you say so. After I blackmailed him into allowing me to accompany him to London, I'm afraid my darling duke is feeling a bit sore."

Glancing to where Jane's hand lightly rubbed the top of her swollen middle, Maureen felt her heart squeezing around a hollow place. The queer, twisting spasm had occurred more frequently over the past year as she'd watched first Annabelle then Jane prepare to become mothers. "He loves you. He only wants you to be safe and well."

"Perhaps that is your answer with Lord Dunston."

Maureen jerked her gaze up to her sister's, blinking fast and breathing faster. "I—he does not love me, Jane."

Jane, by contrast, blinked not at all, merely tilting her head. "No?"

"After your midsummer ball, I thought perhaps ..." Maureen swallowed hard and bent her head to examine the two small crumbs on her skirt. "I wrote him. Did I ever tell you?"

"Yes."

"A mistake. It's not done, is it? Unmarried girl writing a man with whom she's only danced twice." Maureen chuckled and brushed at the crumbs with busy fingers. "I wrote his mother first, of course. His sister. They were unkind to you during their visit at Blackmore Hall, but I thought ..."

"It would give you a connection. A reason to hold on to him."

Maureen stared across Jane's bright, spacious drawing room to the centermost of the five windows. The sun was streaming today. Henry loved to ride on sunlit mornings. He'd not been at the park, however, when she'd gone earlier hoping to find him.

She pushed to her feet and ambled toward the window, pausing to gaze down upon Berkeley Square. "At last, I gathered my courage. My first letter was cordial, of course, begging his pardon for overstepping. In his reply, he sounded as though we'd been friends forever. I was certain he was ... that we were ... I'd never felt anything like it, Jane. I still have found nothing to compare. He ... he has a piece of me."

As usual, Jane understood only too well. "When you are together, you are more than yourself. And when you are apart, you've lost yourself."

*Just so,* her heart despaired. *Just so.*

Turning to her sister, Maureen straightened her spine and folded her hands. "He was gentle in his explanations. Tender, even. I still have the letter. The tenth one he sent. Christmas before last."

"I remember," Jane said, her eyes now shimmering behind her spectacles.

"So you see, he does not love me. Not the way a man loves a woman." Her answer choked her, squeezing the bones in her throat until they ached. "But he is kind. And he is my friend. And I believe I have insulted him. I cannot bear it."

She needed to see him. Because he had a piece of her, and no matter who else she might kiss or how many times she read his tenth letter, she was less herself without him. Less Maureen.

What to do? She hadn't seen or heard from him in ten days. She'd hoped to waylay him in Hyde Park, but he'd not been riding there either in the mornings or afternoons, as he customarily did. She could not very well knock upon the front door of Dunston House. An unmarried woman visiting an unmarried man in his residence would be a scandal. They might be forced to marry.

What a disaster that would be. Married to Henry? She wanted to laugh. Well, not laugh, precisely. More moan. And perhaps find something to drink, for she was suddenly quite parched.

A shiver floated over her, raising the hair on her nape and arms. She rubbed at both and absently watched Jane sip her creamed coffee. Her sister rested the cup upon her babe-swollen abdomen as she picked through a basket of books their butler had deposited on the sofa earlier.

Squinting at Jane's protruding belly, Maureen pondered a sudden, ticklish thought. No, she could not approach Henry in his home. But, perhaps she would not have to. He was not the only one living in Dunston House, after all.

"I shall call upon his mother," Maureen announced with a nod. Relieved to have the decision made, she sighed away the tension from her shoulders and returned to the sofa, taking care to keep her voice and hands steady. "Lady Dunston suffers with gout, and she hasn't many visitors. If he is at home, we may find a moment to speak. I shall apologize, and all will be well."

"Maureen." Jane's dark brows pulled together in a tiny frown. She returned her book to the basket. "Perhaps you should let matters remain as they are. Lord Holstoke appears a most promising prospect."

"Holstoke? Well, yes, of course. But he has nothing to do with Henry."

"Really."

"Nothing whatever."

"Are you certain?"

It was Maureen's turn to frown. "What are you implying?"

"You and Dunston have enjoyed a certain closeness over the past two seasons. It may be time to allow some distance to fall between you. Make room."

Her frown deepened as she considered Jane's words. "For Lord Holstoke." She pictured him—tall and ascetic. Intelligent and serious. Interested. In her.

Jane did not reply, apparently certain that Maureen had received her message. Lord Dunston would never be her husband, for he did not love her. She must nevertheless marry someone, and Lord Holstoke was a good prospect. More than that, she liked him. His low voice. His pale eyes. His odd intensity on the subject of fish ponds and Greek follies. He was the nearest thing to a suitor she'd had since last season, when Sir Barnabus Malby had ogled her bosom and offended her mother at Lady Gattingford's second ball.

Jane was right, of course. Lord Holstoke should be Maureen's focus. Further, she should be glad to gain some distance from Henry, for he was always distracting her. Maddening her. Tempting her.

But, in the end, he was her friend. She wished to ensure he did not despise her.

Giving Jane a quick smile, Maureen bent to retrieve her tea, took a drink filled with soggy crumbs, and allowed her sister to believe she'd won.

REGINA WAS NO ORDINARY LADY'S MAID. FIRST, SHE WAS BOTH as tall as a man and nearly as broad in the shoulders. Maureen had taken to her immediately upon their interview the previous year, enjoying the contrast of Regina's gruff voice and wiry chin hairs against her talent with hair tongs and slipper repair.

At certain moments, however, Maureen wished Regina would disappear. Not forever, mind. An hour or two would do.

"You needn't have come, you know," she said to the maid walking beside her. Regina had a habit of glaring, as she was now at the carriages rumbling along Maddox Street.

She often appeared to be anticipating threats. Maureen had once asked why, and Regina had answered sternly, "Cannot fight what you don't see, m'lady."

Maureen had not inquired further.

Now, she heard the sullen crack of knuckles as Regina clenched her fist before waggling long fingers at her side. "And neglect my lady's safety? Her reputation?" Dull blonde hair, scraped stringently away from a narrow face and topped with a white cap did nothing to gentle those heavy bones and prominent brows. "Never."

"Really," Maureen insisted, smiling and gesturing to the quiet row of houses leading to Hanover Square. "Dunston House is a short walk from Berne House, and I have visited there many times before. Last time, only Lady Eugenia accompanied me."

"I was ill, m'lady. It shall never happen again."

"Nonsense, Regina." Maureen patted the maid's arm, vaguely astonished, as she often was, by the hard muscularity beneath the gray sleeve. "How dearly I value your loyalty. But your duties do not include digging yourself an early grave." She clicked her tongue at Regina's stubborn expression. "I refused to take you with me. You were hardly derelict."

"If you say so, m'lady." Regina resettled the bundle of Chelsea buns on her hip and squinted suspiciously at a gentleman exiting one of the houses ahead of them.

A waft of cinnamon and yeast and sugar crowded Maureen's senses. Briefly, she closed her eyes, savoring the sweet, rich smell pluming amidst crisp, sun-warmed air.

She'd added fewer currants and more cinnamon this time. She thought the change rather a good one.

The double-chinned man exiting a brick house tipped his hat in greeting. She nodded in return, hoping he was not offended by Regina's intimidating stare.

Deliberately quickening her pace, Maureen hurried toward Dunston House, a white-stoned, five-storied affair spanning thrice the width of its neighbors. One half featured evenly spaced rows of tall, gleaming windows while the other was a gracefully rounded bow. On the flat half, a Grecian-style, arched pediment framed the dark-green door and elaborate, fanlight window. Topping the fourth floor, a cornice of carved acanthus leaves spanned the width of the house.

The place was like Henry himself—a bit ostentatious, perhaps, but elegant and unique. Certainly, none of the other houses in Hanover Square compared to it, in Maureen's estimation.

She climbed the few steps to the green door and knocked, her stomach growling at the sweet-spicy scent of the buns. Behind her, Regina's shadow loomed broad and tall.

The door opened, revealing Dunston House's butler, Kimble, a servant even more shockingly stout, towering, and muscular than Regina. "My lady," Kimble intoned, bowing and waving her inside with one gargantuan hand. "Her ladyship will be most pleased you've come."

As Maureen entered, she marveled, as always, at the lovely entrance hall, a circle of curved, blue-paneled walls and golden mahogany tables atop a floor of white and gold marble laid in a starburst pattern. Bright sun shone through the fanlight window behind her, casting a glorious web of shadow on the walls.

Distantly, she loosened the ribbon of her bonnet and listened to the byplay between Regina and Kimble.

"Shall I carry your package for you, Miss Fielding?" the butler inquired, his voice deepening to a rumble.

"No," replied a suddenly tart Regina. "You may keep your hands to yourself, Mr. Kimble."

Maureen fought a grin and spun on her heel to see the burly pair glaring daggers at one another. She cleared her throat. "Is Lady Dunston well enough for visitors, Kimble? I wouldn't wish to tire her, the poor dear. Gout is a dreadful malady."

"Her ladyship will be most pleased to see you." He nodded to the package Regina clutched tightly against her robust hip. "Delighted, I daresay."

Chuckling, Maureen followed the butler as he led them upstairs to the drawing room. Regina trailed, grumbling under her breath about "men with presumptuous airs."

Barbara Thorpe, the Countess of Dunston, was a substantial woman of middle age, her dark hair liberally streaked with gray, her straight brows and tight lips giving her a look of constant disapproval. Indeed, where she sat in her usual chair by the fire—feet propped on a needlepoint stool, head cocked to peer down at her embroidery—one had the impression she'd been subjected to bothersome antics from ill-behaved children.

However, as Maureen had learned with time and patience, that was simply Lady Dunston—a bit sour, a bit disgruntled with life's inequities. Upon delving further, one realized the toll that pain, both physical and emotional, had taken on the matron. One also grew to appreciate that, despite appearances to the contrary, Lady Dunston was a woman of good heart.

"I pondered whether you had been struck down by a runaway coal cart," the countess said now. Her eyes remained on her embroidery needle, those plump fingers deft and graceful as they guided the floss. "What else might explain your interminable delay?"

Maureen took the package of buns from Regina and approached Lady Dunston. She wafted the confections beneath the matron's nose. "Ah, but it is always worth the wait, wouldn't you agree?"

Familiar dark-blue eyes flew up over brown paper. Prunish lips softened into an O. A refined nose twitched. "You did not."

Grinning, Maureen nodded. "I did."

Lady Dunston tossed her embroidery hoop aside and tore into the package with childish glee. Her eyes closed as she revealed the sugar-glazed, cinnamon-speckled treats. "Kimble, we shall require tea."

A half-hour later, Maureen relaxed upon an ivory striped

damask chair, sipped tea for the third time that day, and wondered how long she could wait before inquiring about Henry. Was a half-hour sufficient? She thought so. "The weather has been quite fine today."

"Hmmph." Lady Dunston waved the tip of her cane at her elevated feet. "I must rely upon your reports, dear. The gout has rendered me housebound, you know."

Knowing better than to encourage Lady Dunston's complaints with too much sympathy, Maureen sipped her tea and continued, "Rather surprising that Lord Dunston has not been riding these past several mornings. I know how he fancies a rare bit of sunshine."

The countess sniffed. "Well, even a man of Dunston's constitution must be given time to recuperate."

Maureen blinked. "From?"

"Why, the injury. The fever." Lady Dunston's straight, dark brows lowered into a scowl. "Clumsy boy. How many times have I told him to take care if he is to play with swords? Does he suppose such mishaps impossible?"

Struggling against the vise seizing her chest, Maureen focused on the delicate handle of her cup. Breathe. She must breathe. "Henr—that is, Lord Dunston was ... injured?"

"Mmm. He has been dreadfully ill. It is enough to give a mother apoplexy."

"How?"

"His arm was cut in a friendly spar with Blackmore."

Maureen frowned. Blackmore was Jane's husband, and while he and Henry had once been friends, they had scarcely spoken, much less engaged in a friendly bout at Angelo's, for well over a year. "Are you certain it was a fencing injury?"

"So he said. Had to be stitched back together. Seems reckless for one of Dunston's skill, I daresay." The woman shrugged. "Still. How else might he have acquired such a deep wound?"

How else, indeed. "He—he has been here, then. Recuperating."

Not snubbing her. Perhaps not angry at all, but instead sickened with fever. She should have inquired sooner. Only her fear of his rejection had kept her away when he might have needed her.

"Weak as that tea you are struggling to drink, but yes. His fever appears to have broken at last."

She must see him. Now. Her heart pounded out the demand. *Find him, Maureen. Now, now, now.* Tightening against the urge, she forced herself to remain seated. No, if she was to see him—and she refused to leave until she had—she must be clever. She could not very well demand he present himself. He was weak, likely confined to his bedchamber.

She knew where said bedchamber was, as Lady Dunston had once given her a tour of Dunston House, grumbling all the while about the number of stairs and the fanciful imagination of architects. But if it was scandalous for an unmarried lady to visit an unmarried man in his house, it was positively forbidden to visit him in his bedchamber.

Scandal came in varying degrees of extremity.

However, Maureen's intentions were hardly prurient. She wished to ensure he was well and not vexed with her. That was all.

She cast a sidelong glance at Regina, sprawled in the curved end of the room with her arms crossed, glaring out the bow window. How to rid oneself of an overprotective lady's maid for the brief time required to sneak upstairs and ascertain Henry's wellbeing? A conundrum, indeed.

In the end, Maureen opted for honesty, not out of moral considerations but because she was a talentless and incompetent liar, turning red-faced and high-voiced at the knowledge of her deception. Apart from which, she hoped she might rely upon Regina's overprotective nature.

First, she concluded her visit with Lady Dunston, bending to kiss the woman's rounded cheek and squeezing her outstretched fingers. "I shall come again next week, if you wish."

"Do," came the arch reply, accompanied by a wave toward the empty, cinnamon-dappled paper wrapping. "This time, bring more than a mere half-dozen, dear. My son's house is not one of austerity, you know."

The corridor outside the drawing room was hushed and blessedly free of servants. Regina excepted, of course.

Maureen halted to gather her courage while Regina retrieved her bonnet.

Faced with the maid's hard glower, she nearly abandoned her plan. But a quick breath and a thought of Henry's suffering forced the words from her throat. "I must see him, Regina."

"Mr. Kimble? Doubtful he'll take offense. If we leave without saying farewell, he can blame himself. A butler has one task, and that's to be present when guests arrive and depart. Were I his employer—"

"Not Kimble." Maureen glanced around and lowered her voice. "Lord Dunston."

The maid froze in position, disapproval shrouding her raw-boned features. "T'would be a grave risk."

"Not if you help," Maureen whispered.

Flat lips nearly disappeared as Regina visibly battled her reaction.

"I must see that he is well. Please, Regina. A few minutes. All I ask is that you wait outside the door." She rushed on despite the woman's ominous glare. "Oh, and tell no one. I promise to do nothing untoward."

"Forgive me, m'lady, but every bit of this is untoward."

"Be that as it may, I shall do it. Would you endanger my reputation needlessly, knowing that this is simply one friend ensuring another's health?"

"Friend."

"Of course. What else?"

Regina gave a skeptical sniff.

"His affections are not of an amorous nature, I assure you."

The hard expression gentled. "And yours?"

Giving her head a tiny shake, Maureen replied with the only answer she had. "He was injured. I cannot leave without seeing him. Please help me."

Finally, Regina relented, promising to wait "no more than ten minutes. *Ten*, m'lady. Any longer, and I shall assume a transgression has occurred and act accordingly."

Patting the maid's shoulder, Maureen resisted a grin. "No need to storm the gates. I'll be done in a trice."

Swiftly, Maureen made her way to the staircase and up to the master chamber. For a moment, standing outside his white-paneled door, she considered whether this was entirely wise. Of course, it was not. He might be attended by a physician or his valet. He might be asleep.

Or naked.

She shivered and flushed. The height of embarrassment would be seeing Henry Thorpe in the altogether. The lean, muscular arms and flat abdomen and thick, ropy thighs. Humiliating, really. It made her mouth dry just to contemplate.

*Ninny,* she thought. *How much worse will it be if you are caught hovering outside his bedchamber?* With a shuddering sigh, she gave her disapproving maid a nod, grasped the knob and twisted.

Inside, the room was dim, a low fire crackling to her right, a row of windows to her left, draperies drawn. And along the wall in front of her was his bed, massive and canopied. Draped in blue silk. Dark, fathomless blue. Like the northern seas. Like his eyes.

She leaned back against the paneled door, cringing as the thing shut with a loud bang.

"You harangued me to rest, Stroud. Am I to understand now you wish me to awaken?"

Although the voice from beneath the blankets was spotted with rasp and rust, it was unmistakably Henry's. She would know that amused baritone anywhere.

Before she thought better of it, she found her feet carrying her forward, her own voice answering, "Alas, I have never performed the duties of a valet. Care to instruct me?"

# Chapter Five

*"Of late, more scandals are caused by humdrum breaches of decorum than scandalous acts. Given the choice, I daresay the latter is preferable. If one is to pay the price, one might as well enjoy the transgression."*

—THE DOWAGER MARCHIONESS OF WALLINGHAM to Lady Gattingford regarding the sad decline in the quality of gossip at her weekly luncheon.

HE MUST BE DREAMING. AGAIN.

Bloody hell, he'd thought the fever gone for good. His muscles were shaky and weak, his body wrung out like a stained tunic on laundry day, but he no longer felt the deep-boned aches and flashes of hot and cold.

Sighing, Henry slid one hand beneath his head and stared up at the blue silk canopy. Why was it dark inside his dream?

He blinked. Frowned. It should not be dark. He always envisioned her in the light—moonlight, torchlight, sunlight. She was made for it, and he dreamed of making love to her with every inch bare and perfectly illuminated. Dreamed it with disturbing frequency.

"Are you ... are you going to simply lie there in silence?"

The sheer femininity in her voice made him hard. Predictable, that. Her tone struck him as oddly uncertain, though. In his dreams, she was usually more assured, more seductive.

"Henry." She drew closer, mere feet away, bringing with her the scent of vanilla and orange blossoms and ... cinnamon? "Say something."

Curious, he eyed her shadowy outline. The curves were the same. But she was fully clothed, wearing white muslin beneath a violet-hued spencer with too many frog closures. Her hand came toward him.

It settled on the skin of his biceps, warm and bare and ...

Real.

He bolted upright with a rusty shout, "What the devil, Maureen!"

Simultaneously, she squawked and fell back, her eyes round and fixed upon his bare chest.

Quickly, he snagged a stray pillow and settled it over his lap. No sense in alarming the chit further. "I repeat," he snapped once he'd collected his senses. "What the devil are you doing here?"

"Visiting your mother."

"In my bedchamber."

"Well, no, of course not. I am here to see you. To verify that you are well." She scooted closer, her fingers tangling and twisting at her waist as though she struggled to keep them occupied. "I'd no idea you were ill—injured, in fact. Henry, you must believe I would have come sooner."

He couldn't seem to get enough air. She was here. Standing beside his bed. And he was wearing nothing at all. Well, aside from a blanket or two.

He glanced down.

And a convenient pillow.

"You should not have come," he growled, unsure what to do. He needed to dress. She needed to leave.

"I was worried. Your mother said you've suffered a dreadful fever. I haven't seen you in so long, I thought you were vexed with me." Again, she inched closer until the folds of her skirts flattened between the mattress and her thighs. "I am sorry for what I said, Henry."

He tried to recall what she might have regarded as offensive enough to warrant an apology, but at the moment, his entire being was focused upon lush thighs, delineated by low firelight, thick shadows, and thin muslin. "You are forgiven, pet."

"I should not have asked you to inventory my flaws."

"You haven't any."

She ignored him. "Further, I should not have described my love of bathing. While true, it was inappropriate."

Finally, he shut his eyes, focusing considerable will upon drawing sufficient air. It evidently took more than he had to fuel both a clear mind and a towering erection. "Think no more of it."

"You are not vexed with me?"

"No."

Her sigh heaved with relief as though his anger had weighed upon her, heavy as a millstone.

Then she sat on the edge of the bed, jostling his hip with hers.

Next she brushed the hair away from his forehead with a feathery touch.

"You feel a bit hot," she observed in a whisper. "Are you certain the fever is gone?"

He fisted the pillow covering his lap. Forced himself to remain still. Not to grasp. Not to take. "Maureen."

"Who is your physician? Perhaps I should speak with him."

His eyes flared open. This time, her name was a grinding snap. "Maureen!"

Her hand poised like a startled bird above him. Her skin flushed as she met his eyes. She was an innocent, he knew. Sweet and soft and naïve. The sort who mothered a man and stroked his brow while hers gently furrowed. But her body read his well enough, understood the threat, even if she did not. It was there in her quickened breath, her beaded nipples pressing muslin and violet silk.

"Henry."

"You must go now, pet. Before anyone finds you here."

Her hand fell to her lap. "The rules are silly," she declared. "As silly as Lord Burnley's waddling bum."

He rubbed his temple with impatient fingers and fought to remove his eyes from her breasts. The chit was maddening. "Not silly. Designed for your protection. What do you suppose happens when a lady enters a man's bedchamber?"

"Kissing, I presume."

Perhaps he should not have asked.

"And copulation, most likely."

Definitely. He definitely should not have asked.

"But that is why the rules are rubbish," she continued in a perfectly rational tone. "They make a great many assumptions about individual circumstances. You and I will neither kiss nor copulate, will we?"

"You should go," he repeated, though he knew it was useless. Maureen had decided she wanted to speak with him, so she had used the pretext of visiting his mother to arrange a private meeting in his bloody bedchamber. She might be soft. And sweet. And rather the maternal sort. But she rarely allowed anything to stop her from doing what she thought was right.

"I don't see why I should avoid speaking with you simply

because you are lying in bed, too weakened to do anything more scandalous than sip tepid broth." Now she was showing signs of dudgeon, her neck lengthening, her rounded chin tilting, her generous mouth flattening.

And what was all that about being too weak for scandalous acts? The woman had no notion of his capabilities, let alone his thoughts. "Disagree with the rules all you like, pet, so long as you remember that breaking them has—"

"Consequences." She sighed. "Yes. I know."

"Do you?"

Her eyes flashed in the low light. "I am not daft, Henry."

"Risking ruin in order to speak with me is worse than daft. It is reckless. Why not send a note?"

"A note conveys neither tone nor expression. If you were angry, as I feared, the only way to set matters right was to see you."

He glanced pointedly down at his naked chest. "In my *bedchamber.*" Henry rarely allowed his temper to surface, but right now, the cold sear of it gnawed his insides. She had placed herself in greater jeopardy than she knew. In seconds, he could have her flat on her back, her skirts tossed up, and all her options ground to dust. He could quench this everlasting need, trap her into becoming his, now and forever. All it would take was giving in to his darker nature.

Deep inside, that part of him roared its approval.

"Your bedchamber is merely a room. Four walls and a fireplace." Once again, she reached for the hair that slumped across his forehead.

He grasped her wrist before her fingertips made contact, perversely enjoying the startled jerk of her body. "Even you are not that naïve, pet." Stroking the silken skin of her inner wrist, he murmured, "Being here is an invitation."

"Nonsense. I was concerned." Her eyes fell to his bandaged arm. "How did you manage to acquire such an injury, anyway?"

"Unimportant. What matters is that you leave. Now."

She sniffed and raised a brow. "Evidently, being bedridden

saps your good humor. I like you better when you are healthy."

Being bedridden and naked and unable to protect her from her own soft heart did more than sap his good humor. It made him rage. But, as with so many things, he couldn't allow her to see. Slowly, he forced himself to release her.

"I like me better when I am clothed," he lied, keeping his tone light. "Turn round, if you please. Mustn't ravish your virginal eyes with my splendid nakedness."

She blinked. Then blushed. Then stood and did as he instructed.

He threw aside the blankets and pillow, leaned on his uninjured arm, and rolled to his feet. "Say what you came to say," he tossed over his shoulder as he padded to the dressing room.

While he contemplated the array of brilliant waistcoats hanging neatly in color groupings from red to blue, he waited for her to break her silence. Choosing a shirt of fine linen, a pair of buff trousers, and a brocade waistcoat in green and gold, he dressed and managed to persuade his erection to fall to half-staff before she spoke a single word.

"I—I don't know what to do, Henry."

Those solemn words gutted him more deeply than any man's knife. He returned to the bedchamber, running a hand through his hair.

Her back remained turned, her head bowed, the nape of her neck white and vulnerable in the low light. It drew him within feet of her.

"About what, pet?"

She spun. Her eyes were beseeching. Tormented. Her mouth opened and closed. Opened. Closed. Finally, the word escaped on a breath. "You."

SHE HADN'T MEANT TO SAY IT. HADN'T INTENDED TO OPEN herself to him this way again.

Good heavens, he'd already rejected her once. Why did her foolish heart refuse to accept that he did not want her?

When would she stop dreaming of him, worrying about him, craving the silken way he called her "pet"? She hated the little endearment and yet loved it. She loved ... Henry.

But she must find a way to let him go. She had endangered her reputation by coming here. Regina knew it. She knew it. Henry knew it. In truth, loving him had only ever been a risk without promise of a reward. He preoccupied her mind to an unwholesome degree. With every gown she chose, she wondered whether Henry would like it. Whenever her sister Genie crafted another ridiculous hat, she lived in anticipation of describing it to Henry, longing to hear his rich laugh. All manner of life events, big and small, felt real only when she could share them with him.

Somewhere between conversing with Jane and seeing him today, rumpled and naked and pale with the ravages of fever, it had become obvious what stood between her and a good match—Henry.

Those northern-sea eyes and the playful grin. The teasing affection and clever mind. The feeling of rightness, of being more herself, the moment he came into sight. She hadn't been lying when she protested that his bedchamber might as well be any other space bounded by four walls and a fireplace. No, indeed, for her, the room did not matter.

Anytime she was near Henry, she was his. If ever, for one blessed instant, she believed he wanted her, she would be in his arms before he could blink. Ballroom, billiard room, bedchamber. Location mattered not at all.

She knew he felt differently. Even now, as they faced one another in the darkness of his private domain, he gave no signs of lust or adoration. Rather, his expression was clouded by caution. Concern. It was the look of a man dreading her next sentence.

"I have tried, Henry," she confessed into the long silence, knowing he would understand the struggle to which she referred. She still had his tenth letter, after all. "Mere friendship has not come easily for me. In some ways, it hasn't come at all."

He moved closer, his countenance white, stark, and unsmiling. She saw his hands lift to touch her then drop as though he'd thought better of it.

"Now, I fear other gentlemen sense my ... attachment." She swallowed. "This may explain why their interest wanes so quickly."

Turning his head and propping a hand on his hip, he gazed toward the window and said nothing.

"I realize it is unfair of me to burden you with this. You cannot change your feelings any more than I. But if I am to marry, I must distance myself from that which can never be mine." Her throat burned and her eyes filled, but she refused to let tears fall. It was humiliating enough to reopen her heart's wounds and bleed for him. Perhaps this would be the last time.

"What are you saying?" he asked, his jaw tight and flickering.

That Jane was right. She had to make room. It was time.

"Goodbye," she rasped, those hot tears spilling without her permission. "I am saying goodbye, Henry."

His reaction was one she'd never imagined seeing in Henry Thorpe—violence. Without a word, he pivoted, stalked to the window, fisted the blue velvet and yanked so hard, the draperies tore. Daylight—bright and harsh—flooded the room, blinding her.

She swiped at her cheeks and held her hand up to the glare. When she lowered it, a stranger loomed in front of her.

Eyes of the darkest blue flashed like steel under moonlight. Pallid skin shadowed by a day's growth of beard flexed and tightened over a bladed jaw. A mouth made for smiling and laughing and kissing flattened until it was white.

She'd never seen this man. He made her heart kick, flop, twist in her chest.

"Do not ever say that word to me again." His voice was sibilant and sleek, a cold warning as though she'd threatened to destroy him.

"I—I do not want to," she whispered, swiping more tears with her knuckles. "You are my friend. My best friend."

"In the habit of abandoning your friends, are you?"

"Oh, Henry. Do you think I would leave you if it were not necessary?" She took a chance and laid her hand on the swirling silk of his unbuttoned waistcoat, just to the right of his heart. He flinched away and she withdrew. "You have made me laugh on days when I wanted only to weep. When Annabelle lost her first babe. When Sir Barnabus Malby told me he expected I would grow fat like my mother. When I attended four balls without a single invitation to dance. You bring me a great deal of joy, Lord Dunston."

"Then do not do this."

"I must."

"So you can marry some daft fop like Hastings? Have a brood of bald, dimwitted children?"

"So I can marry someone." This time, she did not let him pull away. She grasped the lapel of his waistcoat and tugged him closer. "Someone," she repeated, her voice contorting and pleading, her fist gently striking his chest, clutching his silk. "Someone, Henry. Because it cannot be you." *And you are the one I want.* She did not say it, but it was there, breathing the air between them.

His face was a barren, wintry moor.

"My fault," she whispered, her eyes dropping to where her hand still clutched him, unable to let go. "There is not enough room for you and for ... another. I'm sorry."

She did not know how it happened. One moment she was apologizing for ending their friendship, and the next she was plastered against him with his mouth grinding into hers. His hand cupped the base of her skull. His chest flattened her breasts. His supposedly injured arm banded her lower back, forcing her hips into his.

Sensations piled one upon the next—full lips she'd expected to be soft, instead eating at her mouth. Hard fingers pressing the hinge of her jaw. Bristly chin chaffing hers. Hot breath against her cheek. Slick, hot tongue invading upon her gasp. Steel arm tightening around her waist until her slippers left the floor.

Henry was all that existed. His scent—herbal and soapy and warmed by sandalwood. His taste—rosemary and salt and heat.

He weakened her until she could only clutch the silk of his lapels and open for him. Open wide.

*This is not Henry,* she thought distantly. Not gentle. Not amused. Not affectionate.

This was a merciless stranger bent on conquest. He hoisted and shook her whole body with a single arm, grinding her against his mouth and chest and hips and ... hardness. Pressing between her ...

Right against her ...

*Oh, my.*

Her eyes flew open.

If he didn't want her, why was he kissing her? And why was there so much *hardness?*

Her tongue retreated from where it been stroking his with unseemly relish. "Ehrmr?"

Not-soft lips continued their devouring. Not-weak arms fastened tighter.

She wriggled her hands against him, writhing to loosen his hold.

He didn't budge. No, indeed, his tongue renewed its mission to claim her mouth for its own, sliding and pressing and heating and pleasuring.

"Mmm. Ehrnry," she moaned, flattening one of her palms against him, wondering if this achy, winding heat in her middle was quite normal. Certainly, she'd never felt it with other gentlemen.

Of course, those kisses had been ordinary kisses. Sweet and gentle. A soft pressure of lips upon lips. A respectful caress of hands upon hands.

No man had ever grasped a handful of her backside as Henry was doing now.

She grunted into his mouth, her thigh rising along his hip. Her hand slid up to his shoulder. Circled to clutch his nape. Speared through cool, chestnut strands. She'd meant to grasp and pull him away, but her fingers liked the feel of him. Silk and steel and hot, hard flesh.

Good heavens, she was melting like butter over a sumptuous, rosemary-herbed roast. She wanted to devour him. She wanted him to fill her until she was satiated.

Gasping again, she fought to free her other hand, sliding it from between their bodies and winding her arm around that surprisingly arousing neck. Naked without his cravat. Exposed to fingers that stroked and pressed and marveled.

He was stronger than she'd ever supposed, to be able to hold her this long. The idea set her on fire. Fancy that. The dapper Lord Dunston was almost entirely muscle. What a peculiar way to make such a discovery.

"I knew it!" Both a bark and hiss, the accusation was flung at them from across the room and punctuated by a slamming door.

Henry froze. Withdrew his tongue. Then his lips, which had softened the more she'd opened for him, she realized. With greater gentleness than he'd previously demonstrated, he lowered her to the floor, giving her backside a fond pat before sliding his hands to her waist.

"R-Regina," she panted, squeezing her eyes closed. "I can explain."

"No need, m'lady," the maid barked. "I've seen rutting before."

Whatever portion of Maureen's face might have retained its normal color now throbbed with pure Huxley Flush. She could not bear to look at either of them. Especially Henry.

He still held her, his breathing fast but steady. "You should not have let her come here, Regina."

She scarcely recognized his voice, deep and coarse as dry gravel.

"Aye, m'lord. 'Tis clear she's in need of protecting."

Maureen cleared her own throat and opened her eyes, perturbed with being discussed as if she were absent. Henry's glare at Regina accused the maid of committing a grievous lapse. Regina returned the glare in full measure. Maureen frowned and inched away from his grasp. His fingers dug into her ribs briefly then let her go.

"Regina," she said as firmly as her breathless state would allow. "Give us a moment alone, if you please."

"Appears you've had too many of those already, m'lady."

She met the maid's eyes steadily. "A moment. Please."

With a grunt, the maid backed out of the room, leaving the door open a crack and glowering all the while at Henry. His demeanor remained both rigid and volatile—two qualities she'd never associated with the man she knew him to be.

"Henry."

Finally, he looked at her. His eyes were shockingly hard. Opaque. Foreign.

Several breaths were necessary before she continued. Confrontations always made her skin cold, her stomach burn, and her palms sweat. But this was Henry. Surely she could speak plainly to Henry.

"Wh—what on earth?"

She didn't have to say more, for his expression told her he comprehended her question well enough: *What on earth would compel you to kiss me? What on earth have you been thinking to deny your desire for so long? What on earth caused you to change so radically from the man I know? The man I love?*

Hands braced on his hips, Henry pivoted and strode to the window, where the draperies hung half-torn and sagging. His shoulders heaved on deep breaths. Sunlight lit his lean, flexing jaw.

She wanted to soothe him, to run her hands over him again. Her fingers still felt the skin at his nape, the bristles along his cheek, the cool strands of his hair. Her lips still tingled from his mouth's hungry pressure.

"Henry," she whispered.

"Go, Maureen."

"Not until you explain." He said nothing, so she answered for him. "You didn't want me, and now"—she raised her hands in a helpless shrug—"you do? Rather sudden, I daresay. Was it something you ate? The rosemary in your soup, perhaps?"

He gave a dry chuckle. "Tasted that, did you?"

"I have a sensitive palate."

"Indeed you do." Now he sounded more like the old Henry. Playful. Teasing. And yet, a darker, more sensual edge remained. He lowered his head and ran a hand through his hair. The profile of his jaw shone tight in the midday sun. Russet whiskers dusted the bones and muscles there. He'd always been lean, but amidst the glare, she noted the blue circles beneath his eyes, the lines of strain and fatigue around his mouth. "I am selfish, pet. A bloody selfish bastard."

She frowned. "What does that mean?"

"It means you should go."

Frustration, raw and acidic, began its ascent from her stomach to her throat. He did not intend to explain himself. She sensed it in his stance, his voice.

"Think me a naïve dolt if you prefer, Henry," she snapped. "Even a dolt deserves better than to be lied to. Then kissed. Then discarded."

"You are the one leaving, as I recall."

"I am leaving because I thought you were not an option." She liked enunciating her words with a little slice at the beginning and end. It conveyed a satisfying level of dissatisfaction with his responses. "Had I known you *were* an option—"

"I am not."

Breath turned to stone in her chest. She breathed anyway, the stone heavy and thick.

So, there was the truth, as baldly as he intended to state it. He liked her, but only enough for friendship. He desired her, but not enough to marry.

Had she been anyone other than an earl's daughter—an actress or washwoman or lady's maid—he might have deigned to take her as his mistress. Not a wife. Never a wife.

"I see," she said, squeezing the words past the stone. Her eyes dropped to her hands, folded at her waist, stacked one atop the other. She let them fall to her sides. What point was there, really, in posing like some Grecian statue? It was one of the little changes she had made over the years, one of a thousand tips she had read in the pages of *The Ladies' Repository of Fashion, Amusement, and Instruction.*

But no more. In truth, all her changes—her scent and her hair and her gowns and her slippers and her hands and her conversation—all had been in vain.

Because the problem had never been that Henry didn't want her. He simply didn't want her enough.

She straightened her back, forcing her chin to rise.

Henry might not wish to marry her. But others would. Holstoke, perhaps. Handsomely ascetic. Intrigued by serpentine lakes. Interested in her.

Clearing her throat of its infernal tightness, she swallowed again before finishing what she had started. "There is only one thing left to say, then." She breathed out. Then in. She gathered her strength and did as she must. "Goodbye, Henry. I wish you well."

Before the tears burning the backs of her eyes could emerge, she found the door, pulled it open, and left Henry Thorpe behind.

Regina, slumped against the wall with her arms folded, turned a harsh look of condemnation upon her. It softened instantly into concern. Then one stout arm circled her shoulders, gathered her close, and patted her awkwardly. "Let us return home, now, m'lady. You'll feel better when you've had some tea and biscuits."

Maureen let Regina guide her down the corridor. Let her intimidate Henry's bespectacled valet, Mr. Stroud, as he passed them with a curious stare.

Just before they turned the corner for the staircase, she heard Stroud open a door. And then came the strangest sound.

It was the noise of Henry Thorpe—the fastidious, fashionable, dapper, unflappable Earl of Dunston—smashing his bedchamber to pieces.

# Chapter Six

*"My sources are superior to all others.*
*Question this fact at your peril."*

—The Dowager Marchioness of Wallingham to Lord Dunston
in reply to said gentleman's skepticism about a certain gaming club
proprietor's implausible bloodlines.

"Looks like the devil ran you to ground and trampled you with the four horsemen of the apocalypse."

Ordinarily, Henry might have laughed at Sebastian Reaver's extravagant description—the club owner was better known for hard calculation than florid rhetoric—but it had been weeks since he'd felt the slightest amusement. Weeks since she had stood in his bedchamber and told him ...

He shied away from the thought, unable to remember without losing his mind.

Stroud still had not forgiven him for shattering the dressing mirror or dismantling the draperies.

Henry sat in the plain, wooden chair in front of Reaver's plain, wooden desk and crossed his legs with feigned insouciance. "The devil would have to catch me first."

Reaver grunted. Dark, heavy brows lowered over assessing eyes. The man was massive—yard-wide shoulders, flagrant muscularity, rough features, and nearly six-and-a-half feet of height. Henry knew of only one other with a similar frame. Rumors had been swirling for months about a connection between the two men. Such a link seemed improbable to Henry.

The man in question was the Earl of Tannenbrook, a Scot who had inherited an English title, whereas Sebastian Reaver was an orphaned commoner who had clawed his way up from rank poverty with an unusual combination of brute strength and ruthless cunning. Reaver was vocally prejudiced in favor of commerce and against the privileges of nobility. He'd been a thief, a workman, a bruiser, and now, the owner of a gaming club that regularly stripped wealthy bloods of their fortunes.

Apart from which, the source of the information was Lady Wallingham. Henry remained skeptical.

"Devils tend to excel in that regard." Reaver paused, appearing to calculate his next word. "Sabre."

Henry grinned but kept it cold. "Cannot say I own one, old chap. Not even for ceremonial purposes."

"Regardless, it is what they've dubbed you. Some say you are deadly as a blade."

Holding that dark gaze with unflinching directness, Henry tsked. "Some say your blood is nobler than your current vocation would suggest." With satisfaction, he noted the glint of surprise, the faint narrowing of Reaver's eyes.

*Ah, so the rumors are true,* he thought. *Well done, Lady*

*Wallingham.* "Perhaps we should cast aside speculation and return to the business at hand."

That business was information—and Reaver's was both expensive and worthy of the price. "Chalmers knew something, that much is certain." Blunt-fingered hands lifted a stack of papers and extended them across the desk.

Henry took them, quickly scanning for pertinent names. Syder, mainly. But also anyone who might know of Syder's ward.

Reaver continued, "He was paid well for his silence while Syder lived. Quarterly installments. Those payments ended December of '17. That was when Chalmers began living beneath his brother's shop."

Henry glanced up from the papers. "Why keep him alive? Syder was—"

"A butcher. I know." Reaver lifted a finger toward the documents Henry held. "They were chums from boyhood, it appears. Chalmers was the reason Syder became a solicitor in the first place. This, according to Chalmers's brother and sister."

The door to Reaver's office opened and Drayton entered, his chest heaving, his houndish face more haggard than usual. After a quick nod of greeting, he said, "No easy way to say it. Bow Street is compromised."

Henry frowned. "How deep?"

"My men are clear of it. But at least four others have received notes like Boyle's."

Reaver's bass rumble intruded. "Higher demand for Sabres than I might have predicted."

Ignoring him, Henry glanced down at the papers. "And Mrs. Boyle?" he asked, his tone suggesting it didn't matter in the slightest. Drayton would know better, of course.

The runner's silence was too long.

"When?" Henry said softly, rubbing the corner of one page between his thumb and forefinger.

"Three days ago. She left the cottage you purchased to visit her mother. My men found her on the road to Manchester."

Henry nodded, feeling his gorge rise. "The babe?"

"Alive. Mrs. Boyle must have hidden him before the attacker caught her. We'd not have found him at all but for his cries, the poor mite. He's with his grandmother now."

Silence fell like freezing fog in the room. Reaver, with stillness and patience, waited for Henry's reaction. Henry could almost hear the hum and tick of the other man's calculations. Reaver was nothing if not opportunistic.

But today, he surprised him. "When I spoke of the devil running you to ground, I'd not intended it literally. This Investor. Worse than Syder?"

Henry raised his head. Met the bruiser's gaze, surprised to find it glinting with a hard edge. Reaver had known Syder personally, for they'd operated in the same underworld of gaming hells, albeit on different planes of depravity.

Sebastian Reaver might be ruthless, but he was no butcher.

That description belonged to Horatio Syder, a mundane solicitor who had been hired, funded, and directed by the Investor to establish a vast series of illicit "businesses," ranging from distilleries and stockyards to gaming hells and houses of ill repute. He'd catered to the lowest perversions, installing both women and children in his brothels, many against their will.

One of those women had been Drayton's sister. A week after Syder was killed, Drayton had taken five men—six if Henry counted himself—into the crumbling, vermin-infested warren where she was being kept, and had carried her out like a limp, vacant doll.

Betsy Drayton had died four months later, weakened and ravaged by disease.

She'd been but one of Syder's victims. The list was lengthy.

In his hells, he'd prayed not upon the careless and wealthy, but rather young, green men newly arrived in London, fleecing them of their few measly pounds, leaving them destitute. Some had taken their own lives.

He'd run thievery rings all over the city, murdered and brutalized with no more care for the lives he took than for an insect one crushed under one's boot heel. In short, he'd been a monster. A clever, conscienceless monster.

"Yes," Henry replied to Reaver's question. "The Investor is worse than Syder."

Drayton grunted his agreement. "Might have said otherwise at one time. More elusive, for certain. But it is clear now that without the Investor, Syder would still be wielding a quill in some windowless office in Cheapside."

With a headshake and a half-smile, Reaver leaned forward, his massive forearm braced on his desk. "How much longer can you keep up the chase, Dunston? Now that the devil is chasing you, I mean."

Henry had asked himself that question countless times—more often over the last several weeks. He had no answer.

Ten years he'd been pursuing the Investor. He'd paid a bloody fortune for information from men like Reaver. He'd entangled himself first with the Foreign Office, then the Home Office in a bid to expand his reach. He'd risked his life and, more importantly, the lives of good men to lure Horatio Syder out of hiding. He'd lost lifelong friendships.

He'd lost ... her.

*How much longer can you keep up the chase?*

"Took us years to bring down Syder. But we did it, didn't we?" answered Drayton from behind him. He heard the Bow Street runner shifting, a signal of his imminent departure. Drayton was the restless sort, having worked himself nearly into the grave while searching for his sister. Even now, the runner was struck by a queer urgency whenever he'd been in one place too long.

Reaver possessed similar energy, except his was a furnace of ambition and drive he kept well hidden. Seeing him now, the massive shoulders tensing and relaxing as the man worked to contain himself, Henry could only conclude he needed a new challenge. It made sense. Reaver had spent his life fighting for every inch of ground. Now, his club was one of the most exclusive and lucrative in London. He was richer than most titled men. But a conqueror's desire to test himself did not abate simply because he'd reached one pinnacle.

"Well," Henry replied, holding Reaver's shrewd, churning gaze. "Colin Lacey brought him down, to be precise. Syder attempted to cut his wife's throat. Lacey was most ... displeased."

Reaver didn't blink. "How was the Duke of Blackmore's brother involved?"

"That, my dear fellow, is a long tale, indeed." Henry brushed imaginary lint and smoothed an imaginary wrinkle from his sleeve. "Let it suffice to say Lacey lent me invaluable assistance, and when Syder learned of it, he attempted to persuade Lacey to reveal the identity of his pursuer."

"You."

"Mmm."

"And Lord Colin Lacey—a man constantly in his cups until his brother cut off his funds—protected you." It was hard to blame Reaver for his skepticism. During the period when Lacey had patronized Reaver's club, he'd been a scapegrace with few redeeming virtues. One would never expect him to withstand hours of torture for the sake of doing the honorable thing.

Henry sniffed. "I am an excellent judge of character. Lacey was always better than his poor choices. He simply needed a reason to realize it."

"So, Lacey dispensed with Syder. And now, he knows the truth. Does Blackmore?"

"The truth about ..."

"You. That you are Sabre."

Henry merely stared back at the other man, letting his gaze slowly deaden.

Drayton answered for him. "His lordship doesn't much fancy that name. Best leave off."

To his credit, Reaver didn't shrink, instead straightening in his chair and donning an unexpected pair of reading spectacles. Perched on the man's twice-broken nose, the silver-wired rims were delicate and ridiculous.

He slid open a drawer and plucked another page from inside, shaking the paper briefly and glancing down to read. *"Mr. Syder appears to have kept his ward, a girl of fourteen at the time of his death, confined to a house twenty miles outside Bath. According to the housekeeper, one Mrs. Ann Finney (lately of Bristol), he retained three tutors and two governesses for the girl over a period of ten years. All retainers have subsequently disappeared, presumed dead. Mrs. Finney expressed her desire for additional funds sufficient to travel to Canada. However, upon our return with said funds to her residence in Bristol, we discovered Mrs. Finney to be deceased."* Reaver lowered the paper and removed his spectacles. "This report was delivered to you last year."

Henry did not reply. God alone knew how Reaver had acquired it. The man had sources throughout the city funneling secrets to him—in addition to the gentlemen who paid their gaming debts with the ton's treasury of illicit information, Reaver bribed Home Office clerks, Bow Street runners, members of Parliament, and chambermaids in the households of Almack's patronesses. Henry wouldn't be surprised to discover the queen herself was in Reaver's pocket. Secrets were his business as much as gaming.

Reaver lightly tapped the paper with a blunt fingertip, now lying flat on the plain, oaken surface. "She is your key, is she not? Syder would scarcely have kept her hidden without a bloody good reason."

"Of what import should it be to you?" Henry replied, his tone nonchalant. "I pay you well for the information you provide. That is the extent of our association."

Dark eyes narrowed and glinted with menace. "Someone is

keeping Syder's name alive. That someone is of interest to me and those who work for me."

Behind Henry, Drayton snorted. "Protecting your territory, eh?"

Reaver speared the runner with a black glare.

"Drayton, perhaps you could make a few inquiries," Henry intervened. "There may be a thread leading to the Investor. Or, at least, the Investor's new venture."

Nodding, Drayton pivoted with a flare of his greatcoat and exited Reaver's office, taking his bristling energy with him.

"You don't believe his inquiries will lead anywhere, do you?"

Henry sighed. "They rarely have before."

"What about the ward?"

"No trace." Henry waved a finger to indicate the paper lying beside Reaver's thick wrist. "That was the last we knew of her. We don't even know her proper name."

"Perhaps you've not been asking the proper questions."

Reaver's rumbling reply dug a burning furrow beneath Henry's skin. What in bloody hell would a Cumberland-born bruiser with too much money and too little concern about methods of acquiring it understand about chasing devils?

Nothing. Not a single, bloody thing.

Henry's seething gut wanted him to lay the bruiser flat with a blow to that granite jaw. Every man he'd lost, the blood he'd spilled, the threads that had been abruptly cut every time he came within a breath of his quarry. Years upon years of hunting smoke, and nothing to show for it.

He could not react the way he wished, of course. He could not spew bitterly about everything he'd sacrificed, nor break the man's nose a third time, nor rage about how many ways he'd asked "proper questions."

Because he was Dunston. A harmless, albeit dashing lord fond of hosting hunts and sporting new waistcoats. Dunston was wit and charm, humor and flair. He was not permitted bouts of fury.

Fury conjured an image of her. Maureen. Tears had

reddened her eyes and nose. Her voice had been wrenchingly hoarse. *Goodbye, Henry. I wish you well.*

He shoved to his feet and stalked the length of the room to the single, narrow window. To either side were oak shelves. The right one held a clock, conspicuously ornate with filigreed gold hands. Reaver's office—in contrast with the opulence of his club—was as plain and blunt and spare as the man.

Henry waited for the hands to move, noting as they did that the light outside the window shifted from yellow to gray. Rain was coming.

"I can help you."

"No."

Reaver's rumble deepened. "Damn you, Dunston, you've been at this too long. Too many people can connect you to Sabre—Lacey, Blackmore, Drayton. How long until the Investor knows?"

"Not long, I expect. He has already tracked my connection to Bow Street."

"Aye. It's obvious you've some personal stake in the matter, but you need help. Give me what you have. Let me chase the devil for a while, eh? Perhaps I'll have better luck."

Henry first let silence yawn with only the faint tick of the clock to mark the time. Then, he answered, keeping his voice gentle but sparing no quarter. "You are unmarried. No children or family. So the Investor will start with your staff here at the club." He turned away from the clock and clasped his hands loosely behind his back. "First, your majordomo will go missing. Shaw, yes? Then your secretary, Mr. Frelling. Newly married last month, I believe. His wife would be taken. He would attempt to kill you in a vain effort to save her. A knife, most likely. Quieter that way." He looked Reaver up and down, taking his measure. "Frelling would die in the process, of course. And yet, you would be the one defeated."

Black hair had fallen over Reaver's lowered brows. The proprietor leaned forward in his chair, his fingers interlaced upon his desk, listening intently while trying to appear relaxed.

"The Investor loves that game best. Playing love against loyalty, affections against duty. It amuses him to make you choke to death on your own heart."

Reaver shook his head. "All the more reason you could use my assis—"

"The information you provide is sufficient. We shall keep our arrangement as it is."

He sat back, ran a massive paw through his hair, and released a gust of frustration. "You cannot protect us all, your bloody lordship." His fist dropped to the desk with a solid thud. "If you want to catch the devil, you'll need someone like me."

"I have Drayton. That is enough."

"It hasn't been, though, has it?"

Ignoring the point, Henry turned back to the clock. Watched filigreed hands move incrementally. "Have you anything else for me?"

A loud sigh. Chair legs scraping. A drawer opening.

"Not on the Investor. But I took the liberty of acquiring information on Holstoke."

Henry frowned. "Holstoke?"

"Aye. Appears he's seeking a wife. It is what brought him and his mother to London after all this time. No debts. No drink. Not even a mistress, at present. Peculiar interests, gardens and such. But little cause for alarm."

Henry faced him again, chills chasing bewilderment. "Why in blazes would I need information on Holstoke?"

One heavy, black brow lifted. "I assumed you would want it. She has been seen with him on at least seven occasions in the last fortnight."

*She.* He could only be referring to one *she,* for Henry had only ever purchased information on one woman's suitors.

*Goodbye, Henry. I wish you well.*

"Was I mistaken, then? Shall I cease further inquiries?"

He thought of her. The lips pursed as though upon a secret. The sunlit hair and helpless laugh. The silly observations about willow trees and walled gardens. The scent of vanilla and orange blossoms. The gentle stroke of her fingers upon his brow.

Upon Holstoke's brow. Upon Holstoke's ...

"No," he gritted, scarcely able to breathe past the constriction in his chest. "I want everything. Get me everything you can find on Lord Holstoke."

# Chapter Seven

*"Astonishing, indeed. One marvels at a man's tolerance for the intolerable when faced with the prospect of wifely deprivation."*

—THE DOWAGER MARCHIONESS OF WALLINGHAM to Lady Berne upon learning of Lord Berne's acquiescence to acquiring another feline companion.

BY ALL RIGHTS, MAUREEN SHOULD HAVE BEEN WATCHING THE man standing atop a pair of galloping black horses, waving a red banner and shouting taunts at the clown spinning madly in the center of the ring. It was an astounding feat, one that made her younger sisters, Genie and Kate, clap and laugh and lean over the railing of their box with bright-eyed delight.

Instead, she gazed upon Phineas Brand, the Earl of

Holstoke. Seated beside her in the row behind the two girls, the black-haired lord held himself still and expressionless, those pale eyes following the circular route of the acrobatic rider as though analyzing the man's use of centrifugal force. He neither laughed nor smiled nor shifted in his seat. Rather, he sat calmly, like a quiet lake on a windless night, content for the commotion to occur around him.

*What would it be like to kiss this man?* she wondered. *To marry this man? To bear his children?* For, surely such a fate was coming.

This evening at Astley's Amphitheatre constituted an escalation of their courtship—previously, they'd confined themselves to the landscaped parks, Kensington Gardens, and the British Museum—venues which facilitated their shared interests. This outing, however, proved the seriousness of Holstoke's intent.

He wanted to marry her. He wanted to please her by pleasing her sisters. There could be no other reason to subject himself to a performance of such lighthearted revelry. Silliness was the opposite of Holstoke.

She frowned. Perhaps it was time to begin thinking of him as Phineas.

Eerie green eyes met her own. "What is your question?"

She smiled slowly. He did that often—guessed her thoughts without her having to say a word. The only other man who had ever done so was ...

No. She refused to think about him. Not this evening.

Licking her lips, she shook her head and widened her grin. "Whether I should begin thinking of you as Phineas, rather than Holstoke."

He took her statement as the declaration it was, his eyes flaring with surprised heat. "I should be glad of it," he murmured, his low voice drowned by the thunder of hooves, the raucous play of the orchestra, and the roar of the audience's laughter.

But she heard him.

For a man of few words and exceptional seriousness, it was virtually a vow of passionate devotion. She felt the Huxley Flush wash hot over her face. Forcing herself to remain connected to him, she held his gaze and nodded. "Very well, then."

A face leaned past Holstoke's opposite shoulder, intruding into Maureen's vision. Despite creases around the liquid blue eyes and ivory forehead, it was jarringly beautiful—delicately sloped nose, symmetrical brows, dramatically high cheekbones. The cheekbones were, in fact, the sole feature marking her as Holstoke's mother. "Have your sisters never been to Astley's, dear?"

Maureen's flush intensified. She glanced at where Genie and Kate leaned over the railing. Then, she answered Lady Holstoke's implied criticism with a tight smile. "Forgive them their excitement, my lady. They are young, and Astley's performances are spectacular."

The older woman nodded, smiling placidly. "Ah, of course. To be expected, I suppose. I'm afraid I am unaccustomed to excitable children. Holstoke was tediously silent as a boy."

Maureen did not know why the answer chafed her temper so sharply, any more than she understood why she had failed to warm to Lady Holstoke. She watched the woman sit back in her chair and applaud the rider as sawdust flew upward from the ring, showering the front of their box and driving Genie and Kate to retreat to their seats.

Holstoke's mother was beautiful. Polite. Certainly, her demeanor could be both silken and cool, as it was now, but she was far more agreeable than Lady Dunston, whom Maureen had befriended even after that lady's poor treatment of Jane. Puzzling, indeed, that she would continue her visits to Henry's mother and yet be bothered by a hint of censure from Lady Holstoke.

Drat. She was doing it again. Comparing Holstoke and Henry. Or, rather, Phineas and Henry. Good heavens, why must she dwell upon him? Their friendship was over. She hadn't seen him in weeks. Interminable, crushing weeks.

Deliberately, she returned her attention to the man beside her—the man who wished to marry her and father her children. With a deep breath, she stared hard at his high cheekbone until he sensed her regard and looked her way.

"If I haven't already said so, thank you for this evening." She swallowed, wishing she was better at reading those unreadable green eyes. "Phineas."

His head tilted. He leaned closer, smelling of lemons and mint leaves and soap. "It is my pleasure, Lady Maureen."

With a quick smile, she turned back to the show, wondering why she was suddenly chilled and a little queasy.

An hour later, as their coach pulled up in front of Berne House, her nerves had settled, but her thoughts had not. She considered how wrong it would be to pilfer a bottle of wine from the cellar and drink until she was sotted. Being sotted made one forget, didn't it? How she longed to forget. To let go of what could never be.

Kate exited the carriage first, her brown ringlets bouncing merrily as she continued recounting the horseman's final flourish. "Oranges! Can you imagine, Genie? He tossed oranges into the air and caught them all! I must learn the trick of it. I *will* learn it."

"Papa would sooner lock you in a tower, ninny," Genie replied, following Kate and giving Thomas, their newest footman, a lingering smile.

Maureen sighed and rubbed her temple as Kate protested that learning to juggle oranges posed little danger to which Papa might object, and Genie replied with her usual acerbity that doing so while standing atop a galloping horse might change his assessment. Their bickering was giving her a megrim.

She accepted Thomas's help to descend from the carriage, but before she'd taken two steps, the front door opened and Mama appeared, dabbing her cheeks with her handkerchief and waggling her fingers toward the carriage. "Back into the coach, girls," she said, beaming through her tears. "Our Jane needs us."

Maureen gasped and reached for Genie's hand automatically, comforted at once by the sisterly squeeze. "Is she well, Mama?"

Thankfully, Mama nodded, shooing them all back toward the carriage. "The babe is coming. We should go now. Your Papa is already at Clyde-Lacey House. It seems Harrison is in need of a father's support."

By the time they arrived at the elegant house in Berkeley Square and ensconced themselves on the sofas in the drawing room, Genie and Kate had already chosen names for the child. Kate proposed Oberon for a boy and Titania for a girl.

"You cannot name a duke's child for characters in that silly play," complained Genie. "Oberon, Duke of Blackmore. What a fanciful farce that would—"

Kate reached across Maureen's lap to swat Genie's arm. "Better than your suggestion! You would name our nephew after a footman!"

Genie shoved at Kate's hand and grumbled, "Thomas is a fine name. A *normal* name for—"

Maureen grasped each of their wrists gently, watching their mother dab her eyes and disguise her trepidation as she stared down into the fireplace. "Hush now, both of you," Maureen admonished. "Jane and Harrison will choose their child's name, and we will have nothing to say about it apart from felicitations."

The younger girls subsided, finally noticing their mother's tension. Maureen rose and laid a hand in the center of Mama's shawled back. "All will be well, Mama. You mustn't worry."

It was rare to see Mama so distressed. She was a merry sort, full of good humor and twinkling charm. She must be remembering the tragic loss of Annabelle's first child two months before he should have been born. A year had passed before Annabelle and her husband, Lord Robert Conrad, had conceived again. Their daughter had arrived just before Christmas, a healthy little cherub they had named Beatrice.

Presently, Mama sniffed and nodded and dabbed her reddened, rounded nose. "I'm certain you are right. Our Jane is strong."

From the drawing room's open door, Papa replied, "That she is, dearest."

Maureen's heart warmed to see him, quiet and jovial, lean and tall with his thinning, silver hair only a bit mussed. He crossed the room to gather Mama into his arms before reaching out to clasp Maureen's hand. As usual, Papa managed to reassure his girls with his mere presence.

"Oh, Stanton," her mother cried. "Is Harrison terribly distraught?"

"He is fretting, as any husband awaiting the birth of his first child would. Jane ordered him from her chamber after he threatened to disembowel both the physician and the midwife. But John is plying him with drink in the study, so I expect he will soon either be less fretful or less conscious. Either way, an improvement is imminent."

John entered moments later, a younger, slightly taller, more robust version of Papa, with the same distinguished nose and ready smile. Now, however, he was running a hand through Huxley-brown hair as though his wits' end had come and gone. Behind him, an even taller man followed.

Jane liked to describe him as the Apollo of the aristocracy, blond and hard-jawed and so handsome that one was tempted to commission a marble sculpture of his likeness. It helped, Jane often said with wry affection, that his bearing was as stiff as stone. This evening, Harrison Lacey, the eighth Duke of Blackmore, was in disarray, his blue-gray eyes bloodshot and stormy, his over-starched cravat missing, along with his tailcoat.

Maureen blinked twice upon seeing her brother-in-law, a man who never lost command of himself, weaving in place just inside the doors of his drawing room.

Her brother reached back to steady the teetering duke.

"John, how much brandy did you give him?" Maureen asked.

"A better question is how much did he drink," John said sardonically, patting Harrison's shoulder. "By the time I had anything to say about it, half the bottle was gone."

"How did you bear it, Stanton?" Harrison asked, his speech slower than normal but not slurred. "Six. Bloody. Times."

Papa gave him a grin and approached with a sympathetic chuckle. "It gets easier, son. You'll see." He and John helped Harrison navigate the length of the room and eased him into a winged chair near the fireplace.

All the while, Harrison shook his head, appearing stricken. "No. Never again."

Mama, unable to contain herself, knelt beside him and stroked his cheek with the backs of her fingers. "Dearest boy. When you meet your babe, all of this fear and worry will seem little more than a dream. You must trust me on this point."

Harrison closed his eyes. "It is a nightmare, Mama. Jane suffers and I cannot ..."

His concession to calling her "Mama" was a measure of either his drunkenness or his turmoil. Perhaps both. For two years, he'd resisted Meredith Huxley's maternal overtures. Only since Jane had announced she was with child had he softened, gradually permitting Meredith to mother him as she longed to do.

Maureen understood Mama's impulse. Harrison was a proud man, one who'd been scarred by a frigid upbringing and a cruel father. His love for Jane had opened his heart, but accepting affection from their family, especially her parents, remained difficult for him. Which only made Mama more determined.

Harrison's sandy-haired butler, Digby, was next to appear in the doorway. He cleared his throat discreetly before announcing, "I do beg your pardon, your grace, but you have a visitor."

Harrison blinked slowly and frowned. "Who?"

"Me."

Maureen's blood fired hot as a red iron, lighting her skin and scalp with tingling sparks. Henry. Oh, God. It was Henry.

Her eyes devoured him—chestnut hair longer than she'd seen it in months, cheeks leaner, dark coat and trousers looser on his athletic frame. But his waistcoat drew her notice above everything else. It was the dull yellow-brown of half-rotted leaves. Not a single gold thread. Not a single flourish of embroidery.

"Go away," Harrison snarled.

"I cannot," Henry replied, nodding to Mama and Papa before sauntering closer to Harrison's chair. "I was summoned."

"Not by me."

"No. By your wife."

A muscle flexed in Harrison's jaw. "Bloody hell."

"Are you sotted?"

"Yes."

Henry raised a brow and quirked his lips. "Excellent. Perhaps now you'll be reasonable."

Harrison's eyes narrowed. "I have misplaced my watch."

"Good God, man. *You* without a watch? Alarming state of affairs, I daresay. How will you judge whether it has been five minutes or ten since you last set eyes upon the duchess?"

"It has been an eternity. A watch merely assures me that eternity may be measured, and therefore, may end."

Ambling nearer with his usual grace, Henry pretended to search his pockets before lifting out a gold-colored watch with two fingers and dangling it before Harrison's nose. "Here, now. A man needs his comforts, I suppose."

Harrison took it, grumbling about how it was "strangely made" and "gilt brass rather than gold."

Henry merely rolled his eyes and crossed his arms over his chest. "Tedious lot. I recommend drinking either more or less to achieve the desired effect, for this melancholia cannot possibly have been your aim."

Observing the byplay between the two men, Maureen wondered again what had caused the rift between them. They'd once been as close as brothers. Henry had been Harrison's best man at his wedding to Jane.

She remembered it well. She had stood as one of Jane's attendants, and during the "with my body, I thee worship" portion of the vows, he had caught her eye and shot her a glittering, rakish grin from across the aisle. She had blushed and gone buttery inside, thinking the dashing Lord Dunston was flirting.

He hadn't been, of course. It was simply Henry's way to smile and laugh and charm. Except right now, the only smile he seemed able to manage was a wry twist of his lips. In truth, he looked quite unlike himself, as though a light had been snuffed out.

She dropped her eyes to her hands, which were stupidly folded one atop the other at her waist. *Preposterous Grecian pose.*

Digby interrupted again to announce that Jane had requested that both Lady Berne and Harrison return to her chamber. Mama immediately bustled out of the room, clutching her handkerchief to her bosom. Upon hearing his name, Harrison bolted to his feet, only to tilt alarmingly like a tree unmoored from its roots.

Swifter than a blink, Henry was by his side, grasping his arm and bracing him expertly. "Time for old sobersides to return, I think. Come now, your grace. Let us gather our watches and our senses."

Harrison leaned on him heavily for a moment before regaining his customary rigid posture. "The room is spinning."

"Let it spin. Jane needs you."

Harrison nodded and blinked. "Right you are."

Henry released his arm and slapped his back. "See? Reasonable. Perhaps the brandy you imbibed was sufficient, after all."

Stepping to Harrison's opposite side, John battled a grin. "I shall take him, Dunston. Already made this journey twice tonight."

The two men moved with care and deliberation to the drawing room doors. At the last, Harrison braced his hand on the casing and turned around to spear Henry with a glance. "Do not leave."

Henry nodded. "I'll be here."

After Mama and John and Harrison left, Papa gathered Genie and Kate together at the corner table to play a game of loo using Genie's stash of ribbons as the pot. Maureen elected not to join them, remaining in her position on the periphery of the room, near the windows.

Henry had not looked at her once. Not once. Perhaps it was too much to expect that he would at least glance her way, or cross the room and say ... something. Anything. *You're looking well, pet. New gown?*

A faint smile tugged her lips, imagining the conversation.

*No, Henry. I'm afraid only the most extravagant among us purchase a new waistcoat for every occasion.*

*Ah, there's the problem with the world. Appalling lack of variety.*

They had said their goodbyes weeks ago. After he had kissed her. Shocked her senseless. Made her burn inside her skin and then told her to go because he would never be an option.

She stared at his shoulders, the hair that brushed his coat's collar. His back was to her as he stood gazing down at the fire, one hand braced on the mantel, one on his hip.

Was he eating enough? Had his arm healed properly? Did he miss her?

She'd visited Lady Dunston every week, those questions eating a hole inside her throat. She never asked them, instead drinking weak tea and nodding in agreement at the injustices and indignities of gout.

No, she decided. He was not going to look at her. He was

going to pretend they were strangers. And wasn't that what she'd wanted? To make room?

Distantly, she heard Genie crowing as she acquired another blue ribbon. Papa chuckled and Kate protested and the fire crackled.

Chilled, Maureen gathered her knitted shawl closer around her shoulders. With measured force, she dragged her gaze away from where firelight spun its shadows through Henry's hair. She turned to the window to gaze upon the blackness shrouding Berkeley Square. In the golden reflection, she glimpsed her own face and knew. She might never speak to Henry Thorpe again. But, despite her best efforts, a piece of her would always be his. She only hoped it was possible to live without it.

HE HADN'T BEEN ABLE TO LOOK AT HER SINCE ENTERING Harrison's drawing room. Vaguely, he knew she wore blue. Knew she was close. Felt her eyes upon him.

An hour passed before Lord Berne approached him, leaving his two youngest daughters to divide their ribbon pot and settle the terms of loo disarmament.

"Dunston," the older man murmured. "Cannot recall the last time you were silent for this long."

Henry's mouth quirked. "I've heard ladies fancy a brooding poet. Must practice the brooding, as it does not come naturally."

Berne's eyes warmed and sparked with amusement. Henry had always liked Maureen's papa, whose easy humor and hazel gaze reminded him of his own father.

"Ah, yes. That explains the longer hair. Byron sported a similar style before he fled to the Continent, as I recall."

Raising a brow, Henry replied, "Perhaps his valet was vexed

with him. Mine is expressing his displeasure by misplacing the shears."

"You could speak to her, you know." Berne kept his voice low, his head tilted in a fatherly fashion. "Her mother and I might be opposed to marriage between you, but not to a conversation."

At the reminder of their disapproval, Henry went cold. Lord and Lady Berne knew of his past work for the Home Office—a tidbit gleaned from Lady Wallingham, no doubt. Because Harrison was their son-in-law, they also knew he'd hunted Horatio Syder and that his pursuit had endangered Harrison's brother. Naturally, they opposed his interest in Maureen.

Who could blame them? He was a danger to her. Every time he spun her about in a waltz, every time he rode with her in the park, every time he persuaded one of her suitors to abandon his suit, he risked the Investor realizing her importance. Yet, he'd been unable to stop. To his great, everlasting frustration, her nearness was akin to breathing. Without it, he drowned.

"No. Better I should leave her be," Henry said now, keeping his back to the windows.

"Perhaps you're right. What would you talk about, after all? Tales of her outing with Holstoke, one supposes. Astley's Amphitheatre. A man stood on the backs of two horses at full gallop. Remarkable trick."

Sharpening to razor fineness, Henry's gaze flew to Berne's. Hazel eyes crinkled at the corners, warmed with a knowing glint.

"Takes a committed rider to brave such a feat. Seriousness of purpose, wouldn't you agree? Eugenia and Kate went along, incidentally. And Holstoke's mother."

Henry's jaw tightened until his teeth ground as Berne's message became clear: Holstoke intended to offer for Maureen. He would not have arranged an outing involving Maureen, her sisters, and his mother for any other reason.

Without a word, Henry nodded his thanks for the older man's warning and crossed the room to where she stood. Maureen. Looking ethereally lovely in long-sleeved cerulean silk and a white knitted shawl. The firelight played with the light-brown curls at her nape.

Blast. His heart was pounding like a great drum. She made him dizzy. Made his skin prickle with heat. It was bad enough when he didn't look directly at her, worse when he did.

As he approached, he watched her reflection in the dark window. Watched his own reflection come behind her. They'd always been a perfect fit, well matched in height and humor, synchronized like two watches keeping time together. He wanted to wrap his arms around her waist. Kiss that lovely nape and hear her whisper his name.

"Henry," she breathed, meeting his eyes in the window's reflection.

He stopped inches away. "Are you well, pet?"

She turned to face him. He devoured her beauty—the petite, rounded nose, the golden-brown eyes, the secretive lips.

"I should ask that of you. Your arm is improved, I trust."

He shrugged. "Wounds heal, don't they?"

She swallowed and dropped her eyes to her hands. "Sometimes."

"Astley's was a spectacular lark, I hear."

Her chin inched up. "It was. Genie and Kate laughed themselves silly."

"Did you?"

She blinked, her eyes darkening. "Of course."

She was lying. The corners of her mouth twitched down in precisely that way whenever he asked if she approved of his puce waistcoat. Maureen loathed the shade, and she possessed no talent for deception.

"Thinking of me, pet?" he taunted, unable to help himself. Astley's had been theirs. He had escorted her, his mother, and his sister, Mary, last season. Maureen had laughed and applauded and gasped until he'd thought he might burst into flames from watching her, imagining similar breathless, open-mouthed delight as he thrust inside her body.

"No," she answered, her lips twitching downward at the corners.

He grinned for the first time in weeks. "Liar."

Her mother chose that moment to bustle back into the room and announce with a sob, "We have a grandson, Stanton. A grandson!"

As Berne rushed forward to embrace his wife, Genie and Kate leapt up and surrounded the pair, chattering like magpies. Minutes later, John entered the room, harried and beaming. "It is twins. Jane has delivered twins. A boy and a girl."

Lady Berne covered her mouth with both hands and spun with a gasp. "Twins? Good heavens! In my eagerness to report the news of our grandson, I didn't realize she hadn't finished!"

The entire Huxley family burst into delighted conversation all at once. Genie and Kate argued about whether Titania was an appropriate name for a girl. Lady Berne exclaimed her motherly pride at Jane's fortitude. John laughed about the moment Harrison had turned whiter than a freshly starched cravat. Lord Berne marveled at how much his family had grown in only an hour.

Every Huxley was exclaiming, laughing, smiling. Everyone except Maureen. He knew because he hadn't torn his eyes from her. Upon her gentle features he saw raw longing. Reluctant envy. Conflicted joy.

Inching closer, he lowered his head, the compulsion to erase her suffering burning through him. "For you, it will be a dozen, pet. Let us hope they do not arrive all at once."

Her eyes flew to his, but rather than softening into amusement as he'd wished, they flared with agonizing doubt.

"Come now," he murmured, nodding toward her family. "You are a Huxley. Huxleys breed. I shouldn't be surprised to find hares in the Berne crest."

There. He could see a spark of laughter in her eyes, the beginnings of a curve on her lips.

Discreetly, he slid a hand to the small of her back—his favorite spot—and savored the way she melted toward him. "One day, you will be round as a cabbage with a swarm of toddling, toothless little ones haranguing you for biscuits and marmalade. On that day, you will curse the Huxley name to the heavens, mark my words."

She snickered. "Daft man. It will be scones and strawberries. Biscuits are too dry."

He smiled. "There's my girl. Sensible, as always."

"Dunston," John called sharply.

Henry stiffened and let his hand fall away from Maureen. He turned with a brow lifted in inquiry.

"Jane would like to speak with you."

Frowning, Henry asked, "Do you mean Harrison?"

"No. Jane. Be thankful it is not Harrison, as he refused to let me leave the room until after the babes arrived. Something about sharing the misery. Deuced uncomfortable, I don't mind telling you." John rubbed his neck. "Come, I shall take you to her."

Henry glanced back at Maureen, who wore a similar confused frown. She shook her head. He turned back to John. "Well, never let it be said I kept a duchess waiting. Lead on, my good man."

Moments later, he entered the master bedchamber with a vague sense of trepidation. Facing an assassin in a black corner of London? A simple matter. Facing the Duchess of Blackmore after seven hours of labor and the delivery of twins? Terrifying. Particularly given he had little notion of what she wanted from him.

The room was well aired by an open window and warmed by a crackling fire. Gowned in white with her long, dark hair plaited neatly over her shoulder and her spectacles perched neatly upon her nose, Jane was propped up in the bed, surrounded by far too many pillows. Harrison sat in a chair next to his wife, staring down at the hand he held and looking as though he'd been brained with a copper pot. Nearby, a pair of cradles held what Henry presumed to be the future Duke of Blackmore and the boy's twin sister, who would never marry because her father would never allow it.

"Oh, do come in, Henry," said Jane, waving him closer with her free hand. "You must see the babes."

He bowed formally and muttered, "Duchess. It is good to see you looking so well," before approaching the pair of cradles.

What was it about infants that made one's chest tighten? They were tiny. Gowned in white. Wrinkled and scrunch-faced like wizened old men. Both had a tuft of dark hair. One's head was alarmingly cone-shaped.

"The pointier one is our son. We're calling him Gabriel. I wanted Fitzwilliam, but Harrison was adamantly opposed. The midwife assures us his head will normalize in time. The angel with the long lashes is Emma." Jane's voice choked alarmingly. "Isn't she b-beautiful?"

The girl's mouth pursed and worked as though seeking her supper. Then she sighed. A tiny, shuddering sigh. And her miniature, delicate fingers fluttered like a harpist's strumming.

"An angel, indeed, your grace," Henry agreed, smiling down at the wrinkled, splotchy, perfect little human. "However did you persuade heaven to release her into your care?"

"Oh, Henry," she sighed, reminding him of Maureen. "You always know the right thing to say."

He turned his smile up to her. Jane was sniffing and brushing away a tear beneath her spectacles. Harrison was glaring daggers at him. Henry cleared his throat. "Well, the brandy wore off, I see. Old sobersides returns."

"The very reason I asked you here," Jane said, the fatigue of her long labor evident in her rasping voice. She drew Harrison's hand to her lips and kissed his knuckles. Then, she leveled upon Henry a look of startling directness. "You are Harrison's dearest friend. It is past time that bond was restored."

Henry sighed. "Harrison is not the forgiving sort."

"You deceived me for years," Harrison gritted. "I believed you to be the man you pretended to be."

Rubbing his forehead with his thumb and finger, Henry wondered why conversations with Harrison Lacey often ended in a headache. "I am that man."

"You turned my brother into bait."

"Yes, well. I am also that man."

Harrison's eyes narrowed.

"We do not all have your purity, Blackmore. You forget that the world you inhabit—the world of unblemished honor and parliamentary maneuvers and efficient household management—has no answer for a man like Syder. Vanquishing such a creature requires weaponry of an entirely different sort."

Harrison stood, held in place only by Jane's grip upon his hand. "So you have claimed."

Henry raised a brow. "It is true."

"Colin could have died. His wife nearly did."

"Your brother *chose* to help me. Grant him credit for wanting to do something noble. After his appalling descent into the brandy bottle, I should think you would welcome his change of—"

"Now, you wish to marry Maureen."

Henry's voice abandoned him.

Harrison's voice grew quieter. Icier. "Yes. I know."

Cold fury rose inside him, emerging as a snarl. "Everything I have done—everything I am doing—is for her protection. Hers."

Jane intruded gently. "That is not in question, Henry."

Feeling as though they'd flayed him open and begun poking about his entrails, Henry ran a hand through his hair, peering at the pair before him. Jane, the plain wallflower who could scarcely speak a word in the presence of strangers. Harrison, the golden duke so proper and rigid, Henry marveled that he didn't crack when he walked. They'd been no one's idea of a good match. Their marriage had been one of necessity. Honor. And yet, they were perfect for one another.

He pointed at Harrison. "You are in no position to sit in judgment. You took advantage of Jane's mishap to claim her."

Harrison's lips went white. His jaw flickered.

"Ah, you didn't think I suspected, did you?"

Jane blinked, first at Henry, then up at Harrison. "What is he on about?"

Henry did not let up, holding Harrison's roiling gaze. "I have known you since you were in leading strings, old chap. Did you suppose I would not see how you maneuvered her into marriage? Your urgency every time she was near? The way you monitored that bloody watch—"

"Henry," Jane said, stroking her husband's hand soothingly. "Leave off, if you please. Harrison is protective of Maureen because he regards her as his sister, not because he finds you unworthy. If the decision were his, he would lock everyone he loves inside a cushioned palace and set an army outside for good measure." Jane nudged her spectacles and nodded toward the cradles. "They are why I asked you here."

Forcing himself to relax, Henry quipped, "I'd be an appalling nursemaid, Duchess. Infants leak. Damaging to waistcoats, you know."

Jane's mouth curled up at the corners. Then, she giggled and shook her head. She never resembled Maureen more than when she laughed. "A brilliant notion. Perhaps you could wear an apron." Her expression sobered. "In truth, we value your friendship, and we have missed it. Harrison is a father now. It is time you reconciled."

Henry sighed and crossed his arms. "In other words, you wish my help in managing his tyrannical tendencies."

"No," answered Harrison.

"Yes," said Jane. "But that is not the only reason." She glanced up at her husband. "You need him, my love. I am perhaps the only person who understands you quite so well. What happens when I am indisposed, as I was today?" Harrison's jaw clenched stubbornly, so she tried another tack. "He is your oldest and dearest friend. If you cannot forgive him, then you cannot forgive anyone. This bodes ill for our son and daughter, as they are bound to vex us eventually."

Frowning as he often did when faced with impossible choices, Harrison sat and brought Jane's hands to his lips. Then, he leaned forward and kissed her forehead. "Ruthless to make such a demand now, when you know I can deny you nothing," he murmured.

"For your happiness, I shall use every bit of leverage I possess. This should come as no surprise."

Harrison gazed down at his wife in a way that made Henry want to leave the room. "Very well," he said before turning in Henry's direction. "Your apologies are accepted."

Henry raised a brow at the gruff concession. "Did I apologize? I do not recall."

"Henry," Jane groaned. "Do not spoil this by being droll."

He sketched a bow. "Never, your grace."

Rising from his chair, Harrison approached. His eyes were reddened by fatigue and strain, but they remained steady and resolute. "Jane asks this of me, but she also asks something of you. We both do, in fact."

Henry looked to Jane, who wore a solemn expression, then back to his recently restored best friend. "What is your request?"

"I have three. First, take this back." He tugged the watch from his pocket and lowered it into Henry's outstretched palm. "Whatever you paid for it, you were fleeced. If you cannot do better than this piecemeal effort, I shall introduce you to my watchmaker at the next opportunity."

As Henry tucked the thing into his waistcoat pocket, he couldn't suppress a grin at yet another display of the Duke of Blackmore's exacting standards.

Harrison raised a brow and clasped his hands behind his back. "Second, never lie to me again."

"Hmmph. I predict you shall regret that stipulation. And third?"

Harrison braced a hand on Henry's shoulder, gripping hard and exhibiting an alarming degree of concern. "Abandon this fool's errand. Cease your pursuit of Syder's benefactor before you get yourself killed."

The unprecedented plea knocked away his next breath, lodging his usual denials inside his throat.

"I say this as your friend," said the man he'd known since boyhood. Those blue-gray eyes bored into his, reminding him of every time Harrison had done what was right and honorable, rather than what satisfied him. Now, in a voice abraded by worry, he spoke the hard truth, as only a friend would do. "You may have the mission you've assigned yourself. Or you may find happiness with Maureen. You may not have both."

Finally, Henry spoke, but found his own answer wretchedly inadequate. "I am doing this for her, to protect her from becoming a target. Why is that so hard to understand?"

From the bed, Jane called softly, "Your intentions may be noble, and we do not doubt your love for her, but she will not wait much longer, Henry. And you should not ask her to."

Harrison released his shoulder and nodded. "Either claim her affections or let her go. The choice belongs to you. It is time you made it."

SEBASTIAN REAVER HAD A HEAD FOR NUMBERS. PROBABILITIES were a particular specialty. He knew, for example, that a hazard caster's odds improved marginally with a main of seven. As the owner of a gaming club, rapid calculation was a talent worth having. But knowing the odds could also be a burden.

Especially when they involved death.

"Four members are delinquent in their dues," said Reaver's majordomo, extending the evening's credit slips across Reaver's desk. "An improvement to last month, I daresay." Apart from coal-black hair and skin the color of strong tea, Adam Shaw looked every inch the proper British butler. He dressed like one—black coat and trousers, white cravat—and spoke like one, too, his lofty vocabulary pronounced with overweening crispness. Reaver suspected the man did it to annoy him, but Shaw insisted it was his mother's influence. His mother had been adamantly English.

Reaver took the slips between two fingers and donned his reading spectacles. A distraction was welcome, but he had trouble focusing. His usual interest in the mewling lords clamoring for credit was being swarmed by news of another death.

He'd been galvanized by one. Grown suspicious after two. This made three. The odds were now longer than credulity could bear.

Three elderly men dying unexpected, yet seemingly natural, deaths. All of them possessed either titles or estates waiting like ripe plums to drop into the eager hands of their kin. Reaver would have taken little notice if the first plum to fall hadn't been a friend. The one bloody aristocrat he'd been able to tolerate.

George Gilmore, the Baron Gilmore, had been an iron-haired rascal fond of gaming, bawdy rhymes, and, oddly enough, gin. Every Friday for the past three years, the baron had summoned Reaver to a table in the club's smallest parlor, where they shared a bracing round of vingt-et-un, a glass or two of Old Tom gin, and the latest obscene poem the baron had committed to memory. Reaver had no particular liking for vingt-et-un, Old Tom, or vulgar poetry, but he'd liked the baron very much, aristocrat or no.

So, when Gilmore had missed their Friday appointment, he'd made inquiries—and discovered the hale, robust, humorous baron had been found dead in his bed the morning prior. He'd been lying with his hands folded across his chest, lips curved in a disturbing grin.

Immediately, Reaver's neck had begun to itch. It was a sensation he'd learned to heed as a fighter early on. The baron's heir, as it happened, suffered significant debts resulting from investments in a shipping company that sank. The inheritance buoyed the new baron's finances rather conveniently.

Whatever his suspicions, Reaver had no proof. Gilmore had been four-and-sixty. Some might say he'd lived longer than many and better than most. Natural thing. No cause for undue inquiry.

Then, it happened again. This time, the death was a lord Reaver knew only because the man had been a member of the club, and what he knew worsened the itch along his nape considerably. Elliott Hastings, Lord Lilliworth, had an ambitious heir with a spendthrift wife and two useless sons, along with an estate dangling like a ripe plum. He had died suddenly two days after his heir made inquiries about selling his fashionable Mayfair house.

The death had been widely reported as a natural, peaceful end to a long life.

Reaver had asked Frelling to search for other deaths that matched the first two. Now, there was a third. Another greedy family. Another wealthy, elderly victim.

"Shaw," he called to the departing majordomo. "The Investor Dunston is pursuing."

Shaw raised a brow. "Yes?"

"Have you discovered anything about his next venture?"

Retracing his steps halfway back to the desk, Shaw frowned. "It's all a bit ... murky. Syder's name has been kept alive deliberately, used as a cudgel to keep his thievery rings in place. Drayton suspects this is the Investor's work. Maintaining an army of ready messengers, I suppose."

Tapping a finger on the year-old newspaper he'd been reading moments ago, Reaver removed his spectacles. "I suspect the Investor has found a new enterprise."

"Oh?"

Reaver slid the newspaper across the desk and pointed to the article. "This man died last year. Read the description."

Leaning forward, Shaw spun the paper beneath his finger and read. His brows lifted. His head came up. "Bloody hell. They were all poisoned."

"Aye. I don't know what substance would produce such an effect, but the odds of these deaths being unrelated to a common cause are—"

"Long, indeed. What makes you think it is the Investor?"

"Something Horatio Syder said."

"You only met him once. Shortly before vowing to bring him down, as I recall."

He grunted. "Strangest thing. He *looked* like a solicitor. Thin. Inconspicuous. Carried a walking stick. Twirled the damn thing incessantly. You'd think nothing of him, eh? Until you looked a bit deeper. Aye. Then you'd see what nothingness really was."

"Yes, well, I was glad you asked me to remain here, comfortably ensconced with my brandy and my books." Shaw gave his usual white, toothy smile. "So, what did he say in this singular meeting?"

"He mentioned a name. A man he said had recently ceased to be of use to him. At the time, I thought it was an odd bit of boasting, implying he had more powerful men in his pocket, should he require them."

"The name?"

Again, Reaver tapped the article, his blunt, ink-stained finger settling just beneath the third man's name.

Shaw met his eyes. "Bloody hell."

"Syder was killed two months before this."

"So, you think the Investor was cleaning up the mess, as it were."

"We know he did so with others during that time."

Shaw rubbed the corners of his mouth. "What do you want to do? We can take it to Drayton, but—"

"No. Bow Street is compromised. Dunston is the only way."

Shaw scoffed. "No help from that quarter. You'll have to wait until he needs another report on Lady Maureen Huxley's suitors."

Reaver sat back in his chair, recalling one such report he'd delivered to the Earl of Dunston only yesterday. "Perhaps not," he murmured.

"Think he will change his mind, do you?"

Repositioning his spectacles, Reaver threw open his account book and began calculating. "I think sooner or later, the odds catch up with us all."

# Chapter Eight

*"Some things are not so much probabilities as inevitabilities.*
*Weak lemonade at Lady Gattingford's ball.*
*Demonstrations of a cat's disagreeable nature.*
*And my assertions being proven correct."*

—THE DOWAGER MARCHIONESS OF WALLINGHAM to her son,
Charles, regarding predictions that said gentleman's first child
would be a boy.

THE FLUFFY GRAY KITTEN HISSED AND SWIPED AT MAUREEN'S hem. She scooped him up and smoothed his fur before he could shred the primrose muslin. Holding him at eye level, she frowned a warning. "Behave yourself, Erasmus, or I shall toss you out with the onion scraps." The cat hissed again and clawed her hand. She rolled her eyes, extending the wriggling creature toward her sister, who stood smirking in the library doorway. "Genie, would you be so kind as to carry Erasmus to the kitchen garden? He is unfit company this morning."

Genie nodded to Regina. "She is the maid. Let her do it."

Maureen eyed Regina's thunderous glower as the maid snapped a thread with her teeth. "She is busy mending the last garment he destroyed."

Huffing indignantly, Genie relented, stomping into the room, snatching the irascible Erasmus from Maureen's hands, and stomping out again in a show of pink-ruffled protest.

In the dark-paneled corner of the room, Phineas watched them with puzzlement, as though he'd never seen an ill-tempered kitten before, let alone an adolescent girl's display of hauteur. She was finally beginning to read Holstoke's moods, though the ability had been slow in coming. He often studied her and her family with the air of a scientist examining a bewildering specimen.

But he hadn't yet lost interest in her after six weeks. A welcome reassurance, certainly. He continued inviting her on outings, continued their sparse and stilted conversations, continued advancing in a matrimonial direction.

In fact, minutes earlier, they had returned to Berne House after a pleasant, privately arranged visit to the Chelsea Physic Garden. He'd spoken little as they had enjoyed touring the lovely gardens near the Thames where master apothecaries obtained plants for their medicinal formulations. Walking with his hands clasped behind his back, he'd assessed the wide variety of specimens, ranging from poppies to autumn crocus, pausing here and there to smell a flower or rub a leaf between his fingers. As they'd marveled at the clever heated greenhouse and the central rock garden, which included volcanic stone from Iceland, he'd cast infrequent glances to where she walked at his side. She'd wondered several times whether he sensed her thoughts drifting away from him, but he'd given no indication of it.

Indeed, she had spoken little more than he had. She had been preoccupied with thoughts of Henry.

"The creature appears a tad feral," Phineas observed now, his gray wool coat nearly the same color as Erasmus. "Is it yours?"

"Oh, no. My mother's." Maureen chuckled. "Papa was not in favor of the addition, as cats cause him to sneeze uncontrollably, but he wishes Mama to be content, so he agreed to allow Erasmus to live here whilst we are in London for the season."

Phineas nodded his understanding, although she sensed he did not quite comprehend why a man would subject himself to discomfort for the sake of his wife's whims.

"Well," she said, waving toward the pair of winged chairs near the fireplace. "Shall we sit? Perhaps you would care for tea."

"I should like to marry you, Lady Maureen."

She froze with her hand extended and her mouth open in an O.

He took two steps toward her and stopped, leaving six feet between them. "We have a good deal in common. It is rare to find a lady so inclined toward proper plantings."

She could not catch her breath.

*You knew this was coming. You knew. Why are you surprised?*

But she was. Shocked down to the soles of her half-boots.

Pale green eyes fringed with short, dark lashes examined her from flushed face to yellow hem. He took another step closer. "We are different, too. But I like those differences. Your family, for example. I have never contemplated such ... unruliness. Yet, it presents rather a disarming character."

She swallowed, her hands now dangling beside her hips, her mouth dry and useless.

He closed the last few feet between them, lowering his head and his voice. "I admire you," he said. "I would be gratified to know you feel a similar regard."

Deep in those eerie, unreadable eyes, she saw something that unstuck her throat. It was subtle. Barely hinted at. But it was there. A flicker of uncertainty.

"Of course, I do," she assured him.

He waited a long while before nodding. Then, he reached for her hands.

She swallowed hard and allowed him to take her limp, indecisive fingers in his.

"I should like to marry you, Lady Maureen," he repeated. "I should like to make you my wife."

Someone was binding the bones of her chest, making it difficult to breathe. "Y-You honor me, Lord Holstoke." Her words emerged as a puny wheeze, and she dropped her gaze to his chin at the end, but at least she'd managed to say something.

"Do not answer now." His warm breath washed over her forehead, scented with something green. Mint or parsley. "You must have time to contemplate a matter of this import. I shall wait to speak with your father until you are certain."

She nodded, fixing upon his lips. They were thinner than Henry's. Phineas's features all had a spare quality, as though the hand that shaped him had been opposed to excess. If she married him, he would kiss her, likely with some frequency. How could she agree to be his wife without knowing what it would feel like?

Henry's kiss had not resembled her imaginings in the slightest. It had been harder. Darker. More.

Not that she was comparing the two men, she assured herself. This was nothing to do with Henry at all. Rather, she simply wished to ascertain whether or not those ascetic lips were acceptable to press against hers for a lifetime. What if Phineas's kiss repulsed her? What if he tasted of tobacco and port, two of her least favorite flavors? Surely she could not marry him.

Those thin lips curved up in a subtle smile. "I can see you thinking," he murmured. "What do you wish to know?"

Before the last word left his mouth, she was reaching for his neck. Drawing him down. Meeting thin lips with hers. Feeling his open gasp against her skin.

No tobacco. No port. He tasted clean and tannic, like good tea flavored with mint. Or parsley.

He took control from one heartbeat to the next, sliding strong arms around her waist, drawing her flush against him, warming her mouth with his tongue, stroking her lips with his in a shocking display of skill.

This was the kiss she'd expected from Henry. Smooth. Controlled. Sensual. The kiss of a man who wished to pleasure and seduce.

A loud throat-clearing and a louder *thud* tore them apart. "Perhaps I should fetch her ladyship, my lady. Seems another chaperone might be necessary." Regina's gruff rebuke was overloud in the silent room.

His breathing was labored, she noted distantly. His lips were fuller, the lofty cheekbones redder. And the dark centers of his eyes had swallowed a goodly portion of the green.

"Beg your pardon, Phineas," she said softly. "I wished to know what it would be like."

"And?"

She licked her lips and swallowed. "The answer was ... satisfying."

He drew a deep breath and nodded. "Right. I shall await your response to my query with the greatest anticipation."

When he departed, Regina's vocal displeasure cascaded over her. Occasionally, she heard select phrases amidst her own whirling thoughts: *For your reputation's sake ... cease kissing men willy-nilly ... what would your mother say ...* and on and on.

Her fingers hovered over her lips then slid to cover her cheeks. Regina's deep voice became a drone beneath the whoosh of her blood and breath.

Genie entered just as Regina threw up her hands, snatched up her sewing, and stomped from the library. Holding a bonnet in freshly bandaged hands, her sister blinked and frowned first at the retreating maid then at Maureen. "What sort of insect did you put in her tea?"

Maureen shook her head and tried to smile, a wobbly effort that twisted at the end.

"Maureen," Genie said sharply, striding toward her with her customary brisk force. "Tell me what happened. You are overset. Did Holstoke—"

"I kissed him," she whispered.

"What in blazes?"

She looked at Genie. Brown hair, artfully curled around soft cheeks. A nose straighter and longer than Maureen's. The Huxley brown eyes and pale skin. She was sixteen, just beginning to bloom, really. But she was the most forthright of all the sisters. As a rule, Genie did not mince words, which made her an ideal confidant when one wished to hear the truth.

"I kissed him. And it was ... good."

Genie frowned. "Well, bloody hell, Maureen."

"Mind your tongue."

"You first!"

"I cannot marry a man without knowing whether kissing him will cause me to cast up my accounts."

Genie's eyes rounded. "He asked you to marry him?"

Maureen nodded.

"Splendid." Genie blinked. "Right?"

She began to pace, a slow back-and-forth from chairs to window. "I don't care for his mother."

"Yes. The bonnet she wore to Astley's was very plain. A feather or two would not have gone amiss."

Maureen halted and rolled her eyes at her sister. "Focus less upon hats and more upon the matter at hand, if you please."

Sniffing, Genie gestured toward Maureen with her beribboned bonnet. "You are not casting up your accounts. I presume this means Holstoke's lips are acceptable."

"I wanted them not to be."

"Hmm. That would have made your choice a simple one. Can't be huddled over the chamber pot every time you—"

"Yes."

Genie set the bonnet on a table near the entrance before crossing her arms and narrowing her eyes. "There is only one Dunston, you know."

Her heart twisting, Maureen bit her lip. She had asked for Genie's bluntness. She could not now regret hearing the truth from her sister's unfiltered mouth.

"However," Genie continued. "Holstoke seems a decent fellow. Not so handsome as Thomas, certainly. Nor Dunston, for that matter. But he is tall. Given more to silence than boastful accounts of his hunting exploits." She shrugged. "Tell him you wish to live separately from his mother. Perhaps he will balk."

"She already spends most of the year at a house in Weymouth. His seat is a half-day's ride away, and he claims she never visits. Further, she rarely comes to London, and is only here for the season because he is seeking a wife."

Frowning, Genie nodded. "Appears you must decide if you like him well enough to bear his offspring, then. No help for it."

Maureen sighed and rubbed her temple. "He is the only one who has offered, Genie. If I do not accept him, I may never have another opportunity to marry."

"There is that."

"You are not helping."

Genie released a frustrated sigh. "This is hardly a choice between cheesecake and pudding, Maureen. I cannot make the decision for you."

"If you could, what would you do?"

"Simple. I would marry Thomas and open a milliner's shop."

Maureen laughed and shook her head, then collapsed into

the winged chair and buried her face in her hands. Moments later, she felt Genie wedging her hips next to hers and wrapping a pair of slender arms around her shoulders.

"A tall, respectable earl whose kiss does not cause you to cast up your accounts wants to marry you. This is happy news, not the end of all good things."

Maureen rested her head upon Genie's shoulder. "How I wish it felt so, dearest. How I wish it felt so."

PHINEAS BRAND, THE EARL OF HOLSTOKE WAS BLOODY PERFECT. Not a single scandal, not one hint of sexual perversion or brutish behavior or drunkenness. The man had employed two mistresses in his life, each for five years, each amply compensated, comfortably settled in seaside cottages, and offering only praise and gratitude for their former protector. Further, Holstoke eschewed gaming and had no debts of any sort. In point of fact, he was far wealthier than he let on, with properties all over England and the Continent. Yet, he lived like a lord of middling means. That and his preoccupation with plants and gardens were the only two oddities Henry had discovered in Reaver's entire sheaf of research. Neither of them would dissuade Maureen Huxley from marriage. Quite the contrary.

Slamming his empty glass down on his desktop, Henry shoved the papers away with a disgusted sigh. One page flew up and drifted to the floor. Another slid to a stop just shy of the desk's edge. Henry wanted to burn the whole useless lot.

"Mr. Drayton for you, my lord," said Kimble from the study door.

Drayton shouldered his way past Kimble's bulk. In the runner's hand was a package wrapped in brown paper and twine.

"What do you have?"

Drayton grinned and placed the thing in the center of Henry's desk. "Open it."

The package was a cylinder roughly ten inches long and four inches in diameter. Henry used his penknife to cut the twine and quickly peeled back the paper to reveal a metal case engraved with elaborate, swirling figures of peacocks, dragons, bejeweled shields, and vines. It had a hinged lid at one end. He popped it open and peered inside.

At first, the cylinder appeared empty. Then, Henry ran his fingers along the interior surface. "Vellum," he murmured, meeting Drayton's eyes. "What the devil is this, man?"

"Pluck it out and see."

Henry did, withdrawing the rolled vellum carefully. The pages unfurled a bit as they landed atop Reaver's reports, but they remained curled enough that he had to unroll them and smooth them with his fingers.

The first page was a botanical rendering of a spire of purple, tubular flowers. Beneath the depiction was a notation of the plant's name: *Digitalis purpurea*. It looked like foxglove to him. Other drawings in the curled stack were less familiar— *Hyoscyamus niger* and *Conium maculatum* and *Taxus baccata*. The latter resembled yew branches. There were more sketches he did not recognize at all, but then, Henry had never paid much attention to plants.

"Taking up botany, are you?" Henry inquired with a raised brow. "Or drawing, perhaps."

Drayton indicated the sprawl of curled papers and engraved case. "Chalmers had that delivered to his sister upon his death. He attached a note with one word: Sabre."

Henry waited for the usual surge of fire, the prickle of incitement at the prospect of a new path for his hunt. He felt nothing.

He glanced down at the case. A coiled dragon stared up at him, cold and flat. "You have examined everything, I presume."

"Aye. Little to lead anyplace, upon first viewing. Case is London made. Sketches are unsigned. Fine work, but nothing distinctive." Drayton sniffed and shuffled his feet. "Must be important, though. I reckon Chalmers went to a good deal of trouble."

Nodding, Henry rubbed a finger over the peacock's tail. His eyes slipped past the case to the papers beneath—Reaver's reports on Holstoke.

A knock sounded at the door a moment before Kimble opened it a mere six inches. "Another visitor for you, my lord." The butler jerked forward as though he had been shoved.

"How many times must I tell you, you great clodpate?" came a gravelly female voice. "I've news he must hear immediately. Now get out of my way!"

Henry blinked at the woman who had managed to shove his exceedingly large butler three feet into the room. "Regina," he said wryly. "Lovely surprise."

The butler smoothed his hair and straightened his coat with a jerk, glaring at the gray-clad lady's maid with an odd blend of irritation and admiration. "I do beg your pardon, my lord. She was most insistent."

"Hmm. Thank you, Kimble. Would you show Mr. Drayton out?" Henry met Drayton's eyes. "Wait until you hear from me." The runner nodded and left.

Henry eyed the bristling maid. "It's been weeks, Regina. I assumed you no longer wished to provide the services for which you have been so amply compensated."

Regina snorted. "You pay me to protect her. That's what I have done, even when the greatest threat is you."

He chose not to respond to the provocation. "What has happened?"

"Holstoke. He wants to marry her."

Swallowing his visceral response like hot ash, Henry replied softly, "I am aware."

"No, my lord. He has *asked* her to marry him. This morning."

All the fire he'd expected to feel earlier upon receiving Drayton's news blazed in upon him, vicious and consuming. The light sharpened. His skin stung and burned. Every muscle seized with the need to tear something apart.

"Her reply?"

The maid, previously insistent to the point of rudeness, fell back a step. She swallowed and glanced nervously behind her at the closed door.

"Come now, Regina. You mauled my butler in order to deliver your news." He stood and leaned forward, bracing his hands upon his desk. "Tell me."

"She—she neither declined his offer nor consented. But ..."

"But what?"

Regina's jaw firmed, her spine straightening as though expecting to be lashed. "She kissed him, my lord. Right there in front of me, bold as one of your waistcoats. Lady Maureen kissed Lord Holstoke. And I think she found it ... agreeable."

# Chapter Nine

*"Strict adherence to convention is more apt to make one tedious than virtuous, my dear."*

—THE DOWAGER MARCHIONESS OF WALLINGHAM to Lady Berne upon said lady's lament about daughters with unusual preoccupations.

OCCASIONALLY—AND WITH GREATER FREQUENCY OF LATE—Maureen longed to ignore the rules. Now, for example, when her arm ached abominably from beating eggs into a froth to leaven her orange cakes. She resented the need to disguise her fondness for cookery, waiting until the most ungodly hours to cook in secret without help from the maids. An earl's daughter simply did not work in the kitchens, whisking eggs and kneading dough and measuring out cinnamon and sugar for her version of Chelsea buns.

The shame of doing something useful! She snorted her derision.

Clutching the crockery bowl to her to her chest, she swiped at her forehead with her wrist and eyed the light-yellow froth she'd produced, satisfied with the result.

The rules were silly, much like the admonitions against kissing gentlemen. How was one to decide whether to marry a man? One might judge his riding skill or his intelligence on matters botanical from chaperoned outings. But heaven forefend one should be curious about whether kissing him would produce a nauseous reaction. She would only be kissing him for the rest of her life, after all.

She sighed. The rules were rubbish. This was not in doubt.

With gentle strokes, she folded the eggs into her creamed sugar and butter, taking care not to deflate the hard-won air bubbles. Then, she added the flour bit by bit, wondering at the arbitrary nature of societal strictures. Why should Mrs. Dunn, their beloved cook, be permitted to instruct her employer's curious daughter in the finer points of braised beef, but only in secret? What made Maureen so bloody different? Furthermore, she thought while adding a dash of nutmeg and a dram of orange-infused brandy, what made "bloody" such a forbidden word for ladies? She did not know. No one did. No one questioned these things. They obeyed the rules because the rules had been set and everyone followed them.

Sighing, she set her bowl on the work table and wiped her hands on her apron. Fetching the small cake tins she had buttered earlier, she arranged them in neat rows upon a sheet and began pouring the batter.

Outside, the steady patter of rain had formed a curtain of sound. By the time she placed the tins in the oven and stoked the coals sufficiently, the wind had joined the symphony, whistling and thrashing against the high windows. She stood with her hands on her hips, glancing about the dark periphery beyond the glow of her lamp. Berne House protested the sudden gale with creaks and groans. She fought a chill as she gathered up the dishes for cleaning, carrying her stack into the scullery.

The wind grew stronger, rattling the door at the opposite end, which led to the kitchen yard. She eyed the thick blackness as she moved past the questionable comforts of lamplight to the scullery sink, wondering at her own nerves. *Steady now,* she admonished herself. *You are overtired and overwrought. It is only wind.*

Still, she moved swiftly back into the kitchen, busying herself with tidying up the work table and trying to ignore the shivers that prickled and sang over her skin. Sighing, she rubbed her forehead and leaned against the table's edge, enjoying the warmth from the range oven and the glow of the lamp.

Like a tongue testing a sore tooth, her mind drifted back to her most pressing quandary. By all rights, she should marry Holstoke. Perhaps he lacked conversation. Oh, very well, the man was approximately as charming as cold milk. But he was a *good* man. Perceptive and thoughtful. Unquestionably intelligent, if a bit odd.

She smiled, recalling their Kensington Gardens visit when his awkward attempts at describing a particular plant's beauty had forced her to cover a sudden cough. Flagrantly swelling anthers and beckoning stigma, indeed. She would never look upon lilies the same way again.

No, if one wanted witty banter, one must marry a man like Henry.

A familiar ache settled in her chest. Slowly, she slid her hand inside her apron pocket and withdrew the twin sheets of paper, folded into quarters, yellowed and careworn.

His tenth letter. Silly to keep it with her—she'd read the thing so many times, she could recite it from memory. Unfolding the pages, she forced herself to read his words again. Forced herself to remember why her quandary was no quandary at all, as marrying Henry Thorpe had never been an option.

*Dearest Pet,*

*Rec'd your letter of 12th December. Happy Christmas, lovely one. How kind of you to speak of my humble self in such fond terms. There is no earthly creature whose admiration I more fervently desire, for your discernment in the debate between damask and brocade is distinguished by its rarity. You are, in short, remarkable.*

She paused, smiling. Henry had always taken pains to spare her feelings, and this was no exception. Her letter of 12th December had been rife with passionate declarations of affection for "quite the finest gentleman I have ever encountered." In four pages, she'd devoted one sentence to his discriminating taste in waistcoats, simply because she'd needed to round out the list of reasons why she loved him. Posting her missive—a bold departure from their prior correspondence—had soon drowned her in a sea of apprehension. Even now, her cheeks heated to recall her words, florid and adoring as only an infatuated young woman could be. In his response, he'd elected to focus upon the point about his waistcoats, making her laugh and setting her at ease.

Henry did that often.

Taking a deep breath, she forged on to read the rest of the letter. It had never been more important to remember why marrying Henry was a fruitless fantasy.

*For this reason, I must protest your magnificent portrayals, as I am wholly unworthy of your generous regard. It has been the singular honor of my life to be counted your friend, and I should be hanged were I to mislead your affections. In truth, you are as splendid as the first spark of sunlight awakening the sky. You deserve a husband who will gaze upon you each morning, knowing your light is the only one he shall ever require.*

*With the profoundest sorrow, I must tell you I am not that man.*

Again, she stopped reading. He'd written more—descriptions of her sterling character and claims about his shortcomings—but none of it mattered.

*I am not that man.* Those words had shattered her foolish, besotted heart. The letter had arrived on Christmas Eve. By February, Maureen had managed to resume eating normally and sleeping through the night. She'd even maintained a correspondence with his mother. The following spring when she'd seen him in London, he'd behaved as though nothing had occurred, teasing her about her fondness for yellow silk and asking her opinion of walking sticks as foppish affectations.

At first, she had responded with cool formality. But Henry had been relentless, seeking her out at every gathering she'd attended—even Almack's—prodding her with amusing anecdotes and wry observations until she'd lost all resistance. Over the course of months, he'd ensconced himself in her life, treating her as a beloved friend. Some had even mistaken his attentions for that of a suitor. She, however, had kept his tenth letter, so she would never again suffer such a delusion.

Folding the letter now, she rubbed her thumb over the broken seal and slipped it back inside her pocket. She sniffed and wiped her eyes.

Henry had done a noble thing. Other gentlemen might have taken advantage, perhaps even compromised her to satisfy their own selfish desires. She knew now, of course, that he was hardly immune to lust. His kiss had proven as much. Those lips. That tongue. The unrelenting hardness. In truth, had Regina not interrupted them, he might have taken her to his bed then and there.

Swallowing against a parched throat, she brushed at the sudden sweat along her brow. The kitchen was rather warm. Perhaps she should check the oven.

She was moving to do just that when something hard snagged across her waist. Something sleek and cool and damp slid across her mouth. And someone very, very strong clasped her tightly against a muscular frame.

Ice bloomed in her veins. Every fiber seized up, prepared to fight. An instant later, she clawed at the hand over her mouth, jerked forward at the waist, and used all her weight to drive the back of her head up toward the intruder's face. Rather than shouting in pain, however, the man grunted and shifted his head to the side, his grip tightening until she squeaked.

"If I hadn't been the one to teach you that maneuver, pet, you would surely have brained me," said a silken voice into her ear. "Well done."

Blood pounding, heart imploding, Maureen struggled to suck air into her burning chest. The arms around her gentled. The gloved hand slid from her mouth.

"H-Henry?" She shoved away, spinning to face him. He was drenched, his hair dark and plastered to his skull, his skin sheening in the lamplight.

He raised his hands to motion surrender. "Only trying to prevent you waking the dead with your screams."

"What in blazes ..." she panted, still struggling to understand. Henry was here. In her kitchen. In the middle of the night. "... are you about? You scared the life out of me."

He shrugged out of his greatcoat, tossing it over a chair. Then, he removed his gloves. Beneath, he wore his usual ensemble of dark tailcoat, shimmering waistcoat, and white cravat. Shaking droplets from his hair, he heaved a sigh. "I needed to speak with you."

"It is half-past two!"

"Yes, well. This could not wait."

"And you are in my kitchen. How did you—"

"Through the scullery door. You should speak to your butler about repairing the lock on the mews gate. I might have been anyone—a burglar or a nefarious intruder."

"You *are* an intruder!"

"Shh, pet. Let's not wake the footmen from their slumber. I've no taste for violence." He glanced around nonchalantly. "What is that heavenly scent?"

She crossed her arms and leaned her hip against the table. "Orange cakes. How did you know I would be here, Henry?"

He grinned. "Orange cakes. Those do sound delicious."

"Answer me," she snapped. "No one knows about—"

"About your little cookery habit? Oh, some of us do. Your mother likes to pretend ignorance, but she's known for years. So have your sisters. Jane, for instance. And Harrison."

She sighed. Then laughed. Then rubbed her tired eyes. To think she'd imagined only Mrs. Dunn and a few maids and footmen knew her secret—the maids because they insisted on cleaning up after her, and the footmen because she baked sweets to bribe them into providing frequent baths. As it turned out, her secret sessions in the kitchen had been no secret at all. They all must think her perfectly daft. Perhaps they were right.

Shaking her head, she focused on Henry. Lean, damp, tempting Henry. "Why are you here?"

A single chestnut brow lifted. "To see you privately."

"You could have seen me in the morning. In the drawing room. Like a normal visitor."

He sniffed and swiped his own wet cheek with the backs of his fingers. "Perhaps you have a cloth? And tea. Tea would not go amiss."

"If you had wanted tea, you should have come at a decent hour!"

"This hour seems decent enough. Unless you'd care to make it *indecent*. We could, you know."

With a huff, she spun and stomped to the oven, ensured the cakes had risen sufficiently, and transferred them onto the table to cool. All the while, Henry wandered about, examining this and that, behaving as though he were an invited guest rather than a bothersome interloper who had frightened her out of her wits.

Now, he came to stand beside her, bringing with him the scents of rainwater and sandalwood. "How did you learn, pet? These look divine."

"Mrs. Dunn tired of shooing me from her kitchen. After a time, I was permitted to stay and watch. Later, she agreed to instruct me." She glanced up at him, noting how one lock of hair fell over his forehead, darkened and dripping. Offering up the linen cloth she'd used to handle the pan, she fought the urge to run her fingers over him. "You should have worn a hat in this downpour, silly man."

His grin grew as he accepted the cloth. The stroke of his fingers against hers felt deliberate—and tingly. "Carried away by a gust, I'm afraid." He wiped at his face with quick swipes and ran the cloth over his hair before tossing it onto the table.

Why he should weaken her to the point of breathlessness, she did not know. Perhaps his lips, full and shining, were to blame. Perhaps it was the muscled arms revealed by a coat tailored precisely to his contours. Or the assurance with which he moved, every motion swift and contained, agile and efficient.

Dash it all, she did not know why he'd always been such a temptation. She only knew she must tear herself away before something happened. Something irreversible.

She dropped her eyes and took up the towel, busying herself with transferring the cakes to a sideboard a few feet away. Then, she moved back to the table and began sweeping the surface with more vigor than necessary.

"You cannot marry him, pet."

Half-bent over the table, she froze. Then straightened, clutching the towel in her fist. And breathed. In. Out. In. Out.

"I realize it is a lot to ask, given our ... history together." As usual, his rich baritone sent shivers over her scalp and down her spine.

Fresh from reading his tenth letter, however, his words had a different effect. They filled her with fury.

"No," she managed through a tight throat. "It is an insult to ask. An *insult*, Henry." She wrung the towel into a knot and threw it at his chest. He caught it without looking. "You do not want me, have *never* wanted me. Yet, you've kept me close, even knowing how I f-feel about you. Knowing how I yearn to be a wife and a mother. Perhaps you did not intend to be cruel, but that has been the result."

In the golden light, his dark eyes held a hard intensity she'd rarely witnessed. The last time had been a bright afternoon in his bedchamber when he'd torn the draperies from his windows.

"I accept my failures," she continued, busying her hands with removing her apron. "If some men find me displeasing, you are hardly to blame for that. But this may be my one chance at happiness, and I do blame you for trying to spoil it."

"I am not trying to spoil anything, Maureen." His voice was pure steel, his eyes flashing as he moved in close, crowding her with his heat and scent. "I am trying to tell you—"

"He is a good man," she insisted, retreating to gain some distance. He granted her nothing, advancing until the table's edge was at her back and a hard, lean, volatile male was at her front. "He will be a good husband."

"He is not me," he gritted. "And I am the man you want."

The arrogance of his claim made her want to strike him. Mutely, she shook her head, surrounded by his strength and heat, watching a bead of water wend its way from his jaw to the hollow at the base of his throat. "Even if that were true—"

"It is."

"—nothing is changed."

He refused to release her, holding her captive with eyes that flickered and burned. "Marry me instead."

In the silence that followed—pounding, fraught silence—she wondered if he was drunk. Or worse, jesting. A cruel sort of mockery, indeed, given her feelings for him. But as she explored his face from high-bridged nose to tempting lips and back up to midnight eyes, she detected no signs of humor. Quite the contrary. She'd never seen him more sober.

"Henry," she whispered. It was the best she could do without proper air.

"I've tried to spare you, pet. Unlike Holstoke, I am decidedly *not* a good man." He cupped her cheek, his thumb stroking her brow tenderly, his fingers caressing her jaw and ear. "But you insist on tormenting me, and I cannot allow you to marry anyone else. Which leaves only one choice. You must marry me. God help us both."

MAUREEN HUXLEY SMELLED AS DELECTABLE AS HER ORANGE cakes. Henry longed to devour her bite by bite, starting with the speck of yellow flotsam on her cheekbone and finishing with her trembling, half-open lips. Afire with lust from the moment he'd entered the kitchen, he'd watched her from the shadows for long minutes. He'd traced the contours of her neck, the solemn cast of golden light along her jaw. He'd savored her presence, calming and domestic, watching her sigh and move with natural competence about her tasks. He'd listened to the battering rain, awash in the full force of his love for her.

Now, her eyes searched his, a crinkle forming between her brows. She cradled his hand against her cheek and shook her head gently. "I thought you were sotted," she murmured. "But it is worse. You are mad, through and through."

He laughed, his chest expanding until he thought his ribs might crack. Good God, she was beautiful. Even when she was a mess. "Mad for you, perhaps."

Suddenly, a soft mouth crimped. Dimpled cheeks flushed. Flashing eyes narrowed. And Henry staggered back as a pair of surprisingly strong, feminine hands shoved his solar plexus, gouging him with a waistcoat button and separating him from her delectable self rather convincingly.

"Bloody hell, Maureen." He rubbed the heel of his hand against the likely bruise in the center of his chest.

She was having none of it. No, his sweet prospective bride was furious beyond measure, her skin flushed and vibrating, her fists clutching the table behind her as though to keep herself from hurting him.

"Bloody hell, *Henry*," she spat. "'*I am not that man,*' That is what you said. 'I am not that man.' Not the man who wants me. Not the man who will love me. Not the man I deserve."

He swallowed. "You have an excellent memory."

She snagged her apron from the table without looking, dug into the pocket, and held up a familiar square of paper between two fingers. "No. I have your *letter*, Lord Dunston. Your *words*."

His heart twisted as he saw the worn edges of the paper, the signs that it had been unfolded and refolded numerous times. She'd kept it with her. Read it again and again. His bloody lie, told for reasons he could not explain to her, not without putting her in greater danger.

He wanted to snatch the thing from her hand and toss it on the dying coals. Instead, he could only tell her the truth and hope it would be enough. "I lied."

Her eyes flared, firing incredulity at him like a cannon. "You lied."

"Yes."

"Why?"

"To protect you."

She threw up her hands. "From what, pray tell? Destitution due to waistcoat extravagance?"

For years, he had been frustrated by the need to keep her in the dark. How many times had he yearned to tell her the truth? The day after he'd killed Boyle, he'd drunk himself numb and written her a letter, explaining everything. He'd burned the missive shortly thereafter, of course. The less she knew, the less likely she was to become a target. The Investor preferred not to leave loose ends. Boyle's wife could attest to that.

He moved closer, halting when she stiffened. "You've known one side of me, pet, the side I wish to show you. But there is another. Selfish and dark."

Her subtle frown suggested she'd glimpsed it already—the day she'd come to his bedchamber, most likely.

"Were I a stronger man, a better man, I would keep you from that part of me forever." Again, he stepped closer, watching the hypnotic rise and fall of her breasts, the tiny tug of her brows as she listened. "Alas, all of me wants you too much to let you go."

"So, now I should simply throw Holstoke over for you." She tossed the apron and letter on the table and crossed her arms over her chest. "Because you *want* me."

"No. Because you are in love with me."

"Bloody arrogant bastard."

He sighed. "Yes, well, this is what I've been trying to tell you. God knows what you find so irresistible in me."

"Precisely!"

As they conversed, he'd been slowly inching toward her so that now, he stood close enough to smell her hair. Orange flowers and vanilla. She made his mouth water.

"I only know this," he continued, breathing her in and battling the urge to touch her. "Standing in St. George's on Harrison and Jane's wedding day, I heard the vows and imagined saying them to you."

Her arms loosened as her breath quickened.

"Then, during our stay at Blackmore Hall, I fell so madly in love, I thought it some wicked enchantment." He grinned. "And so it was. Wicked, indeed. You turned me inside out, pet. Made me yours with a single, wondrous laugh."

She was softening. He could sense it. Then, she pushed away from the table and propped her hands on her hips, her breasts dangerously close to his chest.

"Explain it, then."

He raised a brow.

"Go on. Explain why you didn't beg me to marry you two bloody years ago."

"Why the new fondness for vulgarity?"

"I find it bloody satisfying when faced with *infuriating* men. Do not change the subject."

He cleared his throat. "What would you have me say?"

Alarmingly, her eyes began to fill and shimmer, her lower lip to quiver. "Give me a reason to forgive you, Henry. Because, at the moment, I can think of none."

Dark and grinding and hollow, his regrets rose up to fill him in a tide. He had hurt her. He'd done his best to avoid it, of course. But some pain could not be prevented. And every bit of agony he'd ever caused her had lived inside him like a festering thorn.

That force had driven him to finally abandon the course he'd set for himself over a decade earlier. He might have borne his own pain—the bitter jealousy at the thought of another man touching her, the unquenched need to unburden himself, to feel her stroke his cheek and hear her speak his name.

Yes, he might have borne it. But the day she'd told him goodbye, he'd known the severity of the wounds he'd dealt her. His beautiful, funny, naïve Maureen. Bleeding as surely as if he'd run her through.

No longer. He would repair what he'd broken, beginning now. He would bloody well put her heart first, as he should have done from the start.

To that end, he'd spent the afternoon in Sebastian Reaver's office, transferring into Reaver's hands every account and analytical supposition and hard-won bit of information he'd compiled on the Investor. The club owner had been savagely eager, like a wolf anticipating a new meal. Drayton had been there, too, ready to carry on the hunt with a new partner. The runner had given him a rare smile as they'd departed that evening, clapping him on the shoulder and shaking his hand while muttering, "About time, you ask me. Been waiting years for this."

Henry agreed. He'd been waiting years, too.

Hesitating no longer, he now took the woman he loved more than his own life into his arms. She struggled a moment, but he simply held her as she batted his ribs lightly and shook her head against him.

"I am sorry," he rasped into her ear, "for every moment of pain I have ever caused you. I only ever wanted your happiness, and I believed you deserved better than to have me for your husband."

"It is not enough," she mumbled wetly into his cravat, her fists now alternately pummeling and clutching his back.

Cradling her soft warmth against him, he kissed her cheek, trailed his lips along her jaw to her chin. Finally, he caressed her mouth reverently with his. Satisfaction surged as she responded with a little flicker of her tongue. He smiled against her and returned the favor.

"I will spend every day on my knees, begging your forgiveness, pet." He ran his tongue deliberately along her lower lip, stroking and tempting her to follow as his hands drew her hips into his. "I will work tirelessly to bring you unimaginable pleasure, all to express my deep and abiding remorse."

Her tiny, feminine grunt and panting breaths were most encouraging.

"I vow I will earn your forgiveness kiss by kiss by *kimmph* ..." Of a sudden, he found her mouth sealed to his, her tongue caressing his, her hands tugging at his cravat and dragging him down into her.

Good God, she was more than he'd ever dreamed. Delicious as cream-soaked butter cakes. Hot as the brilliant August sun on a long ride across Fairfield Park. His blood pounded at a full gallop.

He dug his fingers into her waist, yanked her harder against him. Loved the sensation of her hands upon his jaw, her mouth demanding more, her luscious breasts flattened against him. His lust demanded that he explore. Expose. Strip her bare and lay her out upon the table like a feast to be consumed.

His hands gathered her skirts, pulling with desperate motions. His hips ground against her softness, trying to ease the ferocious cock that had hardened from iron to steel when his sweet-natured Maureen had taken control.

She was rubbing herself against him now, grinding her hips upward. Obviously, she needed to be higher.

He gladly obliged, grasping her thighs and lifting, settling her backside on the table as she yelped against his mouth. The sound was distant amidst the pounding, relentless need. They both panted, breathing each other, devouring each other. He shoved her skirts higher, forced her thighs wider to accept his hips, and ground himself against the heart of her.

Her head fell back. "Oh, God, Henry. I've never felt anything this good."

He dismissed the assertion. She had no idea what "good" could be. And she'd left her lovely neck open to him. He took full advantage, burying his mouth against the vulnerable hollow beneath her ear then sliding his tongue down to her collarbone.

Between her thighs, he forced her to accept the caress of his cock, albeit through the thin layer of his riding breeches. And one of his hands, only half-satisfied with gripping her waist, contented itself with finally, at long last, learning the full measure of her breast. Soft. Lush. Round. Centered by a pouting nipple he set immediately to stroking with his thumb.

Her groan choked in the middle. She fisted his hair and gasped in time with his rhythm.

He was going to come. He felt it gathering. Good God, he was going to humiliate himself by spending inside his breeches if he did not do something. The answer was obvious, of course. He should take her. She was wet enough to soak him. Aroused and on the precipice of her peak.

He should take her. Ruin her. She would be forced to marry him, then. No more Holstoke. Nor more options.

Panting against her salty skin, he fought himself. Halted his hips. Retreated an inch. Tightened his muscles as she mewled her protest.

"Shh, pet," he whispered, feeling his control slipping like a man's desperate fingers from the edge of a cliff. "I shall see to your pleasure. Always."

Her hips rocked and scooted closer as the table beneath her creaked. She grasped at his hair, pulling his mouth back to hers. Firm thighs gripped him, making his retreat difficult. If he continued, he would either be carrying her or dropping her off the edge.

Instead, he regained control by squeezing the hard, swollen nipple between his fingers.

She squeaked.

He slid his other hand past the bunched skirts at her waist, down to the warm, wet thatch between her legs.

Good God. Fleecy, soft, and slick, her sweet petals had flowered open for him, begging for his cock to satisfy her. He could not give her that—not if he wished to live with himself. So, instead, he gave her his touch. Gentle and brushing at first, as he learned what she liked. Then with a little more firmness as he circled the swollen nub in time with her needy gasps.

She broke from his kiss, open-mouthed and clawing at his neck.

It was then that her scent hit him fully. Vanilla, ripe and lush and sweet. The lighter scents of rosewater and orange blossoms were faint, but the overwhelming rush was vanilla and aroused woman.

He wanted a taste.

He dropped to his knees.

Settled his hands just above her stockings, upon soft, white thighs.

Faintly, he heard her saying his name with a querulous tone. But he couldn't hear much when his pulse pounded like rain on a metal sheet. She was beautiful. Pink and shimmering in the golden light, shadowed by damp, brown ringlets.

He set his mouth upon her, ignoring the sharp tug of her hands in his hair. He needed this—the salty-sweet of her on his tongue and inside his senses. Vanilla and woman. He flickered his tongue over her swollen nub, first taking it directly, then softening as she jerked on a spasm of shocking pleasure. Now, he circled and let her guide him, her fingertips working against his scalp, her thighs relaxing where he gripped them. Too soon—much too soon—her urgent writhing coalesced with her plaintive cries. He thrust his tongue inside the greedy mouth of her sex, determined to feel every small ripple, to be inside her just enough to make her pleasure a part of him.

In the aftermath, he soothed her with a string of kisses along her thighs and the resettling of her skirts. He stood, half-bent with the pain of his arousal. She continued caressing his jaw, now rubbing her thumbs over his lips. Now pulling his forehead down to touch hers.

"I love you," he whispered.

Her eyes, glowing gold, smiled up at him. "I believe you," she whispered back. Then, her eyes grew solemn, sending a chill across his heated flesh. "But this is marriage, Henry. A lifetime. And I fear I cannot give you the answer you desire."

# Chapter Ten

*"Indulgent madness, Humphrey. That's what this is.
Perhaps the consequences to come will be enough to dissuade
her from future insanity. But I doubt it."*

—THE DOWAGER MARCHIONESS OF WALLINGHAM to her boon
companion, Humphrey, in response to Lady Berne's unreasoning
regard for creatures of a feline persuasion.

THE ARGUMENT COMMENCED WHEN A SHOT ACROSS THE BOW
was answered with an indignant volley of objection. Maureen
was already weary, and it was barely noon.

"Cats are useless creatures. Even the least useless among them
leave headless vermin upon your doorstep as though to announce
all that lazing about was a figment of your imagination."

Mama's mouth tightened as she shot a sidelong glare at her dear friend, the Dowager Marchioness of Wallingham. "If I recall correctly, Dorothea, you expressed similar sentiments about dogs."

"As usual, I was right. Humphrey is the great exception, but one does not judge all creatures by a single extraordinary specimen." Humphrey was Lady Wallingham's boon companion, a bloodhound with a cheerful disposition, but no more extraordinary than any other dog. In the dowager's eyes, the fact that Humphrey was hers made him deserving of such exaltation, Maureen supposed.

Mama was not persuaded. "Cats are both cleaner and less damaging than dogs."

Lady Wallingham glanced pointedly to where Erasmus currently arched, sharpening his claws upon the rosewood leg of Mama's chair. The fragile-boned, purple-clad lady raised one imperious white brow.

Mama huffed and reached down to pluck up the gray kitten, stroking his disgruntled fur. "He is young. These incidents will wane after he is trained properly."

"Hmmph. As properly as you trained the last one? Even Berne is not so indulgent as to refurnish an entire house with new draperies a *second* time, my dear."

Letting their tiresome debate retreat into the background, Maureen crossed the expanse of the drawing room to the corner where Genie sat at a small table, sketching a pattern for the twins' christening caps. Maureen tilted her head and blinked down at the emerging image. "Do you think it wise to add long plumes, dearest? These are infants, after all."

Genie's pencil paused and hovered. "Hmm. A sound point. Perhaps the feathers should be smaller. Proportionality, and all that."

"Sometimes simpler is better."

"Very seldom."

Maureen sighed. "But *sometimes*."

Releasing a hiss of exasperation, Genie tossed her pencil

onto her sketchbook and glance up at Maureen. "Why do you not simply say, 'Remove the dashed feathers, Genie, for they shall look preposterous upon the heads of babes in a church'?"

"I prefer to be kind."

"Yes, well. Kindness wastes too much time. Holstoke, for example. You should decline his offer now. Delaying is cruel, in my estimation."

Stiffening at the reminder of her impossible quandary, Maureen swatted Genie's shoulder. "My decision is not yet certain, brat. I knew I should not have confided in you."

"Oh, rubbish. Firstly, you confided in me because you wanted honesty, not coddling. Secondly, your decision was made last night, as you know very well. You have been in love with Henry Thorpe since Jane's house party."

As her face heated, she swatted Genie again, who swatted back. Over her shoulder, Maureen eyed Mama and Lady Wallingham to ensure they hadn't witnessed the spat. Fortunately, they were still sipping their tea and debating whether Erasmus was destined to be "a prized mouser" or "the fatal test of Stanton Huxley's affections."

Maureen sat in the chair across from Genie and leaned forward, keeping her voice low. "The fact that I am in love with him—"

"At least you admit it."

"—makes me a sentimental ninny. He deceived me about *his* feelings for over a year."

"Punish him if you like. Use Mama's tactic of serving his most despised dish for dinner each night. Or, better yet, apply shears to a few of his waistcoats."

Maureen winced at the image. Genie could be diabolical.

"But do not punish Holstoke. He's done nothing to deserve it."

"You think being married to me would be a punishment?"

"I think marrying a woman in love with another man would be torment."

And there it was—the reason she had confided in Eugenia,

perhaps the least diplomatic person she knew, save Lady Wallingham.

Content with her argument, Genie returned to her sketch, her dark hair shining warmly in the midday light. The strokes of her pencil filled the silence while Maureen's mind spun and circled and tilted.

"As Lord Holstoke's wife, I would do all in my power to bring him happiness," Maureen choked out, despite an ever-tightening throat.

From behind her, she heard a small meow. It was all the warning she received.

"Holstoke? Good heavens! He has offered marriage? Why did you not say?"

She watched Genie's eyes fly up from her sketch and go round as tea saucers. Maureen's own eyes closed briefly as the words "bloody" and "hell" danced repeatedly through her head.

"Mama," she said without turning around. "It—it has only been a day or two, and I—"

"Holstoke!" came the trumpeting cry of Lady Wallingham, drawing closer than before. "Peculiar fellow."

"Maureen Elizabeth Huxley! You should have told me immediately. I am your mother."

"The eyes are a family trait on the father's side," Lady Wallingham continued, her overloud voice growing louder as she arrived to stand beside Mama. "Possesses more land than God and His Majesty combined, of course, which increases his attractiveness considerably."

"How did you answer?" Mama demanded. "Surely you consented. Tell me you consented."

"If one desires offspring who resemble spectral apparitions, he is a splendid catch. Does he know you fancy Dunston?"

"Dorothea!" Mama snapped.

Lady Wallingham harrumphed. "The question must be asked, Meredith. Unlike his father, Holstoke is far from a dithering fool. And that mother of his, while unpleasant, is shrewder than most. They will sniff out such conflicts faster than Humphrey scenting a squirrel."

"It is neither here nor there," replied Mama with waspish tension. "Dunston is out of the question."

"I fail to see why. He is an earl. Sufficiently plump of pockets. A good deal handsomer than Holstoke. Apart from which, he and your daughter have been infatuated with one another for years. You can scarcely pry them apart with a cannon blast. All that laughter and carrying on. Nauseating, really."

"Out. Of. The question, Dorothea! I'll not have my daughter marrying a ... well, a man like him."

Unexpectedly, Mama's statement caught Maureen's temper. She rose from her chair and turned to face the pair of matrons—her pleasantly round mother and the birdlike Lady Wallingham, whose plumed turban should please Genie immensely.

"What precisely do you mean, 'a man like him,' Mama?"

Mama's rapid blink and darting gaze signaled a good deal more discomfort than seemed warranted by Maureen's question. She bent to place Erasmus on the floor with a pat while formulating her response.

"He is frivolous. A dandy."

Maureen could not explain her fierce indignation at her mother's charge. She only knew it billowed like smoke inside her, acrid and burning. "Henry Thorpe is an exceptional man," she said tightly. "Generous of heart. Powerful of intellect. Charming as a siren's song."

Mama took her hands. "Yes! And just as dangerous, my darling girl."

Frowning, Maureen shook her head and tugged her hands free. "Dangerous? In what way?"

When Mama pressed her lips together and refused to speak, Lady Wallingham intervened. "A spendthrift, my dear. Too much puce silk. Then there is his annual hunt at Fairfield Park.

Having attended last winter, I can attest it is *quite* extravagant. Imagine if he should take up even costlier entertainments. You would find yourself pockets-to-let in a trice."

Maureen examined the pursed lips and sharp green gaze of the woman many had dubbed a dragon for her fearsome cleverness and candor. Lady Wallingham rarely lied so explicitly. There was little need, as her formidable nature ensured no one dared rebuke her for her blunt assessments. But it was there in her eyes, direct though they were. She was coming to Mama's rescue, for Mama obviously had some hidden objection to Henry that she'd no intention of sharing.

"From everything I know of Lord Dunston, he is no greater danger to me than Erasmus," Maureen answered, nodding toward where the cat had begun rolling about on the carpet, batting at dust motes.

Behind her, Genie snorted. "A good deal less so, I should think. The scratches that little menace gave me are still smarting."

Maureen ignored her sister, raised her chin, and calmly addressed her mother and the dragon. "If either of you have insights to impart—reasons why I should refuse to marry Dunston or Holstoke—now is the time to speak."

Mama opened her mouth, only to have Lady Wallingham intrude again with the declaration, "I have nothing more to offer on either man. I do, however, have this to say about the feline menace your mother insists on keeping here at Berne House: You must consider the damage that shall be wrought by acting in haste, Meredith. Consider it well, for it cannot be undone."

With that ominous pronouncement, the dowager gave an imperious sniff and retreated to her seat across the room.

For her part, Mama regained her pinch-lipped expression. "I take it you have not yet given Holstoke your answer," she said.

"No. He has granted me time to ... think it through."

"And Dunston? He has proposed as well?"

Maureen nodded, swallowing at the reminder of her quandary.

Sighing, Mama slowly softened. She gathered Maureen into her arms, rocking her back and forth as she'd done when Maureen had been a child. "All will be well, dearest. Let us see what we might have for luncheon, shall we?"

That, too, was an echo from her girlhood. Maureen squeezed her mother tight and drew back, chuckling. "I fear this is one dilemma that food may not resolve, Mama."

"Nonsense." Mama's rounded chin rose. "Everything is improved by a good meal."

As she and Genie followed Mama and Lady Wallingham from the drawing room to the dining room, Mama turned back. "Oh! A question, dearest."

"Yes, Mama?"

"Lord Holstoke's offer. Was it made during your visit to the Physic Gardens?"

She smiled and shook her head. "In the library after we returned. He was most sincere, as you might expect from such an esteemed gentleman."

"Hmm. And Lord Dunston? How did he propose?"

Maureen felt the beginnings of the Huxley Flush rising as prickling heat in her cheeks. She cleared her throat. "H-he too was sincere."

"Sincere? Well, at least may I know whether he tendered his offer on bended knee?"

Oh, dear God. The Huxley Flush was going to send her swooning. Visions of Henry on his knees offering her unspeakable pleasure flooded her head, along with copious heat and, presumably, crimson color.

Brows arching, Lady Wallingham swept Maureen a single, assessing glance and promptly moved to Mama's side. Clasping the arm of her bewildered friend, she tugged sharply in the direction of the dining room, spinning Mama around and all but dragging her down the corridor. "Come, Meredith," the dragon trumpeted. "Let the girl have her secrets. Luncheon awaits!"

As Mama stumbled and protested, Maureen pressed her hands to her cheeks and breathed to dissipate the heat.

"So," began her smirking sister. "An intriguing shade of red you have there."

Maureen held up a finger in front of Genie's nose. "Do not ask, or I shall bury your favorite bonnet somewhere you will never find it."

A sigh. "No matter. I tend to discover these things eventually."

"One hopes 'eventually' comes after you are married, brat." She looped her arm through Genie's and followed in Lady Wallingham's wake. "After you've been married for a good, long while."

HENRY HAD A SIMPLE PLAN—NOT EASY, BUT SIMPLE. AS WAS his long practice, he'd begun with his ultimate desire: He wanted Maureen Huxley. As his wife. In his bed. He wanted her baking orange cakes in his kitchen and filling every room with her laughter. He wanted this all quite ferociously, as it happened.

He'd next identified all possible barriers and set about dismantling them one by one.

The first barrier was Maureen's infernal resistance. The previous night's interlude had worn away a goodly portion. Although he would have preferred her immediate assent, that might have been asking too much.

The second barrier was proving more intractable—he required her father's consent. This had brought him to the coffee room at White's on a bright Sunday morning better suited to riding.

Lounging in a seat near the windows, he took a sip of

strong brew and eyed his future father-in-law. "What more can I offer to set your mind at ease? I have abandoned my prior pursuits. We shall leave London for Fairfield Park immediately after the wedding. My staff there is well trained. Prepared for any eventuality."

Lord Berne gave a small smile and set his own cup on the white-clothed table. "You are not yet a father, Dunston, so I will forgive you for thinking anything less than perfect certainty will 'set my mind at ease.'"

"I love her. I would die rather than see her harmed."

Typically a man of good humor and gentle mien, Berne now resembled only a stern father. "The likelier eventuality is that *she* will die for you." After that soft-spoken kick to his nether regions, the older man demonstrated no remorse, instead giving him another whack. "She is better off with a man like Holstoke."

Henry crushed the snarling reply he wished to give. The goal was persuasion, not a shouting match. "Safer, perhaps," he conceded. "But she does not love him."

Henry watched hazel eyes twitch. Good. He had him thinking. Stanton Huxley knew his daughter's soft heart, knew she would suffer more than most in a loveless union.

"In two years or four, when all possible danger has passed," Henry continued, "will you be glad to have denied her the man she truly wanted? Will she thank you, do you suppose?"

"She will be alive. I can content myself with that."

Henry had no answer. Berne was correct in thinking Holstoke was the safer choice, barring a mishap involving Greek follies or one of the man's blasted fish ponds.

"True, the risk to her is greater as my wife. Precisely the reason I have hesitated to advance my suit until now." He leaned forward, bracing his elbow beside his empty cup. "If I believed for one moment that I could not protect her, I would let her go to Holstoke. It would damned near kill me. But I would do it."

For a long while, the older man sat in silence, holding his gaze as though trying to hear his thoughts. Then, Berne slowly eased back in his seat, nodding faintly. "You have managed to keep your mother and sister safe. How?"

"With great diligence," Henry answered. "And unusually skilled servants. Former soldiers, for the most part."

Berne's brows arched. "Given such a penchant, and your declared affection, I'm a bit surprised you haven't assigned a guard to Maureen."

Henry held his tongue.

Berne blinked. And blinked again. "Regina?"

He loathed revealing his methods, but in the interest of gaining the man's cooperation, he inclined his head.

"Good God! I've been paying her to be a lady's maid, not a—"

"She is worth every penny of what we both pay her, I assure you."

Huffing an exasperated chuckle, Berne sat back and shook his head. "I've little knowledge of these sorts of intrigues, Dunston. I would be trusting in your capabilities."

Again, he had no answer. So, instead, he waited.

Berne tapped his finger rhythmically on the white tablecloth, alternately gazing out the window and shooting Henry speculative glances. Finally, he sighed and stilled his hand. "I will not give my approval, but neither will I stand in your way. If she accepts you, then you may marry." He held up a finger, stalling Henry's wave of relief. "One condition. You have vowed to never take up such pursuits again. But you must also keep Maureen safe."

"I have promised this already."

"Not merely her life. Protect her innocence, Dunston. Do not burden her with knowledge of this dark world you inhabit. Were she more like Annabelle or Jane or even Eugenia, I might suggest otherwise." His smile was wistful. "Her heart is both soft and pure. To sully it would be a kind of poison, I suspect. Slow, perhaps. But fatal."

Henry considered the demand. It would mean continuing the charade, keeping a great many secrets from the woman he least wanted to deceive. Not that he'd intended to burden her with tales of wretched woe on their wedding night. Certainly not. But vowing to hide a significant part of himself from her forever? It was no small thing.

Necessity, however, rarely complied with one's desires.

"Very well," he said to his future father-in-law. "She will not learn of these things from my lips. I will protect your daughter, my lord. Even from myself."

WHEN DUNSTON AND DRAYTON HAD FIRST ENTERED Reaver's office with boxes of correspondence and reports and documents and journals, Reaver had been elated. Finally, he would have what he needed to pursue the Investor, if not the direct assistance of Dunston himself.

"Have it all," Dunston had said, waving to the piles of paper. "Be warned I am using you, old chap. As a married man, I cannot have the Investor hunting me any longer. With any luck, he will hunt you in my stead. Congratulations. And my condolences."

Reaver had wondered at Dunston's decision to abandon a decade-long pursuit rather than simply partner with Reaver and complete his mission. But he'd seen other men change course over a woman before. He scarcely understood it, as few women he'd ever known merited such a shift, but he'd shrugged away the question and dug into the reports on the Investor.

Now, having read through the lot, he was sickened. With hatred. With disgust. With helpless rage. It wasn't enough that the Investor had poisoned at least five old men at last count.

No. The bastard had targeted a little girl for slaughter.

By all accounts, Syder had kept her hidden for ten years. At Syder's death, she'd been fourteen. God only knew what that butcher had done to her, but had the Investor laid hands upon her first, she would have been dead.

She'd been Syder's bargaining chip, near as Reaver could determine, and he'd played it well. Most who entered the Investor's sphere perished the moment they were no longer of use. Syder had lasted ten years.

Reaver sighed now as he leaned one shoulder against a fluted column in the main parlor of his club, watching the fevered glint in a young lordling's eyes as the dice rolled across green baize.

Beside him, Shaw nodded to the croupier. "Fair business today. Frelling thinks we should add another hazard table to the east parlor."

He might have said more, but for once, Reaver didn't care a jot for business.

The bloody Investor had planned to kill a child. At least the poisoning victims had been old. They had lived privileged lives. Syder's ward had been four, perhaps five when she came into Syder's hands.

"Reaver."

"I want to find the man who manufactures the poison."

Shaw cleared his throat. "We have all our sources working—"

Reaver turned a dark glare upon his friend and partner. "He aims to kill a young girl. If we cannot find the maker, we cannot find the Investor. If we cannot find the Investor, then sooner or later, she will die. Simple thing."

Much like Reaver, Adam Shaw had begun his life in squalor, scraping and fighting for every inch of ground. He'd eventually gained a position with the East India Company and journeyed to England, his mother's homeland, at sixteen.

Neither Reaver nor Shaw had a drop of innocence left, but both found threats to children particularly motivating. Now,

Reaver watched Shaw's amber eyes shift. The other man nodded, his lean features hardening with the ruthlessness Reaver felt. "I shall put Frelling on it. His wife's father is a physician, I believe. He may know something."

Reaver glanced to the ceiling, where crystalline chandeliers glittered precisely as he'd envisioned. He surveyed the closed silk draperies and the hushed fervor of the club he and Shaw had built. For years, this place had been his wife, his mistress, and his babe. He'd thought of little else. Certainly, he had aided Dunston in bringing down Syder, but that had been partially self-interested. Syder's butchery had blighted all club proprietors.

Now, the Investor had Reaver's full attention.

He narrowed his gaze upon a man laughing triumphantly and pointing at the latest turn of the dice. Blond, thinning hair. Expansive forehead. "Bring me Hastings," he said to Shaw.

"Are you certain?"

Reaver nodded.

Minutes later, Christopher Hastings approached, flushed from his win. "Mr. Reaver," the man said in a reverent tone. "It is my honor to make your acquaintance, sir. I am a great admirer of your club."

Shaw raised an ironic brow, but he stood behind Hastings, so the insipid man did not see.

Inclining his head, Reaver gestured toward the doors. "Come. I'll show you the east parlor."

Hastings trailed him eagerly. As they strode by, Shaw motioned to Duff, the nearest sentry, to keep others from following them down the corridor. Soon, they passed the doors to the east parlor. Reaver kept walking. He nodded to another of his sentries, who nodded in return, before rounding a corner and entering Shaw's office. The room was small but classically English, as Shaw preferred: white-paneled, blue-draped, and centered with a golden mahogany desk Shaw had paid entirely too much for.

Reaver waited only for the click of the door closing before clapping a hand upon Hastings's shoulder and pulling the confused man closer. "Your grandfather was a member here."

Hastings's eyes darted toward Reaver's hand. "Er—yes. That is, yes, I do believe—"

"He died recently, did he not? Leaving your father the new Lilliworth."

"I-is this the east parlor? Rather smaller than I—"

Shaw chuckled.

Reaver shook Hastings until his brows arched into his broad forehead. "Who is your father's physician?"

Hastings blinked. Glanced at Shaw, who tilted his head expectantly. "W-why do you wish to kn—"

The question ended in a squeal as Reaver's hand dug into his shoulder at a tender spot along the joint.

"Just answer, Hastings. Your father's physician."

"Fenwick! Dr. Fenwick."

Reaver loosened his hold. Patted Hastings's shoulder. Ignored the man's sputtering outrage. "Best not mention this conversation to anyone," he warned. "Your friend Walters owes a substantial sum. He is fortunate we allow him past the door."

Hastings rubbed his sore shoulder and glared first at Reaver then at Shaw. He waved a finger between them. "Is this about Lord Dunston?"

Shaw answered first. "Dunston. No. Why do you ask?"

"He accosted me, as well. Cup-shot at the time. I assure you, my intentions toward Miss Andrews remain entirely honorable!"

Reaver frowned. Looked to Shaw, who was equally bewildered. Then answered, "Good. Now, leave."

Hastings hovered, appearing confused.

Reaver lowered his voice. "Leave, man. I'll not say it again."

Shaw opened the door, and Hastings scurried out.

"Miss Andrews?" Shaw queried, amusement coloring his voice.

Reaver sighed and shook his head. "No idea. Perhaps Hastings made advances toward Lady Maureen. Dunston loses all perspective where she is concerned."

"Well, at least we have the physician's name." Shaw chuckled. "And a guarantee that Miss Andrews will be treated honorably."

Reaver grunted and flexed his fingers into fists then flared them out. "Thought this sort of work was done."

"Using your fists, you mean?"

"Aye."

"It saves time. Not to worry." Shaw's grin was white and annoying. "I shan't be scheduling any bouts for you anytime soon."

Reaver shoved his partner's shoulder and started out the door. "If you're the opponent, I might just accept."

Laughter was Shaw's only answer.

"Find the physician, eh?" Reaver threw over his shoulder as he headed back toward his office to comb through the boxes of paper once again.

"And if a few quid fails to persuade him?"

"We'll see whether my skills have rusted or not."

Shaw shot him a speculative glance.

Reaver kept walking. "Find him soon, Shaw," he said. "A girl's life hangs in the balance. Remember that and act accordingly."

# Chapter Eleven

*"Two strapping men testing one another in a battle of strength
and will? Hmm, yes. How brutish. Step aside, dear boy.
You are blocking my view."*

—THE DOWAGER MARCHIONESS OF WALLINGHAM to her son,
Charles, on an otherwise uneventful stroll in Hyde Park.

"I AM MISSING A BOUT AT GENTLEMAN JACKSON'S FOR THIS.
*With* Gentleman Jackson."

Maureen glanced across the open carriage at her brother,
who wore a brown coat, black hat, and disgruntled expression.
She raised a brow. "Pity Mama could not be here to wipe away
your tears, John."

He released a sharp laugh and glanced over his shoulder at their driver, perched above them. "You might at least have agreed to let me drive. Something other than this old barouche, of course."

"The phaeton has room only for you and me. Where would Phineas sit?"

John grinned rakishly. He'd been doing most things rakishly since returning from his tour of the Continent. "Phineas, is it? I thought the purpose of this outing was to cool the flames of familiarity."

"Do not jest. This is difficult enough."

He sighed and relaxed against the seat. "Holstoke will recover, Reenie."

She gazed out upon the passing houses of Mayfair, glad for the damp-scented breeze in the growing heat. Perhaps John had been the wrong choice of chaperone, but she'd had few other options. Genie would have blurted something inappropriate at the worst possible time, no doubt. Probably a hat metaphor. *As it happens, Lady Maureen prefers a bit more color in her bonnet, Lord Holstoke. You should seek a wife who enjoys the plain black hats one wears for mourning. Incidentally, she snores. Be grateful for all the undisturbed slumber you have regained this day.* Maureen cringed to imagine it.

Mama, of course, had been out of the question. She disapproved mightily of Maureen's decision, which had come in the middle of the night after a dream in which Henry kissed her breathless then left her alone, standing in a gazebo beside a lake. She'd next seen him striding to the water's edge, wading in and disappearing beneath its moonlit surface. She'd been inconsolable, awakening with guttural sobs wrenching her chest.

She might be vexed with Henry for deceiving her, but the truth could not be denied. She loved him. She wanted to marry him. And although she admired Phineas, might even have been content as his wife, he was not the man who held her heart.

Now, as they turned onto Park Lane, her stomach churned and frothed. Her fists clenched in her lap.

A hand covered hers.

John was leaning forward with his elbows propped on his knees. "You were always meant to marry Dunston," he said quietly. "Anyone with eyes could see it. This day, this moment, may be trying, but it will end, Reenie. And then you shall have your long-awaited happiness."

She bit her lip and squeezed her brother's hand tightly, nodding her thanks.

Perhaps John had been the right chaperone, after all.

They entered Holstoke's house minutes later, only to be greeted by Lady Holstoke, who insisted they have tea while waiting for Phineas to complete some urgent task. Now, Maureen was left to perch on the edge of an emerald sofa in Holstoke's drawing room, sipping bitter, over-steeped tea and listening to Lady Holstoke describe in excruciating detail how she had selected the flowers for the table in the entrance hall.

"Lilies overwhelm the senses." Liquid blue eyes swept from Maureen's waist to her nose. "Holstoke enjoys them, but then, he favors a certain vulgar fulsomeness. Roses are pleasant enough, I suppose, if one lacks all originality."

"Oh, I adore roses. I have since I was a girl."

The lovely, placid features of Lady Holstoke smoothed into a benign smile and a long blink. "Of course you do, my dear."

Before Maureen could reply to the veiled insult, John cleared his throat and remarked, "Fine day for a drive. May has been warm all round, I daresay. Summer promises to be remarkable."

Holstoke's mother drank her bitter brew and nodded. "The lilacs have bloomed early. That is what I selected for the entrance hall. Lilacs."

There was no help for it. She could not make herself like Lady Holstoke. Her reasons were subtle—unexplainable, even. But at the moment, she pined for Lady Dunston's griping about gout or even Lady Wallingham's supercilious pronouncements about the uselessness of cats.

She was so relieved when she spotted Phineas entering through the southernmost set of doors that she sprang to her feet still holding her tea. Tall and pale-eyed and frowning, he strode across to her, bowing stiffly before nodding to John and, lastly, his mother. Was it her imagination, or did those eyes acquire a coating of frost?

"Lady Holstoke, it was kind of you entertain my guests whilst I was occupied," he said to his mother before turning to John and Maureen. "We should be off now, however. I anticipate a storm by this evening."

That was another oddity. He always referred to his mother as "Lady Holstoke," as though the woman were as much a stranger to him as she was to Maureen.

Regardless, the stilted exchange resulted in their swift departure, which served her purposes nicely. Except that now, she must confront the reason for their outing—a task even more distasteful than sipping bitter tea with Lady Holstoke.

On the short drive down Park Lane to the Cumberland Gate entrance of the park, John and Phineas discussed weather and carriages while her stomach cramped and her palms sweated inside her gloves. She should have written out what she would say, for the words now escaped her.

*Dearest Phineas, how dear you are to me. So dear, in fact, that I must decline your dear, dear offer.*

Perhaps she should have brought Genie.

Or Lady Wallingham. The thought alone nearly made her burst out laughing. Both Genie and the dragon were instruments best employed judiciously, and only when one cared nothing for the feelings of the target in question.

She cared very much about Phineas's feelings. She did not wish to hurt him.

No sooner had the thought flickered through her mind, however, than John was ordering the coachman to halt just inside the park entrance.

"Well, now. I fancy a bit of a ramble on such a fine day.

What say you, Maureen?" He was staring pointedly at her.

She took a shuddering breath and nodded. Both John and Phineas helped her down from the barouche, each taking a side. Phineas's hand was strong around hers, and she squeezed his fingers a moment before releasing him.

She hated this. Hurting anyone made her stomach sour, her throat tight. John ambled ahead while she took Phineas's arm, pretending to fuss with her skirts to delay and gain some distance, some privacy for their discussion.

Before they'd taken more than ten steps, Phineas said quietly, "You have decided to decline my offer, have you not?"

The cramping in her stomach worsened, becoming a searing pain. She fought unexpected tears and pressed her lips together before gathering her courage to look at his face. His eyes shone brilliantly in the vivid sunlight, the dark centers mere pinpoints. As they strolled into the rippling shadows of one of the park's trees, the eerie effect diminished, leaving only the proud strain around his cheeks and mouth.

"I am so very sorry, Phineas." She swallowed hard, her mouth dry. "But yes. I must decline."

He looked away and nodded.

Beneath her fingers, she felt the muscles of his arm flex and relax. Flex and relax.

For a while, they walked together in silence, disturbed only by the crunch of gravel beneath passing carriages, the rustling murmur of leaves, the shouts of children watching a man fly a kite.

"Well," he said finally. "A disappointment, of course. I should like to have shown you my greenhouse in Dorsetshire."

Despite the pains in her stomach and the twist in her chest, her lips curved into a smile. "I've little doubt there is none finer in England, my lord."

He glanced down at her with one of his opaque expressions. "Quite."

A moment later, she heard hoofbeats. Two moments later,

she was turning. Three moments later, her heart seized to a stop as she recognized who had come riding up alongside them. How could she not? He was the man who held her heart. Although, at present, he bore little resemblance to Henry Thorpe, apart from the green riding coat and copper waistcoat.

No, in fact, this man displayed none of Henry's customary good humor. This man was as dark and ominous as a seaborne squall.

HENRY'S DAY HAD GONE APPROXIMATELY AS WELL AS ONE might expect—if one were cursed.

It started at the breakfast table with his mother commenting that her swelling toes had begun to recede. "They now resemble cauliflower boiled in a broth of beets. An improvement, I daresay," she stated matter-of-factly.

Halting a forkful of kippers four inches above his plate, he sighed and consigned himself to tea and toast. He then sent his mother occasional glances before announcing his intentions to marry Maureen.

Mama stopped with a roll dripping with butter and marmalade half-delivered to her open mouth. She slowly closed said mouth and stared at him in stunned silence for long minutes. Then, she stared down at his waistcoat, then back up at his hair, then to his hands, then to his cravat. "Are you ... are you *certain,* Henry?"

"Yes." He raised a brow and sipped his tea. "Why do you say it like that? I thought you liked Lady Maureen."

Stroud entered, insisting on brushing the shoulders of his riding coat, since "your lordship was in such a rush this morning, I was given no opportunity to attend it properly." After a few swipes of the brush, Stroud nodded, eyed his handiwork, and left.

All the while, Henry's mother watched through suspicious eyes. Again, she examined his waistcoat with visible consternation. "Henry, I ... I don't quite ..."

Returning his tea to its saucer, he frowned at the woman who had birthed him. "What is it?"

"I wish your father were here."

She rarely mentioned him. Too painful, Henry supposed. "As do I, Mama."

Reaching for his hand, she looked down at his fingers. "There was a—a boy when I was young. He was the son of a landowner. A neighbor of ours. We—we spent a great deal of time together."

He wondered if he shouldn't simply leave the table before something horrifying was revealed.

But she continued, "He was a delight, Henry. Dashing and handsome and fastidious. Over time, it grew increasingly evident that he ... well, he preferred ... the company of others." She paused meaningfully. "*Male* others."

Alarm pealed through him. "Good God, Mama. Cauliflower toes and men who prefer other males. Has the gout infected your mind as well as your feet?"

She stiffened, pulling away and sniffing. "My only intention is to convey that I understand your ... peculiar circumstances. And I do not find them as objectionable as you might suppose."

"Objectionable."

"However." She raised a finger. "While I should adore having Lady Maureen as my daughter-in-law, that dear girl deserves more than a ... platonic marriage. You must have an heir, of course. But perhaps you could seek out another young lady. A spinster, perhaps, for whom marrying one such as yourself would be a mercy."

"Mama," he gritted, finally realizing what his mother had obviously presumed about him. Perhaps keeping so many secrets from her had been unwise, for she could not possibly have woven the mysterious gaps into a more erroneous conclusion. "I do not prefer the company of male others."

Her eyes fell again to his waistcoat.

"Oh, for pity's sake. I love women! How much more clearly must I state it? Specifically, I love Maureen Huxley. And I intend to marry her."

Mama gave him a blinking frown as he rose from his chair and tossed his napkin on his plate. "So, Stroud really is your ..."

"Valet," he snapped. "My valet, Mama."

Arched brows emphasized her skepticism. "You haven't retained a mistress in two years, Henry."

"Good God," he repeated, running a hand through his hair.

"Well, what else was I to think?"

"What sort of question is that? Never mind. Do not answer. I am leaving before you decide I have too much fondness for my horses." Despite her outlandish assumptions and the discomfort of their conversation, he leaned down and kissed her cheek before departing for Doctor's Commons.

Once there, he discovered obtaining a special license would be much more expensive than he'd anticipated. The Archbishop, as it happened, had recently dined with the Home Secretary, who was still complaining about Henry's "unpredictable nature" a year-and-a-half after the Horatio Syder debacle ended his association with the Home Office. In short, Henry would not be permitted a special license without paying thrice the normal rate and giving assurances of future generosity toward the Church.

Next, he rode to Reaver's club after receiving a cryptic note written in Reaver's scrawling hand. Upon entering the modest brick house with the red door and luxuriant interior, he was shown by the majordomo, Shaw, upstairs to Reaver's chambers. There, the glowering giant with the tiny spectacles regaled him with tales of disappearing barons and sinking fortunes, exotic poisons and illnesses without explanation. Henry raised a hand to stop Reaver mid-sentence. "What has any of this to do with me, my good man?"

"The Investor is behind everything, I am certain of it. One need only examine the botanical sketches—"

"Again," Henry replied calmly. "It is my concern because ...?"

Reaver's mouth tightened. He tossed his spectacles onto the desk and folded massive arms across his chest. "Right. You are out. I should have remembered. Apologies for disturbing you, your *lordship*."

Yes, he was out. And as he left Reaver's club, glancing up at the statue of Fortuna on his way to the door, he pondered the hollowness of it. The nagging sensation that he'd left something important unfinished.

Seeking to forget, he took his horse, Dag, to the park for a brisk ride.

Only to find Maureen strolling arm-in-arm with the Earl of Holstoke, pretty as you please. Dag—a dark-bay Thoroughbred who was both steady and responsive—sidled nervously as Henry's grip on the reins tightened.

Henry pulled even with Holstoke, spun in a circle and dismounted smoothly. Holstoke was taller, of course. Younger and probably richer. But Henry had something he didn't. Henry had claimed Maureen's heart first. It belonged to him. *She* belonged to him.

"Splendid day, is it not?"

Maureen appeared unreceptive to his jovial demeanor. Perhaps he should smile.

"You are ravishingly lovely in that gown, pet. Where did you manage to find such a color?"

"It is white, Lord Dunston."

"Mmm." He ran his eyes slowly over her curves, tracing every swell and hollow revealed by the light breeze. "No, not white, merely. The embroidery is the sweetest primrose, if I am not mistaken." Deliberately, he settled his gaze upon her bosom, covered in a yellow silk spencer with tucks and ties from shoulder to wrist. "It matches your spencer."

"Dunston," came the one-word greeting from the man at her side.

Reluctantly, Henry moved his attention to Maureen's tall,

ghostly-eyed nuisance of a companion. "Holstoke! Didn't see you there, old chap. Glorious weather."

Before Henry had read Reaver's file on Holstoke, his impression of the earl had been ambivalent. They'd first become acquainted earlier in the spring while waiting for a heated debate about the cash payments bill to run its course in the House of Lords. Henry would have fallen asleep for that one, but his friend from Commons, Robert Peel, had come along to perform introductions. Holstoke had struck him as an odd sort of chap—cool and assessing, curiously devoid of color—but Peel seemed to like him quite well. Of course, Robert was a bit mercurial himself, so perhaps it was a poor measure.

Now, however, Henry thought Holstoke could better be described as a bloody pale-eyed poacher who was both freakishly tall and painfully plain. What Robert—or Maureen, for that matter—found to like in the other man was a mystery for the ages.

"Your waistcoat is the color of a bronze coin," Holstoke commented, staring as though he'd never seen silk before.

Or as though he were a predatory serpent playing with his food.

Henry noted the blackguard hadn't moved an inch away from Maureen, who watched them with horrified fascination.

"I collect them," he replied.

"Bronze coins?"

Grinning wide without really smiling, Henry met the other man's gaze with a challenge of his own. "Waistcoats. Lady Maureen is fond of them, aren't you, pet?" He took in her outrage before returning to Holstoke. "Or perhaps it is me she is fond of."

"Henry!"

Ignoring her rebuke, he watched with satisfaction as Holstoke's face hardened, the eyes going flat.

"Lady Maureen's compassion is one of her many admirable

virtues," Holstoke replied. "She demonstrates patience with feral creatures. Her mother's cat, for example."

Maureen cleared her throat. "You flatter me, Lord Holstoke. Perhaps we should resume our walk—"

Henry tilted his head, this time letting the full weight of his darker nature emerge. "Ah, but a feral creature may return her regard. He may claim her as his own. He may grow dangerous when others seek to usurp such a claim."

Distantly, he heard footsteps approaching from behind him. Then, John's voice. "Dunston!" A hand clapped hard upon his shoulder. "Out for a ride, are you? What a fine mount. Is he new?"

"You rode him not more than a fortnight ago, Huxley."

"Of course. Now I remember. Dunston's Dagger, yes?"

Henry did not bother to reply. Instead, he continued matching Holstoke's deadly glare.

"Yes, a prime bit of horseflesh, indeed," John continued, his grip hardening. "Capital. Maureen, let us make our way back to the barouche. Leave these two *gentlemen* to their conversation."

With a slow blink and a subtle head tilt, Holstoke stated flatly, "I must go. Matters to attend." He turned to Maureen, bowing over her gloved hand. "Lady Maureen, I do hope you will forgive my rudeness. Your fair company has been both a privilege and a pleasure."

"Of course," she murmured sweetly, making Henry want to break the fingers that held hers one by one. "Farewell, Phineas."

*Phineas? Phineas!* He watched the freakishly tall earl stride away, wondering how someone could hit him in the stomach without taking a single swing. She'd just done it, and it left him gasping.

"Henry Edwin Fitzsimmons Thorpe." Her displeasure clipped every word. *"What* was that?"

John coughed into his fist. "Perhaps we should return home, little sister. We are drawing undue attention."

Henry tossed Dag's reins to John and stalked toward Maureen until her head tilted back and her eyes rounded beneath the brim of her bonnet. He stopped when there was scarcely a breath between them.

"I do not like hearing his name on your lips, pet."

"I do not enjoy watching you behave like a rival stag during rutting season, but it seems we both are doomed to disappointment."

"Er, Maureen," said John. "Everyone is listening. Good afternoon, Lady Darnham!" He gave a friendly wave. "A fine day, is it not?"

"Huxley," Henry gritted. "The horse is yours if you will give us two minutes of bloody privacy."

A brief pause. "Come along, Dag. Let us speak with Lady Darnham and her lovely granddaughter, shall we?"

In John's absence, Henry crowded even closer to Maureen, who smelled like orange flowers and sunlight. "There should be no need of rivalry," he said, keeping his voice low and his eyes upon hers. "The problem is merely one of title. Yours should be Lady Dunston."

"I was saying goodbye to Lord Holstoke."

"Yes. I heard." It was all he could do to forget.

"Forever."

He blinked. "You were—"

She released a sigh of exasperation. "Declining his offer, you great lummox."

"Because?"

Secretive lips pursed and tightened. A gentle brow lowered over troubled, flashing eyes. "What sort of husband will you be, Henry?"

His heart stopped. Then soared. Then roared. She was going to agree. She was going to say yes. Bloody hell, he wanted to take her in his arms and kiss her breathless.

"The best sort, pet. The grateful sort who wishes to spoil and pleasure you. The sort who will build you ten fish ponds and five kitchens and erect a ridiculous assemblage of Greek columns upon the lawn at Fairfield Park."

Her mouth quirked. Then quivered. Then broke into a dimpled smile. "Silly man."

His hands found hers. Interlaced their gloved fingers. The brims of their hats brushed, forming a shaded canopy. "I will live upon your laughter, for it is as necessary as sunlight to me. I will give you children because that is who you are—a mother. And I will love you, my beautiful Maureen. Until my last breath."

He felt her answer upon his lips, warm and sweet, as she whispered, "Then marry me, Henry. For I love you madly, and I can scarcely wait another moment to be your wife."

# Chapter Twelve

*"Watchmen, constables, and magistrates. Bah! Incompetents, all. I daresay a new Home Secretary could make a name for himself were he clever enough. A more systematic approach to confronting London's criminal element is long overdue."*

—THE DOWAGER MARCHIONESS OF WALLINGHAM to Mr. Robert Peel regarding thievery perpetrated by a recently dismissed lady's maid.

"BLOODY, BLEEDING HELL," MUTTERED DRAYTON AS HE AND Reaver entered the apothecary's shop jammed between a public house and a cobbler.

The shop was narrow and dark, but the light from the

windows was enough to see broken, amber glass strewn across the counter and wall of shelves. Drayton rushed forward, heading for the opening to the back room. Reaver followed, a rancid sensation invading his gut.

He heard a thud. Watched Drayton's head swivel in the same direction—toward the corner of the room near the garden door. They found the apothecary slumped in front of copious labeled drawers, eyes dilated, chest heaving. He wore a linen tunic and his smallclothes. Nothing else.

Drayton shot Reaver a glance. "Looks like we found the Investor's man."

"Aye. A bit late." Reaver reached down and grasped a handful of tunic, pulling the man up and wedging him against the cabinetry. The apothecary's head lolled to one side, his tongue and lips working as though he wished to speak but could not feel his mouth. "You are the one manufacturing the poisons, eh?" Reaver waited for the near-insensible eyes to meet his and the wheezing, "Yuzsh," before hoisting the man higher.

"Who hired you? Give me a name."

Drool slicked down the man's chin. Wheezing became choking. The mottled face darkened further then began to blue. Dilated eyes rolled. Bare feet thrashed.

Drayton gritted a curse. "He's gone."

Reaver lowered the dying man to the floor. "He'll have an apprentice. Find him."

Immediately, the Bow Street runner exited to the garden while Reaver began searching both the small storefront and the back workroom, opening drawers and sifting through notes and receipts. Both spaces were tiny, so it took only minutes—long minutes in which he tried mightily to ignore the sounds of the apothecary's death throes.

Brushing aside broken glass, Reaver examined the labels on the stoppered bottles that remained intact, squinting and holding the bottles at arm's length. Apart from laudanum, he recognized few of the terms. Glass crunched beneath his boots, echoing in the small space. He gathered the papers and took them into the front room, arranging them into a neat stack and anchoring them beneath a mortar and pestle.

He wanted to ram his fist into the top of the counter. The Investor was always and forever one step ahead. How, he did not know. Perhaps Drayton was being tracked. If so, the runner might be a liability.

Just then, he heard Drayton shouting.

A shot rang out.

Reaver ran. Rounded the apothecary's worktable. Threw open the garden door. Saw Drayton staggering toward a slim figure dressed in two shades of brown. Saw the figure slip through the gate, leaving it ajar. Drayton slowed, limping drastically, red dripping from a wound in his leg.

Racing toward the gate, Reaver used his long strides to eat up the distance. Once in the alley, he glanced to either side, scanning the refuse piled behind the pub, the leather scraps littering the area behind the cobbler's shop. But no slim man wearing brown and toting a smoking pistol was anywhere in sight.

Carefully, keeping a steady but urgent pace, he sidled with his back to the brick walls on the opposite side of the alley. He continued to where the alley met the street, glancing up and down. A coach-and-four lumbered past. A trio of mounted gentlemen and an assortment of Londoners going about their daily business passed shops along the street. But, again, no one who resembled Drayton's attacker.

He moved back into the alley, now loping to the opposite end where the narrow path widened into a small mews. Nothing there, either.

Bloody hell, he wanted to strike something. Grab hold and squeeze until it gave him the Investor's name.

Distantly, he heard Drayton call out, the runner's voice hoarse and more breathless than it should be.

Running back through the gate, Reaver saw Drayton on his knees in a bed of herbs, hat lying on the ground next to him.

The Bow Street runner was wrapping a kerchief around his thigh, knotting and cinching it with shaking hands. Dark trousers were soaked and dripping red.

Reaver stalked to his side and, without a word, looped the man's arm across his shoulders, hoisting him up.

Drayton groaned. "Ah, devil take me."

"Not yet," Reaver growled. "Not bloody well yet."

Hours later, having delivered a gray-faced Drayton to the surgeon and retrieved the apothecary's papers, Reaver thought his mood could not possibly get blacker.

He was wrong.

Upon entering his club through the well-guarded rear door, he was greeted by Duff, whose protruding brow furrowed alarmingly. Duff was a big man of few words and a stoic disposition. If something disturbed him, then it was something to worry about.

"What is it?" Reaver demanded.

"Shaw is ill, Mr. Reaver. Never seen the like."

A piercing chill coiled along his spine.

Dunston had warned the Investor would come for everyone closest to Reaver. *It amuses him to make you choke to death on your own heart.* The words rang in his head, repeating and repeating.

"Where is he?" Reaver barked.

"His chambers."

Reaver hurried as fast as he dared, taking the back stairs three at a time, then ducking beneath two low lintels before turning the corner into the main corridor. Upon entering Shaw's chambers, the smell hit him first.

Foul and sour, it reminded him of all the men he'd known who had poisoned themselves with drink. It reminded him of the apothecary's horrific final moments.

Shaw lay in his bed, his brown skin ashen, his eyes closed. Beside him in a wooden chair, a gray-haired man with hunched shoulders and palsied, spotted hands stirred a cup of tea.

Reaver stomped toward the old man. "Who are you?"

Behind him, Frelling spoke. "My father-in-law. It is all right, Reaver. Dr. Young helped Shaw expel the poison. He believes he will recover." Frelling stepped into the light from the open window. Behind his spectacles, his eyes were hollow and stark. "It was close. Very close."

The physician tapped his spoon on the edge of his teacup. "Mr. Reaver, you have a determined and clever adversary." The old man's eyes gleamed as he took a sip with a trembling hand and swallowed. "I was not about to let him win, however."

Eyeing Shaw's still form and slow breaths, Reaver propped one hand on his hip and forked another through his hair.

What a deadly mess he had invited inside. How in bloody hell had Dunston managed for so long? Remaining hidden had likely helped, he supposed, but to continue the fight for years while the Investor evaded capture over and over. Even after a week or two, Reaver was frustrated beyond measure, sickened by the Investor's tactics and the depraved glee with which he rid himself of those who might endanger his plans.

Reaver thanked the physician and offered to provide the old man whatever he needed.

Dr. Young smiled and nodded toward Frelling. "Matthew tells me you went to see the apothecary who has been preparing the poison. Did you find anything worthwhile?"

Sighing, he shook his head. "My adversary, as you call him, arrived first. Poisoned his own man. When we found the apothecary, he was minutes from death." Reaver reached inside his coat and withdrew the half-folded wad of paper. It was wrinkled, some of the smaller slips torn. "This is all I have. His shop was wrecked."

The old man reached for the papers. Reluctantly, Reaver handed them over.

Palsied hands unfolded them and began sorting into piles, placing each page and slip one by one on the bed next to Shaw. "I shall have a look." Dr. Young waved his fingers dismissively.

"Go on, now, both of you. Leave me to my tea."

Reaver looked to Frelling, who chuckled fondly and headed for the door. As he followed his secretary out into the hushed corridor, Reaver muttered, "How Dunston pursued this bloody demon for so long without losing his mind, I've no idea."

Walking beside him as they made their way to Reaver's office, Frelling nodded. "Extraordinary, indeed. Strength of that sort inspires a certain awe."

"He described the frustrations I would face, but it was hard to credit. Worse than Syder?" He shook his head. "How could anyone be worse, eh?"

Frelling did not reply. He didn't have to.

"Dunston was right," Reaver said quietly. "The Investor must be brought down, and that requires patience. More than I've shown. The poisonings will likely slow now that the apothecary is dead, but both Shaw and Drayton have been laid low."

"Drayton?"

"He was shot pursuing the apothecary's killer. The apprentice, most likely."

"Dear God."

Reaver grunted his agreement. "Aye. I suspect we have drawn dangerously close. If what Dunston told me proves true, we must prepare well. Be ready. The Investor's war will only get bloodier from here."

# Chapter Thirteen

*"Wedded bliss? Rubbish. We are all adrift on a sea of alternating misery and contentment, Eugenia. Marriage merely promises that we neither float nor drown alone."*

—The Dowager Marchioness of Wallingham to Lady Eugenia Huxley upon said girl's assertion that ivy should be incorporated into all bridal wreathes to ensure a happy marriage.

STEAM CHOSE A CURLING PATH UPWARD FROM THE COPPER TUB. Tendrils of sensation took a similar route up Maureen's spine as she brushed her hair and eyed Henry's massive bed in the dressing table mirror.

"Hmmph," grunted Regina, laying out towels and soap on a small table. "T'would appear Mr. Kimble manages his footmen better than he manages his duties at the front door. Never seen a bath delivered so quickly."

A smile tugged at Maureen's lips. "Does this mean you won't mind being a member of the staff here at Dunston House?"

Busying herself lining up the pitchers of fresh water so that the handles all faced the same direction, Regina huffed again. "My loyalty remains with you, regardless of your new residence or new title, Lady Dunston."

Hearing Regina refer to her in such a way was a startling jolt. Lady Dunston. She was Henry's wife. It hardly seemed possible, let alone real.

Only two days ago, she had stood in Hyde Park, gazing up at the vexatious man she loved and agreeing to marry him. This morning, they had spoken vows in the light-filled, bowed drawing room of Dunston House. At Henry's behest, she had worn the same canary gown she'd worn to the Holstoke ball, and Genie and Kate had woven her a crown of rosebuds, daisies, and orange blossoms for her hair. Henry had worn his best midnight-superfine tailcoat, black trousers, and a sky-blue waistcoat with silver embroidery. His sapphire cravat pin had glimmered from within the snowy folds of his cravat, but it paled in comparison with his eyes. By turns, they had sparkled with shared humor and glowed with adoration. From time to time, she thought she'd glimpsed something darker—possession, perhaps, or hard ferocity. But no sooner would she peer deeper than the light would shift, and the strange glint disappeared.

Henry had surprised her with the special license, of course, and with his insistence on marrying her as swiftly as possible. She'd felt a similar urgency, so had not demurred, but her mother had been apoplectic. It had taken the combined forces of Maureen, Jane, Genie, Kate, John, and Papa to calm Mama's nerves.

In the end, surprisingly enough, it had been Lady Wallingham who had persuaded her that all would be well.

"Oh, do calm yourself, Meredith," the dowager had barked. "She is marrying Dunston whether you attend with a smile or lie prone and alone with only your wretched cat and your smelling salts for company. I recommend the former."

Maureen grinned now, recalling the dumbstruck expression upon Mama's face. She'd occasionally doubted Lady Wallingham's power, but no longer. Clearly, the dragon was capable of magic.

Mama had dutifully attended the ceremony, sniffling softly beside Papa, John, Kate, and Genie. Lady Wallingham also had been present, along with her son, Lord Wallingham, a good friend of Henry's, and Wallingham's radiant new wife, Julia, who appeared well on her way to motherhood. Annabelle and Robert, unfortunately, could not travel from Nottinghamshire to London on such short notice, but Jane and Harrison had attended, of course, with Harrison standing as Henry's best man. And Lady Dunston—now the dowager countess—had been the proudest of mamas, dabbing at the corners of her eyes, seemingly overjoyed.

At least, that was how Maureen interpreted her new mother-in-law's peculiar comments about how much Henry enjoyed Maureen's distinctly feminine company.

"He *adores* females, you know," Barbara Thorpe had whispered as though revealing a salacious bit of gossip. "You in particular. Otherwise, why would he wed you? No, it is only because you are female and lovely. A lovely, feminine bride, my dear. And Henry loves you."

Maureen supposed the reassurance had been well-intended.

Barbara had been flanked by Henry's sister, Mary, and brother-in-law, Lord Stickley, who had rushed from Surrey to London for the wedding. Mary, a spoiled-yet-pleasant young woman with chestnut hair a shade or two brighter than Henry's, had welcomed Maureen to her family with an embrace and a promise to "take Mama with us back to Surrey for a nice, long visit."

As fond as she was of Henry's mother, she was glad they had done so. Stickley had gone so far as to help three footmen lift Lady Dunston into his travel coach. He'd appeared quite winded and dismayed at his dented hat, but it had been a generous act to arrange for Maureen and Henry's post-wedding privacy.

As Maureen had watched the coach pull away, Jane had leaned closer and murmured, "I simply cannot like her."

Maureen had chuckled. "Mary? Still? You did win Harrison's heart rather handily, you know. I think her past rudeness toward you was merely disappointment at losing a prize she believed she had secured."

Jane had sniffed and knuckled her spectacles higher on her nose. "I fully concede my enmity is irrational. Harrison is mine. He never was and never will be hers. But you've not had a similar rival for Henry's affections. Had there been one, doubtless you would comprehend why I feel as I do."

For a moment, Maureen had tried to imagine it—Henry with another woman. Instantly, the wedding cake in her belly had turned to vinegar. She'd never had to face it. For as long as she'd been in love with Henry, he'd only courted ... her. He'd danced with her, laughed with her, flirted with her. He'd focused so much attention upon her—the full force of his wit and charm and care—that she'd had little opportunity for jealousy. Her only concern had been trying not to fall more deeply in love with him.

What a ninny she had been, believing one blessed word of his tenth letter.

Now, gazing down upon the flower crown lying on the dressing table and listening to the clink and splash of Regina's preparations, she coiled and pinned her hair loosely atop her head with swift, practiced motions.

She found her small valise in the dressing room, retrieved the letter, and unfolded it, caressing the worn paper with her fingertips. She traced the words that now felt precious—*you* are as splendid as the first spark of sunlight awakening the sky. Her finger slowly drifted to the words she now knew to be false—*I am not that man.* False because he *was* that man. The man she loved. The man who loved her.

She pressed the letter between her palms then pressed it to her heart. She went into the bedchamber and stood between the tub he had bought for her, filled with the bath he had arranged for her, and the lit fireplace. Every detail was perfect.

She lowered the letter to gaze upon it one last time. Then let the pages flutter gently down onto the flames.

"Are you ... quite well, my lady?"

She bit her lip and nodded.

Regina's callused, bony hand intruded in her vision. It offered her a cloth.

"Ready to climb in?"

Maureen sniffed. "Yes."

With Regina's help, she quickly disrobed and slipped into the steaming water, scented with rose oil and orange blossoms. The heat was almost too much, causing first her feet and legs, then her torso to flush pink. She sighed and leaned back into the curve of the tub as the silken water began its work on the sore muscles of her neck and shoulders.

The day, while long, had been wondrous—she loved nothing more than being surrounded by her family, except perhaps being surrounded by her family while she married the handsomest man in the world. A smile took her lips.

Regina handed her a cake of her favorite honey-vanilla soap. It was fresh from the paper and unmarred. Newly purchased. She hadn't had time to purchase new soap. She sighed, her grin widening helplessly. "Oh, Henry."

"Yes, pet?"

Eyes flying wide, she jerked and splashed, scrambling against the slick metal to grasp the edge of the tub as she twisted toward his voice. She slipped and half drowned herself in the process, but she now pressed her naked front to the tub's side. Glaring at the devil who stood in the shadows near the door, leaning one shoulder against the casement with his arms crossed, she noted he'd discarded his tailcoat and cravat, and now was garbed only in a white shirt, blue-and-silver waistcoat, and black trousers.

Oh, and a wicked grin.

Dear heaven, he was delicious.

"It appears you've lost your soap. Perhaps I can help retrieve it."

Wicked. Delicious. And hers.

"Regina ..."

"Yes, my lady. The towels are here on the table when you need them. I'll bid you good night, then."

As soon as the door closed behind the maid, Henry nudged away from the casement and moved toward Maureen with his usual prowling grace. She swallowed and licked her lips, watching him stalk closer and closer until he towered at the side of the tub. Slowly, he crouched until those midnight eyes were more level with hers, bracing his elbows on the tub's edge.

"How do you like your bath, pet?"

Her breath quickened, the steam swirling, her skin flushing. She clutched the copper edge and dragged herself higher. Closer to him. "Kiss me," she begged.

Dark eyes crinkled at the corners, lit by dancing flames. A lean, strong hand cupped her cheek. Full, kissable lips swooped down to capture hers. Firm, sensual strokes of a sleek tongue melted her in the middle. She grappled for purchase as she clutched his neck. His resulting chuckle echoed against her mouth.

"Easy, love."

"I want you."

"I know."

She shook her head and used her grip on his strong, curiously arousing neck to drag herself higher. "No. You could not possibly. I ache, Henry. I *need*."

His nostrils flared and all amusement disappeared, leaving the man she had glimpsed only rarely staring back at her. "We will go slowly. To do otherwise will cause you pain."

"I don't care."

"I do."

"Kiss me again."

Rather than answer her, he grasped her wrists, gently forced her hands away from his neck with disturbing ease, released her, and stood. With jerking motions, he stripped off his waistcoat and flung it onto the carpet ten feet away. He reached behind his head to tug his linen shirt, pulling it off, wadding it into a ball and tossing it after his waistcoat.

While she devoured the muscular, chestnut-dusted contours of his chest, those elegant hands worked at the fall of his trousers. She had only seconds to absorb the magnificence of his shoulders and flat, rippling belly—it had been too dark to see more than an outline on her previous visit to his bedchamber—before the trousers disappeared, as well.

Which left Henry Thorpe naked to her eyes. All of him. The lean, muscled arms. The trim waist and hips. The aforementioned chest. And, of course, the alarmingly sizable appendage rising flushed and hard from a chestnut nest between his thighs.

She blinked, struggling to reconcile it with others she had seen on statues and such. Odd how different it was. More colorful, certainly. And larger. Much, much larger. The ballocks beneath were similar in shape to those modeled in Greek statuary, but likewise larger than she'd expected. Perhaps it was her angle of view and her proximity.

That was when her gaze caught upon another oddity. A puckered, paler furrow of flesh on his thigh. A scar. Deep and dreadful, running from the outer edge near his hipbone, across the bulging muscles at the top of his thigh, and disappearing high along the interior, near his ballocks.

"Henry," she gasped, reaching automatically to trace a

finger along the silvery slice. "What happened to you?"

His entire frame jerked at her touch, his belly rippling in a fascinating fashion as his male member swelled and arched even more. The turn came so suddenly, she could scarcely credit it. One moment she was stroking his thigh, picturing all manner of injuries that might explain the scar. The next, her wrists were seized, her body turned to face away from him, and his voice was in her ear, silken and hard.

"Blades are dangerous, pet. Caution is advisable whenever they are near."

His arms wrapped around her shoulders from behind, his hands manacling her wrists. Her body's reaction to the abrupt shift in their relative positions and the strength of his hold astonished even her.

She lit on fire.

Where her breasts swelled above the water's surface, her nipples peaked and flushed. Beneath the water, between her thighs and low in her belly, the ache sharpened and clawed to be eased. She let her head fall back into the crook between his neck and shoulder, then turned to press her lips against the pulse in his throat.

His grip on her wrists loosened, but only so his hands could slide beneath her arms, diving beneath the water and reemerging to cup her breasts. She moaned against his skin. Licked the bead of sweat forming beneath his jaw. He tasted of salt and Henry.

She gripped his forearms, distantly noting the ridged scar from the injury that had caused his fever. She wanted to see it, demand to know its true cause, but his fingers were too distracting. They squeezed and tightened around her nipples, sending spiraling pleasure outward in pulsing waves.

Her heels scraped and scrambled along the tub's bottom, struggling to push her body higher, to force her swollen breasts more firmly into his grip. She raised her arms to clasp his neck, locking tightly with one hand and grasping his hair with the other.

"Oh, God, Henry."

One of his hands slid from her breast down over her belly and between her thighs. His middle finger delved between the folds there, stoking a new, hotter flame. He stayed to fan it higher, sliding and circling, dipping and pressing. When one finger pushed inside, she arched and gritted her teeth. Squeezed against the invasion. Groaned her pleasure. It pulsed and climbed, wound tighter as the heel of his hand joined the fray.

All the while, his other hand busied itself torturing her breast, squeezing and playing, plucking and strumming. It was so much. Too much. The heat and the pleasure. The tightness and the pressure. She was going to …

She was so close to …

"Are you clean enough yet, pet?" He added a second finger, stretching her with just a hint of pain. "Perhaps I can help. I am most thorough, you know."

His words and his fingers and his taste and his scent and his knowing, skillful hands pushed her higher, filled her deeper, drove her further than she'd ever thought possible. The crisis arrived in a swirling rush, seizing her in its grip and thrashing her mercilessly. There was nothing else. No one else. Only pleasure and Henry. She sobbed his name and squeezed his wrist between her thighs until she feared she might break him.

He didn't seem to mind. His lips were upon her neck, his teeth skimming her shoulder, his whispered words in her ear. "That's it, love. Let yourself feel it. My God, you are the most beautiful thing I have ever seen."

Minutes later, while she lay limp and boneless, he washed her with a cloth and soap he'd managed to retrieve from its watery prison—after a detour or two, of course. He was diligent, skimming over her breasts and along her inner thighs, over the soft curve of her belly and the expanse of her back. For this, he bent her forward and spent an inordinate amount of time exploring the area just above her buttocks, where her spine met her hips.

Then, just as her breath and skin and tingling arousal began to quicken once again, he tossed the washcloth aside, helped her stand by simply grasping beneath her arms and lifting her directly upward like a child. She squawked, but as the water sluiced down her body, he banded her waist, collected her against him, and lifted her free of the tub without so much as a by-your-leave.

Rather than release her, however, he hauled her toward the bed, all but tossing her wet form onto the soft mattress. She landed with a whump, causing her to giggle in surprise. "Henry! What are you—"

Without a word, he clasped her knees, spread her thighs, and climbed atop her, bracing himself on outstretched arms. She gazed up at his face.

He was not laughing. He'd obviously pushed himself too far. His skin was stretched upon his bones. His eyes were black and ferocious with arousal. His lips were full yet tight, his jaw twitching, his chest working like a bellows.

She reached for him.

He forced her knees higher alongside his hips, widening her thighs. Without a word of warning, he sheathed himself inside her with a ragged thrust. The pinching pain was less vicious than she'd anticipated, for he'd prepared her well. But the fullness, the stretching was a surprise. With a firm series of thrusts, he pushed deeper and deeper. One hand cupped the back of her right knee and pressed her legs wider. Then, his rhythm grew harder, slamming into her with a force that burned and ached and left her gasping.

"Kiss me, Henry," she panted, grasping at his neck until he collapsed down onto his elbows.

Closer. Ah, yes. Closer was better.

She stroked his flexing jaw. Nibbled his bristly chin. "Kiss me."

Finally, after several hard thrusts, he gave her his mouth. In return, she gave him her tongue, sliding in and out, tasting her irresistible husband. Between her thighs, inside the core of her, the burning ache of his invasion and their combined friction transformed. Grew. Bloomed into something larger than itself. It gathered like thunder. Swelled and roiled. Darkened and turned.

Her nipples, sensitized earlier by his fingers, now reveled in the pressured chafing of his chest. She tilted her hips, working upward along with his. Finding an astonishing angle at which lightning struck. And struck. And pulsed. And struck again.

Until, at last, the pleasure burst open in a deluge. She sobbed into his mouth. He thrust impossibly deep. Once. Again. Again. Then, as her sheath clenched and demanded every drop of pleasure, he gave it to her in full measure, growling and shuddering and trembling against her mouth and beneath her hands. His mouth slid away to bury against her neck as he groaned her name and undulated helplessly between her thighs. Deep inside, she felt the warmth of his seed, felt it multiply her own pleasure until, at last, the rippling shudders slowed and stilled. With their ebb came a peace unlike any she'd ever known.

Later, as she fell asleep with her husband wrapped around her like a possessive vine, she wondered how she could make this happiness last forever. Surely it was possible, she thought, her fingers absently stroking Henry's forearm—the one with the vicious scar. Her hips snuggled back into his as her eyes drifted closed.

Yes, surely all it would take was her love and his love and the will to see them through.

# Chapter Fourteen

*"The trouble with your fanciful stories, my dear, is they all end with a wedding. One might as well propose the day ends at noon. Night always comes eventually, you know."*

—The Dowager Marchioness of Wallingham to the Duchess of Blackmore in reply to her grace's suggestion that *Pride and Prejudice* might one day be regarded as a classic tale.

THE SCREAM AWAKENED HER. BLOOD-CHILLING AND HIGH, IT was followed by distant thuds. A crack. A crash. Broken wood and shattering glass.

Disoriented, Maureen froze, blinking in the darkness as her chest worked to breathe, shallow and quick. Heart racing, she reached for Henry. Nothing. Just bedsheets. Cold, empty.

She was cold, too. The fire had died down to coals hours earlier. But it was more than that. Panic had iced her through from the inside out. In the dark, Henry's bedchamber was unfamiliar, filled with shadows and menace. And she was naked.

Gathering herself, she listened for more sounds. They had seemed to echo, she thought. Perhaps from the main floor. The entrance hall?

Slowly, she sat up, gathering the coverlet around her. The bedchamber door was closed, but the dressing room door stood ajar. She lowered her feet to cold wood planks, dragging the coverlet behind her like a cape as she tugged forward on shaking legs. Inside, every inch of her quivered. She did not know why except that being awakened from a dead sleep by disturbing noises on her wedding night was more than a bit unnerving. In all likelihood, a servant had simply taken a tumble on the way to the kitchens and was injured, perhaps in need of help.

The explanation did not slow her breathing or warm her skin or calm her racing heart. Moving carefully in the dark, she was glad for the sliver of moonlight that illuminated the dressing table. She'd left a lamp there earlier. Now, she patted the edge of the table, feeling her pin box and knocking her hairbrush several inches before she found it. She carried it to the fireplace, banging her shin painfully on the edge of the copper tub.

Cursing her love of bathing, she bent to rub the spot and lost her hold on the coverlet. It slid off her shoulders onto the floor. "Blast," she hissed, retrieving the thing and huddling inside it once again. Feeling her way to the mantel, she found the container of spills and used one to light the lamp from the dying coals.

Just as golden light built a circle around her, she heard masculine shouting. Kimble, she thought. Where was Henry? Was he safe? Her heart twisted hard.

Oh, God. What if he was hurt? Based on the number of

scars she had discovered on his naked body throughout the night, the man was a walking disaster—the slashes on his arm and thigh were just the beginning. He'd had a circular scar on his ribs about the size of a coin, a series of two-inch flat scars near his lower back, and a jagged slash on the underside of his left arm. Every one of them was a genuine oddity for someone whose physical prowess and athletic grace she'd long admired.

If he had injured himself again, she would kill him. She didn't care how he came by those wounds. He belonged to her. She loved him, and he would bloody well take more care from now on.

Rushing toward the dressing room, she stumbled on his discarded clothes. She plucked up his shirt and waistcoat.

More shouts echoed from downstairs. The words were unclear, but the urgency was bright and obvious.

She threw off the coverlet, tossed aside his waistcoat, and pulled his shirt over her naked body. It gaped over her breasts but covered her knees. Swiftly now, her heart throbbing a repeated warning, she donned the dressing gown Regina had laid out for her earlier. She cinched the ties at her waist with a jerk and stuffed her feet into her yellow beaded slippers before taking up the lamp and running out of the bedchamber into the corridor.

As she drew closer to the stairs, she was better able to pinpoint the direction of the voices. They sounded not from the entrance hall, but further toward the rear of the house. The parlor, perhaps, or the morning room.

She reached the entrance hall, the golden light of her lamp dancing madly.

*The morning room. Definitely the morning room.*

Her slippered feet slid to a stop as she arrived at the open door. Then, her heart similarly skittered to a stop.

For there, shirtless and bleeding in moonlight made jagged by the broken window, stood Henry. Except that this was not her Henry. This was some other Henry, twirling twin daggers in his hands as though he planned to toss them in the air like an Astley's performer standing atop a pair of galloping horses.

More shocking than the blood or the long, wicked blades was his face. It was the face of a man she simply had never seen. Grim. Cold. Teeth bared like a ferocious animal's. Stance wide like a towering conqueror.

Her eyes drifted down to the figure he stood over, his knives dripping dark fluid on the floor. It was a man. White-faced. Eyes open. Blank.

*Dead, Maureen. He is dead.*

She could not look away.

There was a man. He was dead. Henry wielded knives like an extension of his arms. Dripping. Dripping. Dripping.

Sound receded until she only heard the whoosh of her own blood. Distantly, she recognized movement in the corner of the room. Kimble, crouched next to something near the sideboard. Another figure. Large. With callused, bony hands lying curled and empty and still in a shaft of moonlight.

Hands whose gray sleeve she recognized. Hands she knew could stitch a spangle onto a slipper as easily as they could wield a water pitcher or build a fire or carry Maureen's specially made Chelsea buns without crushing them.

The lamp thudded to the ground. Maureen followed, all the strength leaving her legs.

Vaguely, she heard her own voice, a formless cry covered by her fingers. Broken in the middle.

Regina. It was Regina. How could it be Regina?

No. No, no, no, no, no. This was some horrible nightmare. She would wake any moment now. She would feel her Henry's arms wrap around her. The other Henry would disappear and Regina would be ...

Alive. Not dead. Not lying so dreadfully still.

"...reen."

*Wake up*, she begged. *Wake up, wake up, wake up.*

"Maureen!" The shout was harsh. Sharp. It was not-Henry.

His knives were gone. No, not gone. Lying on the table. "On your feet. Now."

She swallowed and blinked away the moisture that made moonlight swim and dance around him. He was nodding to someone behind her.

A moment later, strong hands grasped her arms and lifted her to her feet, moving her from the doorway where she had collapsed. Two footmen filed into the small room, edging around the table to where Kimble crouched over ...

She looked away from the curled hand.

A shoulder bumped hers as Stroud, too, entered the room. He handed first a damp cloth then a fresh shirt to not-Henry, who swiped at the splattered blood on his bare chest and shoulders before donning the shirt in one swift motion.

"... return to our bedchamber, Maureen."

She shook her head.

"Do as I say," he snapped. "There is nothing for you here. Go back to the bedchamber and wait for me."

"R-Regina." She began to crumple, her voice collapsing, her eyes filling.

Not-Henry came toward her, gripped her arm firmly, and led her out of the room. He bent and retrieved the lamp, wrapping her fingers around its handle. Grasping her chin with his fingers, he forced her to meet his eyes. "Listen to me carefully. You cannot help her. You will only be in the way."

She hated that she could not see anything familiar in him. No glow of tenderness. No spark of love or gentleness. No hint of softness. She hated not-Henry.

"I do not like you," she whispered.

His head tilted. "I expect you don't. But you will obey me, wife. Now, go. Return to our bedchamber. Wait for me."

He released her without another word, turning his back and stalking toward the prone figure bleeding on the morning room floor—the man not-Henry had evidently killed.

She stumbled backward, the circle of golden light bobbing

and receding from the horrific scene. As she braced a hand on the opposite wall of the corridor and turned to make her way back to the bedchamber, she heard not-Henry call out, "One last thing, Maureen. Begin packing. We leave before sunrise."

THE MOTION OF THE CARRIAGE JARRED HER AWAKE JUST IN time to see the disappearing sun painting the sky pink and orange. They'd been traveling since before daybreak, stopping to change horses only when necessary. Not-Henry had offered few explanations and fewer reassurances. None, to be precise.

"Pack only what you need. Nothing more," he'd said upon entering their bedchamber. Then, without waiting for her compliance, he'd emptied one of her trunks, piling two gowns and a pair of stockings on one side of the bed, then plopping her valise beside the paltry collection. He'd walked to the dressing table and tossed her silver-handled hairbrush onto the mattress from across the room. It had landed precisely an inch from the valise.

Having managed earlier to coil and pin her hair and to dress herself in her dark-blue cambric travel gown and leather half-boots, she had dutifully begun folding the gowns and placing them into the valise, adding a spencer and pelisse and extra petticoat, then stuffing and pressing until the case closed properly. While he'd stripped off his shirt and used the ice-cold bathwater to wash, she'd ignored the howling ache at the center of her chest and said as calmly as she could manage, "Explain what is happening, Henry. Please."

Donning a new shirt and carelessly tied cravat, he had taken long minutes to reply. She'd watched him stalking like a restless cat from dressing room to window to copper tub and back to the dressing room, gathering up his things and stuffing them into a case of his own. Finally, he'd stopped beside the window again, looking grim and cold. "We had an intruder. The blackguard attacked Regina."

She'd winced upon hearing her maid's name spoken aloud.

His finger had dropped away from where he'd held the draperies aside. He'd turned his gaze to her.

Her heart had turned to ice.

"This will not be the end of it. To keep you safe, we must leave London immediately."

"I don't understand."

"You don't need to understand. You need to do as I say."

She'd opened her mouth to protest that he was being unreasonable.

He'd cut her off immediately, closing the distance between them with shocking speed. "This is not a game, Maureen." His hand had cupped her nape with chilled fingers and forced her to meet those steel-sharp eyes. "This is the blackest reality. If you wish to survive it, you will do precisely as I instruct. No hesitation. No delay. No protests or willfulness. Do you hear me?"

She had heard him. And she had elected to trust him, nodding her agreement even though it seemed the man she had married and the world she had known was gone.

Now, as the sun set beyond the windows of the carriage—a small, rented travel coach with unforgiving springs and a tendency to creak when turning left—she wondered if she had made a mistake in not demanding answers before their departure. She'd expected them to travel north to Henry's country estate, Fairfield Park. Surely, she'd concluded, he would take her there, for what sort of criminal would pursue an earl and countess all the way to Suffolk?

But, no. They had, in fact, been traveling in a westerly direction for more than fifteen hours. Her backside was numb, her lower back longed to be numb, and her only refuge from the agony of her memories was fitful bouts of napping with her rolled-up pelisse for a pillow.

Not-Henry had chosen to ride outside the carriage like a sentinel. She spotted him through the window now and then, resting Dag and mounting another horse to keep them fresh. The other men he'd brought with them—Stroud and five strapping footmen—similarly surrounded the carriage like a contingent of mounted guards. They had all abandoned their livery in favor of plain woolen coats, broad-brimmed hats, and riding breeches.

Oh, and weapons. Pistols. Knives. One even carried a hunting rifle across his lap.

She had exhausted herself trying to guess what was going on. Now, she rubbed her eyes and cataloged her theories. First, it was possible Henry was mad. In fact, that had been her first thought. But she'd abandoned the idea almost immediately. The broken window, cracked table, and dead intruder all suggested the danger was real.

*And Regina. Oh, God. Regina.*

She shook her head. She could not dwell upon Regina, lest grief's greedy abyss swallow her up.

Instead, she reviewed theory two: thievery. Perhaps Henry had overreacted to a common burglar, and now they were traveling west to heaven-knew-where because there were fewer people—and, thus, fewer thieves—in the farthest reaches of Cornwall. But that brought her back to theory one, Henry's madness. And Henry was not mad. Right now, he was also not Henry, but that was neither here nor there. Even not-Henry was sane—vexing, forbidding, hard, and a bit frightening, but sane.

Her third theory consisted of silly fancies in which Henry was secretly battling a mysterious villain who would stop at nothing to defeat him. She snorted at that one. Even young, imaginative Kate would balk at such a tale.

She had no fourth theory, for she'd run out of notions. Her head and body ached with exhaustion. The ale she'd imbibed at the last coaching inn sat frothy and unsettled in her stomach. And she suspected Henry had no intention of stopping until they reached Land's End—perhaps not even then. She wouldn't be surprised to find herself hip-deep in seawater before he called a halt.

Four hours, two coaching inns, and one rat-ridden public house later, she was proven wrong, much to her relief. The darkness had grown thick and suffocating inside the coach, though the air was now damp and cold. She'd sat for hours, remembering too much, shivering and huddled beneath the dubious warmth of her wrinkled pelisse. Then, the travel coach creaked as they turned sharply left. She blinked, trying to make out the shadowy landscape. She thought she glimpsed a low wall covered in moss, but who could say for certain in the relentless black?

The men outside called to one another, repositioning as they all maneuvered onto the narrow lane. Less than a quarter-hour later, the coach came to a rocking stop outside a large, mismatched manor house surrounded by looming trees. As best she could make out, one half of the house was constructed of dark stone with diamond-paned windows, several of which were lit. On the right side, running perpendicular to the main structure, was a half-timbered wing clearly built in a different era.

The coach door opened, giving her a start. It was not Henry, his face shadowed from the lantern light by his hat's brim. He stretched an arm toward her. "Come," he ordered, his voice broken and rusty. "Let's get you inside, pet."

Hearing him call her "pet" again made her want to weep. She flew into his arms, crushing her pelisse between them and knocking his hat to the ground. He grunted and staggered backward, but his strong arms held her blessedly tight against his muscular frame as he dragged her out of the carriage and lowered her feet to the ground.

He smelled different, and yet the same. Like horse and sweat and salty air, but also like sandalwood and her Henry.

His hand came up to cup her head as she buried her nose in the spot beneath his ear, near where his jaw muscle flexed.

Her breath was ragged against the creases of his cravat and collar, her chest tight with circling tension. She swallowed down the rising sobs and held her breath to regain control.

"We must go inside," he murmured in her ear. But, she noted, he did not loosen his grip.

Finally, she nodded her agreement, and he slowly released her, his hand settling along her lower back to nudge her toward the great oak door. Two broad-shouldered footmen were already using the large brass knocker. Moments later, the door opened to reveal a short, round, rosy-cheeked woman wearing a mobcap and a weary expression. The woman greeted them with a nod and a quick curtsy.

"Welcome to Yardleigh Manor, my lord," she murmured to Henry.

"Mrs. Poole," he answered, urging Maureen forward into the well-lit interior. "My wife will require a bath straight away." Dimly, she moved past the woman who was apparently the housekeeper, given the ring of keys that jangled as she bobbed another curtsy.

"At once, my lord. Your ladyship, it is our pleasure to provide whatever you may need after your long journey. Would you care for tea? Perhaps a bite to eat?"

Rendered numb and speechless by the day's events, Maureen blinked and swayed on her feet, trying to bring the oak-paneled walls of the large, octagonal entrance hall into focus. Light and sound flickered in and out. Or perhaps she imagined it.

Dimly, she heard Henry telling the housekeeper—Mrs. Poole, was it?—to deliver a tray to their bedchamber along with the bath. Then, without asking, he bent and scooped Maureen into his arms, one bracing her back and the other cradling her knees. She clung to his neck, sick with fatigue and dizziness as he strode through a doorway, down a dark corridor, and up a set of stairs.

"Henry," she whispered in his ear, her fingers sifting the chestnut strands just above his nape. "Where are we?"

"East Devonshire."

Ahead of them, a liveried footman carried a lantern. He led them to another oak door. She felt the scratchy wool of Henry's coat against her cheek, the cool air of the new chamber as they entered. But her eyes were dry and heavy, the voices of Henry and the footman faint in her ears.

Beneath her now, the softness of a mattress—so much better than the stiff seats of the rented coach—invited her to rest. But Henry would not allow it. He rolled her onto her side and began plucking at the closures of her gown, then at the laces of her corset, then at the pins in her hair.

"I can do it," she murmured, embarrassed at being undressed like a child. But her words slurred and slid, her eyes weighted against opening.

"Don't bother with the bath, Mrs. Poole," she heard Henry say. "Just bring warm water, bread, and tea."

Frowning, she grunted as her sleeves were tugged down her arms in sharp motions. "Where is Regina?" she grumbled. "She is so much better at this."

The motions stopped.

Darkness beckoned. She thought she might have fallen asleep, because the next thing she knew, she was naked beneath a set of sheets and blankets. The room was dark, but she was no longer cold—exceedingly warm, in fact. She lay on her side facing a window. Between her legs was a hard, muscled thigh. At her back was a hard, muscled chest. Wrapped around her waist and banding upward between her breasts were hard, muscled arms.

They held her so tightly, she could scarcely breathe. She explored the one between her breasts, fingering the puckered scar amidst a dusting of hair.

He was all heat and strength, his muscles tightening reflexively as he squeezed her tighter. Semi-hardness prodded her backside, but he made no move to touch her more intimately. He simply held her, his warm breath rhythmic against her nape and ear.

She clasped his hand, interlaced her fingers with his, and tucked her chin to lay a kiss upon his palm. Slowly, she relaxed into the curve of his body, breathed deeply of his familiar-yet-unfamiliar scent, and interlaced their fingers to draw his palm over her heart.

As the darkness swept over her once again, she soaked in his heat the way she would a deliciously warm bath. And just before the faint memory of horror and violence could take hold, she heard him whisper, "Sleep now, pet. I shall keep you safe. This I promise you."

# Chapter Fifteen

*"The charm of your snoring is lost
when it interrupts my slumber, Humphrey."*

—THE DOWAGER MARCHIONESS OF WALLINGHAM to her boon
companion, Humphrey, upon awakening to a
less-than-charming racket.

BEHIND MAUREEN'S EYELIDS, THE WORLD WAS PINK AND
bright. But she was having trouble breathing, at least through
her nose. The stoppage forced her from the pleasant oblivion
of sleep.

The first thing she noticed was a pair of round, thickly
lashed eyes mere inches from hers. Then, she took in the
button nose and rosebud mouth. Then, she felt the small

fingers pinching her nostrils closed. That explained the breathing problem.

Blue eyes widened further. Small fingers withdrew. "You were rumbling," the little girl explained. "Ladies aren't supposed to rumble."

Maureen blinked, struggling to recall what had happened and who the girl might be. She knew she was naked beneath the bedclothes, lying on her side in an unfamiliar room. She remembered Henry holding her. She remembered she was in Devonshire, a county she had never occasioned to visit before.

"Good morning," she ventured, drawing the sheet further up her shoulders.

The little girl—an adorable moppet with dark, frayed plaits and a smudge of jam at the corner of her mouth—frowned in pronounced concern. "It is not morning any longer. Are you ill, then?"

Despite everything, the girl's blunt question made her smile. "No, darling. I was simply catching up on the sleep I missed. What is your name?"

"Biddy. Your hair is a pretty color. It is messy, though."

She smiled wider. Biddy reminded her of Genie at the same age—perhaps five or six. Of course, Genie had never quite outgrown the tendency to blurt whatever she was thinking.

"Bridget, what have I said about your wandering?" The gentle reprimand came from across the unfamiliar, green-draped bedchamber. The woman standing inside the door resembled a slender pixie, complete with uptilted nose and glimmering gold eyes. Rich, honey-brown curls fought their pins ruthlessly. She wore an apron over a dark, long-sleeved gown and carried a tray with a steaming bowl and a small teapot.

Biddy grunted her little-girl annoyance. "Not to do it."

The woman set the tray on a table in the corner near the window. "And?"

"And if I were to do it again, I shall be peeling a great many potatoes. I hate peeling potatoes."

"Perhaps you should cease your wandering, then."

Biddy's button nose wrinkled. "She was rumbling. I wished to know why."

The woman ushered Biddy out of the chamber, admonishing her to return to the music room for her lessons. Then, she closed the door and faced Maureen. "I do apologize. Bridget has not yet learned to restrain her curiosity."

Maureen sat up, clutching the sheet and a lovely green quilt to her bare bosom and running fingers through her wildly looping hair. "She is precious. My younger sister was much the same when she was a girl. Is Biddy your daughter?"

"Oh, no." The pixie chuckled. "Merely my charge. And a bit of a handful, I must say."

Maureen nodded. That made more sense. The woman must be a governess, for she spoke with perfect diction and possessed a genteel command Maureen had commonly seen in her own governesses. This one had a tidy, efficient air about her despite the unruly hair, coils of which formed a halo around her delicate features. She arranged the items on the tray, pouring a cup of tea then moving toward a chair where a familiar yellow gown was draped before addressing Maureen again.

"I am Sarah, by the by. I've brought you a bit of soup and some tea. The maids delivered hot water earlier, though it is likely cooled by now. I thought I might help you dress, if you are agreeable."

"Yes, thank you." She watched the pixie gather up her gown, corset, stockings, and petticoats and lay them upon the foot of the quilt-draped bed.

Sarah ran a hand over the yellow sprigged cotton of Maureen's favorite day dress. "This is excellent work. Who is your modiste?"

*Gray sleeve. Open hand. Still, still, still.*

The bright light from the window turned liquid. A lump rose into her throat. With a heaving breath, she squeezed her fists and forced the memories to retreat again.

"My maid crafted it from a bolt of cloth I purchased on impulse." Maureen swallowed. "I often told her she should have been a seamstress."

Sarah's golden gaze was solemn and understanding. "Well, it is lovely. Let us get you dressed properly, shall we?"

With the practical efficiency that seemed inherent in the pixie's nature, Maureen was gowned and coiffed within minutes. As she sat at the table and forced down a bit of white soup, buttered bread, and moderately acceptable tea, they chatted about sewing—Sarah was avid about the subject—and Devonshire. Sarah described her childhood in a nearby seaside village, distracting Maureen with tales of cricket matches on the village green and shops offering more fish nets than fine fabrics.

All the while, Maureen smiled and ate, sipped and stared curiously at the pixie. She had a thin, pale scar on her neck, running from beneath her ear across her throat to her windpipe. Maureen wondered what could have caused such an injury.

That made her think of Henry, who also bore scars he'd never properly explained.

"Sarah, I should like to speak with my husband. Lord Dunston. Do you know where he is?"

The pixie smiled gently. "Yes. I'll take you to him as soon as you finish your soup."

Maureen glanced down at the remains in her bowl. She did not feel like eating any more. She opened her mouth to protest that she'd had enough, but the pixie governess crossed her arms, one finger tapping an elbow, and preempted any denials. "All of it, now. You need your strength."

A half-smile curled Maureen's lips. Sarah was indeed a governess through and through.

She did as she was instructed, and a short while later, Sarah led her downstairs to the octagonal entrance hall she remembered from their arrival. In the daylight, it was a large, warm space paneled in oak and offering doors or passages in every direction. Sarah opened a set of double doors along the far wall and waved her through.

Inside what must be a drawing room, for it was enormous and richly paneled, was Henry, rising from a green-striped sofa. Her first glimpse of him unwound the coil inside her chest. He had shaved, she noted. He wore a blue riding coat and buff breeches. His waistcoat was a simple brown weave.

He looked wonderful—drawn and weary, his mouth unsmiling, his eyes squinting as though he'd not slept a wink—but wonderful. She wanted to sigh his name. She wanted to run into those strong, lean arms. She wanted him to explain how he could be both Henry and not-Henry. How he could leave her feeling so alone.

Instead, she stood in place, catching her breath.

"Lady Dunston."

She dragged her gaze away from the stranger she had married to the man rising from the green-striped sofa's mirrored twin. Her brows arched in surprise.

"My, it is strange to address you as Lady Dunston," said the handsome, smiling blond man she recognized instantly as Lord Colin Lacey, Harrison's younger brother. "The last time I saw you, I was escorting your sisters to the museum."

"Lord Colin," she said faintly, staggered at the incongruity of seeing him here in ... Devonshire. Oh, dear. She did recall Jane telling her Lord Colin had moved to Devonshire after marrying a vicar's daughter named ... Sarah Battersby.

Her eyes flew wide before streaking to the pixie governess. "Oh, good heavens. Lady Colin. I had no idea ..." The Huxley Flush swarmed her cheeks.

Sarah waved a dismissal and smiled. "Sarah, please. And do not worry another moment. We wish you only to feel safe and welcome here at Yardleigh Manor, Lady Dunston."

Maureen protested that she must likewise call her by her first name, and after they'd each taken their seats on the sofas beside their husbands, Sarah explained the presence of not only Biddy but twenty-five other girls at Yardleigh. Sarah and Colin, along with Sarah's mother, had established St. Catherine's Academy for Girls of Impeccable Deportment in the half-timbered wing of the house.

"Occasionally, Biddy escapes and goes wandering about," explained Colin with an amused chuckle. "Little imp. We find her in the oddest places. Once, we discovered her asleep in the larder, clutching a loaf of bread. She later claimed it resembled a doll and demanded that Cook make doll loaves for everyone."

Maureen laughed along, but half her attention was occupied with Henry. He hadn't spoken or touched her, merely sitting at her side like a stone sculpture. Still and grim and silent.

She felt his heat. Wanted to place her hand atop his where it splayed on his thigh. Wanted to hear him laugh at the anecdotes about Biddy and her attempts to dress a loaf of bread in a linen napkin. But he was thrumming with volatile energy. His muscles were tense, his gaze hard.

Abruptly, Henry shot to his feet and prowled to the doors. He closed them with a click and strode back to the sofas. "My wife and I will be relocating to the hunting lodge. Lacey, we shall need the supplies I mentioned. And a maid or two. Strong. Reliable. An additional footman, as well. Mine will be unable to assist with menial tasks."

Maureen expected Lord Colin to balk. She did not imagine a duke's brother was accustomed to another man barking orders at him like a field general. Especially in his own house.

But Colin Lacey merely nodded. "Already done. We sent Francis and David to the lodge this morning with the supplies. Sarah will ensure a suitable pair of maids follows."

Leaning forward, Sarah caught her eyes. "Lord Dunston, how much have you told Maureen about your ... circumstances?"

Henry began to pace. The agitation reminded her of the

afternoon she'd said goodbye in his bedchamber. It reminded her of not-Henry.

"As little as possible," he muttered, running a hand through his hair.

Maureen watched him for a few moments before answering, "Nothing at all, in fact. Isn't that right, Henry?"

He shot her a blazing look before pacing away again.

Calmly, she returned her attention to Colin and Sarah. "On our wedding night, I awakened to find my new husband standing over a dead intruder in the morning room. He held a pair of knives in his hands. Henry, I mean. Not the intruder. Nearby, I saw my m-maid ..." She took a shuddering breath. "Regina. She'd been ... killed. Henry did not explain. He ordered me to pack then stuffed me into a rented coach alone. Why we should rent a travel coach when he owns two that are both larger and better sprung, I do not know. But, then, why should I know? I am only his wife." She chuckled without a drop of humor. "We traveled west. I knew this not because he told me where we were going, but because I watched the sun both rise and set. He has spoken fewer than twenty words to me since we left London. I still have no idea what happened or why we are here."

She glanced up at her husband, who now stood with his hands on his hips, scowling at her.

"You appear perturbed, Henry. Perhaps I missed something. Do tell."

HENRY WAS BURNING INSIDE A HELL OF HIS OWN MAKING. First, he had allowed his desire for her to cloud his judgment. He could keep her safe, he'd told himself. Reaver would draw the Investor's attention away, and Henry would take Maureen to Fairfield, where he would make love to her and surround her with an army of capable guards until Reaver and Drayton tracked down the Investor or enough time had passed that the blackguard would have died.

God, what a fool he'd been. Blinded by love and lust and jealousy.

He should have let her marry Holstoke.

The thought tightened his gut, made his hands clench with the need to throttle someone. He calmed himself with the reminder that she belonged to him now. She was *his* wife, and that could not be undone.

His second mistake had been to avoid warning her about his past. He'd listened to her doting father rather than his instincts. Bloody stupid.

Now, he ran a hand through his hair again and gazed down at his pale, stricken, justifiably indignant bride. She was calmer than he would have been had their positions been reversed. And she was right. He'd told her nothing. Stuffed her in a rented coach and ridden for Yardleigh as though the devil were chasing them.

Which was true, but she hadn't known that. No, she'd seen her beloved maid lying dead on the floor while her new husband stood with twin daggers over the corpse of a Bow Street runner. On her wedding night.

Briefly, he glanced at Colin and Sarah. Both wore expressions of sympathy and concern.

Henry took a deep breath, trying to force the thrumming urgency to recede for one blasted minute. Long enough to regain control. Long enough to explain in a way that she would understand. He rested his hands on the back of a green velvet chair, gripping the carved wood frame.

"The danger to you is real, pet."

"I gathered as much. What I do not understand is why."

He released a breath and gripped the chair harder. "It is complicated. Hard to explain."

"Try."

He considered keeping things simple, eliminating the parts

of the story that might disturb her most, but in the end, ensuring her safety meant telling her the whole wretched tale. She needed to know the peril she faced.

"My father was murdered," he began. "A highwayman on the road to London."

She nodded. "I remember the stories. The man was caught and hanged, was he not?"

"Within two months. Killing an earl is no small matter. He claimed the murder had been a hired task, that someone had paid him well, but his claims were dismissed because he could not name the supposed employer. He said the matter was arranged through a series of deliveries. Notes. Coin."

Maureen nibbled her lower lip, as she often did when distressed. "You were there, weren't you? When your father was ... shot."

He swallowed. Dropped his gaze to green velvet, then back up to her beautiful face. "Yes. Bloody awful day, pet. Bloody awful."

He'd rarely discussed it with anyone, even his mother.

He pushed away from the chair to resume pacing. "I was a boy at the time. My mother and the magistrates and the estate's solicitors—everyone decided the matter had been settled, the murderer caught and punished. Having identified the man myself, I had no reason to doubt them until I reached my majority and all my father's papers became mine."

He explained how he'd discovered his father's work for the Foreign Office, stacks of correspondence dating back to the period immediately preceding the Revolution in France. Fearing the mobs and guillotines and radicalism might spread to its own shores like a violent plague, England's most powerful men had worked to undermine the fledgling French Republican government. They had funded and facilitated a clandestine web within France, collecting information and using it to thwart the expansion of French influence.

His father had been one of those powerful Englishmen

with "a strong preference for stability over bloodletting." In the course of his work for the Crown, Edwin Thorpe had learned of a threat to English spies—a smuggling operation benefitting those who were systematically killing one Englishman after another. One spy, before he'd been killed, had managed to trace the origin of the operation to England's shores. To England's aristocracy, in fact.

"My father knew the smuggler was funded and organized by someone highborn," Henry continued. "He had the blackguard's name, was delivering it to London when our coach was set upon. He was murdered for what he knew. Unfortunately, that information was lost with him."

Colin frowned, leaning forward with his elbows on his knees. "You never told me this. The smuggler's employer. Was he the same man who funded Syder?"

Henry nodded. "Near as I have been able to determine, this was the Investor's first foray into criminal enterprise on such a scale. Obscenely lucrative, particularly if the conflict between our two countries should continue. But I knew nothing of the Investor's methods then. I was one-and-twenty. Still a boy, really. When I first discovered my father's true murderer—a traitor to England, no less—had escaped punishment, I vowed he would not elude me. That is when, like my father, I began working with the Foreign Office. They were glad for my eagerness. By then, the wars with Napoleon were blazing."

Maureen glanced at Colin then back to Henry. "But you were never a soldier." She shook her head. "The only time you would have spent in France was when you ..." Her eyes widened. "Your grand tour. You—you were a spy?"

"Nothing so official. Think of me as a diplomat. With a gun."

Outrage flared in her eyes. "But that is *dangerous*, Henry. You might have been killed."

God, she was sweet. So sheltered. So deuced naïve. "Yes, pet. Like a pup nipping at a stallion's hooves, I was kicked more than once. It taught me a great deal, however. The brutality of man. The value of deception."

"I don't give a fig for what you learned. I care that you risked your life—"

"I am still here."

"Covered in scars!"

Colin cleared his throat. "I take it the Investor remained hidden, despite your efforts to track him. Did you discover anything useful?"

"He places a great many layers of protection between himself and his crimes. The smuggling operation was dismantled shortly after my father's death. I chased the trail in France until it was clear anyone who might know his identity had been"—he glanced to Maureen—"dispatched. Every useful thread was swiftly cut. In time, this proved to be a pattern. One enterprise would be crushed, and the next would begin within a year. The new enterprise is always illicit, always managed by a hired man. That is why I call him the Investor. He does nothing himself, merely planning and funding his operations from inside a nest of anonymity."

Sarah clasped Colin's hand and murmured, "Within a year. It has been nearly two years since Mr. Syder's wretched businesses were shuttered. Do you suppose ...?"

Maureen's gaze darted between Colin, Sarah, and Henry. "I'm sorry. Who is Mr. Syder?"

Silence fell as Colin's jaw tensed and Sarah rubbed her husband's hand, her brow crinkling into a frown that was both worried and haunted.

"Horatio Syder was the Investor's most recent hired man," Henry said quietly.

"He was a bloody butcher," snarled Colin, biting down on any further descriptions. Sarah laid her cheek on Colin's upper arm and stroked him with soothing motions.

Maureen looked from them to Henry, back and forth, until finally, she sighed. "I feel a bit lost."

Henry came around to perch on the edge of the velvet

chair, directing Maureen's attention solely to him. He'd asked enough of Colin and Sarah Lacey. He could not also ask them to reopen old wounds. "Syder ran a number of businesses in London, most of them either illicit or meant to disguise something illicit. His empire was expansive. He preyed upon others to line his pockets. The poor. Women with few alternatives. Desperate men. Children."

Maureen frowned. "And he was funded by the Investor?"

Henry nodded. "Until he slipped his leash. I suspect they had a falling out. Syder grew arrogant in the years before his death. Bold. The Investor would not have approved his increasing prominence in London's more notorious quarters. That is how he caught my notice. Had I captured him, I suspect he might have given me the Investor's name."

"Why didn't you? Capture him, I mean."

Colin sat forward. "I killed the bastard before Dunston had the chance."

Maureen blinked and eyed Sarah's scarred neck, then Colin's fierce expression. She blanched. "He—he hurt Sarah?"

Colin did not answer. Sarah nodded.

Maureen swallowed visibly then pushed to her feet as though uncertain what to do with herself. Henry rose, too, moving to her side, cupping her lower spine. She gazed up at him with bewilderment. Despair.

"Henry," she whispered.

"I will keep you safe," he gritted. "I will die before letting anyone touch you."

"Dear God." She laughed an odd, breathless, humorless laugh. Her hand drifted up to lay over her heart. "Me? *You* are the one who threatens this Investor. *You* are the one he will try to ... " Warm brown eyes lit with horrified recognition. She grasped his forearm, pulled it toward her with a sharp jerk. Tugging his sleeve with solid yanks, she was only able to draw the wool and linen halfway up. It was enough to expose his newest scar. Suddenly, she shoved away from him.

Now, she was the one pacing.

"Henry Edwin Fitzsimmons Thorpe."

Bloody hell. Nothing good ever came of Maureen using all four of his names. "Yes, pet?"

She spun on her heel when she reached the fireplace. Her eyes were lit with fury, but at least her cheeks had more color. "You nearly died, didn't you? From that." She pointed at his arm.

He sniffed. "Of course not. A scratch, really."

"I should like to pummel you right now."

"I don't recommend it. Violence rarely solves problems to any great degree of satisfaction."

"Oh, I don't know," chimed Colin. "I found it extremely satisfying."

Sarah shushed Colin before adding her perspective. "I can only imagine how shocking this must be for you, Maureen."

Maureen turned to her. "Shocking. Yes. My husband is a spy working for the Foreign Office."

Henry cleared his throat and rubbed the back of his neck. "I was never a spy, precisely. And I ceased my work for the Foreign Office long ago. The Home Office was more useful in the years after the war."

Maureen's eyes flared, her hands now on her hips.

He held up a staying hand. "Not to worry. They want nothing more to do with me. The business with Syder was too much for the Home Secretary, I'm afraid. Sidmouth and I are no longer on speaking terms. Granted, Colin did make a dreadful mess."

Colin balked. "So, now it is all *my* doing?"

"Well, you might have waited two bloody minutes for me to arrive—"

"Henry!"

"Apologies, pet."

"Have you any notion of how mad this is?" She waved wildly toward Colin and Sarah. "Sarah's throat was cut. Colin killed a man. You nearly died. More than once, if I am not mistaken. And Regina ... Regina is ..." Those heartbreakingly sweet eyes filled and her rounded chin quivered, searing Henry's insides.

He strode to her, ignoring her upraised hand. Wrapping her small, soft frame in his arms, he cradled her against his body, as he should have done when she'd entered the horrific scene in the morning room, her white dressing gown matching the color of her skin. Every time he closed his eyes, he saw her crumpling to her knees, folding in upon herself as she'd stared at her maid's empty hand.

He wished he'd had the strength to hold her in that moment, but he'd been in no condition to offer comfort. He'd been consumed by rage, driven by primal urgency to see her safe. That urgency had only begun to ease when he'd held her naked body against his last night. It had risen again as soon as he'd spoken with Colin and remembered watching the other man try to staunch his wife's blood.

Remembered hearing Colin beg his wife not to leave him. Not to die.

If Henry lost Maureen, he would go mad. He would tear the world apart until he found whoever had taken her from him, and then he would make that man's death into a thing of artistry. Assassins the world over would write odes in his honor, sonnets to his savagery. Other men might express similar sentiments but lack the will to carry them to their conclusion. Henry Thorpe was not one of those men.

"Henry," Maureen wheezed. "Too tight."

He loosened his hold, but only slightly.

"How have you managed to keep your pursuit of the Investor a secret all this time?" Her words were muffled by his cravat.

He eased a bit more so she could breathe. "Ah, yes, well. That is an excellent question."

She pulled back to blink up at him, the wet lashes fanning repeatedly. "Who else knows?"

He dug inside his waistcoat pocket for a handkerchief.

"Harrison, of course. He was there when Colin ..." He finished his sentence with a pronounced raising of his brows.

"Harrison. So, Jane knows, too."

"Mmm. And Colin's sister, Lady Atherbourne. Her husband. His friend, the large and helpful Lord Tannenbrook."

Maureen put more space between them, wiping her dainty, reddened nose and her damp lashes with his handkerchief. "And the rest of my family?"

Bloody hell. This was not going in an auspicious direction. He rubbed his neck, running a finger beneath the suddenly itching cravat. "Your mother and father know about Syder and the Home Office. Your father perhaps a bit more. I had to give him assurances before we married."

Her lips tightened into a line. No, not auspicious in the slightest. "Anyone else?"

"Men I trust. A Bow Street runner named Drayton. A gaming club owner called Sebastian Reaver. A few others."

She kept staring at him, her glare growing ever sharper.

He might as well get it all out. "And Lady Wallingham."

That did it. "Lady Wallingham," she breathed, shaking her head.

He held up a hand, attempting to stem the tide. "I told her nothing, pet. She discovered my work for the Home Office through her mysterious contacts. I don't know how she—"

"You mean to say that Lady Wallingham knew before I did. Lady. *Wallingham.*"

Why Lady Wallingham should be the deciding drop in Maureen's flood of fury, Henry did not know. But she was. And Maureen—his sweet-natured Maureen—had obviously had enough. Her dimpled cheeks went red. Her chest worked on furious breaths. She shoved him hard as she stalked past, her yellow skirts swaying and snapping before she threw the doors open and slammed them closed behind her. The hard crack echoed for a long while.

Colin, reclining and stretching his arms out along the back

of the sofa, gave Henry a smirk. "Well, that went swimmingly. I'm beginning to suspect you're a bit rusty at this sort of thing, Dunston."

"What sort of thing is that?" he growled, staring at the doors as though she might reappear.

Colin stood and clapped him on the shoulder. "The truth, man. The truth."

Henry grunted.

"Care for some advice?"

"No."

"Don't underestimate her. She's a Huxley. Huxley girls tend toward the extraordinary."

"I do not need you to tell me about my wife, Lacey."

Sarah cleared her throat. "He is right, Dunston. Concealing the truth from her has only made its revelation more devastating. Even so, she has not fallen apart. Quite the contrary."

Henry cast a glance in her direction. "You did not see her after the attack."

"Stunned? Confused? Grieving? Natural reactions, I daresay," said Colin. "Particularly when you gave her no prior warning."

"Your world is a dark one," Sarah interjected. "Many would have accused me of being unable to cope with it."

"Or me," Colin added, grinning. "And yet, here we are. Try a bit of trust, man. Perhaps she will surprise you."

His eyes falling to Sarah's scar, Henry shook his head. "My task is to protect her. That is all that matters. And that is what I shall do."

# Chapter Sixteen

*"Don't let the waistcoats fool you.
He is cleverer than he appears."*

—THE DOWAGER MARCHIONESS OF WALLINGHAM to her son,
Charles, upon said gentleman's astonishment that Lord Dunston
purchased a prized Thoroughbred with a pair of dueling pistols
and a bottle of Bordeaux.

THE MOMENT THE HUNTING LODGE CAME WITHIN SIGHT,
Maureen slumped in relief. At last, she would have something
to do, if only a bit of unpacking. The distraction would be
welcome.

She glanced to the man who rode Dag beside her, a knife
strapped to one lean, muscled thigh, a pistol to the other. His

chestnut hair peeked out from beneath his hat, glimmering copper in the waning sunlight. Despite signs of fatigue around his eyes and the grim set of his mouth, she wanted to leap upon him. Cover him in kisses. Strip him bare and take him inside her again. Take her pleasure with him again.

And then pound his infuriating head into the ruddy Devonshire mud.

Good heavens, she had never been so angry as she'd been in Yardleigh Manor's drawing room. It seethed inside her, even hours later, as she recalled his confession.

Lady Wallingham, of all people. She still had trouble reconciling it. How bloody galling to be kept ignorant. How foolish she must have seemed to everyone, believing Henry to be the charming lord whose greatest concern was planning his annual hunt. They all had known better. Jane and Harrison, Mama and Papa. And worse, the dragon herself, who must have exhausted Humphrey's pendulous ears with complaints about Maureen's lack of cleverness.

"The lodge is just ahead," Henry muttered helpfully.

"Oh, really? Where?" She pretended to look about as though searching for the half-timbered, two-storied cottage standing prominently in front of them. It was on a hill bare of trees, surrounded by rolling green fields dotted with sheep. "Dear me, I must have missed it. We daft types miss the most obvious things, I'm afraid."

"Maureen."

"Why are we here?"

He sighed. "The manor house is teeming with young girls and surrounded by trees. Keeping you there poses too great a risk. The cottage is isolated. Easily defended."

"Not the hunting lodge," she snapped. "Devonshire. Why did you bring me here? Why not Fairfield?"

He shifted in his saddle and cast her a sidelong glance. "Before Yardleigh was Colin's, it was mine. I purchased the estate as a sanctuary for occasions such as this. When I sold it to Colin, we agreed that it could continue to serve that function in the unlikely event—"

"That the Investor tried to kill you."

He nodded and flexed his jaw. "Or threatened someone close to me. The house is uniquely situated miles from any village or anyone who would take notice of my men or me. It is distant from London. The coast is an hour's ride, should we require passage across the Channel."

"It seems you've thought of everything. Wouldn't your name be listed on the deed or some such? Surely a man as clever as the Investor will look for—"

"There is no way to connect the property to me. I made certain of it." Again, his jaw flexed as though he chewed something distasteful. "I am clever too, pet."

"Yet he found you, didn't he? He sent a killer to your house on your wedding night."

His flat, steel gaze was like nothing she'd ever seen. It sent chills rippling across her skin.

"That was not clever. That was the daftest thing he's done in this long bloody war."

Her heart pounded as she stared at the stranger she had married. A man who killed with twin daggers. A man of violence and cold resolve. "What are you going to do?"

He did not answer, merely pulled his hat lower over his eyes and quickened their pace to climb the last two-dozen yards to the hunting lodge. After helping her dismount, his hands lingered on her waist. "Go inside, pet. Have a look around. Decide which bedchamber will be ours."

She gazed up into darkest blue, bewildered by the heat coursing through her belly, swirling and swooping like a banner caught in a playful breeze.

She had no liking for not-Henry. She should be removing his hands from her person. Removing her person from his reach.

Instead, she tingled with the Huxley Flush. She swallowed against a dry throat. She lowered her eyes to his lips—those beautiful, kissable lips—and she licked her own. Unnerved, she drew a breath and pushed him away.

"Find your own blasted sleeping quarters," she said tartly, resettling her skirts before turning on her heel. "For, you shan't be sharing mine."

Entering the cottage behind a pair of broad-shouldered footmen carrying a trunk between them, she glanced right and then left, noting the polished plank floors in twin parlors flanking a central entrance hall. Warm oak paneling similar to that at Yardleigh Manor lined the walls, and weighty, weathered beams striped the ceiling. Substantial stone fireplaces appeared in each room, and a staircase perhaps ten feet inside the door led to the upper floor and, presumably, the bedchambers.

Perhaps she should start with the kitchen. She removed her bonnet with shaking fingers and smoothed her hair. Yes, the kitchen.

She found it precisely where it should be at the rear of the cottage. Much smaller and plainer than the one at Berne House, this kitchen nevertheless had many of the necessities—a heavy work table in the center of the small, timbered space; rugged stone floors; and a wide, open stone hearth with a variety of spits and hooks. No range, of course, but that was no great matter. And the wattle-and-daub walls were lined with haphazard shelving and stacked with all manner of pots, pans, crockery, and utensils.

She sighed. It was lovely. Rustic and clean with two diamond-paned windows looking out on a small garden and a door leading to the same. Setting her bonnet on the heavily scarred table, she ran a gloved finger along the blackened mantel high above the hearth. Then she dusted her hands together and turned in a circle. She could work in here. Yes, indeed. She could happily spend hours in this small space.

"Oh!" cried one of the maids from Yardleigh, a young, blond girl who halted inside the garden door. Nervously, the girl bobbed a curtsy. "M'lady. Beggin' your pardon. Have you lost yer way, then?"

Maureen smiled. "No. I am in the right place. Martha, isn't it? You are one of the kitchen maids."

The girl nodded. "Cook is teachin' me. She said if yer ladyship were agreeable, Oi might perform such duties whilst you and his lordship are in residence."

"I should like that very much. But, I must confess I enjoy a bit of cookery myself from time to time. I do hope you will allow me the use of this"—she glanced around and gestured to the odd assortment of dishes and pots—"lovely kitchen."

Martha appeared dubious. "Y-ye wish to cook." Her eyes wandered from the rough-hewn, blackened hearth to the poorly matched shelving. "Here."

Maureen chuckled. "Peculiar, I know. But I promise I shan't burn the place down." She tugged her gloves off and laid them and her bonnet on a shelf near the window, craning her neck to view the neat rows of herbs and flowers in the garden. "Now, then." She spun on her heel to face a befuddled Martha. "Perhaps you have an apron I may borrow. And bacon. We shall need a goodly amount of bacon."

Within an hour, they had built a roaring fire, chopped carrots, parsnips, and onions, and rolled out a passable paste for the lamb pies Maureen planned for the second course. Martha was a hard worker, sturdier than her slender lines would suggest, but also chatty as a songbird. She hadn't ceased talking in that coiling Devonshire burr since handing Maureen a striped apron and stacking a great lot of wood in the grate.

Maureen didn't mind. Tales of how Martha had burned Cook's favorite wooden spoon to a cinder, or how Martha's younger brother made a fine stable lad, despite having misdirected a shovelful of horse dung onto Lord Colin's boots, wafted around her like so much wind. The flow was a distraction, and a distraction was what she needed. She rubbed her forehead with her wrist and pressed the paste gently into the pan, taking care not to overwork it. The breeze from the open windows cooled her skin.

"... where do Oi find Miss Biddy next but hidin' under the kitchen table with an empty jar of jam, lickin' her fingers clean one by one."

Laughing, Maureen scooped the cubes of tender lamb meat and vegetables, along with a hearty quantity of gravy and suet, into the paste shell and carefully layered a second shell over the top.

"How is the veal coming along, Martha?" She glanced over her shoulder to where the girl was draping bacon over an herbed fillet. "Do you have enough bacon?"

"Indeed, m'lady. Though we'll likely need more sent up from Yardleigh if we wish to have any for breakfast. What did you call this receipt?"

"Veal fillet à la Flamond. A favorite of mine." She blew a puff of air upwards to scatter the stray curls sliding across her brow and grinned while she crimped the edges of the pie. "Probably the bacon."

Martha sniffed. "Hmm. Cook never mentioned a flamin' fillet. She prefers plainer fare. Stewed brisket of beef. Now, there's a hearty dish."

Another breeze drifted in through the windows as Martha continued her chatter and Maureen continued pressing the paste with her fingers. The fresh air felt lovely, smelled of sea and salt and shorn grass and ... sandalwood.

A tingling glissade of sensation rose up her spine, curled along her nape and scalp, then shimmered across her skin. She glanced up.

And collided with deep, burning blue.

He stood with his arms braced on the window frame, chestnut hair tossed by the wind. He wore no hat, evinced no playful grin or mischievous charm. Only hunger. Raw and stripped of its veneer. Voracious eyes bored into her, heating her as surely as fire heated a hearth.

He stole her breath. Stilled her hands. Made her ache.

This was not-Henry. She should turn away.

His eyes dropped to her bosom, her beading nipples, the halting rhythm of her breath. His tongue wetted his lower lip in a slow glide. His nostrils flared. His head gave a predatory tilt.

Good heavens, her heart was pounding, forcing blood to throb and pulse in every inch of flesh. She gripped the table's edge. Leaned toward him as her thighs clenched around an ache she could not explain.

She was in love with the Henry she'd married, dash it all. Not this Henry. He infuriated her. Frightened her. But as those ruthless midnight eyes traveled her length, lingering on her throat and her lips and finally returning to meet her gaze, the quaking in her limbs and belly felt nothing like fear.

One corner of his mouth curled upward ever-so-subtly as though he knew.

He knew she was on fire for him. Not *her* Henry, but the real man, the one he'd always been beneath the dashing wit and brilliant waistcoats.

The arrogant bastard knew how she melted and yearned for his mouth. His hands. That scarred, naked body. How incendiary was her desire. How much sharper than before. Stronger. Wilder.

Distantly, she heard Stroud calling him. Martha chatted away behind her. But despite how dearly she would like to sever the connection, she remained enthralled.

In the end, it took another shout from Stroud for not-Henry to break his hold upon her. He gave her one last, lingering glance then backed away from the window and disappeared into the garden.

Only then was she able to drop her gaze, feeling as though she'd been seared, breathless and stunned at the power of it.

Two hours later, as she watched Martha carry her handiwork out of the kitchen toward the dining room, she removed her apron and patted her hair, feeling the loosened strands. She tucked them away and smoothed the yellow cotton of her skirt along her waist and hips, keeping her motions light, as her skin was still sensitive to the touch.

When she entered the dining room, she was reminded of why. He was there, standing at the head of the table talking with Stroud. Once again, his eyes followed her every movement, tracking her as she thanked Martha and invited both the staff from Yardleigh and the men who had traveled with them from Dunston House to be seated. She'd offered them dinner as a thank-you for their diligence.

Henry, looking refreshed and wearing his green tailcoat and copper waistcoat, came around the table to aid her with her chair. The air between their bodies fairly crackled as his bare hands came within a breath of her waist and lower back, his lips within inches of her cheek.

"Simply divine, pet. Everything you touch is delectable."

"You haven't tasted it yet," she retorted, blushing.

"Oh, but I intend to," he murmured. "Anticipation is a delicacy in itself, I daresay."

She swallowed and sat, her cheeks not the only parts tingling with heat.

All through the meal, she watched not-Henry take bite after sensual bite. Each time full lips closed around the tines of his fork, his eyes flared in appreciative bliss. Her reaction, intense and immediate, bloomed in her belly. Watching him savor her food was perhaps the most erotic thing she could imagine.

Her gaze lingered long on his hands. She pictured those elegant, capable fingers plucking and stroking and ... Oh, good heavens. She must have downed three glasses of wine trying to cool the fire, but she'd only managed to make herself dizzy.

Presently, a wicked smile curled the devil's mouth. He hadn't said much during the meal, spending most of his time holding her in a sensual prison across the length of the table. Vaguely, she heard the footmen and two maids laughing at

Martha's anecdote about Cook's attempts to swat a bee with an iron pot.

She could not laugh. Even eating had proven difficult, despite her veal having turned out rather well, tender and evenly roasted, the bacon crisp and salty. Everything was delicious, in fact. But for once, she barely tasted it.

Her entire being was consumed with him.

Finally, as the red rays of the setting sun beamed through the window, she set her linen napkin aside and rose from her chair. Everyone else stood with her, and she quickly waved and thanked them. "You've all worked tirelessly to help us settle in here, and I am ever so grateful. Martha, dinner was lovely."

"Oh, no, m'lady," the maid protested, "'Tweren't my doin'. Ye've a rare talent for cookery, ye have."

Ten sets of eyes turned Maureen's direction and widened at once. Silence fell over the table—uncomfortable silence punctuated with the Huxley Flush.

Countesses did not cook. Servants cooked. Maids like Martha. Cooks like, well, Cook. Even in a cottage with a meager staff of two maids and seven footmen, plus one valet, the lady of the house *managed*; she did not labor. Perhaps if she'd been less discomfited by her attraction to not-Henry or less dizzy from the wine, she might have brushed away the embarrassment. But, as much as she might wish the rules of convention away, they existed. Often, they were enforced most strictly by servants themselves.

These servants appeared taken aback, if not appalled.

She swallowed and nodded, her hands clasping at her waist. "Yes, well. Thank you just the same, Martha. I believe I shall retire now, but please continue eating as much as you like." She waved to the remaining food arranged upon the white-clothed oak table and sideboard. "There is more than enough, as you can see."

With that, she exited the dining room, but Martha trotted to her side just as she reached the foot of the stairs. "M'lady, Oi never meant to cause ye discomfort. Beggin' yer pardon, most sincerely."

She shook her head and smiled to indicate all was well.

The girl continued, "Would ye care fer a bath? Oi can heat the water in a trice, and Francis and David will be glad to—"

"No, no. I wouldn't wish to trouble you or them after such a long day. Just some warm water for the washstand would be lovely." She blinked, a thought occurring to her. "Martha, do you know which bedchamber my belongings were taken to?"

"The corner room, m'lady. It overlooks the pond. His lordship said ye would like it best."

Again, Maureen nodded, the motion shaky. Perhaps it was the wine.

She bid the maid goodnight and climbed the stairs, glancing left and right before deciding the corner room must be to the right. She found the door at the end of the hall and opened it to discover a moderately large, oak-paneled room arranged much like her chamber at Yardleigh. The stout oak bed was covered in another quilt, this time in shades of rust and ochre. She walked to the double window along one wall, gazing down through the diamond-shaped panes to the small pond in the distance. From the house's perch high on a hill, one could see the rolling green landscape, both brilliant grasses and emerald woodlands, stretching like a magnificent, quilted masterpiece for miles in every direction. Presently, the land was bathed in gold and crimson by the setting sun.

She hugged herself and sighed, wondering how she had come to this. Standing in a corner room in a hunting lodge in east Devonshire. Married to a man she had loved for years but perhaps never truly known.

A man she wanted with every ounce and inch and breath of her body.

A man who had lied to her again and again.

She'd forgiven him once, thinking he must have had his reasons, that he was still her Henry. But he was not. She refused to pretend he was.

Her body might not care, but she did.

The door opened behind her. "Here we are, m'lady," said a cheery Martha, setting the pitcher and towels on the washstand and a lantern on a table near the bed. "Would ye be needin' a bit of help with yer gown, then?"

"No," came the baritone reply from the doorway. "I shall assist my wife. That will be all, Martha."

The maid bobbed a curtsy and scurried out of the room before Maureen could catch her breath to protest.

Not-Henry closed the door and leaned against it with a dark, unreadable expression.

Maureen raised her chin. "I have no need of your assistance."

"Is that so?"

"Further, I think you should sleep elsewhere."

He didn't reply, his face increasingly hidden within the shadows cast by the waning sun.

She continued, her spine straightening, her hands squeezing her arms reflexively. "It would be better if I had time to ... think things through."

"Things."

"Our marriage, for one. Your deceptions, for another."

Several pounding heartbeats passed before he answered, his voice low and sleek. "Our marriage is a fact, pet. No amount of thinking will change it."

"You lied to me, manipulated me for years. I scarcely know who you are. In my estimation, that renders our marriage fraudulent."

"Hmm. It didn't seem fraudulent when I was inside you."

The shockwave of his silken statement concussed through her bones. For a moment, she thought her knees might buckle.

"Nothing more to say?"

Her mouth rounded to speak, but it took a moment to produce sufficient air. "I married a different sort of man.

Loving and kind. Amusing and affectionate. Perhaps he never existed, but that does not change the fact that I fell in love with *him*. Not you. You and I ... w-we are incompatible."

He was very still, as though he waited for something.

"Had I known the truth before we married, I might very well have—"

"What, pet? Might have what?"

"Made a different choice."

"Ah. Back to Holstoke, are we?" His voice remained even, his stance unmoving. But something about the way he spoke made gooseflesh rise on her skin.

"I—I didn't say anything about Holstoke."

"He was your other choice, was he not? More *compatible,* it seems."

No. In fact, there had been no other choice. Her heart had always been Henry's. From the moment in St. George's when she'd clutched her bouquet of white roses, her palms perspiring and her middle melting as he'd flashed her his wicked grin.

She wished to stop this infernal longing, to drive him away from her.

And draw him closer.

She wanted to punish him for his deception.

And take his tongue with hers.

The two forces were tidal in nature, ripping her apart.

"Perhaps I can help," he said, pushing away from the door. With slow, gliding strides, he came toward her, the lantern's glow at last lighting his features.

What she saw rendered her weak and molten. Charming, handsome Henry was gone. In his place was a man who had been pushed past his limits. A man as hard and deadly as a steel blade.

He halted when mere inches remained between them. "Compatibility is a complex measure, requiring numerous elements to align. Fit together like a lock and key, you might say." He ran a fingertip along her temple, playing with the curls there.

Her breath quickened. She wanted to withdraw, but she couldn't. It simply felt too good.

"Turn round, Maureen."

She swallowed, eyeing his mouth.

"Turn. Round." His lips quirked. "Please."

Slowly, she complied. Then, she felt his fingers deftly loosening the hooks of her bodice. Her hands came up automatically to clutch the gown to her breasts. He next removed the pins from her hair, the plucking motions sending thrills over her scalp.

"Now, then." He brushed past her, casually shedding his tailcoat and tossing it across a cushioned chair near the window while he piled her hairpins neatly on the sill. "The first element to consider is origin. A common language, common stature within society." He worked on his cravat next, unwrapping that curiously arousing neck with deft motions. "Not strictly necessary, of course, but swimming downstream rather than up lends itself to greater endurance over time."

His waistcoat followed, catching the dimming light from the window on its path to the chair.

"Second, one must examine the intersection of one's interests and tastes. Riding, for example. Dancing. Excellent food. Intellectual pursuits. Again, perfect alignment is unnecessary and often tedious, but direct conflicts should be avoided. Off with your gown, if you please, pet." He nodded toward the window, where one could see twilight descending in shades of violet and rose. "You'll wish to be comfortable."

She swallowed and clutched the yellow cotton harder.

He shrugged and stripped off his shirt, tossing it, too, upon the chair.

"Henry," she breathed, unable to tear her eyes from his chest. Good heavens, how she adored it—the dusting of chestnut hair, the rippling of the muscles along his belly, the tapered waist and coppery nipples.

"The third element involves a confluence of essential character. This is where true compatibility lies. Shared humor requiring no explanations. Instinctive understanding of one another's thoughts and desires. Patience with one another's faults. Such synchronous alignments are both rare and miraculous, pet."

Her eyes flew up to his, her heart twisting. Rare and miraculous. Yes, she'd thought so from the beginning. What she felt for Henry had been everything she'd ever dreamed—a dance in which one's feet never touched the floor. Gliding and effortless, soaring and wondrous.

"Now, one might suppose if the first three elements converge, eternal bliss cannot be far behind." He held up a finger. "But that is to ignore the fourth element."

"Which is?" she asked, if only to bring him to the point more quickly.

With grace and purpose, he moved toward her, blue fire igniting a blaze in her core. "The flesh, of course."

She wasn't certain, but she thought she might have moaned. Unquestionably, she panted, all but gasping for breath.

"Release your gown, Maureen."

Her hands obeyed him without a thought. The gown sagged to her waist.

His arms came around her shoulders, but he did not hold her. Instead, those talented fingers drew the straps of her petticoat down past her elbows and then lightly plucked at the strings of her stays.

His voice, a wash of heat and low, rumbling sound, brushed her ear. "These determinations require a great deal of study."

His lips found her pulse, throbbing in her throat. They nibbled and suckled and slid.

"Contemplation at great proximity."

His hands gripped the sleeves of her petticoat and gown, yanking firmly until the garments fell past her hands and puddled around her feet, leaving only loosened stays, her shift, and a pair of stockings.

"And experimentation with great frequency."

Lean, elegant fingers traced a path across the upper swells of her aching breasts, sliding inside the cups of her stays and shift to skim the perimeter of her nipples. Those fingers scissored and squeezed, putting insufficient pressure on the throbbing, sensitive tips.

She jerked and held her breath, thrust her breasts toward him, arched her throat into his mouth.

His fingers stopped. His head lifted. He stepped back. "If we are to continue our study, pet, I must insist upon dispensing with the remainder of your garments. Full proximity is required, if you recall."

Ordinarily, she might tell him to go to the devil. But the lust rampaging through her blood would not allow it. She needed him. Needed his hands and his mouth. His touch and his tongue.

Within seconds, she had thrown her stays and stockings and a shift that would likely need mending upon the pile at her feet.

"Now you, Henry," she said, her own voice thickened and hoarse, her hands kneading at her sides as though she were preparing dough. "Remove your breeches."

Eyes locked on his fall, she watched those fingers loosen buttons, each tiny movement causing her flesh to pulse as though he touched her instead.

"Oh, God," she groaned, covering her cheeks. "Why do I want you so much?"

The breeches disappeared, and in their place was his nakedness, centered by a towering stalk, dark with arousal, arching along his abdomen. "The wanting is mutual, as you can see." He moved closer, muscular thighs both thick and defined. "A critical aspect of compatibility. Come, let us explore the subject in greater depth, you and I."

# Chapter Seventeen

*"Brace yourself, Humphrey. Such provocative behavior
invariably garners a reaction of equal severity."*

—THE DOWAGER MARCHIONESS OF WALLINGHAM to her boon
companion, Humphrey, upon said companion's ill-advised
incitement of a prospective mate's temper.

HE WAS GOING TO TORTURE HIS WIFE WITH PLEASURE.
Before the end of this night, she would understand she
belonged with him and no one else. Not Holstoke. Not daft
Hastings. Not any other man.

Him.

Bloody hell, he'd never been so incensed as the moment she'd
implied she regretted their marriage. He suspected she'd only said

it to hurt him, but that did not make the wound any less severe.

He began where he knew she was most sensitive—those round, blushing breasts with their tight, pink nipples. "When judging fleshly compatibility, one must consider, above all, one's response to stimulus." With one hand bracing her lower back, he used his other to plump and tease her left breast, watching her eyes fall to half-mast as his thumb repeatedly stroked the ever-hardening tip. "There, now. You see? Perfect."

Her hands came up to his shoulders. She stood on her toes and tried to rub her body against his.

"No, no, pet." His arm secured her waist and kept her in position. "One experiment at a time, if you please."

"Kiss me, Henry," she pleaded.

He resumed stroking her nipple, giving it subtle little pumps of pressure between his thumb and finger. "Are you feeling warm?"

She moaned and nodded.

"How are your legs? A bit weak?"

"God, yes."

"Perhaps you'd care to lie down."

"Only if you are on top of me."

His cock throbbed like a pulsating wound in agreement. "Not yet," he whispered into the orange-blossom curls at her temple. His fingers lengthened and kneaded her nipple, drawing the sensation deeper, pushing her harder. "First, why don't you lie on the bed, and we shall resume our study of compatibility."

"R-resume?"

He removed his hands.

She swayed in place, her eyes flaring at the sudden loss. "Henry!" she snapped hoarsely.

"Lie down, pet." His voice was quiet, but his tone deliberately firm. She responded well to commands, at least when he promised her pleasure. It was something to remember for the future.

She huffed irritably, but walked to the bed and threw back the quilt, climbing onto the mattress and lying on her back. He took a moment to savor the creamy curves and rosebud nipples and downy thatch that matched her sunlit brown hair.

This time, she expressed her impatience by groaning his name and grinding her lush hips into the mattress. "I have done as you asked. Touch me now."

The white-hot magnitude of his arousal made the light brighter around him. Made his skin unbearably tight, his cock unbearably hard.

He moved to the bed, his head filled with all the ways he could ensure her surrender—watching her wrap those secretive lips around him, take him deep inside her mouth, for example.

No, he was too close to the edge for that. He needed to control both himself and her.

"Place your hands above your head, love."

"Why?"

"So we might see whether we are compatible."

Her eyes grew mutinous. "Don't be silly. I want to touch you."

He crossed his arms and waited.

Within seconds, she hissed in annoyance and did as he'd requested. The position of her arms stretching upward raised her breasts higher. "Happy?"

No. He'd be happy when she admitted she was *his* wife, and that nothing could ever take her from him. "Better," he murmured. "Now, keep them there."

"Henry, are you going to kiss me?"

He traced the nipple he'd neglected earlier with a fingertip. It grew pearl-hard in appreciation. "Yes, pet."

Sighing and squirming, she thrust her breast toward his hand. "When?"

He met her eyes. "Now."

With that, he gripped her behind her knees and spread her beautiful white thighs. He climbed between them and wedged them wider with his shoulders.

"Oh, dear heavens." She panted as though she'd raced uphill. "Like in the kitchen?"

"Hmm." He drew two fingers down through her glistening folds. She was pink and wondrous, wet and swollen. "I watched you today, you know." He slid two fingers inside her.

She arched on a keening cry, gripping the pillow beneath her head and grinding her hips upward. "I—I saw you, too. Through the window. I thought I was ... going to burn to ashes inside my own skin."

For the first time that evening, he grinned. He'd seen her response. In her eyes. Her lush, open lips. He'd wanted to bend her over that old, scarred table and make her scream in pleasure. He'd feared burning to ashes, himself.

"I like watching you cook, pet." Had she any idea how much, she would never let him in her kitchen again, at least not if she wanted to finish preparing a meal.

"I like watching you eat," she whispered. "So very much."

The confession surprised him. He rewarded her with a firm thrust of his fingers and a long stroke of his tongue upon her needy little nub. She gifted him with another high, breathless moan, and her tight sheath gave a warning ripple.

She was close. He repeated his strokes, taking her pleasure on his tongue. Vanilla, honey, and Maureen. How she obsessed him. How she maddened him.

Sudden and sharp, her peak came. He suckled and stroked and pumped his fingers inside her, letting her sob and writhe and clench, giving her the completion she needed. When she relaxed into the mattress, panting and flushed, he kissed her inner thigh and asked, "So, pet. How compatible would you say my fingers are with your—"

"Henry!"

"Perhaps we should try again."

Her head rocked side to side on the pillow. "No. I can't possibly."

He tsked and flickered his fingers, curling them just so. "Nonsense. Compatibility is important. One must be diligent."

She swallowed, eyeing him nervously. "What—what are you ...?"

He found the spot he'd been seeking.

Her back bowed and her hoarse shout echoed across every inch of oak paneling.

He pressed harder. Leaned in to suckle her sweet nub with firm draws of his lips and tongue.

Her thighs squeezed his shoulders with astounding force. Her heels dug hard into the mattress. She cried his name over and over, every syllable leaching another drop of his anger, easing the edge of his temper. Finally, the rush of blood in his ears dimmed, and he could hear her sobbing that the pleasure was too much. She was begging him to let her rest.

He would not, of course, but he would pause for a moment before resuming. "I shall require an answer, wife. Compatible?"

She groaned.

He pressed again.

"Yes! Yes, Henry. We are compatible."

It was not enough. He withdrew his fingers and climbed her silken belly. Worked his way north to her nipples. Began suckling and nibbling the firm, luscious tips, using his teeth and tongue while she moaned incoherently and attempted to force her hips up into his. He growled, "My mouth and your nipples, pet. Compatible?"

"Oh, God. Yes. Yes. Yes. Compatible."

He flipped her onto her belly. Pulled her up onto her knees. Gathered her lush, silken hair into his hand and swept it over her shoulder so he could position his mouth near her ear.

"Now, I want you to focus, love. Concentrate very hard."

He took his cock in hand and slid it slowly into her drenched sheath. She was swollen and fist-tight. He gave her a moment to accommodate him, and himself a moment to regain control, for he'd never been quite this aroused before.

"How does it feel?"

Soft white hands clawed into the bedclothes. "Henry," she sobbed. "Please."

He gave her a hard thrust. "Tell me, Maureen." And another. And a third. Each deeper and harder than the last. "Compatible?"

She grasped his wrist where his arm braced beside her. "Com-compatible, Henry. So bloody compatible I think I shall go mad."

He nibbled her ear, teasing the lobe with his teeth as one hand came up to caress her pouting breast. "Then, I daresay to call us incompatible would be a lie, would it not?"

To emphasize his point, he pounded inside her several more times, letting her hitching moans soothe his outrage at her earlier claim. She squeezed him rhythmically now, her sheath desperate, her fingers clutching and clawing his wrist. She turned her head and bit his biceps, then soothed the nip with her tongue.

He was not the only one feeling savage, it would seem.

In reward, he gave her what he could—a drumming cadence they both seemed to need. And as she began to seize upon him, arching her back and sobbing, he extracted what he most desired from her—a confession. "Say you are my wife, Maureen."

"Ah!" Her breath sawed in and out, her skin damp and her scent filling his head to the exclusion of all else. "I—I am yours, Henry."

"My wife."

"Yes, your wife."

"And I am your husband. I love you more than you will ever understand. More than anything in heaven or hell. More than anything on this bloody earth. I will kill ten thousand men before allowing anyone to harm you. So long as I live, you will be safe. Do you hear me?"

The hand that had been around his wrist reached up to cup his cheek. "I hear you," she whispered.

He shoved deep inside her, sinking to the root. He cupped her wondrous breast and kissed her beautiful neck. And he felt the first signals of her culmination quaking around him as her soft hand threaded his hair and drew him to her mouth.

He kissed his wife fully, tenderly. Loving her secretive lips and savoring the stroke of her hand along his cheek. Finally, as her belly began to ripple and her soft cries of ecstasy echoed against his mouth, he let the undulating force of Maureen's pleasure carry him willingly—happily—into the shoals of his own pinnacle. It battered him. Shattered him. Wrung him dry.

When the waves receded, he took his Maureen into his arms. Held her as tightly as he could. She laid her head upon his shoulder and gently brushed the damp hair away from his brow. Her lips found his neck. Her thigh covered his. Her sighs soothed him.

In the dark, he heard the soft, snuffling strains signaling her descent into slumber. And for the first time since awakening to a nightmare, he kissed his precious, passionate, snoring woman, and fell asleep with a smile.

OVER THE FOLLOWING TWELVE DAYS, MAUREEN FELL INTO A rhythm with Henry. She awakened each morning in his arms having spent the night in pleasurable splendor. He often began by kissing her neck or whispering devilish things in her ear that made her laugh and then groan and then turn over to trap him in a kiss.

At the hunting lodge, breakfast was a simple affair prepared by Martha and laid out on several trays in the dining room. Maureen at first avoided cooking another meal, worried that she'd embarrassed herself with her dinner their first night, but Henry wouldn't have it.

"Don't be ridiculous, pet," he said as they strolled along the banks of the pond on the third day, tossing scraps of stale bread to the ducks. "Martha was right. You have a remarkable talent for cookery, and anyone who tastes your food would be daft to say otherwise. You love it. Why should you avoid doing something you love?"

She sighed and threw a cube of bread as far as she could, watching the ducklings swim behind their mother toward the treat. "Countesses don't cook. That is the rule."

He cast her a look over his shoulder, raising a brow. "I seem to recall a friend telling me once that the rules are rubbish."

She glanced at his face, trying to judge his sincerity. Despite having known the man for years and being in love with him for the last two, she found herself curious about him—the real Henry. She'd decided that regarding him as not-Henry was to imagine that no part of the man she'd fallen in love with had been real. And that was wrong. The Henry with whom she'd been infatuated—the charming, dapper, amusing Lord Dunston—*was* a part of him, she discovered. It was his hidden half—the darker, quieter, deadlier part—that she was now coming to know.

"Well," she answered pertly. "Your friend sounds very wise. If she says it is permissible, then I suppose I should dispense with concerns about propriety. Dreadfully old-fashioned, in any case."

He laughed and caught her around the waist, kissing her lips and knocking her bonnet askew.

That very day, she took his advice and began helping Martha prepare dinner. At first, the questioning frowns from the other servants disturbed her—not all households were as tolerant of eccentricity as Berne House.

However, Henry made a cake of himself demonstrating his appreciation as they sat at opposite ends of the table. With loud sighs and groans and rolling eyes, he expressed delight in every morsel, lavishing her with praise, making her Huxley Flush rise and her belly ache with laughter. After his show of support softened the disapproving frowns of the staff, the devil spent another hour teasing her by devouring her creations with lingering, sensual bites.

Each night, of course, he made love to her with thrumming intensity and urgent purpose, as though his mission was to wring every ounce of pleasure from her body that she could bear. And then, another ounce more.

In turn, she explored every inch of him, including his scars. "Tell me truly," she murmured on the fourth night, lazily stroking a fingertip the length of the scar on his thigh. "How did this happen?"

He grunted and shifted in the bed. "Why do you want to know?"

She kissed his belly and gazed up the length of his chest to meet his eyes. "Because you are so reluctant to say."

His mouth quirked. "Curious little cat."

"Tell me."

He sighed. "A colleague and I were meeting a man who worked for Syder. After we concluded our ... negotiations, my colleague departed, and I was set upon by three brigands."

"Th-three?"

"Mmm. Should have been more, but one suspects they were not the sort to study mathematics." His fingers sifted through her hair.

"More." She snorted. "Really, Henry."

He chuckled and shrugged. "My talents are legion. An onerous burden, but one I bear willingly."

"Continue, please."

"Ah, yes. Well, I was set upon, but I fear it was after I had imbibed too much Scottish whisky. My colleague was fond of the stuff at the time. In any event, the three chaps took their chances. They lost."

"Henry," she prompted when a long silence signaled he thought he had finished the story. "The wound to your thigh. How did you get it?"

"One of them had a sword. He attempted to ... well, let us say, as my wife, you should be profoundly grateful he was a poor marksman."

"Oh, dear God."

"Yes, my sentiments precisely. I retrieved the sword from where it was lodged—"

"In your *thigh.*"

"—then I put the thing to better use. Slayed the dragons, as it were. Hoisted them on their own petard. Gave them their just—"

"Henry."

"Apologies, pet."

"Why should you hesitate to tell the story? You were wounded whilst defending yourself. That sounds heroic to me."

She watched in fascination as Henry's face grew suspiciously ruddy and his eyes dropped away from hers.

"Ghastly wound. Dreadful memories. I may be haunted forever."

Narrowing her eyes, she muttered, "Rubbish. Do not make me use your full name. I shall do it, I warn you."

He laughed, deep and delicious, his belly rippling beneath her cheek. "The aftermath of the story is rather less heroic, I fear. Unbeknownst to me, a crowd had gathered from a nearby tavern. It was dark where the battle began, but we soon came within the periphery of a streetlamp. The audience arrived in time to see the brigand thrust his blade in a location one scarcely likes to contemplate. Apparently, it was in shadow, so they assumed I had been ..."

She swallowed her nausea. "Oh, my."

"Hmm. I staggered nearer the light for the second act."

"Removing the sword and—"

"Dispatching the evildoers. Yes."

"So, they thought you had killed three men with the same weapon used to—"

"Render me a fine soprano."

Her fingers covered her mouth.

"Pray, contain your mirth a moment longer, pet," he said. "That is not the worst part."

"What is the worst part?" she mumbled, caught between laughter and horror.

Sighing, he took on a look of weary resignation. "They gave me a moniker."

No, disgust better described his expression. Disdain. Annoyance.

"A moniker?" she squeaked.

"Sabre." He spat the word. Rolled his eyes. "I do not even own one. A man uses a sabre one bloody time to defend his most precious cargo, and forever after, he is known by that ludicrous title."

She covered her face with both hands, seized by gasps of terrible, rising mirth. "Oh, God."

"Go on, then. Laugh. But I warn you, wife, your punishment will match your amusement in severity."

"It—it could have been worse."

"You shan't be comfortable walking for days, love. I shall bind you to this bed—"

"What if"—she stifled a series of giggles—"the tavern had instead been a theater? What if they had decided their hero was a performer?"

"Do not say it."

"A lover of music."

"Maureen."

"*Il castrato.*"

"Good God, woman. Have you any idea how loathsome this subject is for a man?"

Only when her laughter had subsided did he trap her beneath him and begin her punishment. Unsurprisingly, he was a man of his word.

On the seventh night, she awakened to find him standing with his hands braced wide on either side of the window. He was painted silver by moonlight, the naked contours of his back and buttocks, muscled legs and sculpted arms a feast for her eyes.

"I love you, Henry Thorpe," she whispered.

His head turned. A grim mouth eased and curved upward in a smile. "And I love you, Maureen Thorpe."

On the tenth night, he tossed their quilt over his shoulder and coaxed her to follow him outside where a full moon held court among a thousand stars. Tugging her along behind him, he drew her down to the bank of the pond where the grass grew thick and high. The breeze was cool and soft, his hand warm and strong around hers. He laid the quilt atop the grass, then laid her atop the quilt, then stretched out beside her and tucked her close.

She listened to his heart beating through linen and flesh. Gazed up at stars sparking white trails through a sky the color of his eyes. Felt his palm settling possessively along the small of her back, his lips pressing her hair.

Suddenly, she knew.

He was leaving.

He was making memories for her because he was leaving.

"At Fairfield, there is a valley much like this one," he murmured. "Ideal setting for a fish pond, I think. You must confirm my supposition when you see it, of course. But I think you will agree."

She breathed his name.

"Shh, love." He stroked her hair with the softest touch. "Let us lie here a while. Nights like this are a rarity. The last one I remember was your sister's midsummer ball. God, you were an enchantress. The most beautiful thing I'd ever seen."

Squeezing her eyes closed, she held him tighter, soothed herself with the sounds of the night—wind sighing through grass, frogs singing, owls hooting—and prayed she was mistaken.

On the eleventh morning, her suspicions were confirmed.

She found him talking with Stroud in the small stable behind the cottage, his chestnut hair lit by the graying light. Clutching her shawl around her shoulders, she slowed her pace, catching a piece of their conversation.

"... anywhere alone. You must remain by her side at all times, understand? Do whatever is necessary, Stroud. Nothing is more important."

"I will keep her safe, my lord. Upon my honor."

Henry set a hand upon the other man's shoulder and nodded. He pushed away from the rail fence upon which he'd been leaning and moved to where Dag happily munched his breakfast.

Maureen watched him stroke Dag's neck and give the animal a brisk pat with a lean, elegant hand.

"Please don't go, Henry."

He stiffened. "I must, pet."

Fear—grinding and roiling—swelled inside her chest. The pain of it was a devouring void. "No. What you must do is stay with me. Here. I am your wife."

He slowly closed the distance between them, coming around the edge of the stall to where she stood in the wide entrance. A strong wind buffeted her back. The line between shadow and daylight moved like a rising curtain across his features as he approached, revealing his solemnity. His resolve. "My wife, indeed. And you shall be at risk until the Investor is eliminated. That is unacceptable to me."

"Leave the matter to Mr. Reaver. Hire more men to pursue him."

"That might take years, love. We cannot hide here forever. And what of our children, hmm?" His palm settled over her belly, warming her there. "They must be safe, as well."

She grasped his hand and pulled it to her mouth, laying a kiss upon the flesh at the base of his thumb, then another in the center of his palm. "Just a while longer, then. I beg of you ..." Her voice contorted. She swallowed upon her fear, the gnawing agony at the center of her chest, her heart's demand that she hold him. Keep him with her.

He gathered her close. Gently kissed her forehead. "You are all that matters to me. I need you to be safe."

"I need you to be here."

"Here will not help us. The Investor disposes of anyone who has knowledge of him. A boy who delivered a message. A woman who received it. Anyone. I must find him before he finds you." He rubbed her back with soothing strokes.

She was not soothed. She was quaking for him. The fear gripped her insides until drawing breath was painful. "What are you going to do?"

"Return to London. Reaver is expecting me. I should have left days ago, but ... well, you are an intoxicating minx, Lady Dunston. The extremity of my desire would shock your sensibilities."

"Doubtful," she said, laying her cheek against his chest and sliding her arms around his waist. "I find even your neck arousing."

He chuckled, the sensual rumble echoing through whorls of her ear. "Bloody hell, Maureen. Little wonder I am mad for you."

She wanted to beg him not to go. Blackmail him with complaints about his duplicity. Bribe him with endless lovemaking. She wanted to tie him to their bed and force him to remain where he would be safe. Unharmed. Alive.

His lips settled on the crown of her head then trailed down to her temple. "I would never leave you were it not necessary, love."

The refrain of her own words from months ago forced hot tears to spill onto her cheeks. The raw wound in her chest expanded until it swallowed her.

Letting him go was going to tear her in two.

She wasn't strong enough. All her life, she'd had her family surrounding her. Papa protected and indulged her. Mama directed and coddled her. Her brother and sisters counseled and commiserated with her. Then there had been Henry, hiding a part of himself and, yes, deceiving her in a most unforgivable manner. But he'd also been her friend, giving her strength and solace and shelter from the darkness lurking at the edges.

Now, Henry needed her to stand on her own. To be stronger than she'd ever been. To send him into battle with that darkness, knowing he might never return.

She wasn't strong enough. God, she wasn't strong enough for this.

The weakness shook her muscles and closed her throat. But for him, somehow, she found the words and spoke them anyway.

"Henry Edwin Fitzsimmons Thorpe. Come back to me whole and alive, or I shall never forgive you."

# Chapter Eighteen

*"By all means, ignore my advice. Perhaps you would also care to poison your tea and toss your bank notes in the fireplace and invite Sir Barnabus Malby to your next fete. So long as you are practicing idiocy, I see no reason not to strive for perfection."*

—THE DOWAGER MARCHIONESS OF WALLINGHAM to Lady Berne upon said lady's insistence that a certain feline companion will learn proper behavior eventually.

THUNDER CRACKED AND ROARED AS SEBASTIAN REAVER stalked through the antechamber and threw open the door to his office, letting it bounce on its hinges and swing closed behind him.

"Bloody, bleeding hell." He'd picked up the epithet from Drayton. At times, it was particularly useful. Now, for example.

"Ill tidings, I take it."

Reaver stiffened halfway to his desk. "Dunston. I expected you a week ago."

The lean man sat in the darkest end of the room, one leg crossed over the other, one hand stroking his chin thoughtfully. Reaver noted the shine of rainwater on his boots.

"Hmm. A matter of urgent necessity required my attention."

Reaver frowned and moved to light the lamp on the shelf behind his desk. "How did you get in here without Shaw noticing?"

Dunston's slow grin was an answer in itself. "I've methods you cannot comprehend, old chap."

Grunting, Reaver yanked his chair away from the desk and sank into it, rubbing his hands over his face. "If you've come hoping to find the Investor's head on a pike, I regret to say neither of us is so fortunate."

"I've come to change our luck, you might say."

Sitting back, Reaver rested his elbows on the arms of his chair. He examined Dunston's posture, still and nonchalant. His expression, flat and deadly. Clearly, the man had been provoked.

Outside his window, the rain began pelting in earnest. A white flash lit the room.

Reaver had been waiting for the Investor to make a mistake. It appeared he finally had. The blackguard had gone after Dunston's wife. Judging from the look in Dunston's eyes, that error would carry a heavy price.

"What did you have in mind?"

"Tell me more about these poisonings."

Giving the other man a long look, Reaver leaned forward and opened his second drawer, lifting out the cylinder case and setting it atop his desk with a clack. He pointed to it and said, "This is what I have. A bloody case. And a bloody lot of sketches showing poisonous plants."

"But you suspect the Investor's new scheme involves these very poisons, if I recall."

"Every death follows a pattern. Wealthy nob with greedy, murderous kin eager to lay their hands upon his purse. He dies peacefully in his sleep. Few question it, for who bothers to wonder why an old man dies?"

"You did."

He rocked back in his chair. "Aye. The baron was a nob, but a decent sort."

Dunston sighed. "A poison no one would question—apart from you, of course. One that gives the appearance of a natural death. Sold to wealthy families for, presumably, a fat sum."

Reaver nodded and described what he'd managed to gather thus far. Knowing the Investor was either titled or wealthy and would have needed some knowledge of plants, he'd questioned every member of the London Horticultural Society. One elderly, gout-ridden baronet had sniffed disdainfully and informed Reaver the plants depicted in the sketches were hardly of any note, as they were common throughout England, either growing wild or cultivated in gardens.

He bloody well could have figured that one out on his own.

Next, he had attempted to trace the origins of the cylinder case. While ornate, the thing was not connected to any aristocratic family that he could find.

"You examined crests and insignia, I presume," Dunston murmured.

"Aye. Nothing similar that makes any sense. Spotted a few dragons here and there, but nobody of a proper age or location or disposition to be the Investor."

"Mmm. What of the maker?"

Reaver leaned forward again to tip the cylinder on its side, exposing the small mark on the bottom. The cylinder rolled to and fro as he sat back again in disgust. "Man with that mark says he's never seen the case, nor does he do such fine work."

Dunston's brows rose. "And you believe him?"

Rolling his shoulders, Reaver sighed. "Hard not to believe a man when he's pissed himself and begged you to kill him."

Dunston pushed to his feet and moved to pick up the case. He turned it this way and that, holding it up to the meager lamplight. A minute passed before he set it down and sighed.

"Aye," muttered Reaver. "Precisely."

Pacing in front of the desk, the earl began firing questions. "Anything on the ward?"

"Nothing. It appears Chalmers acted as her solicitor for a brief time following Syder's death, transferring funds and such, but the trail dies into bloody oblivion thereafter. Little wonder. The girl is in grave peril, should the Investor ever find her."

Dunston nodded. "What of the poison? Have you located the supplier?"

"Apothecary choked to death from the inside out while we spoke to him."

Halting, Dunston raised a brow. "Rather alarming."

Reaver grunted his agreement, preferring not to discuss it. "Before his death, he admitted preparing the formulations. After a fashion." He swallowed at the recollection. "I gathered his papers and showed them and the sketches to a physician I trust. He believes there were at least four formulations, all incorporating laudanum. The Investor attacked us because we were too close. The apothecary would have given us a name had he not ..."

"Yes. Inside out and all that." Dunston braced his elbow on his opposite wrist and stroked his chin thoughtfully. "The sketches denote the components of various poisons. But the case must also have some significance. Otherwise, Chalmers would not have bothered to send it."

"Pity Chalmers ain't here to explain himself."

Dunston huffed his agreement and resumed pacing. He paused by the window, apparently watching the flash of lightning and the angry spray of rain. Or, perhaps he was enchanted by the ormolu clock on the adjacent shelf.

Reaver didn't know why he'd kept the frilly thing—he preferred an object to be nothing more than what it was—except that it reminded him of the day he'd opened his club.

"Perhaps Chalmers did explain himself," Dunston murmured. "Only I misheard him." He reached into his waistcoat pocket and withdrew a watch.

Reaver frowned. "Explain."

Dunston turned the watch this way and that, opening the outer case and running a finger around the rim. "The night I was to meet him, he had no papers on his person, nothing of any real value. Only a handkerchief, some snuff." He presented the open watch to Reaver, holding it out in his palm. "And this."

"Most men in London have a watch."

"My thoughts precisely. Additionally, this watch is of lesser quality than one might expect of a solicitor. Gilt brass hunter's case. Inferior etching. A poor replica of finer pieces."

"The watch of a man who has run out of blunt, in other words."

"Mmm. Easily dismissed." Dunston came toward the light, lowering the watch into the direct glare of the lamp. "But the movement is a repeater. Expensive. Masterfully crafted, some parts gilded, even. I assumed Chalmers had sold the original case to replenish his purse after Syder's funds evaporated."

Reaver leaned forward to examine the timepiece. Dunston was right. The two components were not well matched. "Is the case marked?"

Dunston withdrew his dagger from the sheath beneath his coat and used the tip to open the back of the case. Inside, the case was inscribed with an S, denoting a familiar London maker known for imitating more expensive watches. Of interest, however, was the mark on the back of the movement—a double-F contained inside a W. It looked like the one on the cylinder case if the W were enclosed and more stylized. Inconveniently, the maker had neglected to inscribe his full name. Perhaps he had done so on the original case.

Tilting his head to get a better look, Reaver grunted. The mark, having been protected from wear, retained detail that changed its appearance considerably from the one on the cylinder—the one Reaver had mistakenly attributed to the craven jeweler he'd questioned last week. "It will take time to track this," he said. "But knowing the craftsman is a watchmaker of some skill should narrow our field."

"Find him, Reaver. I want every man you have on the task." The edge in Dunston's voice brought Reaver's head up. Dark eyes flashed with a fiery glint.

Dunston was an affable sort, sometimes cold, sometimes droll. But now, he resembled one of Reaver's fighters in a match that neared victory. This was bloodlust, pure and simple.

"Calm yourself, man. The Investor's apothecary is dead. That should slow him down for—"

"We haven't time to waste."

"Bloody hell. Acting in haste has already resulted in Drayton being shot, Shaw being poisoned, and an innocent jeweler wetting himself and wailing for his mother. I've no desire to break anybody else's fingers when we cannot be certain—"

The dagger appeared at his throat so suddenly, he hadn't time to blink. "My wife is in danger while we dally, old chap. A sense of urgency would be wise."

Reaver did not tolerate threats, particularly those issued at the point of a knife. But the man known as Sabre was far from ordinary. And that man had been goaded one time too many.

Holding himself motionless, Reaver opted for reason over force. "We will find the maker. It will take some time, but none will be wasted, I assure you." Slowly, he reached for the tip of the knife, pressing it away from his neck with a finger while taking care not to alarm its volatile owner. "Meanwhile, you could help by leaving my skin intact, eh?"

The dagger was tossed in the air and sheathed with a snick. "Apologies." The word was flat, but his tone sincere. Dunston ran a hand through his hair. "Having Maureen in danger has turned me into a madman, it seems."

Reaver raised a brow.

Upon seeing his expression, Dunston chuckled wryly. "You may not understand now, my good man. But one day, you will."

His response was another grunt. To Reaver's mind, that was more than the daft prediction deserved.

Dunston clapped him on the shoulder with the same hand that had held a knife to his throat moments earlier. "You'll see. If you are very fortunate, you'll see I speak the truth. Some women are worth going mad for."

TWO WEEKS AFTER HENRY'S DEPARTURE, MAUREEN LOST HER grip on her temper.

"Stroud! Lord Dunston instructed you to remain at my side, but I doubt very much that he intended you to follow me to and from the privy." She brushed at her skirts and glared at the hawk-nosed, bespectacled valet who straightened from his position beside the privy door.

"I do beg your pardon, my lady. His lordship was most explicit."

She sighed in exasperation and stalked the length of the garden toward the kitchen door. "Is the cart ready? We need much more flour than last time."

"Indeed, my lady."

The morning Henry left for London, Maureen had spent an hour weeping like a ninny. But it hadn't taken long for her to tire of the hot face and swollen eyes and hollowed, aching chest. An hour more of gathering her thoughts and penning a letter to Jane had resulted in general dissatisfaction with her circumstances.

She had little to do at the hunting lodge, apart from fret and miss Henry. The two maids and two footmen from Yardleigh Manor seemed determined to prove themselves more efficient than a staff twice the size. She'd even ceased preparing dinner each night, as it was far too much bother for only her. And, in any case, the reward of cooking was the delight of those eating her food. Despite the staff's softening censure toward her eccentricities, they did not appear to relish the dishes she prepared as she might have hoped. Rather, they ate largely in silence and left the table quickly.

As for other distractions, the footmen from Dunston House positioned themselves like watchmen around the cottage. If she dared go for a ride or a walk, Stroud and at least two footmen followed. Such vigilance diminished her enjoyment considerably.

This was why—four interminable, misery-filled days after Henry's departure—she had elected to take command of the kitchen once again, but this time for a different purpose.

"I shall begin baking for the girls at the academy," she'd declared in answer to Martha's querulous inquiry about why Maureen was donning an apron.

Martha had opened her mouth, perhaps to protest, but Maureen had merely reiterated that she intended to deliver treats to Yardleigh Manor upon their next trip for supplies, and that was that.

The next morning, Maureen patiently peered out the diamond-paned window of the east parlor, and when the footmen hitched up the cart for said journey, she took up the basket filled with her strawberry tarts and Chelsea buns, and ventured outside. Stroud protested. So did two of the Dunston House footmen. She raised her chin, ignored the queasy feeling in her belly, and declared, "I am going, gentlemen. You may come along if you like. But I am going."

They all came along—Stroud and the Dunston House footmen. Her Palace Guard, as she'd begun to think of them, surrounded the cart on three sides with Stroud seated beside her on the cart's bench, managing the reins and casting her furtive, questioning glances.

Upon their arrival at Yardleigh, she entered the massive kitchens, uncertain of her welcome. However, Cook was a steady sort, round and friendly. She reminded Maureen of Mrs. Dunn, which made her miss her family, though not as deeply as she missed Henry.

Despite her melancholy, she soon fell into an easy rapport with Yardleigh's cook and several of the kitchen maids, who agreed to distribute Maureen's creations to the girls of St. Catherine's Academy. One of the maids fetched Sarah, who likewise expressed delight at Maureen's idea.

"They will be over the moon," exclaimed a halo-haired Sarah, sighing as she took another bite of a Chelsea bun.

"I promise to keep my distance," Maureen assured her. "My visits will be confined to the kitchens. I wouldn't wish to endanger anyone, especially you or your students."

Sarah's mouth quirked wryly as she licked cinnamon and sugary glaze from her fingers. "I doubt such precautions are necessary. Yardleigh is rather isolated." She nodded to where Stroud stood beside the door to the rear courtyard. "And adequately protected."

Maureen's answer halted when she glimpsed dark curls and round blue eyes peeking around the edge of the archway behind Sarah. Biddy spotted the basket upon the table and came forward to investigate. Offering the girl first a Chelsea bun then a strawberry tart, she felt a surge of delight at seeing

Biddy's greedy gleam and waggling little fingers. She gave her two tarts, which swiftly disappeared.

So had begun a daily ritual. Maureen, accompanied by her Palace Guard, delivered a basket of treats to Yardleigh's kitchens each morning. While the cart was loaded with new supplies, she visited with Sarah and Cook and Biddy. Between the visits and the planning and the baking, she managed to confine the clawing worry and longing for Henry to the background of her thoughts.

Except at night. Then, it rushed in upon her like dark water.

This morning, after the incident outside the privy, Maureen was bristling with unaccustomed irritation, gripping the handle of her basket, and struggling to remember why using it to bash Stroud's head was a bad idea. She glanced his way as he resettled his spectacles on the bump at the top of his nose. Minutes later, as they strolled into the kitchens at Yardleigh, she slammed the basket onto the table and tugged at her gloves with snapping motions.

Stirring something in a copper pot, Cook glanced over her shoulder. "Another delivery, eh, m'lady? Biddy will be right pleased. Girl does love her strawberries."

Maureen forced her irritation aside and huffed a chuckle, tugging at the ribbons of her bonnet. "She does, indeed. Where is little Biddy? She is usually here to greet me."

"Ah, she's like to still be at her chess lesson. Miss Gray's been teachin' her every morning of late."

Miss Gray was one of the older girls whom Biddy had befriended. According to Biddy, she kept to herself, watching everyone but speaking little and laughing less. Sarah had clarified that, in the year Miss Gray had been at the school, she had struggled to engage with other girls her age.

"She is brilliant," Sarah had said, shaking her head in wonder. "Any subject, be it dance or music, sewing or household budgets, she masters effortlessly. Where she finds difficulty is in relating to others beyond the most fundamental politeness. Her affinity with Bridget is the first improvement we've seen, really."

Maureen's heart had immediately twisted, thinking of all the years Jane had struggled with shyness, immobilized and silenced in the presence of strangers. Maureen had asked Biddy more about Miss Gray, to which Biddy—licking tiny fingers after finishing a strawberry tart—had replied simply, "She is odd."

After admonishing the little girl to cease wiping her sticky hands on her Sunday dress, Maureen had pressed her to elaborate. "Odd how?"

Biddy had shrugged. "She thinks Lord Colin is a hero." Round blue eyes rolled dramatically, accompanied by a heaving sigh. "That is silly. I like when he plays the pianoforte. And when he teaches us about dancing and such. But she says he is a valley knight."

Maureen had puzzled over why a knight's location should make any difference until she'd realized Biddy had misinterpreted "valiant."

"Everybody knows he is just a duke's brother," Biddy had continued. "That is why they call him Lord Colin. Knights are called sir. Lady Colin has been teaching us about it. Proper titles are very important."

Miss Gray's fascination with Colin Lacey was more understandable to Maureen, perhaps because she'd once been sixteen and susceptible to handsome features, golden hair, and sky-hued eyes. It told her that the girl, rather than being odd, was normal but quite shy, as Jane had been. Maureen had seen Biddy's long-suffering eye-roll numerous times in her sisters. Miss Gray must have bent the little girl's ears at some length about "valiant knights."

Now, as Maureen smoothed her hair and gazed curiously toward the pot Cook was stirring, she wondered if Biddy would manage to coax Miss Gray to come to the kitchens at last. Sarah and Maureen had agreed that Maureen's experience with Jane's shyness might be of some benefit to the girl.

Sarah entered through the brick archway, her pixie face smiling a greeting. "More tarts, I hope. Bridget has taken to hoarding them. I don't know what she is promising the other girls for their share, but it cannot be good."

Maureen chuckled and removed the cover from the basket. "Even better. I have a surprise for her."

Sarah came alongside Maureen to peek into the basket. "Oh! She will adore it. Simply adore it." Beaming, Sarah squeezed Maureen's arm. "What a marvelous talent you have. So thoughtful. Thank you."

Maureen waved away the praise, feeling the Huxley Flush rise. "It is my pleasure. A welcome diversion, you might say."

Sarah's warm, honey-gold eyes softened with sympathy. She gave Maureen's arm another squeeze. "You miss him."

Blinking away sudden tears, Maureen swallowed and cleared her throat. "Yes. I do." Her eyes landed upon Stroud, who was now chatting with Cook, gesturing toward the larder and explaining the need for more bacon. Maureen sighed, her temper swelling again.

Sarah followed her gaze. "Has Mr. Stroud done something to vex you?"

"He is ..." Maureen gritted her teeth and attempted to be reasonable. "He is only doing his job. I realize that. But he is always near. He even stands outside the privy whilst I ..."

Brows arching and mouth quirking, Sarah replied, "Gracious me."

"Yes. At first all this vigilance was ... but now I am ..." She released a heavy sigh, lowered her voice, and turned her back to Stroud. "I am furious, Sarah. So bloody furious I want to scream."

With a sympathetic nod, Sarah guided her through the archway, down a corridor, and into a small room with a rough-hewn table and several mismatched chairs. Maureen plopped down into one of them and covered her hot cheeks. "I am sorry."

"Why should you be?" Sarah pulled back a chair of her own and sat, folding her hands neatly on the table's surface.

Squeezing her eyes closed, Maureen clenched her fists several times and tried to regain some control. "It is not Stroud's fault, but if I see him adjust his spectacles one more time, I shall brain him with the baking basket."

"Are you certain Stroud is the man you are furious with?"

Her eyes flew open. She breathed and breathed and breathed, but it didn't help. She pictured a calm pond with a lovely gazebo and plenty of ducklings, as she'd taken to doing on nights when the fury took hold of her and kept her awake, but that didn't help either. The Huxley Flush worsened, tingling in her skin.

"No." Tears—helpless, blasted tears—caused Sarah's pixie face and halo hair to swim in her vision. "I am furious with Henry."

"For?" Sarah prompted gently.

"Leaving." The word was hoarse and contorted.

"And?"

"Lying to me."

"Mmm. For how long?"

"Years." Tears streamed now. She swiped them away. "Bloody years. How could he do that, Sarah? How could he not trust me enough to tell me the truth? How could he pretend not to want me? Pretend that I was alone in my feelings for him? Watch me mourn the loss and search for another to marry?"

Rather than reply, Sarah simply listened, steady and calm.

"He lied to me about who he is," she whispered. "And yet I love him. The real Henry. Even knowing ... everything he's done. I love him. I miss him until I ache. Until I cannot bear it another moment."

For a while, they sat together in the silence, the creak of the house's floorboards above their heads and the distant bustle and chatter of the servants the only intrusion. Then, Sarah sighed. "You *should* be furious, you know. He had his reasons, there can be no doubt of it, but sometimes even the best reasons are insufficient."

"At least I understand now why Harrison refused to speak to him for so long."

Sarah smiled. "Blackmore is protective of Colin."

Maureen frowned. "How is it that you and Colin have forgiven Henry? It seems to me you would have the best reason of all for resenting his intervention in your lives."

Sarah folded her arms across her middle, each hand resting on the inside of the opposite elbow. As usual, one of her fingers began a rhythmic tapping on her sleeve. "Oddly enough, I never blamed him for Colin's involvement with Syder. Colin has made it abundantly clear joining the cause to defeat that monster was his choice. Dunston gave him an opportunity, one he badly needed at the time."

"But *you* did not choose it." Her gaze settled on Sarah's neck, where a thin, pale line marred her flesh.

A warm hand covered hers. Sarah's expression was mixed with patience. Grief. Understanding. Love.

"I chose Colin. I would do the same a thousand times."

"You might have died."

Sarah nodded. "I might have done. So might have Colin. He was tortured, you know. Syder wanted Dunston's name very badly."

"T-tortured?"

"Mmm. I found him lying on the side of the road. It was a chance thing, as it was not the route we'd originally intended."

"You saved him."

Smiling, Sarah replied, "We saved each other." Her smile faded as she squeezed Maureen's hand and lowered her eyes before tracing her scar with a finger. "My memories of the moment Syder gave me this are ... limited. I remember only pain and then nothing. Later, Colin told me a bit about what happened. Dunston, too, at my insistence." Golden eyes lifted to meet hers. "Your Henry remembers it all too well, Maureen. Colin believed Syder had murdered me. He went ... mad. Killed the butcher with a knife. Nothing could stop him. Do you know what Dunston told me?"

Maureen shook her head.

"He said, 'Colin is a better man than I. For, if my wife's throat had been cut while I watched, I would have slaughtered the entire world.'"

She swallowed a sudden lump. Now that she knew the full Henry Thorpe, she believed every word. He was a good man, but a dangerous one.

"In any event, matters ended rather well, all things considered. I have only the slight scar. Dunston's surgeon and physician are both excellent. I was mostly healed in less than a month. We enjoyed a lovely Christmas that year with your sister and Blackmore."

Maureen blinked. "This was ... two Christmases ago."

"Yes. Is that significant?"

The tenth letter. Henry had sent it shortly after he'd witnessed Colin's wife being abducted and nearly murdered by the monster he'd been chasing. A monster who was supposed to give him the Investor's name so that Henry could, at long last, end the threat to him and to anyone he loved. Instead, the trail had gone cold yet again.

"He—he wanted to marry me, I think." Maureen murmured the words more to herself than to Sarah. "He loved me, even then."

"Oh, I've no doubt in the slightest. The man left all of his guards here with you, including Stroud."

Her stomach lurched. Her lungs tightened. "If he is hurt, or k-killed, I don't know what I shall ..."

"Do not forget, you are also furious with him. It is all right, you know. To love a man and also see his faults, ask him to do better. If marriage teaches you anything, it teaches you that we are all constructed of faults—cracks and fissures in rather interesting shapes." She leaned closer. "With the occasional spot of grace to make things bearable." Chuckling, she shook her head. "You love him. He loves you. At times, you will be furious. Or enchanted. Or frightened for him. Or in need of his arms around you. The love remains, so long as you remember to leave room for both the faults and the grace."

"I wonder at your strength," Maureen whispered. "Henry believes me to be naïve. Too soft for such an ugly, brutal world. Perhaps he is right."

"Gracious me. What a lot of nonsense." Sarah clicked her tongue. "Strength is not instilled at infancy. It is built over time as we face hardships and either flail about or find a way through. You didn't always know how to bake strawberry tarts, did you?"

She shook her head.

"There you have it. We learn, Maureen. We decide what we want, what we believe to be right, and we strive for it. If we become resilient along the way, so much the better. Never believe your softness is a fault. I daresay it takes a good deal of courage to remain soft in a world determined to drum it out of you."

The knot in her chest loosened. Not much. Just enough so that she could tease her friend. "You should be an instructor, with all that wisdom."

Sarah laughed, her eyes dancing. "If only more of my pupils were similarly appreciative, rather than obstinate and willful like Bridget, I should be most pleased."

Maureen's eyes flared. "Oh! I suppose I should return to the kitchens. Biddy may have come down. And Stroud will be wondering where I've gone."

When they entered the kitchens, they discovered Stroud still arguing with Cook, apparently unaware of Maureen's brief disappearance. They also found Biddy investigating the contents of the baking basket. Maureen felt a glow rise in her chest as the little girl gasped and giggled and twirled in delight, clutching the doll-shaped loaf of bread dressed in frilly linen napkins and wearing a bonnet constructed from an old reticule.

Biddy's thick-lashed blue eyes locked upon her. "Lady Dunston! It is perfect! Wherever did you find it?"

"I made her, Biddy. She is yours."

The little girl hugged the bread baby tighter, then extended the silly thing out to her companion, a slender young woman with raven-black hair arranged in a lovely spiral of curls along the back of her head. The older girl was peering into the basket but turned when Biddy nudged her hip with the bread baby's leg.

The light caught first on the shoulder of her gown—a rose-petal pink muslin day dress with white embroidery—then on the curve of her jaw, sloping to a delicately pointed chin. As the girl faced Sarah and Maureen, however, all her features blurred into inconsequence. All but one. The light centered on a pair of eyes so eerily familiar, she would swear she was staring at a specter.

Maureen blinked. Lost her breath.

At her side, she heard Sarah greet the girl as though nothing was wrong. "Ah, Miss Gray. How good of you to join us."

With a strangely still, opaque expression, the girl nodded. Maureen should have reciprocated. She should be approaching the young woman, attempting to speak with her.

But she could not. For, she'd only ever seen a pair of eyes that particular shade on one other person—Phineas Brand, the Earl of Holstoke.

# Chapter Nineteen

*"Deny the resemblance if you prefer, dear boy.*
*Truth does not require acknowledgement for its existence.*
*A man may swear to the heavens that there is no rain,*
*but that does not make him any less wet."*

—The Dowager Marchioness of Wallingham to Sebastian
Reaver during a discussion of undeserved bloodlines, undesired
obligations, and unexpected connections.

After fifteen wretched days of hounding the
Goldsmith's Hall and various guilds for answers about the
maker's mark, Henry and Reaver entered a tiny shop in a
timbered brick building on the fringes of Clerkenwell. The

sign above the door read Wolff & Sons, Watchmakers. Inside, plank floors creaked beneath their boots and the air smelled of acrid dust. A small counter stood a few feet in front of them. Behind that was a door.

Henry started toward the door, ready to obtain answers, but was stopped by Reaver's massive paw grasping his arm.

"Wait," Reaver rumbled. "Just wait."

"Why?"

The giant sighed and shook his head, rainwater dripping from the brim of his hat. "No sense breaking things unnecessarily. Let us try a bit of honey before we tap the vinegar barrel, eh?"

"Drowning someone in vinegar sounds tempting at the moment."

Reaver glowered. "Last time you tried that, it cost you twenty pounds and three days before that whey-faced guildsman agreed to speak to us again."

Gritting his teeth, Henry glanced to the closed door. "Very well. How long?"

No sooner had he asked the question than the door behind the counter opened and a balding man with a remarkably triangular face appeared, blinking in a mole-like fashion. "Good morning, gentlemen. How may I assist you?"

Before Henry could answer, Reaver stepped forward, causing the mole's head to tilt back and his eyes to widen as he took in the club owner's size. Reaver set the cylinder case and watch on the counter. "Are these your work?"

The mole's near-invisible brows arched at the blunt question. He glanced down then waved a finger toward the cylinder case. "This is my work, yes." Nudging the watch, he sniffed with derision. "This is not."

Burning with a flare of triumph, Henry plucked up the watch and flipped open the cheap cover to reveal the movement inside. "But this is yours, yes?"

The mole blinked again and frowned. "Yes. Although I cannot understand why someone would choose to house it inside such an appalling—"

Henry grasped the man's lapel and pulled him halfway across the counter. "For whom?"

The man gripped his wrist and shoved, but to no avail. "Unhand me at once!"

Henry drew him closer until their noses nearly touched and droplets from his hat landed on the man's chin. "For whom did you make these items, my good man? Tell me now, and I shall leave you hale and whole."

More blinking. More bluster. "Release me. I shan't be mauled in such a way by any ruffian!"

"Oh, I am not the ruffian." Henry tilted his head in Reaver's direction. "He is the ruffian."

The mole swallowed with an audible gulp. "The movement is not in its case. I would have to examine the number inscribed on the—"

"And the cylinder?"

A furtive glance at Reaver. "It was commissioned perhaps ten years ago, before I had a shop of my own. Not my usual sort of work—"

"The name, man. The name."

"L-lord Holstoke. The Earl of Holstoke."

Henry must have released the man. One moment he was nose-to-nose with the mole, and the next he was standing outside beneath the Wolff & Sons sign, rain pattering on his hat.

"Bloody, bleeding hell," muttered Reaver, tucking the items inside his coat as the shop door closed behind him. "Your vinegar cost me seven shillings. I expect repayment."

His mind scrambling for purchase, Henry shook his head. "How can it be Holstoke?"

Reaver grunted agreement.

"Ten years ago, he would have been, what, seventeen? Scarcely old enough to employ his first mistress."

"Aye. His preoccupation with plants fits, but nothing else does." Reaver glanced around the street and started for the corner where they'd left their coach.

Henry followed, reviewing everything he knew about

Holstoke. "He would have been a small child the year my father was murdered. It makes no sense."

"What about his father?" Reaver asked, his long strides setting a swift pace so that they reached the black coach in less than a minute. "Also Holstoke, if I am not mistaken."

"Dead. More than five years ago."

Henry didn't wait for the footman to clamber down from his perch. He yanked the coach door open and climbed inside while Reaver barked instructions to the coachman. The giant removed his hat before seating himself, but the interior was still too small, forcing Reaver to tilt his head awkwardly. "Next time, we ride," he grumbled. "Rain or no."

A half-smile curved Henry's lips briefly before fading. His mind worked on the puzzle, struggling to make the pieces fit.

"Could Holstoke have commissioned the case as a gift?" Reaver suggested.

"Possibly. But, then, why should Chalmers keep the thing? There's no indication of who might have been the recipient. No, it must tie directly to the Investor."

Reaver shook his head. "Only two Holstokes living during the time the Investor has been active. The son is too young. The father is dead."

"Mmm. And before that, he suffered a wasting illness. It made him"—Henry tapped his temple—"simple, in the end."

"An illness in a man whose kin stands to inherit title and lands. Familiar, eh? Could it have been poison?"

"I suppose. Small doses. Long periods. But, again, his illness began when his son was still a young man." Henry stared out the window at the rain and the street. "He might have done it, were he sufficiently precocious."

"No shortage of intelligence in that one." Reaver shifted on his seat, trying to find a more comfortable position. The result was clearly unsatisfactory as the giant leaned forward and propped his elbows on his knees. Looking down at his hands, he muttered, "What if the Investor is more than one man?"

"I've considered it before, but there would have been a change of pattern. Over time, men always reveal their natures."

"Aye, but father and son are similar enough. Perhaps the elder Holstoke began his enterprise, and the son is carrying on in his stead. You nobs seem to favor such things."

Henry rubbed his lower jaw. "Hmm. It might explain the family's wealth. Still, the Brands have no reputation for scurrilous behavior. They are known to be tediously honorable."

Reaver scoffed. "I've seen *honorable* gents wager their sisters' virginity when the fever takes them."

His response was a sigh. "Nothing would make me happier than believing Holstoke is the Investor. I despise the man."

Chuckling, Reaver turned his head toward Henry. "She married *you*, Dunston."

Battling his own darkness, he did not reply. Reaver could not possibly understand, for he'd never been in love. Yes, she had married Henry. But he would never forget hearing that Maureen had kissed the blighter—and liked it. The very thought turned his stomach, even now.

"You are right," Reaver continued. "The pieces are a troubling fit. My sources did everything but turn the man's breeches inside out. They found nothing of this nature."

"And yet, he studies plants."

"Aye. There is that."

"His father may have been poisoned."

Reaver nodded.

"Only one name is associated with the watch and case."

"Holstoke."

Henry met Reaver's black gaze. "Holstoke."

They fell into silence.

"Is he still in London?" Henry asked.

"Doubtful. Most nobs have scurried off to their country houses."

A chill ran up Henry's back, prickling along his nape. He sat straighter. "Holstoke's country house is in Dorsetshire."

Reaver frowned. "Aye. Along the coast, near Bridport."

All the blood drained from Henry's head, pooling in a painful, expanding mass inside his chest. "Bridport. West of Weymouth, yes?"

"Aye."

"That is twenty miles from where my wife awaits my return."

Rising from his crouched position, Reaver thumped his fist on the ceiling and shouted an urgent command to the coachman.

Henry didn't hear him. His blood was too loud. "How many men can you spare?"

"Not many. One. Maybe two."

Nodding, he forced himself to draw air. "It will have to do. We leave immediately."

"Let me contact Drayton—"

"Immediately, Reaver."

The other man's black gaze was a mix of assessment and sympathy. "We shall protect her. There is no reason to believe he knows where she is."

Henry ran a hand over his mouth and jaw and looked out at the rain. It now formed a misty layer where it ricocheted off the street. Despite Reaver's attempts to calm him, urgency ran like fire in his veins. Nothing would ease it except to see her again, to hold her again and know she was safe.

"You've left her well guarded, Dunston."

Keeping his eyes to the rain, he replied in a voice as cold and brutal as the blade he planned to sink into the Investor's heart. "Let us hope you are right. If my wife is not safe, then I assure you, neither will anyone else be."

"I THINK WE SHOULD TELL HER," SAID COLIN, TIPPING HIS TEA to his lips as he turned away from the drawing room window. "She deserves to know."

Brow crinkling in concern, Sarah sighed and addressed her mother, who sat beside her on the sofa. "Did you locate her guardian's correspondence?"

Eleanor Battersby, an older duplicate of Sarah, nodded. "I can find no mention of the Brand family or the Holstoke title. Mrs. Fisher"—Eleanor turned to address Maureen—"that is Hannah's guardian. An aunt on her mother's side, as I recall." Eleanor's mouth tightened. "Truth be told, she's shown little interest in the girl beyond bringing her here and paying the tuition promptly. It is certainly possible Hannah's father and Lord Holstoke's father were the same man. By-blows are far from rare."

Maureen worried her lip with her teeth and sat forward in her chair. After absorbing the stunning resemblance between Miss Hannah Gray and Phineas Brand, she'd kept her silence, waiting until Biddy had tugged Hannah from the kitchens before informing Sarah. Now, two days later, they were still debating whether to reveal the connection.

The young woman was as fragile as a frozen bloom. Maureen had no desire to shake the ground in which she was rooted.

It had taken mere minutes in her presence to decide that Hannah Gray's silence and eerie stillness were not the result of shyness, but of deep wounds. Shyness, in Maureen's experience, was characterized by tension, like a stoppered pipe. With Jane, for example, if one bothered to draw her out, humor and wit would pour forth, first in a trickle then in a gush. By contrast, Hannah's stillness was seamless armor, her every movement slow and graceful, visibly calculated as though seeking a path through poison-tipped thorns. The only reason a girl of sixteen moved in such a way was out of fear.

Stark, permanent fear.

Maureen wanted to hug her tightly and wrap her in a blanket. She wanted to demand Hannah reveal what had been done to her and by whom. Then, she wanted to tell Henry to fetch his daggers.

Most of all, she wanted to inform Phineas that he had a sister. He would take care of Hannah. Protect her. Maureen did not doubt it for a moment.

"I agree with Colin," Sarah said quietly, then turned to her mother. "Mama?"

Eleanor nodded. "Perhaps she already knows. If not, better that she should be surrounded by those who care for her. I am not certain Mrs. Fisher meets that standard."

Maureen agreed. It was also possible Mrs. Fisher was the reason for Hannah's odd behavior. What if the woman knew Hannah was a bastard? What if she'd mistreated the girl for years, ashamed of her sister's illicit offspring? The very thought made Maureen want to pummel the woman, and not with a basket of baked goods.

Hannah was the same age as Genie. She should be gossiping and giggling and sighing over bonnets and ball dresses, not imitating a marble sculpture—beautiful, pristine, and expressionless.

Maureen could not bear it. Every instinct she possessed longed to give Hannah what any girl should have—a loving family.

Once they'd all agreed, Eleanor fetched Hannah, returning to the drawing room with the quiet, black-haired young woman in tow. Today, she wore a sprigged muslin gown with a blue sash. She was lovely, with delicate features and thick lashes around those extraordinary eyes.

Maureen stood and smiled. Hannah's only reaction was a subtle tilt of her head.

Clearing her throat, Maureen approached the girl, keeping her warmest smile in place. "Good morning, Miss Gray."

"Good morning, Lady Dunston."

"Would you care for tea?"

"No, thank you."

"I so enjoyed making your acquaintance. I was hoping we might chat a bit more."

No reply. No expression. Simply a placid stare of pale green.

Maureen turned to wave toward the chairs and sofas. "Shall we sit?"

Again, no response. The girl did not even blink.

"Miss Gray?"

"You have something to tell me, do you not?"

Maureen's smile faltered, then faded. She licked her lips and swallowed. Glanced behind her to Colin and Sarah, who wore twin frowns of concern. Their expressions matched those of Eleanor, who stood at Hannah's side. Returning her attention to Hannah, Maureen nodded, taking two steps closer.

The girl's shoulders stiffened, the movement so slight as to be unnoticeable.

But Maureen noticed. She halted in place, three feet away. "When I first saw you the other morning in the kitchens, I confess I was a bit surprised. You see, I have a ... friend whose eyes are a most unusual color." She paused, trying to gauge the girl's reactions but seeing only a blank surface. "They are identical to yours, in fact."

At last, those eyes blinked, albeit slowly. Then the slender shoulders trembled. "Who? Who is it?"

Maureen hesitated, startled by the changes in her demeanor, the urgency in her voice.

"Tell me," Hannah whispered, her shoulders now leaning forward as though she wished to move closer but stopped herself. "Please."

"His name is Phineas Brand. He is the Earl of Holstoke."

Pale eyes closed, the dark lashes fanning white cheeks. Beside her, Eleanor murmured, "Hannah, dear. Are you all right?"

Her eyes opened, now glowing with a spark of fervor. "The only one with my eyes was my Papa."

Maureen interlaced her fingers at her waist and clenched them together until they went white. She could not comfort the girl as she wanted, nor ease the sharp pang in her chest.

She could only give Hannah information. It was not enough, but the girl trembled like a doe startled by a hunter's rifle. Information would have to do. "Phineas is seven-and-twenty. Not old enough to be your father. However, he may be your cousin or perhaps even your brother."

Hannah's quickened breaths shook her fragile-boned chest but made no sound in the quiet room. "Brother?" she breathed.

Maureen swallowed a lump. "It is possible, though I cannot say for certain."

"I should like to see him."

"His estate is near Bridport, but—"

Hannah staggered toward Maureen with jerking motions, as though her body and her will were at war. "Please." A tiny crinkle formed between smooth black brows. "I—I must see him."

Colin stepped into Maureen's vision, coming to stand at her side. "We can write to him, if you like. Explain about the resemblance—"

Shaking her head, Hannah's eyes flared wide. Suddenly, she reached out, gripped Maureen's hands in her own, and pulled her forward until they were inches from one another. "Please," she begged, a gloss of tears shining. "Please."

Maureen could not bear it another moment. She pulled Hannah Gray into her arms, ignoring the brittle shudders and wrapping the girl up tightly. "Very well, darling. We shall go and see him." With gentle motions, she rocked the young woman back and forth, back and forth, as she would a babe. Gradually, the shudders began to ease, but they did not disappear. "Shh, now, little one. We shall go, and all will be well."

# Chapter Twenty

*"Rules are designed to contain the feebleminded so as to prevent them wandering into trouble. A woman of good sense knows when to cast aside these arbitrary admonitions and wander into trouble on her own."*

—THE DOWAGER MARCHIONESS OF WALLINGHAM to her son, Charles, regarding her intervention in a private matter between an earl and his unexpected relation.

HENRY WAS GOING TO BE VERY, VERY CROSS.

Maureen swept aside her widow's veil and leaned toward the carriage window to get a glimpse of the sea. "Have I mentioned that this must remain—"

"Strictly confidential," Sarah said wryly. "Yes. You did."

Hannah hadn't spoken a word the entire journey. But every so often, her gloved hand would steal across the seat and grasp Maureen's. She then would allow Maureen to stroke her hand comfortingly a minute or two before withdrawing again, staring out the window at the rolling valleys of the lush Dorsetshire landscape.

Now, Maureen watched soft, misty rain bejewel the grass along the road to Primvale Castle. She hadn't *intended* to thwart Henry's wishes. In fact, she'd taken every precaution she could devise—Stroud and five more of her Palace Guard rode in front and behind Lord Colin's travel coach. Colin himself was armed with both a knife and pistol. And Maureen was garbed in top-to-toe widow's weeds, courtesy of Sarah's mother. No one would recognize her, save Phineas.

But she was reasonably certain both Henry and not-Henry would find her precautions insufficient. In fact, she anticipated much displeasure. Perhaps growling. While in certain instances, growling could be quite enjoyable—even tingly—this would be the angry, fearsome sort. Her one hope was to prevent him discovering she had ever made the trip at all. She sighed. Sarah had agreed to keep her secret, as had Eleanor. Colin had not. Neither had Stroud. All the men, it seemed, did not approve.

Before departing, Colin had nearly barred her from coming along. "I cannot allow it, Maureen," he'd said, looking more like his older brother, Harrison, than the boyishly handsome scoundrel she'd known for years. "Dunston will be apoplectic."

Maureen had argued vociferously that she was the only one among them whom Phineas knew and trusted. Who better to perform introductions? Additionally, Hannah needed her, and she needed to be there for Hannah. Her heart would not let her do otherwise.

Eventually, she'd won agreement from Colin, and she'd used a combination of bribery and threats to persuade Stroud.

Henry would be another matter entirely.

The carriage turned inland and rounded a rise, bringing Primvale Castle into view. Again, Maureen shoved aside her veil.

It was remarkable. Rising five stories, the castle was a perfect square braced by four rounded towers. The gray stone appeared velvety—almost polished. She thought it must be due to the uniform color, a soft, medium gray. Many castles sprawled outward in an ungainly fashion. This one was a study in symmetry. As they drew closer, she glimpsed the surrounding gardens and sighed. Good heavens. Phineas had done magnificent work, indeed.

"Is that a glass house?" murmured Sarah, her face inches from Maureen's as they gazed out the window. "I've never seen one so large before."

"Neither have I. Phineas spoke of it, but he was modest in his descriptions."

The carriage rounded the fountain at the center of a circular drive and stopped at the foot of stone stairs leading up to the castle's enormous arched entrance.

A small, gloved hand grasped hers. She squeezed and turned toward Hannah, who gazed up at the entrance with little expression.

"He is a good man," Maureen said quietly. "He may be surprised at first, but he is a good man."

The girl took a shuddering breath and nodded.

The carriage door opened, and a damp Stroud inclined his head. "My lady. Your veil, if you please."

Maureen lowered her veil and, together with Hannah and Sarah, climbed from the carriage down onto cobbles. Colin descended after them, grumbling, "Dunston will kill me for this." Ignoring him, Maureen looked to Sarah and Hannah, took a deep breath, and climbed the stairs.

Inside the shadows of the archway stood a set of towering wood doors. Stroud, having come alongside them, used a knocker in the shape of a dragon. The sound echoed sharply.

Hannah squeezed Maureen's hand spasmodically, and Maureen tucked it close, giving her reassuring pats. Slowly, the heavy door swung inward. A liveried, bewigged footman tall enough to make Genie sigh greeted them with an inquiring lift of his brows. "Good day to you."

Colin came forward. "Good day. We are here to see Lord Holstoke."

"I am afraid his lordship is not at home to visitors. Perhaps you would care to—"

"Give him this," Maureen said, extending the note she had prepared in advance. "He will wish to see us, I assure you."

The footman blinked then surveyed the coach and her Palace Guard and, finally, lingered long on Hannah. His eyes flared and sharpened. He accepted the envelope before stepping back and waving them inside. "Do come in. I shall inform his lordship at once."

The entrance hall was a massive, two-storied affair with a marble floor patterned in gray and white squares.

Hannah's hand tightened painfully. Maureen pulled her close and whispered in her ear, "All is well, little one. He will see us soon."

The footman led them past another archway, down a corridor, and through a set of doors into a receiving room. This room featured a wall of arched windows looking out upon an open central courtyard. The walls were yellow. Beautiful, sunny silk. The chairs and settees were upholstered in darker shades of the same color, along with a few pieces in white and cerulean.

Maureen could scarcely credit the castle's perfection. Phineas had often commented on how much he thought she would like his country estate. If anything, he had understated the matter.

The briefest of twinges struck—a flickering stroke of wistfulness. Not regret, precisely, for she loved Henry with all her heart. Wanted Henry with every fiber of her body. Missed

Henry like she would miss air, were she deprived of it. But as they were seated in a room seemingly conjured from her dearest fantasies, inside a castle she'd never dared imagine, surrounded by gardens she itched to explore, she could not help envisioning a different future than the one she'd chosen.

"Appears Holstoke is fatter in the purse than rumor suggests." Colin's low murmur to Sarah floated to Maureen's ears.

Sarah hummed her agreement. "A magnificent place. I am curious why so little is known of it. Have you ever met him?"

Colin shook his head. "We are close in age, but he attended Harrow and Cambridge, whilst I attended Eton and Oxford."

Their murmuring conversation faded from Maureen's notice as she cast a glance at Hannah, who had gone even paler than usual, her lips colorless, her skin white. Maureen stroked her hand, giving what solace she could.

In time, the doors opened. It was not Phineas, but the butler, a tall man with a full head of white hair. He led them all out of the lovely yellow room through a series of doors and corridors, around the perimeter of the central courtyard, past another archway covered in ivy and trellised roses. After two walled gardens, they arrived at the astonishingly large glass house, positioned several hundred yards from the castle.

"Is it too much to ask for a man to receive his guests in proper fashion?" grumbled Colin, shaking his head to dispel the droplets of rain.

For her part, Maureen stood in awe, lifting her widow's veil just inside the door of the massive conservatory. Everywhere around her were leaves and blooms, plants both large and small. The space was warm, humid, scented with soil and water and sunlight. She sighed, the pang of wistfulness striking again.

"Is Dunston dead already? I should have thought he'd have the decency to wait at least a year."

She spun toward the familiar voice. Tall and unsmiling, he strode toward her. He was in his shirtsleeves, the linen rolled up to his elbows, a plain brown waistcoat the sole nod to formality.

"Lord Holstoke." She grinned wide. "Oh, how good it is to see you again."

As he moved closer, it grew increasingly evident he did not share her sentiments. In his hand was her note. He waved it in a sweeping motion to indicate her black ensemble. "What is this all about?"

She shook her head and kept smiling. "Never mind that. I have someone I should like for you to meet."

Coming to a stop several feet from her, he glanced to Colin and Sarah and gave a brief nod. "Is that all? Seems a long journey for that purpose."

Worrying her lip with her teeth, she recognized signs that perhaps he was less amenable toward her than she might have hoped. She had, after all, rejected him in favor of another man. But this was not about Henry or even her. This was about a girl who deserved the chance at a family and a man who deserved to know about her existence.

Quickly, she introduced Colin and Sarah, explaining her connection to them through the Duke of Blackmore, explaining that they operated a girls' school in Devonshire. All the while, Phineas maintained an opaque expression. Beneath it, she sensed his impatience.

"I am pleased to make Lord and Lady Colin's acquaintance, Lady Dunston, but I'm afraid I have matters to—"

"Phineas," she interrupted. "Please listen."

Turning around, she retrieved Hannah from her position tucked behind a broad-leafed potted palm, taking the girl's hand and drawing her forward. "Come, darling. It is all right."

The girl moved slowly, cautiously. Ghostly green eyes fixed upon Phineas, her chest pumping on rapid breaths.

"Phineas Brand, this is Miss Hannah Gray," Maureen said gently, watching his astonishment dawn. "Hannah, this is Phineas. Lord Holstoke."

Hannah's mouth moved, forming a word, but no sound emerged. She tried several times, her lips opening and closing, before the word finally sounded. "Papa." She drew a shuddering breath, and those extraordinary eyes sheened. "Y-you look exactly like my Papa."

His reaction was not what Maureen had expected. Those ascetic features tightened. Hardened. He turned his back and strode several steps before pivoting and returning to stare at Hannah. Finally, he glanced to Maureen. "Who is she?"

"I have given you her name."

"Not her name. You know what I am asking."

Maureen shook her head. "I only know she looks remarkably like you. Too much for coincidence."

He inched forward, frowning fiercely now. "Miss Gray," he said, his voice low and calm despite his obvious confusion. "You say I resemble your father?"

It took several heartbeats for Hannah to nod. She hadn't removed her gaze from him, her eyes roving his long frame again and again.

"Is your father alive?"

She shook her head.

"Your mother?"

The girl went whiter. Shook her head again.

Colin stepped forward. "She has a guardian, Holstoke. Mrs. Fisher. Her mother's sister."

Phineas tilted his head, keeping Hannah's gaze locked with his. "Is this true?"

This time, the shake of her head drew everyone's attention, including Maureen's.

"Mrs. Fisher is not my guardian. She is in my employ."

Maureen glanced to Sarah who peered back with alarm.

"Neither is she my mother's sister. Mama had no family that I remember. I regret the deception, but it was necessary."

As the only one among them capable of speech, it was left to Phineas to clarify, "Who is your guardian, then?"

"Nobody. The man who pretended to be my Papa is dead. I am most grateful for that."

Each placid statement detonated Maureen's assumptions one by one, leaving her reeling. Given Colin and Sarah's expressions, she was not alone in feeling as though a series of explosions had blasted the ground from beneath her feet.

And Hannah was not finished. Abruptly, the girl turned to Colin.

"I never thanked you," she said softly.

Colin blinked before responding with a single, hoarse word. "For?"

"Killing him."

Maureen's stomach dropped from her body. Her fingers lost their grip on Hannah's hand, her vision graying at the edges.

Distantly, she heard Sarah speaking, asking Hannah for details, begging her to reveal the name of the man who had kept her. Hannah said she did not like to speak his name, but Sarah pressed her, insisting that it was important.

With a small frown, the girl answered. But Maureen already knew. As inconceivable as it seemed, she knew the name before it was ever spoken.

"Horatio Syder." Hannah once again addressed Colin, her voice thinning to a ribbon. "Never was a man more deserving of death. At last, I can thank you properly. Thank you, Lord Colin. Thank you for freeing me."

HENRY AND REAVER DIDN'T BOTHER WITH A CARRIAGE. THEY rode furiously through the night, exchanging horses only as often as they must and stopping for few other reasons. By the time they arrived at Yardleigh, both were filthy from mud and dust and rain. Henry slid from his mount, alarmed at the exhaustion in his legs. He hadn't been able to stop. She needed him. That was all he knew.

To his credit, Reaver had kept pace without a single complaint. Now, as they entered the manor house, he stood silently at Henry's back, a solid, looming shadow.

Mrs. Poole bustled forth, yelping when she saw the giant.

"Calm yourself," Henry said. "He is a friend. Is Lady Dunston at the hunting lodge?"

The housekeeper kept her rounded gaze on Reaver.

"Mrs. Poole!"

"Oh! No, m'lord."

"Is she here, then?"

"No, m'lord."

"For God's sake, woman, take your eyes from Mr. Reaver for one bloody second, and tell me where my wife is!"

"I ... I ..."

"Lord Dunston? Is that you? My word, you are caked in mud—"

He glanced beyond Mrs. Poole's shoulder to see Sarah Lacey's mother, Eleanor Battersby, exiting the drawing room with a pile of correspondence in her hand. "Mrs. Battersby. I must see my wife. Where is she?"

The woman's mouth pursed before she answered. "Er—she made me promise not to tell you."

His mood went from dark to pitch in one plummeting heartbeat. "Where? Tell me now."

Reaver's hand gripped his shoulder, holding him in place. "It is best you tell him, madam. Now."

Mrs. Battersby clutched the papers to her bosom. "She departed this morning with Colin and Sarah. They are traveling to Primvale Castle to see Lord Holstoke."

A thick, muddy arm locked his neck in an unbreakable hold. "Easy, now, ye mad nob. Let us discover what's happened before we hie off into the storm again."

Having no desire to gut the giant, Henry nodded and held his hands up in surrender.

"Better." Reaver released him. "What would cause them to

make for Holstoke's estate?"

Mrs. Battersby had gone quite pale, either from seeing Henry nearly lose his mind or from seeing Reaver's brute response. But she managed an answer. "We have a pupil here at the school. Hannah Gray. She bears a remarkable resemblance to Lord Holstoke, according to Lady Dunston. The girl is only sixteen, and quite ... fragile. Lady Dunston insisted on accompanying her to meet Holstoke, and given that she is the only one acquainted with him—"

"Who is this girl?" The question came from Reaver.

"We—we do not know, precisely. She arrived here a year ago. An orphan, by all accounts. Lady Dunston hoped that Lord Holstoke, if he is, in fact, her kin, might wish to care for her."

Henry could scarcely think. He needed to find Maureen. But he also realized the import of Mrs. Battersby's revelations. This girl—sixteen, orphaned, related to Holstoke—must be the ward. There was no other explanation.

And Maureen was escorting her straight into the devil's sanctum.

He needed to regain control. He'd never needed it more. Yet, he felt every ounce of madness Reaver had accused him of. It drove him like a gun to his temple. Chanted like a maniacal chorus: *Find her. Find her. Find her.*

He paced outside, turning his face skyward and letting the steady rain wash his skin. Think. He must think. She'd taken Colin and Sarah with her. Colin, for all his appearance of charming uselessness, was both capable and astute. He would not allow harm to come to either Sarah or Maureen. Or the girl, for that matter.

The ward. He shook his head. After all this time, he'd found the ward. What the devil was she doing at Colin and Sarah Lacey's school? The coincidence was simply not credible.

He lifted his hat and ran a hand through his hair. Glancing back to the open door, he reentered the house to find Reaver questioning Mrs. Battersby about the girl. The woman was now explaining about her eyes, how they were an unusual color, and about her guardian, whom they'd not seen in a year.

"Did my wife take Stroud with her, at least?"

Mrs. Battersby blinked. "Yes, actually. Your five footmen, as well. That is in addition to the coachman and another two footmen from Yardleigh."

It eased him slightly. At least she was surrounded by guards.

"She knew you would be distressed, my lord. But you should be aware that Lady Dunston would not have risked her safety without cause. She has such a way with that poor girl—no one else has ever been able to touch Hannah. If you had met her, you would understand. Lady Dunston ... she felt ..."

"Like a mother." He knew. He knew Maureen's heart better than his own. She had never been able to resist mothering anyone, including him.

Mrs. Battersby's eyes widened. "Yes. Like a mother. Determined to comfort and protect. Determined to help Hannah find her family."

He nodded. It was everything he loved about Maureen. And it may have put her directly in the Investor's grip.

Reaver eyed him warily then asked Mrs. Battersby if they might refresh themselves and exchange their horses before departing.

Less than a half-hour later, they were galloping for Dorsetshire. Henry scarcely remembered a moment of the long journey. He was tipping on a knifepoint between exhaustion and enervation. His thoughts were consumed with a single focus—Maureen. He must get to her and keep her safe.

If he killed Holstoke in the process, so much the better.

# Chapter Twenty-One

*"Can I keep a secret? How insulting, Charles.*
*The fact that you do not know how many I have kept*
*is a testament to my capabilities."*

—THE DOWAGER MARCHIONESS OF WALLINGHAM to her son,
Charles, while discussing plans to surprise said gentleman's wife.

A BOOM AND CRACK SOUNDED BEYOND THE WINDOWS OF THE
lovely yellow room. Thunder matched the mood of the past
two hours as Phineas, Hannah, Maureen, Colin, and Sarah
struggled to reconcile the girl's past and her connection to
Phineas's father and Horatio Syder.

The white-haired butler entered with a tea tray, setting it
on the table in front of the settee where Phineas sat beside

Hannah, quietly quizzing her about her memories of her papa. *Their* papa.

Colin stood beside the window, arms crossed, staring out at the rain. Sarah sat beside Maureen, casting concerned glances between her husband and Hannah.

"There is no way Colin could have known," Maureen murmured. "Hannah was too frightened to reveal anything."

Sarah sighed and nodded. "Nevertheless, he blames himself for failing to see it sooner." Her mouth quirked with a bittersweet twist. "His past weighs heavily upon him."

Maureen did not know much about Colin's past—only that he'd been a drunkard and a disreputable scoundrel in his younger years—but she did know that Hannah Gray had had excellent reasons for remaining hidden.

The girl's story was harrowing. She'd lived with her mother in Bath until the age of five. Her earliest memories were of her mama taking her to buy treats at a small shop near their house. Her papa, a kindly man with eyes like hers, had brought her a new doll each time he came to visit. Those visits had been infrequent but happily memorable, as both she and her mother had adored the gentle, humorous man. He'd been ill, she'd recalled, thin and gray with increasing difficulty remembering things. Her mother had fretted about it, begging him to do more than take the waters. The last time Hannah had seen her papa, he had kissed her forehead, hugged her mother, and promised he would seek a new physician.

A short while later—weeks, perhaps—Hannah and her mother had been returning home from the little confectioner's shop. Their customary route took them through a landscaped park with a steep hill and a long series of stone steps. It had been winter, just coming on dusk, and the steps had been slippery with frost. Hannah recounted how she had run ahead, enjoying the thought of galloping down the hill like a horse. Her mother had called after her, warning her to take care, for there might be ice.

In a thin voice, Hannah had described arriving at the base of the hill, turning back to look for her mama and seeing the figure of a man three steps behind her. She'd watched in horror as the man had shoved her mother squarely in the back. She'd screamed as her mama had landed at the bottom of the stone steps, still and crooked and open-eyed.

Then, the man had picked Hannah up, shoved something over her mouth that made her sleepy, and when she'd next awakened, she'd been inside a coach. The man had introduced himself as Mr. Syder. He'd explained that he was protecting her and that she should not be afraid.

"But I was afraid," Hannah whispered. "He pretended to be my papa, but he was ... not good. Not good at all."

He'd kept her isolated and hidden for nearly ten years.

Hearing her recall the sickening dread with which she'd anticipated his visits, how fearful she'd been of his ever-present walking stick, Maureen had held the girl's hand and bitten her lip until it bled. She'd wanted to cast up her accounts. She'd wanted to revive Horatio Syder and kill him again. She'd wanted to weep for Hannah's mother and, above all, for Hannah.

Phineas had been thunderstruck, of course. He'd spoken little, listening intently to the girl he must have concluded was his sister, for her descriptions matched precisely what he'd once told Maureen about his father's declining health. And there was no denying their resemblance—the black hair, the bone structure, the extraordinary eyes. Even some of their mannerisms were the same, a certain tilt to the head, a certain alert stillness.

During Hannah's account, Maureen had seen bewilderment flicker through Phineas's eyes, but she had also seen his impulse to protect the girl flare brightly.

At least, she thought it was protectiveness. Admittedly, she was less attuned to Phineas's subtle shifts of mood than before. His opaqueness had been easier to penetrate when he had wished to marry her.

Hannah, on the other hand, appeared to have no such trouble. She responded to Phineas with reverence and rare openness. Even now, the girl sat close to him, her knee touching his, speaking more than she had done in the past year, if Colin and Sarah's descriptions were any indication.

When Colin had asked why Hannah had chosen to enter St. Catherine's Academy, she had replied, "I wanted to be safe. He was not good. You were the man who killed him. Therefore, you must be good. It was logical."

Setting aside the simplicity of her thinking, Maureen had asked how she'd managed to hire Mrs. Fisher. Hannah had explained that, before his death, Syder had made arrangements with a solicitor named Mr. Chalmers to provide funds for her and to keep her well hidden. When Phineas had asked why remaining hidden was necessary, she had refused to explain further, saying only that Mr. Chalmers had been most adamant that Hannah should not remain in any one place too long. She had lost contact with him prior to entering the school.

Now, as the storm outside grew in volume, the lovely yellow room where they'd all returned to continue their conversation grew quiet. Maureen rose to pour the tea while Sarah went to whisper consolingly to her husband. Lifting the blue-and-white china teapot and filling each cup in turn, Maureen wondered whether Phineas would want to keep Hannah at St. Catherine's Academy or bring her to Primvale so that they might become better acquainted.

She took up her cup and sat in a cerulean chair with a sigh. The matter was rather a tangle. On one hand, Hannah was his sister. On the other, Lady Holstoke was bound to balk at her dead husband's illegitimate offspring being welcomed into Primvale Castle. The woman did not strike her as particularly motherly, even toward her own son.

Another loud crack outside made Maureen jump and her tea slosh onto her wrist. She turned toward the windows, where Colin was frowning and Sarah appeared startled. In the distance, she heard shouts. Men. Urgent.

She pushed to her feet and started toward the table, but she took no more than two steps before the doors burst inward with dreadful force, crashing into the adjacent walls. In staggered the white-haired butler, reeling backwards into the room.

Coming in after him were two men. One was enormous, garbed in black from head to toe. The other was similarly clothed and, while leaner and not as tall, he wore an expression one could only describe as lethal.

Her heart stopped. Her mouth opened. Her only breath spoke his name.

"Henry."

He was unshaven, ragged, and soaked to the bone. He was stalking toward her with grim purpose, midnight eyes flashing in the dimming light.

He was beautiful. God, how she had missed him.

"Henry," she said again, her voice thready, her hands and throat and stomach shaking.

He swiped the teacup from her hand. It shattered on the floor.

"Henry! What in blazes are you mmmrmph ..." His mouth fastened upon hers, his chilled wet hand cupping her nape and drawing her into his kiss. He smelled of rainwater and mud. He tasted of salty marine air and Henry.

He tasted like heaven.

She clutched him desperately, yanking fistfuls of wet wool coat. Distantly, she heard other people talking. A deep, rumbling voice. Colin and Sarah asking questions. Phineas demanding answers.

But it had been weeks since she had touched him, and she needed his lips and his tongue. She needed to stroke his dripping, bristly jaw and feel his arms band her waist. Tighter. She wanted him tighter against her.

"Dunston! Good God, man, save that for later. We've a thing or two to settle at the moment." It was the rumbling voice. She wanted it to be quiet.

But Henry listened. Slowly, he loosened his arms. Gently, he withdrew his lips and moved his hands to bracket her waist.

"Henry," she breathed. "What are you doing here?"

"How much tea did you drink?"

She glanced down at the long streak of brown liquid and shattered china on the floor. "None." Frowning, she laid the backs of two fingers along Henry's brow. "Are you feverish again? Suffering some sort of plague that turns sane men into candidates for Bedlam?"

He grasped her wrist and laid a kiss on her palm. "No, pet. Apart from exhaustion and worry and missing my wife until I damn well want to thrash someone, I am relatively sound." He pulled away. "We've come for the Investor."

Again, she eyed the remains of her cup. "And to wage war against perfectly good tea?"

"It might have been poisoned. I couldn't take the chance."

"Don't be ridiculous. I thought you went to London to find the Investor. Why would he suddenly be in Dorsetshire?"

"Because Holstoke is the Investor."

She laughed.

He did not. His brows sank low over red-rimmed midnight eyes. "Holstoke is the Investor."

Bracing her hands on her hips, she looked first to his unusually large companion. Then, she examined Phineas's grim glare. Finally, she looked at Henry. "You may repeat it however often you like. You are wrong."

His jaw flexed. "Setting aside your past affections for one moment, wife—"

"Oh, do not dare to bring our courtship into—"

"All evidence indicates he is the man behind—"

"—this. Need I remind you I declined his proposal in favor of—"

"—everything. Well, perhaps his father began the traitorous—"

"—yours. Far from the easiest decision, I'll have you know—"

"—endeavors. But it is clear he has carried on his father's legacy."

"–what with your lying and deceiving and misleading me for years and–"

"One need only note the connection between him and–"

"–years into thinking you were an irresistibly dashing gentleman with too many puce waistcoats–"

"–Horatio Syder's ward. Apart from that, we have a case commissioned by–"

"–when you are really a much more dangerous sort of man. Perhaps I should have recognized–"

"–the Investor. Who bloody well is Holstoke!"

"–your deceit *before* you kissed me in your bedchamber, but I maintain I am ordinarily an excellent judge of character, and I further maintain–"

"Have you listened to a bloody word I have said?"

"–the Investor cannot possibly be Holstoke!"

He threw up his hands, paced away several steps, and promptly paced back again. "You are blinded by naivety and sentiment."

She scoffed. "*You* are blinded by jealousy and false assumptions." She pointed to Phineas. "He was in leading strings when your father was killed."

Henry held up a finger. "A series of poisonings in London have been traced to the Investor. The poisons are all derived from plants. Holstoke has a peculiar interest in plants." He raised a second finger. "A metal case full of botanical sketches featuring common poisonous plants was delivered to me from one Mr. Chalmers, a former associate of Syder who had agreed to share what he knew of the Investor. We located the man who crafted the case. It was commissioned by Holstoke."

She opened her mouth to reply, but Henry calmly raised a third finger.

"Horatio Syder's ward—a girl for whom I have searched for over a year because I have good reason to suspect she knows the identity of the Investor—is related by blood to Holstoke, a fact made obvious by their resemblance." A fourth finger lifted. "Of all the ladies clamoring for a titled husband during the season, Holstoke set his sights upon you."

Maureen frowned. "What has that to do with anything?"

Henry moved closer, his thumb extending outward from his palm. "You. Are. Mine. Above all things, the Investor would wish to have you in his grasp."

She had seen this look before. The lines of strain around his eyes and mouth. The tension in his brow and jaw. Henry had been pushed hard. Much more, and she suspected matters would end rather badly. She grasped his hand in both of hers and held his gaze without flinching. "Before we married, you took great care to persuade everyone—including me—that your affections were nothing more than friendship. Why would he assume I had any more importance to you than Harrison? Or your mother? Or Stroud, for that matter?"

"Because I am a damned besotted fool who could not keep a proper distance from you. If he knew I was the man pursuing him, then it would not take long to discover whom I treasured most. Bloody hell, he launched his attack on our wedding night, Maureen!"

A cold, sick feeling wrapped its tendrils around her stomach. Had she been wrong about Phineas the same way she had been wrong about Henry? Her eyes drifted to the other man. He was standing in front of Hannah, a scowl shadowing the ghostly green. His fists clenched and his bare forearms flexed in response to Henry's giant companion.

Good heavens. If she'd been wrong about Phineas, then she had delivered Hannah to a monster.

But she was not wrong. Maureen might be soft. Naïve. A novice in Henry's world of clandestine intrigue. But her instincts were sound. They had told her Henry was a good man, and he was, despite his deceptions. They told her the same about Phineas, who was peculiar and awkward at times, yet fundamentally an honorable man.

Her chin came up. No, she could not wield a dagger or a pistol. Nor could she deceive with aplomb the way Henry could. However, she possessed strengths that could be of value if only Henry would listen to her. Trust in her.

"Talking of Stroud, where the devil is he?" Henry demanded. "I told him to remain at your side like a bur on a woolen blanket."

Her eyes flew to the doors Henry had thrown open when he'd entered. The white-haired butler leaned against the casing, rubbing the back of his head, but beyond him was an empty corridor.

The cold, sick feeling returned and grew colder. It spread from her stomach outward, chilling her muscles and skin, making the room shift and waver. "He—he and the footmen ... they were supposed to be ... outside the doors. You didn't see them when you entered?"

Henry's eyes sharpened. Hardened. He pivoted and stalked around his large companion, withdrawing a dagger from his hip and leveling the point beneath Phineas's chin. Phineas's only reaction was to tilt his head back and glare down his nose at Henry.

Maureen hugged herself, glancing to Sarah and Colin, who looked on in apparent dismay.

His jaw flexing, Henry asked softly, "Where are my men, Holstoke?"

"I haven't the faintest notion."

"Come now. The game is over. Do let's conclude matters as gentlemen."

"I cannot tell you what I do not know."

"I've no wish to spill your blood in front of the ladies."

"Then we are in agreement."

"But I will. You are a predator, Holstoke. Like your father before you."

Phineas's reply was interrupted by another voice.

Soft and low, scarcely above a whisper. "Do not say such things. Papa was good."

Sidling to see past Phineas's shoulder, Maureen glimpsed Hannah, her skin the color of salt, her slender frame trembling. "Henry," Maureen warned, slowly inching toward the girl. "Have a care."

"I always do, pet."

"Hannah," she said softly, skirting the table where the tea sat, cold and brown in its delicate china cups. Finally, she reached Hannah's side and held out her hands. "Here now, darling. Take my hands."

Hannah did not reach for her, nor did she look away from Henry. "He is wrong. Papa was not bad. He was very ill, and he would sometimes forget things, but he was kind."

"For what it's worth, Dunston, she is right," Phineas said flatly. "Despite the mistaken theories you've conjured, my father—*our* father—was honorable."

Henry's lips twisted into a bitter imitation of a smile. "So was mine. Until yours killed him."

"I cannot believe that."

"Why the pretense, old chap? Surely you realize you are finished. Now, tell me where my men are, and we shall have done with this."

"I do not know where they are. And I am not this Investor, though given the evidence you cited earlier, I can see why you would reach that conclusion."

Henry's eyes narrowed, a considering glint emerging. "Can you, now? How civilized."

Again, Hannah interjected, "The Investor. Is that what you call Mr. S-Syder's employer?"

Henry appeared to bite down on a response. Instead, although he kept the dagger steady at Phineas's throat, his eyes moved to Hannah. "It is the name we gave him, yes, as we did not know his true identity."

Hannah's brow crinkled. She blinked once. Twice. Again. "You are wrong."

Henry sighed. "Miss Gray, you may not wish to believe

your brother is responsible for such villainy, but in time—"

"No. I don't mean about Phineas. About the Investor."

Henry frowned.

Maureen moved closer to Hannah, cautiously taking the girl's hand between her own. "What about the Investor, darling?"

Ghostly green eyes turned to meet hers, blinking as though surprised by everyone's ignorance. "The Investor is not a 'he' at all."

# Chapter Twenty-Two

*"Underestimating women is a time-honored blunder.*
*Deviousness is a human trait, not a male one."*

—THE DOWAGER MARCHIONESS OF WALLINGHAM to Lord Dunston
in a letter explaining how premature assumptions
might lead one astray.

SILENCE FELL, BROKEN BY A PROLONGED BURST OF THUNDER
and sharp, pattering rain. Shadows deepened in the room as
the storm darkened to stygian gray.

Struggling to catch her breath, Maureen was the first to
speak. "A—a woman? How do you know this?"

"Mr. ... Syder gave me a miniature. Painted on ivory. He
said if ever I saw her, I should run. Very fast and very far."

"Do you still have the miniature?"

Hannah shook her head. "I gave it to Mr. Chalmers. She is beautiful. But very bad. Worse than Mr. Syder. She made him hurt my mother. He did not want to give me to her, and so he kept me hidden."

"Why did she want you, Hannah?" This question came from Colin, who, along with Sarah, had drawn closer during the confrontation. The five of them now formed a half-circle around Henry and Phineas.

Her voice fell to a whisper. "He never said. Just that if she found me, she would kill me."

Maureen looked to Henry, whose gaze matched her own turmoil. Slowly, he lowered his dagger. "Bloody hell," he rasped.

The giant who had accompanied Henry edged closer to Hannah, moving with great caution, lowering his head so as to appear smaller. "This woman," he rumbled softly. "You needn't fear her any longer. We'll not let her near you." For such a large, ferocious-looking man, he was surprisingly gentle with the delicate girl.

Hannah blinked up at him. "Who are you?"

"Sebastian Reaver." He nodded toward Henry. "We have been searching for you. Do you know the Investor's name?"

Maureen swallowed. Cleared her throat delicately. "I do."

Phineas spoke then, starkly white and looking ready to vomit. "As do I."

Henry rubbed his forehead between his thumb and forefinger. "I as well. Bloody hell. Of all the miscalculations."

Mr. Reaver frowned, the expression turning his heavy brow into a shelf. "What have I missed?"

Henry waved his blade toward Phineas. "His mother." He then sheathed the dagger and addressed Phineas. "Did you know?"

Phineas shook his head, looking dreadfully ill. "I rarely speak to her. We do not ... care for one another's company."

At Henry's skeptical expression, Maureen came to his

defense. "It is true, Henry," she said quietly. "They have lived separately for years. He calls her Lady Holstoke."

"Since my father's death, she spends most of her time at a house near Weymouth," continued Phineas. "Before that, I was away at Harrow, then Cambridge, then traveling abroad. We are not ..." He sighed. "My mother has never shown particular interest in being a mother. Her request to accompany me to London for the season came as a surprise."

"Weymouth," said Henry. "Is she there now?"

Phineas frowned. "Presumably. I left the London house first, and she said nothing of her plans." Pale green eyes settled on Maureen. "Frankly, my mother was not the female uppermost in my thoughts at the time."

Maureen gave him a small, regretful smile. Although she knew her decision to marry Henry had been the right one, the last thing she'd wanted was to hurt Phineas. He was a good man. Good and honorable. She'd never been so glad to be vindicated in her judgment about someone's character.

Henry stepped between them. "Let us focus on the matter at hand, hmm? I need to find my men."

Phineas moved toward the entrance, but Henry grasped his arm, halting him midstride. "Dunston, I can neither speak with the staff nor arrange to search the grounds if you will not release me."

Slowly, Henry loosened his grip. "I don't trust you, Holstoke."

Colin stepped in, approaching the pair cautiously. "I shall go with him." He looked at Henry. "Provided you and Reaver ensure Sarah remains safe."

He and Henry shared a silent message only men seemed to understand and nodded to one another. Maureen was confused as to what had been decided, but Phineas and Colin left the room moments later, pausing briefly to speak with the white-haired butler.

Reaver went to speak with Henry in low tones while Sarah came around to comfort Hannah. Maureen glanced about, noting the shards of china still on the floor. She had almost finished gathering them up when she heard Sarah's loud gasp.

"Oh! Gracious me!"

Maureen spun just in time to see Sarah clasping Hannah's waist as the young woman slumped onto her shoulder, her arms loose and dangling. In two long strides, Reaver was there, scooping Hannah's limp form into his arms as easily as Biddy lifted her bread baby.

"What happened?" Maureen said, depositing the shards on the tea tray and rushing to where Sarah cupped Hannah's cheek.

"She swooned," Sarah murmured, a frown puckering her brow. "I think the past two days have simply been too much for her."

The white-haired butler approached, moving slowly as though he too was feeling faint, and offered to escort them to a bedchamber where Hannah might recover comfortably. Reaver nodded. Sarah murmured her thanks. Maureen started to follow them.

"Where are you going, pet?" Coming from directly behind her, Henry's deep, hard voice gave her a start.

She spun to face him then glanced over her shoulder as the trio disappeared. "I must make sure Hannah is—"

"No. You must remain in my sight at all times, do you understand?"

The carefully banked fire in his eyes was making her belly swoop and curl. She swallowed. "Henry. Is that really necessary? We know Phineas has nothing to do with this."

His jaw flexed. "If you wish me to maintain a semblance of civility, you will cease speaking his name."

"Don't be silly."

"Not silly, pet. Not amusing. Not absurd. Every time I hear that name on your lips, I want to kill him."

For several breaths, she didn't believe him. What sort of man had such thoughts? Then, she looked up into midnight eyes entirely absent of humor or artifice. Her Henry was weary and worn to the bone. Stripped of his polish. He was speaking the truth of his feelings, however extreme they might seem to her.

She cupped his cheek, savoring the feel of his whiskers beneath her fingertips. "I chose *you*, silly man."

His nostrils flared. His breathing quickened. "It has been this way from the beginning. For two years, it has been the same."

Her hand fell away and confusion made her frown. "Two years." She'd thought his jealousy specific to Phineas. "With such feelings, how did you endure my husband hunt? Had I been forced to watch whilst you pursued lady after lady, I would have been inconsolable."

He backed up a step. His gaze slid away. He rubbed his forehead and turned to the side, one hand braced on his hip.

Heart pounding at her new suspicions, she drew a breath and remembered. Every time she'd prattled on about her suitors. Every time another one had abandoned his suit. Every time she'd changed yet another small habit in a fruitless search for the cause of her unattractiveness.

"Henry Edwin Fitzsimmons Thorpe." Red was rising in her cheeks and her vision.

"None of them was right for you. I told you as much."

"Do *not* make excuses."

He shot her a sidelong glance. "My intention was always that we would be married. I couldn't very well allow you to marry another."

She shoved both hands into his upper arm. Rather than moving him, it earned her a lifted brow and quirk of his lips. Which only made her madder. "I stood like Grecian statuary!" she cried. "I pored over *The Ladies' Repository of Fashion, Amusement, and Instruction*. I changed my hair and my gowns and my speech."

"And, as I advised at the time, none of those changes were necessary. Perfection has no need of improvement."

"Meaningless flattery!"

He frowned as though genuinely vexed. "Why would I flatter you? You were already hopelessly in love with me."

Could a woman burst into flames from sheer rage? Good heavens, it was worse than the Huxley Flush, burning her skin and her insides. She panted through it, her chest heaving, her flesh pulsing.

Henry appeared alarmed. "Perhaps we should postpone this conversation until a more appropriate—"

"You make me furious!"

"Clearly."

She began shaking. Pacing. Raving. "Do you have any idea how long I have loved you? Do you?"

"No, pet. Tell me."

"Jane's wedding."

"Ah, yes, the vows."

"Not the vows. Before." She halted and pivoted and stomped the distance between them until he was inches away. "I fell in love with your hair first. Envied the color. The light through the windows of St. George's made the red shine. You were standing at the back of the church with Harrison, telling him to stop looking at his watch every half-minute." Her chest seized and ached at the memory. "Then, it was the way you moved. Like a dancer. I'd never seen a man so graceful. You smiled in that wicked way of yours." Tears were gathering in her throat. She swallowed them down. Grasped his lapels and shook. Predictably, he barely moved. The man was solid muscle. "I was lost, Henry. I was yours. If you had asked me to marry you there, in front of Jane's wedding guests and that priest who kept prattling on about fertility, I would have said yes."

He held his silence, but a hand cupped the base of her spine.

"I always knew it would be that way for me. I would see the man I was meant to marry, and feel like a bud opening to summer's warmth." She let him go and pushed away, turning to pace ten feet, then spinning back to face him just before reaching the open doorway.

Her stomach hardened and twisted. "How dare you make a jest of it? How dare you behave as though it were merely a fact, like the rain or your distaste for blancmange, and not a woman giving you her heart?"

His eyes had gone hollow, his skin pale, his mouth tight. He glanced at his boots before speaking. "Is that what you think? That I've taken you for granted?"

She pressed her lips together and wrapped her arms around her middle, uncertain if she wanted to answer.

"You are all that matters to me," he said starkly. "Your life. Your heart. I have not made perfect choices. I bloody well should have told you about the Investor long before I did. Before I wrote you that cursed letter."

"Why didn't you?"

He sighed and shook his head, his hands splayed out from his sides in a shrug. "I wanted to keep you ... safe." Another crack of thunder sounded outside. "Away from all the darkness."

"No. It was more."

His brow crumpled. "Please don't cry, love."

She hadn't realized she was. But now she felt it. Heard it distorting her voice. "You didn't trust me, Henry. You thought me weak and naïve."

"I believed you should not have to face it. Life is not simply summer warmth and orange cakes. It is also"—he waved toward the windows—"darkness. Violence. Chaos. I wanted *your* life, our life together, to be as beautiful as I could make it."

"The darkness found me anyway, didn't it?" she whispered. "It found R-Regina."

"I am sorry, pet. So very sorry."

She blinked away the dashed tears, pressing her eyes with her fingers and releasing a breath. When her chest loosened, she breathed again and dropped her hands.

"Am I your pet, Henry? You have called me that from our

first conversation. Is that how you see me? Simple and amusing but ultimately useless? Someone to keep by your side, stroked and fed and contented with your company?"

He bristled. Henry rarely bristled. For some reason, she found the reaction reassuring.

"Bloody hell, Maureen. I call you 'pet' because, of all the people I have ever known, you are my favorite. The one I hold above all others. The one more precious to me than my own life."

Tears filled her eyes again, this time for another reason. If what he said was true, and she suspected it was, then every time Henry had called her "pet," he'd been telling her he loved her.

He ran a frustrated hand through his hair. "I admit to being a jealous fool. I confess I have courted you without your knowledge. I have schemed and plotted against any man who would seek to take you away from me." He held up a finger. "But I haven't killed any of them, and believe me, it was tempting."

She sniffed, smothering a grin.

"But I love you," he said starkly. "I love you." He took a step closer and stopped, his hands flailing at his sides. "I love you."

Her smile was shaky, but it grew. Watery and real.

He loved her. She loved him. Neither one of them was perfect or anything like it. And those three established facts might just be enough to see them through.

He sighed. Then frowned. Then glowered menacingly at something over her shoulder.

Or someone.

A small, round, cold object pressed into the base of her skull.

"I am sorry, my lady," said a familiar voice above and behind her head. "She has my son."

Maureen couldn't place him. One of Phineas's servants. The footman who had answered the door, perhaps. He sounded distressed.

She knew the feeling. Her heart thrashed and sped. Her blood thundered like the storm outside, sending icy prickles flushing out over her skin. But her awareness was remarkably clear. She saw Henry's eyes—blue flickers of horror and anguish and rage and resolve.

She saw him become not-Henry.

She saw him become the Sabre. She understood now why others had given him the name. He was pure steel sharpened to razor fineness. Nimble and precise, cold and deadly.

Carefully, he stepped toward her.

A distinctive click stopped him.

"I'm afraid she was quite specific," said the man with the gun. "She wishes to take the girl. And she wishes your assistance, my lord." The man gripped Maureen's upper arm gently, guiding her further into the room, sidling away from Henry's position. All the while, the barrel's tip remained firmly notched at the top of her nape.

Rustling clothing and tapping boots grew louder, signaling the approach of at least two people. Then came a voice she knew. Low and feminine, precise and chilling. "Lord Dunston. My, you have been the elusive one, haven't you?"

She moved into Maureen's vision, her platinum hair neatly coiffed, her azure silk pelisse swishing like the wind outside. To her left was a man only slightly smaller than Mr. Reaver. He, too, held a pistol, but his was aimed at Henry.

Henry spared no glance for the man. Rather, he kept the elegant, beautiful woman squarely in his sights. "I might say the same for you, Lady Holstoke."

# Chapter Twenty-Three

*"In the worst of all possible circumstances, one must
remain calm. And well armed. Particularly the latter."*

—The Dowager Marchioness of Wallingham to Lord Berne
regarding the anticipated confrontation involving an unreasonable
female and her highly destructive feline companion.

For years, Henry's nightmares had consisted of this—
Maureen with a pistol pressed to the back of her skull. The
Investor brazen and gloating. Except the Investor had never
been a woman.

He examined her face. Beautiful, certainly. He could see
what might have entranced Holstoke's father. Luminous blue
eyes. Flawless skin. Perfect symmetry.

"*You* are the Sabre." She chuckled. "Well, I must admit some surprise. I had my pursuer as Mr. Reaver."

"Hmm. I find your surprise a bit surprising, considering you sent a runner to my home to kill me on my wedding night."

Silver-blonde brows arched. "Oh, not you." She gestured toward Maureen. "Her."

Henry's blood, already cold, solidified into ice.

"My son was much too attached. Had she simply married him, I might not have minded. But she married you. That was unacceptable."

"You failed," he said softly.

"Yes. You have given me a good deal of trouble, it is true. But now, I shall make proper use of your talents."

"I will not help you kill an innocent girl."

She blinked slowly, her lips curling in a grin that made his neck prickle. "I think you will. A pistol can do dreadful damage. Even the Sabre is not swift enough to undo what has been done, should he choose unwisely."

"I've long wondered," he said, keeping his voice casual. "Are you mad or simply evil?"

Luminous blue eyes flared, first with surprise, then with puzzlement. "Neither. I am a gardener."

He waited for an explanation, letting the silence build.

She clicked her tongue. "To cultivate a garden, one must plant and tend whatever one wishes to grow. Nature is unruly, however. Weeds and blight and vermin work against the proper order. They must be eliminated. The concept is a simple one."

"So, mad, then," he confirmed. "I am relieved to have an answer. Thank you."

Frowning her displeasure, she moved toward him. Her strapping companion, holding his pistol like a dead fish, looked on in wary puzzlement.

"Madness implies I lack reasoning. That is both inaccurate and insulting."

"Apologies for the slight, Lady Holstoke. You did murder my father, after all."

She waved a hand. "Oh, that. He discovered my association with a band of smugglers. I could not very well allow him to expose me. The solution was inelegant, I grant you. It was early on. My weeding techniques have since improved."

He pretended curiosity. "How did you become associated with French smugglers?"

She sniffed. "I am French."

Again, he waited for an explanation. The woman was out of her mind, but the longer he could delay, the better the chance either Colin or Reaver would return.

"Your disbelief is flattering. Disguising oneself as a young woman raised from birth in the English gentry was quite a difficult task. Particularly for a French girl whose first proper meal came when she was sold to a wealthy merchant at thirteen." Her chin tilted and a hint of defiance entered her eyes. "I escaped his grasp. I escaped France and all its iniquities. I learned to be as English as your tiresome wife. I even ascended to the aristocracy."

He recalled the reports on Holstoke's family history. Lydia Brand had begun as Lydia Price, daughter of a little-known, deceased English landholder. The impoverished beauty had enchanted Simon Brand into marriage within three months of their first meeting.

At least, that had been the story everyone believed.

Now that he understood her essential nature, he could well imagine her strategy. She had married Simon Brand, a second son, shortly before his older brother had perished in a hunting accident, making Simon the heir apparent. Then, the old earl had suffered a lingering illness over several years. Most had assumed his grief and age to be at fault. Few would have suspected his daughter-in-law's facility with poisons.

"Well," he said wryly. "Your diction is flawless."

She nodded to acknowledge the compliment. "It took three

years, but nothing worthwhile comes without effort."

"So, the French smugglers were ..."

"Old acquaintances. The one who managed the shipments was the same man who ferried me from France to England when I was a girl. He discovered I resided in Dorsetshire and that I was connected to Holstoke. He sought to gain my assistance."

The county of Dorset had been a center of smuggling during the conflicts with France. Henry should have made the connection, looked more closely at Holstoke from the beginning.

Instead, he'd been caught unawares, forced to watch a viper in blue silk play games with Maureen's life. If he wanted to win, he must wait. Calculate. Stall for an opportunity. Above all, he must keep his wife here with him.

"He blackmailed you, in other words," he said now, keeping the game going.

Again, her eyes flared as though she were offended. "A crude attempt. I soon turned the arrangement to my advantage, I assure you."

"Yes, betraying one's country can be lucrative."

"Come now, Dunston. Patriotism is fool's lullaby, sung as he marches to his death. I am subject to no king. Before the Revolution, France was a wretched place for those not born to privilege. England is little better. One is best served by serving oneself."

"Your enterprises were all strictly for monetary gain, then."

She sniffed. "A woman is, by all legal considerations, a nonentity. She is an extension of her husband, and therefore, whatever wealth she earns or property she obtains becomes his. On the whole, if a woman seeks to acquire a fortune over which she maintains control, she must do so in ways which remain, by their nature, hidden."

He raised a brow. "With the help of a capable solicitor, of course."

She smiled that frigid, predatory smile. "Of course."

"Except that Syder did not remain dutifully bound in your garden, did he? No. He sprawled outward, invading where he should not. Drawing attention that threatened to expose you."

Her smile faded as he spoke. Her eyes flattened until they resembled a snake's—empty yet watchful. "Horatio was useful. Quite fond of me for a time. Like most men, however, he fell prey to disturbances of sentiment. His loyalty turned when he grew obsessed with my husband's bastard daughter. A grave error. It made him reckless."

"It appears he was not alone in that obsession. She's drawn you here, where your enemies are assembled. Why do you want her so badly?"

The smile reappeared. "My reasons are irrelevant to your purpose." She raised a finger. "Now, Lord Dunston, I shall ask politely for your assistance one more time. Have a care how you answer. Your wife is waiting with bated breath."

Until now, he had deliberately avoided looking at Maureen. He could not remain lucid if he glimpsed her fear. But his gaze drifted to her anyway. What he saw nearly cut him in half.

Love. Her love for him.

She was afraid, too. He could see her trembling. Her color was papery, lips turned lilac, breathing gone shallow. But her eyes were locked upon him, shining like a beacon. Her head remained proudly upright.

Far from whimpering and swooning as one might expect from a woman unacquainted with such evil, she held herself steady. Held *him* steady.

His own fear felt ancient, a great boulder in his internal landscape, looming and permanent. The Investor loved nothing more than to hone her weapons on the stone of impossible choices. He'd long known that if the choice were Maureen's life or becoming the Investor's weapon, he would abandon all conscience, all civilization. He would be the monster he despised.

And yet, the choice was no choice at all.

"Very well," he said, holding Maureen's gaze with his. Right now, he needed her love, her faith, more than he had ever needed anything. "What would you have me do?"

Minutes later, they ascended to the bedchamber where Hannah had been taken to recover. The footman led the way, with Lady Holstoke's man pressing his gun between Maureen's shoulder blades. Henry followed the pair, savoring the thought of the man's imminent death. Lady Holstoke followed behind Henry, aiming the footman's pistol at his back.

The footman opened the large, oaken door and stood aside. Lady Holstoke gave Henry an imperious nod.

Henry entered first, swiftly scanning the interior. It was a small chamber, the bed on the left wall, a single draped window on the right, and a fireplace at the back. The space was dark except for a small, golden pool emitted by the lantern on the bedside table. But he could see. Even at the edges, he could see.

Hannah lay on the bed, still and unconscious. Sarah sat beside her, dabbing the girl's cheeks with a cloth. Reaver stood beside the bed with his arms folded across his chest, glaring at the white-haired butler, who yammered on about vinegar being quite effective after a swoon.

Henry started there. "Reaver," he said, withdrawing a dagger. "I'm afraid I must ask you to step aside."

Reaver transferred his glare to Henry. He glanced at the blade, dropped his arms, flexed enormous fists, and widened his stance. "What the devil are you about, Dunston?"

Henry waved the knife toward the corner near the fireplace. "Stand there, if you please. The butler, too." He then spoke to Sarah, who had leapt to her feet. "Lady Colin, you as well."

"Dunston," Sarah protested, reaching back for Hannah. The girl did not move.

"I am sorry," he said. "I've no choice."

Behind him, he heard the others enter—the shuffling leather soles of the big man. The lighter, reluctant slide of Maureen's half-boots. The footman's erratic tapping and the swish of Lady Holstoke's silk.

The butler, he noted, had already scurried into the corner. Reaver hadn't budged. Neither had Sarah.

Henry shook his head and pointed behind him in the direction of rustling silk. "This is Lady Holstoke. Perhaps you do not recognize her. Understandable. However, I must insist that both of you leave the girl and move to the fireplace."

"Bloody, bleeding hell," growled Reaver.

"Agreed. However, the large gentleman with the gun pressed into my wife's back is not a figment of your imagination. I will thank you to move, Reaver. Now."

"I promised Miss Gray my protection," came the rumbling answer.

"We all say things we later realize were foolish. Come, man. Do not be stupid. When I tell you to move, you *move*." He dared not convey his meaning more emphatically.

Reaver's scowl did not abate, but his eyes narrowed subtly. He moved.

Sarah sputtered an objection, but Reaver simply grasped her elbow and tugged, pulling her with him toward the fireplace then tucking her protectively behind his powerful frame.

Henry turned to the side and waved Lady Holstoke forward toward the bed.

The woman shot him a suspicious glance then sniffed. "Edward, wait outside the door. If anyone enters, your son will not see the morning."

Raw hatred twitched the corners of the footman's mouth. Nevertheless, he obeyed.

She moved toward the bed, her gaze fixed upon Hannah's prone form, her gun held casually at her hip. Slowly, she reached down and clasped the girl's chin with the fingers of her free hand, turning her head this way and that. Then, she drew back her arm and brought her palm forcefully across the girl's cheek. The crack, loud in the silent room, made Maureen gasp and Sarah cry out.

Henry tightened every muscle in his body against the need to toss his blade into Lady Holstoke's back. His legs and lungs and arms burned with it.

Hannah's dense black lashes fluttered open. She stared up into Lady Holstoke's face. Her mouth opened as though to scream, but nothing emerged. She was frozen like a doll.

"Awake, are we?" said Lady Holstoke calmly. "Good. Your father gave you something that belongs to me, girl. Tell me where it is."

Pale green eyes darted to the side, flaring as they saw Maureen, who covered her mouth with both hands. They came to Henry then dropped to his blade. Finally, they returned to Lady Holstoke. "I—I don't know what you—"

*Crack!* The girl's head snapped sideways, but she remained silent, slowly turning back to face the woman who had struck her.

"Pray, do not bother with lies, dear. Your father brought you gifts every time he visited Bath to see his whore. The object I seek would have been distinctive. A Pandora doll. Red gown. Blue glass eyes. It is mine. Now, tell me where it is."

Once again, the girl's eyes found Henry. She must have seen his hand tightening around the dagger, his muscles readying to strike. She gave a minute shake of her head. "Not here. I keep it in a special box. In my chambers at the school."

"*Putain!*" She gripped the girl's upper arm, her fingers digging until they whitened, dragging until she'd jerked Hannah halfway off the bed. "Up! Get up."

Hannah scrambled to catch herself, but her arm buckled, and she tumbled awkwardly to the floor.

Lady Holstoke hissed and spun toward the man holding

Maureen. She paced to where he stood. "You will have to carry her. Worthless girl."

Henry watched the big man's eyes. Saw the confusion. The uncertainty. Noted the relaxing muscles in the man's arm. Time slowed with each breath as he waited for just ... the right ... moment.

Then it came. The man's gun hand dropped.

Henry shouted Reaver's name. Tossed his dagger end-over-end. Grasped the cool blade. Threw it with all his strength into the big man's shoulder, where the separation of muscle and nerve would render the arm useless. Henry did not hear the man's shout. Sound was dull and slow.

A growling giant rushed past him like a furious bull, swinging a fireplace iron high and swift into the other man's head. Abruptly loosened from the man's grip, Maureen staggered sideways, ramming her shoulder into Lady Holstoke.

Henry watched in horror as the woman righted herself, lifted her pistol, and pressed it to Maureen's temple.

"Reaver!" he shouted as the giant pummeled the other man with boulder-sized blows.

Reaver halted, his shoulders heaving. The other man collapsed in a thudding heap. Behind Henry, he heard Sarah murmuring to Hannah.

But Henry's entire being sharpened upon one thing—his pale, trembling wife.

Lady Holstoke shifted behind Maureen, who swallowed visibly and winced at the pressure on her temple. The woman wrapped one arm across Maureen's shoulders. "Sabre," she spat. "Vermin infesting my garden, uprooting and wreaking havoc. Why can you not simply die?"

Air halted in his lungs. Ice held him fast. His eyes riveted to the spot where the tip of the barrel pressed. A spot he had kissed tenderly dozens of times.

"I will die. Gladly," he rasped, meaning every word. "Give her to Reaver, and you may kill me."

She laughed, low and strange. "Sentimental fools. All of you." She lowered her head to whisper in Maureen's ear. He could not hear what she said, but Maureen swallowed again and lost what little color she had.

Then, his wife spoke. She said his name. "H-Henry."

His gut twisted. "Yes, pet."

"She says I may bid you farewell. This is what I would like to say. I trust you. Do you trust me?"

He was suffocating. Frozen and flailing in the void. "Always."

Those secretive lips trembled into a tiny smile. Golden-brown eyes glowed with love for him. Love and purpose. "Good. When you think of me, I want you to remember one thing: There are storms, of course. Storms big enough to carry your hat away. But there are also orange cakes, my love. And they are divine."

He had a single heartbeat to digest her message. To ready himself. To move.

For, no sooner did he draw a breath than his beautiful, clever, brave Maureen bent forward at the waist, throwing Lady Holstoke off balance, dislodging the pistol from its position against her skin. Just as quickly, she reeled back with all her weight, cracking her head into the other woman's nose.

Blood spurted. The woman shouted in pain. The pistol fired into the floor. Maureen shoved backward with her hips, driving Lady Holstoke into the wall hard enough to snap the woman's skull into plaster.

Henry was there in an instant, his second dagger caressing his palm, his free arm circling his wife's waist and lifting her away. He had every intention of thrusting his dagger into the heart of the viper. But, before he could move, a shot rang out. Lady Holstoke's already battered head jerked back, a dark hole staining the center of her forehead. She slumped and slid down the wall.

Turning with Maureen anchored to his side, her fingers

clinging to his neck, his heart sank as he saw who had managed to retrieve the big man's discarded pistol.

The one who had fired the killing shot.

"Oh, darling," Maureen murmured. "Hannah."

The girl—unsteady on her feet, black hair loosened into haphazard curls, pale green eyes eerily calm—lowered her arm to her side. "For Mama," she whispered, and let the gun clatter to the floor.

# Chapter Twenty-Four

*"I knew there was something about her I could not countenance. I assumed it was her dreadful personality. How gratifying to learn my perspicacity is sufficient to astound even me."*

—The Dowager Marchioness of Wallingham to Lady Berne while discussing the unlikable nature of Lady Holstoke.

THE COACH ROCKED THROUGH ANOTHER RUT, BUT THE jostling did not bother Maureen. She was safe. Warm. Cradled in Henry's arms. Her head nestled in the crook of his neck, the scents of storm and salt and sandalwood easing her from sleep.

"Only a mile to go, pet," he said, stroking her hair. "Not

far now."

She caressed his jaw, smoother since yesterday. Stroud's work.

Colin and Phineas had found the valet and the rest of the Palace Guard lying unconscious in a little-used stillroom. Edward, the footman whose son had been taken, confessed he had served Henry's men ale laced with a tincture Lady Holstoke had given him. He'd used the same tincture in the tea served in the yellow drawing room, though no one had partaken. Fortunately, Stroud and the others recovered after a night's rest.

Unraveling the truth about Lady Holstoke had taken longer. They had remained at Primvale Castle for three days while the dead woman's oversized servant had recovered from his wounds, and the constable and magistrate had performed their inquiries.

The servant, whose name was Albert, was insensible for an entire day due to Henry's well-placed dagger and Mr. Reaver's fists. When he awakened, he took one look at Reaver and began talking. Between Albert, Edward, and Phineas, they pieced together a rough portrait of the woman known as Lydia Brand.

From her beginnings on the streets of Paris, she had escaped to England after killing and robbing the man who'd kept her as a virtual slave. According to Albert, she had boasted about burning the man's house to the ground.

Upon reaching England's shore, she'd developed a new ambition—to join the ranks of the aristocracy. Her stolen goods had purchased gowns and tutors. Her beauty had purchased entry to the uppermost circles of society. Her target had been Simon Brand. In time, she had become Lady Holstoke.

Phineas—white as salt and visibly stricken from both the revelations about his mother and her death—described his memories of her as "remote." She'd assigned nursemaids and governesses to raise him, he explained, while she arranged entertainments for influential neighbors and managed the design of the formal gardens around Primvale Castle.

"It was the one thing we had in common," he said. "The gardens. The plants. Yet, we could not converse on the topic without her finding some fault in my knowledge or opinions. Before long, I ceased speaking to her at all, which suited her rather well."

Her coolness had alienated many, preventing her from rising among the beau monde. Whatever power might be afforded an unpopular countess had been dissatisfying, according to Albert. "She wanted more. Always more," he lamented. The French smugglers had offered her an opportunity to acquire wealth of her own—illicit wealth that she'd needed Horatio Syder's help to hide. When the smuggling operation had been discovered, she'd cut all ties and entered into partnership with Syder instead.

"Syder were in love wi' 'er," Albert explained. " 'Til she sent 'im to Bath to fetch the girl. Day she 'eard he were keepin' the girl ... a bad day, I reckon."

Lady Holstoke had spent years searching for Hannah while maintaining a strained partnership with Syder. She had accrued a fortune, but had been forced to spend a goodly portion to protect herself from discovery.

Albert's narrative paused when he turned swollen eyes toward Henry. "She thought ye were a ghost. Sabre. Only name she 'ad. Ye never let up. Ever' turn, there ye were. Drove 'er mad, ye did."

Listening, Maureen couldn't help smiling in satisfaction. Her dashing Sabre had done more damage than he knew. And she could not be prouder.

When Henry had asked why Lady Holstoke had gone after Maureen, Albert had scoffed. "She 'ad little use fer 'er boy, I reckon. But she didn't care fer 'im bein' cast aside, neither. Said it were disrespectful to 'er. She'd 'ad enough of that."

In the end, Lady Holstoke made one last bid to replenish her funds. She'd used her knowledge of plants to formulate poisons that would mimic a natural death. It had taken months to find an apothecary who could be persuaded into a partnership. More months to develop the formulations. And still more to sell the poisons to families who stood to gain much more than the poison's price.

As an Investor, Lady Holstoke had preferred high-risk, high-reward propositions. With both Henry and Reaver in pursuit, her risks had turned grave. The apothecary's death had been the deciding moment, and she had begun making arrangements to flee England for the Continent.

But not before she located the girl. Albert sighed as he described her intractability on the subject, his swollen lower lip trembling, his voice strangled by emotion. "I told 'er. Said as it would get 'er killed. An' it did."

She had paid servants such as Edward the footman to alert her immediately if ever a girl with Holstoke eyes came to Primvale Castle. Edward claimed that the moment he'd dispatched the message, he'd known it to be a mistake. Lady Holstoke had arrived an hour before Henry and Reaver—time enough to threaten Edward's son if he did not aid her in the girl's abduction.

They still did not understand why Lydia Brand had wanted Hannah so badly. According to Phineas, she'd cared nothing for her husband, particularly toward the end of his life. And to imagine her reasons were sentimental was, in Phineas's estimation, outlandish.

"She would not have cared that he had a mistress, much less a daughter," Phineas said to a glowering Reaver and a puzzled Henry. "If my father gave Hannah a doll that had once been hers, she might have been vexed. But to remain in England over it? Extremely unlikely."

Hannah had been unable to offer any explanation either, as she hadn't spoken since firing the shot that killed Lady Holstoke. When the magistrate wanted to question her, Phineas had been fiercely protective, his pale eyes blazing down at the squat man while stating in clipped tones that Lady Holstoke had attacked the girl, and the girl had fired in self-defense.

The magistrate accepted his answer, and the constable took Albert away. Edward the footman had little information to offer, instead weeping piteously and begging to see his son, who thankfully hadn't been harmed. Phineas dismissed Edward from his employ, of course, but encouraged the magistrate to exercise leniency for his crimes.

At the magistrate's insistence, Henry, Reaver, and Colin attempted to calculate how many murders Lady Holstoke might have committed. They'd ceased counting at forty when the magistrate called a halt.

Now, all that remained was to return to Yardleigh Manor and, with any luck, discover what had been so enticing about a Pandora doll given to a little girl by her papa over a decade earlier. Phineas, Hannah, Sarah, and Colin rode inside the Holstoke travel coach, leaving Colin's coach to Henry and Maureen. Along with Reaver, Stroud and the Palace Guard rode ahead on their mounts. Stroud, in particular, seemed eager to return, complaining that he hadn't had "a decent crumpet" since leaving Yardleigh.

Presently, Maureen stroked Henry's jaw again, nuzzling his throat and breathing in the sandalwood scent of his shaving soap. "You should have awakened me sooner," she murmured. "We might have taken advantage of our solitude."

His baritone chuckle sent thrills over her skin. "Feeling wicked, pet?"

In fact, she had not been able to stop touching him for three days. No amount of distance was acceptable. Not a single inch. Perhaps someday her need to feel his breath and heat and heartbeat would ease. But not yet.

Fortunately, he didn't appear to mind.

He cradled her waist with his hands as she repositioned herself on his lap, straddling his thighs and rising on her knees to cup his handsome face.

"I thought I wanted you before," she whispered against his lips. "When you were merely Henry."

Those delicious lips quirked with wry humor. "Merely?"

She ran her tongue playfully over his lower lip. "Now that I know your true identity, I must confess, dear sir, I am on fire for you."

He groaned and squeezed her waist with strong hands. "God, love. Not this again."

"I am going to make you adore your moniker if it is the last thing I do."

"Yes, well. I suspect shouting it whilst I pleasure you is a sound start." His hands lowered to squeeze her backside.

She kissed his beautiful, sensual mouth. Savored the stroke of his tongue, the pressuring ridge of his hardness between her thighs. Moaning, she clung to his strong, arousing neck and threaded her fingers through chestnut strands, loving him with every fiber of her tingling, Henry-mad body.

As his breathing quickened and one of his hands came up to cup her breast, she broke their kiss on a gasp. Her hips worked against him, writhing of their own accord. "Oh, Henry. Nothing could be better than this."

His lips suckled at her throat while his fingers plucked her nipple through black crepe. Her breath caught and surged as heat flooded and gathered and pressed.

Several gasps later, she managed to finish her thought. "Well, perhaps one thing could be better. If only I knew for certain your sword was as long and steely as they claim."

"Bloody hell, Maureen," he growled, his hands caressing her breasts and backside as though bound by a compulsion. "We haven't time."

"Oh, I beg to differ, Sabre. Your swiftness is legendary, is it not?"

As it happened, so was his skill. He demonstrated both to astounding effect, lifting her easily with one arm while tossing aside her skirts and loosening his fall with his other hand.

When he was seated snugly inside her, she stroked his brow and kissed the corner of his mouth. "There now," she said, her voice hoarse with desire. "Isn't that better?"

He took her hard and deep, his eyes capturing hers, shining like the midnight sky filled with glimmering stars. Strong, elegant hands clutched at her hips, forcing her to take him all the way to the root. The pleasure of it bloomed outward from where they were joined, burning and swelling and driving. She cupped the sides of his neck, wrapping her fingers around the muscular nape. It gave her a perfect hold as she rode him, grasping with her body, kneading with her fingers, grinding with her hips.

"Henry," she whispered, refusing to release his gaze with hers. "I want you to fill me completely."

His jaw flexed, his skin tight and flushed. "I'll have your pleasure first. Give it to me. Now."

She grinned. "Mmm. So forceful. I am yours to command, Sabre."

He gave her backside a playful swat. "If that's true, you may call me whatever you like."

She threw back her head and laughed, breathless and joyful to be in his arms. He groaned her name. Thrust deep and true. Held her tighter than before so that the undulations of her hips sparked an irresistible series of waves.

Her eyes returned to his as the waves began to crest and break. And crest. And break. And ripple. And break.

He gripped her neck so that she could not look away. Held her fast and let her see.

His desperate, consuming love for her.

Unguarded. Undisguised. It shone there in deep, cascading blue.

"God, how I love you, Henry," she said, the words punctuated with hitching moans as she was battered by the aftermath of shimmering sensation.

He didn't echo the words, too caught up in the explosive pleasure of their union. But he didn't have to speak them.

They were there, as vivid as a midsummer sky.

*I love you, Maureen.*

They whispered in her ear as she cradled him to her, held her precious husband close, and took his pleasure inside.

Long minutes later, she kissed his brow and his eyes and his sensual lips. She breathed him in and lingered awhile as the coach rocked through another rut. He sighed and stroked her back. "Why do you want me to adore my moniker?"

She chuckled and sat back, letting him help her move to a spot beside him on the bench seat. "You mean you don't know?"

His forehead creased in a funny frown as he buttoned his fall and smoothed her sleeve up over her shoulder. No, his expression said. He really didn't know.

Clicking her tongue, she ran her fingers through his hair, using the excuse of straightening the rumpled strands to touch him again. "Because, you silly man. I love all of you. Not just the Henry who made my heart race at Jane's ball. Not just the man who makes me laugh until my ribs ache or twirls me through the waltz or settles me when I've had a distressing day." Her fingertips found the corner of his mouth. Traced his lower lip and the edge of his jaw. "I love the man who decided to hunt monsters."

"He's lived in darkness a long time, pet."

She smiled gently and took his hand in hers. "He is you. You are that man. The man I love. The man I am proud to claim as my husband."

"Extraordinary woman."

She would have brushed aside his words as simple nonsense a husband might say to his wife. Except that he spoke them with such perplexity, as though she'd told him she could toss oranges in the air while standing astride two galloping horses. As though loving him completely were a feat of astonishing measure.

The coach rocked to a halt. She smoothed the sides of her hair. "How do I look?"

"Delectable."

"Really."

"Yes, pet. Shall I demonstrate?"

Her lips pursed. "Your word will suffice."

With a fingertip, he repositioned a curl just above her right ear. His grin was wicked enough to make her heart flutter and sigh. "Consider my word—and anything else you desire—yours."

Stroud knocked on the coach door and cleared his throat emphatically.

Henry raised his brow. "Ready?"

She smoothed her skirts, donned her gloves and hat, then nodded.

Upon entering Yardleigh Manor again, Maureen was struck by how little it had changed while the world felt inexorably altered. The warm, oak-paneled walls. The round Mrs. Poole and the smiling Mrs. Battersby. Even little Biddy came running to greet her, hugging her bread baby and chattering about how the poor thing had lost a leg in a battle with an ill-mannered chicken.

Biddy was distracted, however, when the second coach arrived and Sarah, Colin, Phineas, and Hannah climbed down onto the graveled drive. Hannah was pale and solemn. Phineas hovered at her side, tall and unsmiling, holding his sister's hand.

It gladdened Maureen's heart.

Biddy raced directly to Hannah and threw her arms around the girl's waist. The bread baby went flying. Hannah jerked and blinked. But soon, her free arm came up to return the embrace.

That gladdened Maureen's heart even more.

Colin invited them all into the drawing room. They were joined by Reaver and Stroud, who had arrived ahead of them.

Mrs. Battersby served tea and listened as Sarah and Colin explained everything that had happened. "So, this doll," she clarified. "Is it here?"

All eyes turned to Hannah. Slowly, the girl glanced up at Phineas, who sat beside her, their hands linked. Then, in turn, she looked to Reaver and Colin and Sarah and Maureen and, finally, to Henry. Pausing there for a long while, she assessed Henry with an unblinking stare. At last, she nodded.

Phineas spoke first. "Where, Hannah?"

She swallowed, stood, and left the room without a word.

Maureen turned to Henry, who shared a speculative look with Reaver.

By the time Hannah's slim form hovered once again inside the doorway, they had informed Mrs. Battersby about Phineas and Hannah's agreement to keep Hannah on at St. Catherine's Academy for Girls of Impeccable Deportment, and for him to take over tuition payments and visit regularly until Hannah decided whether she would like to live with him at Primvale Castle.

Now, Hannah slowly treaded into the drawing room, cradling a doll. The doll's gown was red brocade in the style of the previous century. The face appeared to be painted wood, the eyes blue glass. Maureen recalled seeing similar dolls in her youth, though she'd never had one. They'd begun as small-scale models for dressmakers who wished to mimic French fashions, but they'd become popular with both ladies and children simply as decorative playthings.

Inching toward the seat she had earlier vacated, Hannah paused. Shifted. Turned. Came toward where Maureen stood. She paused again. Glanced down at the doll that had turned her fate into one of horror. Then, she extended her arms, offering it to Henry.

With reverence and gentleness, he accepted Hannah's gift. Their eyes met. He inclined his head in thanks. The girl's lips gave the barest hint of a smile, and she nodded in return.

The others came closer and gathered around Henry as he began to examine the doll. At first, there did not seem to be anything special about it. Most of the parts were either wood or plaster. The clothing was well made, but no finer than one might expect. It wasn't until Henry began pressing along the doll's waist that he frowned.

"I fear I must perform a disrobing. Ladies with delicate sensibilities may wish to avert their eyes." He wagged his eyebrows in Maureen's direction. "Or quell their jealous natures."

Maureen couldn't help it. She laughed. The giggles sounded loud in the room, and she acquired a bit of a Huxley Flush. But soon Sarah and Mrs. Battersby joined in, and then Colin, too. It dispelled the tension while Henry flipped the doll's skirt up and examined the stuffed cloth that formed the doll's waist. He probed it with his finger and thumb. Within a blink, he withdrew his dagger, pausing to catch Hannah's wide gaze.

"May I?" he asked.

She nodded.

He cut a slit in the fabric, sheathed his knife, and used his thumbs to reveal what lay inside the stuffing. It was a rounded oval. Red-pink. Satiny in sheen. It glowed with a radiance that appeared as a six-point star in the center.

"Is—is that a ruby?" Sarah asked.

"I believe it is. A star ruby, to be precise," answered Colin. "I've never seen one quite so large before. It must be worth—"

"Thousands of pounds," Reaver confirmed. "Tens of thousands, likely. She could have lived the rest of her life in comfort anywhere in the world, had she found a proper buyer."

Henry played a bit more with the stuffing of the doll. He reached inside the gap and withdrew a ring. Gold. With a faceted sapphire sparkling inside two rings of diamonds.

"Gracious me," Sarah breathed.

"Good heavens," Maureen concurred.

Henry dug free four additional items. None were quite so valuable as the star ruby, but all would fetch a "pretty sum" if Reaver's assessment proved accurate.

Phineas's face went dark and tight. "Jewels," he said quietly, his fury contained but palpable. "She terrorized Hannah for jewels."

Hannah turned toward her brother. Went to him and reached for his hand. Twin pairs of Holstoke eyes met. "She did one good thing," the girl said, her voice soft and a bit rusty. "I am most grateful for you, Phineas."

Gently, he gathered his sister into his arms and tucked his chin upon her head.

Just then, a black-haired imp carrying a half-eaten, unclothed bread baby burst into the room, skated across the length of the floor, and threw her arms around Hannah's waist. The now-crumbling bread baby's last leg broke as it collided with Phineas's knee and landed with an ignominious plop.

Maureen tried everything she could think of. She held her breath. She covered her mouth. She even turned her back. But it would not be contained.

A possessive hand cupped the base of her spine.

"Not to worry. Bit of a cough. We'll just step outside."

The hand pressed and guided her out of the room into the entrance hall, then through the door to the graveled drive, where Stroud was shouting directions at the Palace Guard as they unloaded the coaches.

"Oh, God, Henry," she gasped, tears now springing to her eyes. "I shall have to bake her another one. D-did you see ... the leg ...?"

His rich laugh preceded his answer. "Yes, pet. That was your work? The anatomical detail was most impressive."

Another burst shook her. She clung to Henry's arm and buried her face in his shoulder, trying to let the mirth run its course. His hand tugged her forward, prodding her lower back until she was snugged tight against him and he'd maneuvered them into the deep shadows of the stone entrance. He turned her until her back was cooled by dark granite and her front warmed by hard, insistent male. Just as her peals of laughter began to ebb, he swooped in and took her mouth with his.

Her laugh became a moan, humming against his lips. She

cupped his cheek and reveled in the tingling heat that was her husband's kiss.

Retreating a scant inch, he smiled wide and licked his lips.

"What was that for?" she asked, wondering how a man could be quite this handsome and clever and brave and dashing, all at once.

"That was what I should have done last time, pet. It is what I want now. I suspect it is what I will want to do forevermore."

"Kiss me?"

"Make you happy."

She grinned up at him, her stomach swooping and fluttering and melting. "Silly man. All I have ever needed to be happy is you."

# Epilogue

*"Hmmph. I am well past the age at which these silly themed entertainments hold the slightest allure. Although, I must say, the orange cakes are quite delicious, my dear."*

—The Dowager Marchioness of Wallingham to Maureen Thorpe, the Countess of Dunston, at said lady's surprisingly enjoyable midsummer ball.

*August 5, 1819*
*Fairfield Park, Suffolk*

His enchantress was gowned in canary silk, wearing a flower crown and spinning beneath a midsummer moon. She laughed with her whole body. She danced like a fairy sprite.

She entwined him inside ribbons of madness and lust.

And she was making him wait.

A watch dangled in front of his eyes. "It can be helpful," said Harrison. "Trust me on this."

Henry swiped away the offering and chuckled. "You need it more than I."

Harrison tucked the thing in his pocket. "Probably true." Blue-gray eyes drifted to where Jane danced with her sisters in a merry circle. Her spectacles flashed in the torchlight as she pushed them back up on her nose then righted her flower crown, which had slumped to one side of her head. Harrison withdrew the gold watch again and opened the cover with a click. "Almost certainly true."

All five brown-haired, brown-eyed Huxley girls were flushed and laughing—Annabelle, Jane, Maureen, Genie, and Kate clapped and moved in time with the jolly rhythm of a country tune. Maureen consumed Henry's attention, of course. She always did, even when she was asleep and snoring adorably like a short-snouted pup. But on a night like this, when velvet air was warm and close, scented with orange cakes and summer grass, her skin glowed. Her breasts, round and soft, made his mouth dry. And her eyes danced in time with the torches.

His wife riveted him.

The dance ended with a flourish.

A hand clapped his shoulder. "Well, now. Appears Jane is in need of refreshment. I must assist her."

Henry raised a brow as Harrison started past him. "She is two feet from the punch bowl, old chap."

"Mmm. Maureen looks a bit parched, as well."

She had wandered toward the western edge of the terrace where his mother sat talking to one of their elderly neighbors. "Excellent point."

While Harrison made a beeline for Jane, Henry wound his way through the maze of their guests. As he passed, he overheard pieces of their conversations. John spoke animatedly with Charles Bainbridge, Lord Wallingham, and his imminently expectant wife, Julia, about a new Thoroughbred line recently conceived at Wallingham's stables. Henry made a mental note to ask Wallingham about it soon. Steadwick Park was renowned throughout England for its superior horseflesh.

Next, he brushed past Lord Berne, who listened as Lady Berne mournfully explained to Henry's sister the necessity of keeping all things feline outside her house due to "Berne's violent fits of sneezing" and "Erasmus's unanticipated enmity toward silk." Mary suggested acquiring a dog. Lord Berne immediately began coughing, which pulled his wife's attention away from the discussion.

Henry chuckled and shook his head. Stanton Huxley indulged his wife and family, but he had no liking for pets inside his house. The final judgment for Erasmus had come when three of Stanton's waistcoats had been found shredded and soiled. The cat had been relegated to the stables ever since. Henry's sympathy could not have been more profound. *Three* waistcoats. The man's patience was worthy of sainthood.

As Henry passed near the westernmost refreshment table, the scent of orange cakes grew stronger, and the sound of the Dowager Marchioness of Wallingham's declarations grew louder.

"Bah! Flowers and weeds are not improved when woven into a circle and worn upon one's head. They are wilted," the white-haired matron scoffed at an exasperated Genie. "Plumes, by contrast, are regal in nature. Much better suited to someone of my age and wisdom."

"Feathers are a superior adornment," Genie conceded. "But a midsummer ball without flower crowns is like a masquerade without masks."

"Precisely. Much better to dispense with these preposterous affectations altogether." The old woman sniffed. "Perhaps I was mistaken about you, Eugenia. You may have a drop of good sense after all."

He winked at Genie as he passed, smiling when she rolled her eyes toward Lady Wallingham.

Finally, he approached Maureen. She stooped over his mother's chair, murmuring something as Mama beamed up at her fondly and nodded. Maureen kissed her cheek and patted her arm. She turned as he closed the last few feet.

"Oh! Henry. I was just telling your mama—"

He interrupted her with a kiss. She responded with a sweet grunt and a stroke of his jaw with her silk-gloved hand. When the moment began to heat, he pulled away, leaving his hand shaping the small of her back. "You were saying?"

Her eyes, lambent and hooded, blinked slowly. "Oh. I ... I was ..."

"Before your amorous interruption, she informed me of your plans to refurnish the dower house so that my bedchamber is relocated to the ground floor." Amusement threaded his mother's voice. "My feet are most relieved."

He chuckled. "And the rest of you?"

His mother's smile faded into a gentle curve. Her eyes—so much like his—softened as she gazed up at him and Maureen. "Proud, son. Your father would be, too."

Choking on a sudden rise of emotion, he couldn't speak. So, instead, he simply squeezed Mama's fingers and kissed her cheek.

Stroud approached and whispered a message.

Henry looked to his bespectacled valet. "Where?"

"The library, my lord."

Taking Maureen's gloved hand and weaving their fingers together, Henry said, "I have a surprise for you, pet."

Her brows arched in inquiry. His answer was to tug her behind him through the throng of guests, back through the house to the library. By the time they stood before the polished mahogany doors, Maureen was breathless.

"Henry, what is it? We have guests, you know."

"This is important, love. Are you ready?"

Her eyes rounding, she took a deep breath, chuckled, and gave a nod.

He opened the door and ushered her inside.

Kimble rose from one of the high-backed chairs near the fireplace. "My lord. My lady. It is good to see you again."

Maureen's fingers loosened slowly where they entwined with his. Her breathing sharpened, becoming gulps. Then sobs. She covered her mouth with her free hand. Tears overflowed onto her cheeks.

The figure in the second chair—drastically thinner and frailer than before—came to a shaking stand with the help of a cane.

"R-Regina?" Maureen sobbed. Her hand pulled free of his. She stumbled toward her former maid.

Henry moved beside her, reaching over to shake Kimble's hand. "Thank you, Kimble. For everything."

The butler inclined his head.

Maureen was bracketing Regina's shoulders now, patting her to ensure she was real. "I—I thought you were ... dear heavens, Regina, I thought ..."

"I am alive, my lady." Regina's voice was hoarse and uneven, but she smiled down at Maureen and hugged her with devoted affection. "My recovery has been long, but Lord Dunston's surgeon is highly skilled."

"Dunston's surgeon," Kimble grumbled. "It was not his surgeon who stitched you together, carried you to a cart, then tended you in his mother's cottage for two months."

"Calm yourself, Evan. I have agreed to marry you. That is thanks enough."

"Married?" Maureen cried. "You and Kimble? Regina. How could you not tell me you were alive? And getting married!"

Kimble cleared his throat. "Entirely my fault, my lady. Her survival was uncertain for a long while after the attack. And with the Investor growing bolder, I felt it prudent to keep Miss Fielding well hidden, even from his lordship." Kimble cast a sheepish look in Henry's direction. "Beg your pardon, my lord."

Henry's mouth quirked. "If anyone understands the urge to protect the woman you love, it is I, my good man." He quickly explained to Maureen that Regina's wounds had been dire and appeared fatal. Nevertheless, having served as a battlefield surgeon during the war, Kimble had acted quickly to close her wounds and stem the blood loss. He'd saved her life and promptly hidden her from any further danger.

"I discovered Kimble's secret when he wrote to me last week," Henry continued. "Regina had improved enough to travel, and she wished to see you."

Maureen gave a tearful, happy laugh and hugged the maid again. "This is the most splendid surprise I can imagine."

An hour later, after an excruciatingly detailed discussion of Regina and Kimble's courtship and anticipated wedding, Henry was relieved when Kimble insisted that Regina retire. "I'm afraid she needs her rest, my lady."

Maureen sent the weary-yet-happy Regina off with another affectionate embrace. Kimble bid them goodnight as he closed the library doors behind them.

The silence in the room did not last long.

"I cannot believe you neglected to tell me for an entire—"

"Now, let's not imagine conspiracies where there are—"

"—week. You know I have been in agony over her death, Henry, and—"

"—none. The moment I discovered the truth, I made—"

"—yet you wait until now? I should let Erasmus have his way with your waistcoats—"

"—arrangements for them to come here specifically—"

"—or serve blancmange for supper, but I think instead, I should like for you to—"

"—so that you would know for certain. Because nothing matters more to me—"

"—hold me. Yes. Hold me very close. Now, Henry."

"—than your heart. Mending it properly and keeping it safe."

"Henry."

"Yes, pet?"

"Hold me."

He opened his arms.

She ran into them.

They stood, swaying and silent, for a long while.

Then, he took her hand and led her outside again. Beneath the stars and the warm summer night. He took his enchantress out past the terrace where their friends and families still danced, past the stables, through the whispering grass, down a gentle slope to the base of a valley. Neither of them spoke. As one, they lay down in the spot where he had promised to build her a fish pond. She pressed her cheek over his heart, and he settled his palm at the base of her spine.

"I dared not imagine it," he mused.

"What?"

"This. Peace. My battle was very long, pet. Had you not come along to tempt me into a life of domestic bliss ..."

Her fingers stroked his brow, as they often did when she sensed the dark currents beneath his surface. "You would have found your way."

He kissed her temple. "I am not so certain. Even now, a part of me wonders if I am capable of normalcy."

She sighed. Pushed up. Climbed on top of him. Her flower crown tumbled off her hair and plopped on his chin. She tossed it away and sat up to straddle his waist. "Henry Edwin Fitzsimmons Thorpe."

He grinned and rested his hands upon her hips. "Yes, pet?"

"I am your wife."

"Is that so? I was wondering whose gowns those were hanging beside my waistcoats."

"You are not alone any longer. You have me. I am an expert in both normalcy and domestic bliss."

Through the veil of her loosened curls, he could see stars

streaking the sky. He reached up to cup her dimpled cheek. Caressed her secretive lips with the pad of his thumb. And marveled that she had chosen him. "Indeed. Your orange cakes are delectable, love."

Her mouth quirked. She lowered her head until her breath whispered across his lips. "Oh, you have no idea. My talents are legion. An onerous burden, but one I bear willingly." She brushed his mouth with hers and smiled brighter than the midsummer moon. "Come. Let me show you."

What sort of woman could possibly bring the towering Sebastian Reaver to his knees? Find out in Book Eight of the Rescued from Ruin series **now available**!

FIND BOOK EIGHT AT ELISABRADEN.COM!

# Anything but a Gentleman

## ELISA BRADEN

# More from Elisa Braden

*Be first to hear about new releases, price specials,
and more—sign up for Elisa's free email newsletter at
www.elisabraden.com so you don't miss a thing!*

## Midnight in Scotland Series
*In the enchanting new Midnight in Scotland series,
the unlikeliest matches generate the greatest heat.
All it takes is a spark of Highland magic.*

### THE MAKING OF A HIGHLANDER (BOOK ONE)
Handsome adventurer John Huxley is locked in a land dispute in the
Scottish Highlands with one way out: Win the Highland Games.
When the local hoyden Mad Annie Tulloch offers to train him in
exchange for "Lady Lessons," he agrees. But teaching the fiery, foul-
mouthed, breeches-wearing lass how to land a lord seems impossible—
especially when he starts dreaming of winning her for himself.

### THE TAMING OF A HIGHLANDER (BOOK TWO)
Wrongfully imprisoned and tortured, Broderick MacPherson lives for
one purpose—punishing the man responsible. When a wayward lass
witnesses his revenge, he risks returning to the prison that nearly
killed him. Kate Huxley has no wish to testify against a man who's
already suffered too much. But the only remedy is to become his wife.
And she can't possibly marry such a surly, damaged man...can she?

## Rescued from Ruin Series

*Discover the scandalous predicaments, emotional redemptions,
and gripping love stories (with a dash of Lady Wallingham)
in the scorching series that started it all!*

### EVER YOURS, ANNABELLE (PREQUEL)

As a girl, Annabelle Huxley chased Robert Conrad with reckless abandon, and he always rescued her when she pushed too far—until the accident that cost him everything. Seven years later, Robert discovers the girl with the habit of chasing trouble is now a siren he can't resist. But when a scandalous secret threatens her life, how far will he go to rescue her one last time?

### THE MADNESS OF VISCOUNT ATHERBOURNE (BOOK ONE)

Victoria Lacey's life is perfect—perfectly boring. Agree to marry a lord who has yet to inspire a single, solitary tingle? It's all in a day's work for the oh-so-proper sister of the Duke of Blackmore. Surely no one suspects her secret longing for head-spinning passion. Except a dark stranger, on a terrace, at a ball where she should not be kissing a man she has just met. Especially one bent on revenge.

### THE TRUTH ABOUT CADS AND DUKES (BOOK TWO)

Painfully shy Jane Huxley is in a most precarious position, thanks to dissolute charmer Colin Lacey's deceitful wager. Now, his brother, the icy Duke of Blackmore, must make it right, even if it means marrying her himself. Will their union end in frostbite? Perhaps. But after lingering glances and devastating kisses, Jane begins to suspect the truth: Her duke may not be as cold as he appears.

## DESPERATELY SEEKING A SCOUNDREL (BOOK THREE)

Where Lord Colin Lacey goes, trouble follows. Tortured and hunted by a brutal criminal, he is rescued from death's door by the stubborn, fetching Sarah Battersby. In return, she asks one small favor: Pretend to be her fiancé. Temporarily, of course. With danger nipping his heels, he knows it is wrong to want her, wrong to agree to her terms. But when has Colin Lacey ever done the sensible thing?

## THE DEVIL IS A MARQUESS (BOOK FOUR)

A walking scandal surviving on wits, whisky, and wicked skills in the bedchamber, Benedict Chatham must marry a fortune or risk ruin. Tall, redheaded disaster Charlotte Lancaster possesses such a fortune. The price? One year of fidelity and sobriety. Forced to end his libertine ways, Chatham proves he is more than the scandalous charmer she married, but will it be enough to keep his unwanted wife?

## WHEN A GIRL LOVES AN EARL (BOOK FIVE)

Miss Viola Darling always gets what she wants, and what she wants most is to marry Lord Tannenbrook. James knows how determined the tiny beauty can be—she mangled his cravat at a perfectly respectable dinner before he escaped. But he has no desire to marry, less desire to be pursued, and will certainly not kiss her kissable lips until they are both breathless, no matter how tempted he may be.

## TWELVE NIGHTS AS HIS MISTRESS (NOVELLA - BOOK SIX)

Charles Bainbridge, Lord Wallingham, spent two years wooing Julia Willoughby, yet she insists they are a dreadful match destined for misery. Now, rather than lose her, he makes a final offer: Spend twelve nights in his bed, and if she can deny they are perfect for each other, he will let her go. But not before tempting tidy, sensible Julia to trade predictability for the sweet chaos of true love.

### CONFESSIONS OF A DANGEROUS LORD (BOOK SEVEN)

Known for flashy waistcoats and rapier wit, Henry Thorpe, the Earl of Dunston, is deadlier than he appears. For years, his sole focus has been hunting a ruthless killer through London's dark underworld. Then Maureen Huxley came along. To keep her safe, he must keep her at arm's length. But as she contemplates marrying another man, Henry's caught in the crossfire between his mission and his heart.

### ANYTHING BUT A GENTLEMAN (BOOK EIGHT)

Augusta Widmore must force her sister's ne'er-do-well betrothed to the altar, or her sister will bear the consequences. She needs leverage only one man can provide—Sebastian Reaver. When she invades his office demanding a fortune in markers, he exacts a price a spinster will never pay—become the notorious club owner's mistress. And when she calls his bluff, a fiery battle for surrender begins.

### A MARRIAGE MADE IN SCANDAL (BOOK NINE)

As the most feared lord in London, the Earl of Holstoke is having a devil of a time landing a wife. When a series of vicious murders brings suspicion to his door, only one woman is bold enough to defend him—Eugenia Huxley. Her offer to be his alibi risks scandal, and marriage is the remedy. But as a poisonous enemy coils closer, Holstoke finds his love for her might be the greatest danger of all.

### A KISS FROM A ROGUE (BOOK TEN)

A cruel past left Hannah Gray with one simple longing—a normal life with a safe, normal husband. Finding one would be easy if she weren't distracted by wolf-in-rogue's-clothing Jonas Hawthorn. He's tried to forget the haughty Miss Gray. But once he tastes the heat and longing hidden beneath her icy mask, the only mystery this Bow Street man burns to solve is how a rogue might make Hannah his own.

# About the Author

Reading romance novels came easily to Elisa Braden. Writing them? That took a little longer. After graduating with degrees in creative writing and history, Elisa spent entirely too many years in "real" jobs writing T-shirt copy ... and other people's resumes ... and articles about giftware displays. But that was before she woke up and started dreaming about the very *unreal* job of being a romance novelist. Better late than never.

Elisa lives in the gorgeous Pacific Northwest, where you're constitutionally required to like the colors green and gray. Good thing she does. Other items on the "like" list include cute dogs, strong coffee, and epic movies. Of course, her favorite thing of all is hearing from readers who love her characters as much as she does. If you're one of those, get in touch on Facebook and Twitter or visit **www.elisabraden.com.**